LONDON FALLING

ALSO BY PAUL CORNELL

British Summertime

LONDON FALLING

PAUL CORNELL

A TOM DOHERTY ASSOCIATES BOOK
New York

LONDON FALLING

A Tor Book
Published by Tom Doherty Associates, LLC
175 Fifth Avenue
New York, NY 10010

www.tor-forge.com

Tor® is a registered trademark of Tom Doherty Associates, LLC.

The Library of Congress has cataloged the hardcover edition as follows:

Cornell, Paul.
    London falling / Paul Cornell. — 1st ed.
        p. cm.
    "A Tom Doherty Associates book."
    ISBN 978-0-7653-3027-7 (hardcover)
    ISBN 978-1-4299-4672-8 (e-book)
    1. Detectives—England—London—Fiction.   2. Murder—Investigation—England—London—Fiction.   I. Title.
    PR6053.O72 L66 2013
    823'.914—dc23

                                                    2012043356

Forge books may be purchased for educational, business, or promotional use.
For information on bulk purchases, please contact Macmillan Corporate and Premium Sales Department at 1-800-221-7945 extension 5442 or write specialmarkets@macmillan.com.

First U.S. Edition: April 2013

Printed in the United States of America

0 9 8 7 6 5 4 3 2 1

For Caroline, for putting up with me

LONDON
FALLING

ONE

Costain entered the service station and stopped when he saw Quill standing there, not even pretending to look at the chocolate bars displayed in front of him. Costain headed for the toilets, and Quill immediately followed, as if he didn't care who noticed. Costain made astonished eye contact with him just before the door, turning to take in the SUVs he'd left on the forecourt outside, with Mick and Lazlo currently filling up the first two vehicles with diesel. No, nobody was watching. He closed the toilet door behind them.

They stood in the cubicle, with the door bolted: the seat gone, the toilet bowl blocked, everything smelling of shit, a single bulb making it all ghostly white. The cold made their breath bloom around them.

"What the fuck is Toshack doing?" asked Quill. He was speaking too loudly.

"I don't know."

" 'I don't know, *sir!* ' "

"I don't know, *sir*. Do you want me to recite my rank, nick and surname, too, in case Lazlo pops in for some fags?"

Quill looked affronted, as if a detective sergeant had never talked back to him in his entire life. He seemed to choose his next words carefully and, thankfully, they were closer to a whisper. "You know how long it's been for us lot on Operation Goodfellow? Four years

1

now, from you first getting in with Pa Toil's gang. And maybe you ought to have stayed in the Toil, because now you're in Toshack's sodding Chelsea tractor, leading this convoy or whatever it is, and him looking as if he might run for an airport any second."

"He's not going to do that."

"How do you know, if you don't even know what he's doing?"

"'Cos he's looking for somebody. He said we'll be going house to house."

"So you *do* know what he's doing. But earlier you said you didn't."

"I meant that I don't know what he's doing in the wider sense, *Detective Inspector*. I don't know who he's looking for—or why. He went off on his own, and couldn't find them, came back to the Bermondsey house, decided to take us lot with him. He's off his head tonight, playing with his guns. He's been at the supply."

"What?"

"Chisel. Crack."

"What, *now*—as a little treat on New Year's Eve?"

"His first time. Ask the second undercover, if you want."

"I don't want anything unpredictable tonight."

"Well, what you *want*—"

Quill put a finger to Costain's lips. "The top brass are pushing Superintendent Lofthouse to end this right *now*, understand? Right now, *you* are the lead UC in the least successful operation SCD 10 has ever mounted in the capital, and that, my son, is a fucking highly contested honor. The boom is *going* to come down tonight, or tomorrow or the day after. We have run out of money and good will, so the bastards are going to settle just for the small fry. Toshack will laugh his arse off at us again, get off any charges brought against him again, and just a few of his soldiers and toms and lads down the chop shop will get put away, but none of the fucking terrifying ones. The risks you and Sefton have taken for the last four years, and all the working hours of your comrades back at the nick, will have been basically about *nothing*. And if that happens, I will make sure that you *burn*. Now, what do you have to say to me?"

Costain licked his lips. *Oh, piss off: that's what he wanted to say. Don't you think I can see it coming? You're setting me up to take the fall for this. You're going to burn me anyway.* This fucking insane meeting, with no real excuse for being here, could have been achieved by a brush contact or a dead letter box. And never before had Costain dealt with a DI in charge of an operation who'd even known what he looked like. He'd been sold the lack of a handler this time on the basis that Lofthouse had her own way of doing things, and she had been given the freedom to pursue it this way because of all that Toshack had previously got away with. But now Quill was raising the stakes on him, deliberately pushing him. He made himself take a deep breath, then realized that was a mistake. The coke was roaring through him, putting him in charge, but he knew it made him paranoid too. He had no way any more of telling what was true, but, looking into Quill's eyes, he knew he couldn't trust him. "He's not making a run for the airport. *I know it*. So tell Lofthouse that's the opinion of the lead UC."

"Sefton's in there with you, does he share that opinion?"

Why do you want to know? " 'Course he does. We've got a window. In this present state of his, Toshack might start talking about his supply and his connections at any moment, but while I could be listening, you've got me in *here*—"

" 'Cos you've done everything so well already, haven't you? You're in his car and you've established access like that, but, over four years, the quality of the information—"

"You think I've gone native?"

"Oh, you don't catch me out like that, sunshine. I wouldn't dream of using such ill-considered language to a gentleman of West Indian extraction . . . who'd be on to Professional Standards like a shot."

If I had a gun I'd put it on his forehead, see him sweat! "I've tried to tell you. He doesn't talk about the bodies he's dropped, his supply, how he absorbed the other gangs. When it needs to be done, he goes off on his own and *nobody* goes with him. He must hire freelancers, but we've never had a sniff of them. There's been nothing heard over the lines, and obviously nothing from probably a dozen approaches you haven't told me about, or you wouldn't even be here."

"Oh yeah."

"So why do you think I am at fault, sir?" He let a little of the Guyanese accent creep in, the way a lot of soldiers did when they wanted to act hard. *Blam! Quill flew back! Blam!*

"Because you're a wrong 'un."

"Sefton will have corroborated *all* of this."

But, of course, Quill didn't have a word to say about Sefton. "Wrong 'un, I said, and Lofthouse shouldn't have picked you." Quill reached into the pocket of the enormous old overcoat that smelt of mints, and took out a Nagra tape recorder. A bloody Nagra—last century's recording device of choice. "If I were you, I'd be highly motivated to grab one last chance."

Costain considered the device for a long moment. "I don't know when I'd get a chance to switch it on."

"Do it now, then."

Blam. Or else bow your head. Fuck it. Fuck him. Costain dropped his jacket onto the hook on the back of the door, pulled his shirt out of his trousers and reached around to attach the Nagra to his belt, at his back. He hadn't used one of these devices in years, but he remembered the awkwardness of them. He found the little hook on top of the recorder, and flicked it to the On position. Then he tucked his shirt back in and put his jacket back on over it, careful not to touch the hook again. Judges took a dim view of interrupted recordings.

"I am a serving police officer," he said, making eye contact with Quill, who seemed to be wondering if the UC would remember the necessary words, "who for the purpose of this operation will

4

be known as Anthony Blake. I can, should a court require, produce my warrant card. The date is 31 December. The time is twenty-two-oh-four hours, and I have just switched on the tape."

Quill nodded to him. "Two hours of tape," he said. "Last chance— for all of us." He unbolted the cubicle door. "If the suspect heads for the airport . . ." And then, mindful of the recorder, he gestured to Costain and then pointed upward with a grim little smile.

Then you make sure you go with him.

Costain allowed himself another minute after Quill had left. He splashed freezing water on his face. It made him start panting. *Quill had set him up to fail. He needed a sacrifice, letting Costain burn. No, no, keep going. Get through it. Work it out.*

He walked out on to the freezing forecourt, the warm breath billowing out of his mouth, to the sound of the convoy of SUVs revving their engines. UK Grime beats were pumping out through their open doors. A sample of the Clash looped in and out: "London Calling." The Asian blokes at the tills were staring worriedly out at them.

Rob Toshack stepped out of the lead car, holding a pistol in his hand. He was beyond caring who saw it.

The Asian blokes dived for cover.

Toshack was red-faced and sweating. He was shivering like an old horse. For a second, Costain wondered if he would find Quill's corpse lying somewhere out here.

No fear, now. Fear will kill you. Costain made himself become not the hiding, shameful traitor but the star of this picture. With a dirty great supportive soundtrack blasting from those cars, and now this guy with a gun, eyeing him worriedly, not betrayed— nowhere near it—just impatient, and a bit lost, high for the first time in his hard protective old life . . . This guy hadn't just shot anyone.

"I was getting worried, Tony," Rob Toshack explained. "We're running out of time."

"What?" Costain went over to the door of the lead vehicle and grinned at his boss. The star of this picture, yes, but never appearing melodramatic. Always the class joker, always relieving the tension that might one day kill him. "I was only having a shit."

They raced through the London night, heading for somewhere on the North Circular, up near Neasden. Mick had to swing the car back and forth, every now and then, to avoid the potholes. Not much traffic this late on New Year's Eve. Rob was keeping the SUV so hot inside that everyone was now in shirt-sleeves. Sefton had somehow managed to move himself up into the lead car, and was now sitting beside Costain. Which was just fucking perfect. The second UC was looking pretend-concerned for Rob, with that round, frigging black children's television-presenter face of his. Chill out everybody; let's all be friends and play a rap music game!

Costain made grudging eye contact with him. He held on to it a moment too long, taking some small pleasure in making Sefton start to react. *What?* Costain turned back to glance at Rob, at that worried drinker's face, with something weak and unused about the muscles with which normal folk smiled. That lack of tension connected his loose jowls to those lost eyes. The king of London, the first ever. Even gangsters of old, like the Krays and the Richardsons, had had to deal with rivals. Toshack had made his money on drugs and brass, miraculous warehouse and container robbery and high-performance car theft. He was the man for whom it had fallen off the back of that lorry. Or, rather, just vanished from it. It was usually Toshack kit that got auctioned out of cardboard boxes in empty storefronts in the dead-eyed towns of the south coast.

In the last ten years or so, he'd seen off all his rivals or, more often than not, absorbed them. He held actual territory in the thirty-three boroughs, in an age when most Organized Criminal Networks found that much too stressful. He regularly had soldiers coming to him, ratting out their bosses, saying where the money bunched in market folds would be counted tonight. Because everyone knew that in the Toshack OCN you got to do all the posing and none of the getting shot at. It was at that point that Rob would make their bosses a peaceable offer, backed up by some sort of threat, the details but not the results of which were kept from his own inner circle of soldiers. The smaller boss then took the offer and vanished. Always.

Those incredibly efficient freelancers of his.

It made it doubly strange that tonight Rob was out on the warpath with his own people right beside him.

Absorbing soldiers from so many different gangs was how the Toshack set had come to be different from most OCNs, composed of people who'd known each other in the schoolyard, but diverse, like on TV where the producers could imply that these guys dealt heroin but not that they might be a tiny bit racist with it. Costain and Sefton had come aboard when Toshack had taken over the Toil to join Shiv and Mick and Lazlo, the League of Nations. Rob had looked after them, with so many loans and smoothings of the way, and also the taking asides for a little chat that started out with terror, then became about whiskey and good advice from this man who looked at you with eyes that said he'd been there.

Costain liked to feel free. "I'm this guy who's got no karma," he'd once said to Rob during one of those whiskey conversations. "Half of what people think there are laws about, there really aren't. You can do what you like, but people are just afraid."

"Amen to that, Blakey," Rob had said, clinking glasses with him.

He loved the freedom Rob gave him. The freedom of someone who could still afford the diesel for a fleet of SUVs. The freedom of someone who was not a victim. Only now he was carrying a burden in the middle of his back that could bring them both down. One way or the other, this free lunch looked likely to end tonight. Costain glanced at his watch. His tape was going to last up to, what . . . midnight? What was he going to do? He'd put a certain something aside for when he got out of this, and he hoped to

God that neither side had discovered *that*. Was now the time for him to cash in and run?

"What goes around comes around," declared Rob. Then he turned to look at Costain and Sefton. "Well, that's not always true, is it? Not necessarily."

Costain pursed his lips. A sudden memory had been set off by those words, but Quill had planted it in him. *Why he always thought he was going to get burned. Because he was the bad guy.* The memory went like this: he was leaning closer to one Sammy Cliff, taking him into his confidence after the informer had again ranted on about how he felt about himself, describing himself in the most derogatory terms. "But it's not about what you are, is it?" Costain had said, making his tone sound like the sort of kindly teacher he'd seen in old movies. "It's about what you *could* be. One of the good guys—one of *us*—fighting the good fight against gang culture. I think it's time I assigned you a code name, mate. I have been given five randomly generated subject names to pick from, so do you want to choose?"

Sammy had shaken his head, unable to stop himself from looking eager, he'd so wanted to be named.

"I think," Costain had said, "I'm going to call you Tiger Feet."

And then he remembered what had happened soon after that: Sammy Cliff hanging there, the burned remains of his feet, of his face.

Costain shoved that memory down again. "Nah," he said, "you're right there, Rob."

"Depends," said Sefton. "Depends on what he means. What exactly do you mean, chief?" Costain wondered if Sefton knew about the Nagra, if his fucking brilliant strategy now was going to be to ask loads of bloody *questions*. Like UCs never normally did.

"I mean that, for the last ten years, what goes around *hasn't* come around for me. And it *won't* come around now, Blakey, Kev, Mick. I'm going to get out of it this time too, like every other time."

"Sure you are, Rob."

"I got all of this 'cos of my brother. All down to him, oh yes." He laughed gently, as if at some irony that Costain himself wasn't aware of. "I'm not going to let it go." He hit the button to lower the window, inviting a freezing blast of air in, and shoved the gun out. He fired it in the air and kept firing, with an absurdly precise gap between each shot, as if he was waving a flag that fired bullets. Maybe he expected similar from the convoy behind him, but Costain heard nothing. He imagined bullets falling into the streets of semis standing below the underpass. *That* demonstrated real freedom, but he could sense Sefton having the temerity to worry and fear and bridle at it.

Rob closed the window and turned back to them again, laughing. "I'm sorry, boys, I've had some of the other, so I feel a bit free and easy tonight. I used to do that down the shopping centers in Peckham, you know, walking along with a pump-action. Window of a business that's giving us gyp, bang! The glaziers used to love me back then. I'd take down the Neighborhood Watch stickers, saying they no longer applied, and they never got put up again, because everyone was afraid of me. That was before your time, Blakey. It was just me . . . it *is* just me in this city, invulnerable."

Sefton spoke up *again*. "Yeah, boss? We sort of took that as read. So why are you going on about it finishing?"

Costain felt his teeth grind at yet another question. Questions broke the flow of the other bloke telling you something. They weren't part of a normal chat. They just raised more questions. Sefton was Quill's favorite, but the little shit was acting like a bloody amateur.

But Rob had suddenly started yelling at Mick, the driver. "Right here, quick, down here!" And they were off down a slip road, the rest of the convoy blaring their horns and making other cars swerve out of their way as the convoy was forced to follow.

Costain glimpsed a gasometer and rows of neat little houses, some of them still with their Christmas lights up. They were somewhere in the Wembley area, he decided. He used to take his bike up here as a kid: these rows of homes all with their own little gardens, everything in the shadow of the stadium and the dirty great warehouse stores. Little people living here in the shadows of stuff. Rob was meanwhile giving directions to Mick, looking at a map on his phone, but keeping one hand cupped round it. Even now he didn't want anyone seeing their destination.

They roared round a corner, past a square-built pub with a crowd of smokers outside who cheered without knowing what they were cheering. It was the first pub in three streets that hadn't been boarded up. They took a left down a side street.

"That one," Rob pointed. "Park up nice like. Don't disturb the garden."

The suburban street was fully lined with cars, so "nice" meant double parking. A home owner came out, calling that he'd need to get his car out later, but Rob vaguely waved the gun at him and he went running back inside. That was how they were rolling tonight, then. Costain felt the others were up for it, into it, experiencing some action with the boss at last—not just serving as his drinking buddies now. Rob led his soldiers to the door of a house, and they formed up outside, ready to rock.

Rob rang the bell. And then twice more. He turned to them. "Could someone—?"

The soldiers came forward to help, the big Russian trying to do it with one kick. The door went down in three, and then they were rushing inside. Costain hung back, Sefton alongside him, ready to let any shooting start ahead of them.

But, inside, the gang were wheeling about through a bare and freezing lounge and heading into a kitchen with no fittings and with broken windows looking out to the rear. There was thin carpet and a front parlor space with paintwork yellowed from cigarette smoke. "Doesn't look as if anyone lives here," said Mick. "Not even as a squat."

"I know what it looks like, Michael," said Rob. "Just search the place."

So they turned out empty drawers lined with newspaper, and peered under what little furniture there was, the soldiers kicking about inside what looked like their nan's house. Rob himself went upstairs, and Costain and Sefton—always at his shoulder—followed. Empty bedrooms. Nothing. "What are we looking for, then, boss?" asked Sefton. *Always the questions.*

"We're making a noise," said Rob, raising his voice as if to address the ceiling. "Making it clear we're here. Loads of us to choose from." He grabbed a shotgun and slammed the butt up into a trapdoor of what must be a loft, and the big lads helped him up inside it. But a few moments later he was back down again. "Get in there," he said, pointing, "and root around a bit." Costain studied Rob's face as he marched past. He seemed to have come here with hope and then lost it.

Costain managed to investigate the back room downstairs on his own. Then he turned round to see that Sefton had entered. But nobody else. They could hear the sounds of the search continuing in every other room around them, carried out swiftly and offhand as every soldier wondered when he'd hear sirens approach to cut off their limited exit. Sefton closed the door behind him. "How do you want us to proceed, skip?"

"As the tribunal will hear from the tape, I then asked the lead officer in the field to inform me of his plans . . ."

Costain looked at Quill's boy for a moment, then silently blew him a kiss. Sefton stared back at him—apparently astonished that Costain had somehow worked out that Sefton was just waiting for him to fail somehow, that he'd probably been already sending in carefully neutral reports that damned the lead UC only in the details. Quill hadn't actually said that he'd backed up his version of events, had he? Costain was pleased to have finally got under Sefton's skin. "I wouldn't worry. *You'll* be fine."

"So you don't have any . . . particular thing you'd like me to try on Toshack . . . Sarge?"

There came a shout from Rob himself in another part of the house. "Right! Next address!"

Quill sat in the back of an unmarked BMW, heading back to Gipsy Hill at speed, with his detective sergeant, Harry Dobson, in the seat beside him, talking into his Airwave radio. "The helicopter used the opportunity of Toshack's stop-off at that address in Wembley to refuel," he told Quill. "He's now moving to resume surveillance by tracking the bug concealed on Sefton."

"Tell him, if he loses them, he'll be flying Fisher Price."

Harry raised an eyebrow. "He's about to, anyway, Jimmy. This is the last op, the service is getting cut and the crew are taking early retirement. Like with that Nagra you managed to get hold of when there was nothing else; we're riding third-class here. So I'll call him back with your message, shall I?"

"Oh, piss off," said Quill. Harry had been with him since they'd been in uniform together. Quill liked having someone he could yell at but not have it matter.

"You really giving Costain another chance?"

"Nah, I was just trying to motivate the fucker. When this is over, he's done. I'll have him up on a charge, if I can. I do a bit of the necessary paperwork every lunchtime—gives me something to look forward to. If we'd had a better lead in there, or if Sefton had gone in first—"

"Sefton's a DC, Costain's a DS, and Sefton has backed up every single thing that shifty bugger's said about the Toshack firm. You just don't like him 'cos you've got your own lines drawn in the sand—"

"Laws, I like to call them. And where would we be without them? Where we are now, but a bit worse. He had eyes like frigging dinner plates, Harry. He knew I could see that, and all. When this lot falls apart, we'll find there was info going the other way, knowingly or not, stuff that he's been contributing to Toshack's bloody twilight zone that we can't get into. Bet you a fiver."

"Blimey, you *are* serious."

"Operation Goodfellow's falling apart, and we've got this last shindig on triple time. It's the last night of the Proms. When this goes under, Lofthouse won't be able to fend them off no more. The axe'll then come down, and undercover ops in London will end up being about some old dear telling a DCI what she heard down the bingo. It's like Toshack threw us a few coins. There you go, lads, tip for being sodding useless. Now sling your hook."

"Bet Sarah's enjoying it."

"Oh, yeah, Harry, she's ecstatic. I think she's visiting some distant cousin tonight. Maybe she'll stay there."

Harry laughed. "You're never that lucky."

Quill looked at him a bit sharply, then realized that he had done so and cuffed the DS across the shoulder before he could apologize. *Do as I say, not as I do*; they should have that written over the door at Hendon. He banged on the back of the driver's seat, and saw her raising an eyebrow at him in the rear-view mirror. "Faster, love. We want to be back at the Ops Room for 'Auld Lang Syne,' don't we?"

Shit, shit, shit!

Kev Sefton was his *actual* name, and right now he was carefully making himself look out of the window of the SUV because he couldn't look at that bastard sitting beside him. The convoy had gone to two more houses, both within ten minutes' distance of the first. They'd been empty, too. Both times Toshack had headed up into the loft while he got the soldiers to "bang about." Sefton had tried to keep his mind on the job, but . . .

The bastard *knew*. He'd been on his back since he'd joined Goodfellow, and that was the reason Sefton didn't know how Costain came to know about his "protected characteristic," as the blunt jargon put it. He'd always stayed away from the Gay Police

Association, the Black Police Association . . . He hadn't thought much about why he should have joined them, or why he shouldn't. He'd been out, sort of, at his last nick. A few of the lads had asked, so he'd told them. And then his DI, Pete Grieves, had, too, over a pint—deliberately nothing official. "I should think you qualify us for some sort of grant, lad, representing two minorities for the price of one," he'd said. Sefton had laughed along, only realizing later how the conversation had left him feeling . . . he still didn't know *how* he felt about it.

But there was meant to be a firewall between his present UC life and the nick where he'd first worked.

And, however he knew, Costain had decided that *now*, on the night the op was going to crash and burn, was the time to really have a go. He'd been at Sefton ever since he was brought in. That superior look in his eye, 'cos he was the real thing and Sefton was the fraud, the posh boy with the put-on accent. There were so many things Costain had stopped him from mentioning in his reports: so many little infringements that added up to a damning picture. "Let's not mention how long I was alone in there, mate. I might have been a bit rough with him there, mate. Not worth mentioning the toms, is it, mate?" He was always so friendly during that thirty seconds, and Sefton always kept silent, and then the smile dropped away and the mask was back. He had rank on him, but that was no excuse. *He's put a gag on you, and you let him! You keep letting him!*

It was obvious the man was using. Sefton suppressed his fury yet again. You did undercover one of two ways: you either stayed yourself, playing a part all the way; or you became something else, something that suited your undercover situation. *I'm still me. But you've lost yourself.* Undercover was a big deal for black coppers, because so many of the OCNs were of African ethnicity. Maybe you didn't get to do all the management courses, maybe your experience became too narrow to attract promotion, maybe you were just a tool like a phone tap or a surveillance team, but it felt like the most meaningful contribution you could make. And that in a culture where, no matter what anyone said, your opportunities felt narrow anyway. But, when Sefton saw that glazed-eye coldness in Costain's face tonight, he knew: *This bastard's going to bring me down with him.*

Sefton's mum had taught him something, from his earliest days of getting kicked about. "Wish good things at them," she'd said. "Wish good things at them *hard*." Then she'd make a serious, ridiculous face. He had kept that as a habit of mind, like not walking under ladders. He glanced at Costain now and wished paydays and promotion for the sod, contorting his face with the effort of wishing it.

"You all right, Kev?" asked Toshack. Which made Costain look round quickly, and satisfyingly. *There, Mum, wherever you are now, it worked—sort of.*

He instantly dropped the expression. "Come on, boss," he said, in that West London accent he'd sold to Quill as a black kid trying too hard. The voice he hated, if he was being completely honest, because it reminded him of all the kids around him when he was growing up, but not of himself. It was a voice he'd learned to adopt. "We'll move heaven and Earth for you, you know that?" *Yes, sir, master*—Toshack liked that, so Costain gave it to him. "But tell us who we're after. We all want a drink at midnight, don't we?"

There, the look on Costain's face! Fabulous, darlings. 'Cos second UC Sefton kept daring to show initiative, and that was recorded on that bloody tape of his. Assuming Quill had actually passed it to him. And assuming he'd switched it on.

"You'll get to toast the New Year at midnight," Toshack reassured him. "Back at the house. If we don't find it this time . . . it's last orders for me, 'cos I'll be gone soon after."

Sefton looked just a bit worried and puzzled, but inside now he was yelling.

*

As the soldiers strode up the path of their last suburban semi, Sefton finally made eye contact with Costain. They hung back until everyone else had gone inside.

"Your call, skip," he said to Costain, as the familiar crashing noises began inside.

Costain looked splendidly uncertain. His lovely criminal lifestyle was coming to an end, and he was going to have to either call it now or add to the pile of disciplinary charges. "Go on, then," he said.

Sefton looked toward the house, then carefully took his mobile, with the tracer in it, from out of his other pocket. He texted one word to a number which, if called, would connect to a bloke who called himself Ricky, who would ask, "What's up, Kev?"

The single word: *Midnight*.

Costain had placed himself between Sefton and the window, and now he pointed to himself. "*I'm* going to get him," he said, "before it goes down."

Sefton watched the lead UC, as he marched toward the house, and once again he sent all his bloody good wishes after him.

TWO

Gipsy Hill was indeed a hill, and the nick was situated near the top of it; at the highest point above sea level that any police station in London occupied. Quill had just stepped out of his vehicle in the Hill's car park which was, as usual, lit up like a stadium. Well, a stadium where a few of the lights were broken. It was just past 11 p.m., at the very end of the old year.

"Midnight!" he was saying into his Airwave radio, while Harry marched beside him, talking equally urgently into his phone. "So we're assembling at a quarter to, round the corner from the house in Bermondsey, which means we have to be out of here—" He paused when he heard the sound of engines behind him, and turned to see a line of unmarked cars rolling in, followed by an Armed Response Vehicle out of Old Street. "—right now!" He then exclaimed, "You beauty!" before correcting himself, "Sorry, ma'am."

Harry waited until his superior had switched off the radio. "You still reckon Toshack's going to run for it?"

"Not so much now. I've been talking to the uniforms who're moving in on every place he's been to, and he's been making a fuckload of noise at every one of them. That's hardly *sneaking* out of the country. That's more like desperation. He's looking for someone important to him: an old flame, or a kid he lost track of. If he's cashing in, it'll be with a shotgun to his own forehead on the stroke of midnight. Only, instead, we'll be there to hear his confession."

Harry coughed a laugh. "At least then we'll get him for possession of a firearm."

They got into one of the waiting cars. As police officers in Metvests came running out of Gipsy Hill police station to start filling up the other vehicles, Quill waved for his driver to join the convoy.

Costain watched as Rob Toshack stepped slowly down from the cab of the SUV. His last hope had gone with that final house. "What would you do if you were me, son?" the boss asked.

The question you could never answer. You started making suggestions, saying hit them here and here, and a jury would start to wonder if these fine gentlemen would have done any of that without you egging them on. *Run for the airport, Rob. Take me with you. The fuckers who're after you, you're worth ten of them.* "I don't know what the problem is, boss."

"I'm just going upstairs for a minute."

Rob went inside, and Costain walked quickly after him, aware of Sefton catching up, but he didn't look back to check on him. Upstairs meant Rob was going to lock himself into his den. They'd searched that room in the past, and Rob only kept it locked when he himself was inside. He'd spend hours up there, and come down looking elated, telling some new story of how a certain someone either wouldn't be getting in their way much longer, or had been persuaded over to their point of view. Or that would be the moment he'd choose for sorting and then sending out the supply. As if having the supply in his own home wasn't a risk at all; it had proved not to be. Costain followed him upstairs, and heard the other boys switching the telly on down below, their laughter rising; crisis over, they thought. Sefton had stayed down there, too, thank Christ.

"Rob," Costain said, "what's wrong?"

But Rob just shook his head and went on into his den. He locked the door behind him.

Costain waited a few moments, then put his ear to the door.

He didn't hear Rob talking to anyone. Instead he was fumbling with something. The den was actually quite a big space, obviously a spare bedroom from the days when that meant showing off some square feet. Rob had lined it with shelves stacked with cardboard boxes, most of which—as the two UCs had discovered on that day of blissful hope when they'd made a search in there—were empty. Nor, Costain was sure, having had a look at the plans and done some tapping on walls, was there enough room in the house for a hidden den or passage.

There was a sudden noise, and for a moment Costain thought something must have fallen. But then there was silence again. Very aware of time rushing past, Costain kept listening. It was twenty to midnight when he heard another sound from inside, and he had to stand up quickly and get away as Rob's footsteps approached the door. *What had the man been doing in there? What did he ever do in there?*

Rob emerged from the den looking as if he'd had the last tiny bit of hope shaken out of him, but his dignity seemed to have returned as a result. "Having earlier sampled a bit of what we sell, Blakey," he said, "I find I don't like it very much. So, in the next ten minutes, I'd like to get as pissed as humanly possible."

The pair of them sat in an empty bedroom, London cloud glowing dull-orange through the window. From downstairs Costain could hear the sounds of the party getting raucous. Sefton would be sweating now, aware that, just for once, he had to let his colleague make the play.

"When Dad died," said Rob, "my brother Alf was left in charge. He was older than me, and he was shagging the proverbial deer with no eyes—literally had no fucking idea. All these vicious kids,

19

with their crack and their guns, were sprouting up around us. We had no resources to match that. We had community, yes, but community don't mean a thing when it gets in the way of money. Nothing to stop a jeep mowing down the gnomes in the front garden and then some twat from Jamaica chucking a grenade through your window. Here's the secret, Tony: London's always about what's moving underneath, about what's pushing what. It was understanding that which let me get past what Alf left me with." He raised his can of lager, managing a smile as if at some private joke. "To Alf."

Costain joined in. "You never did talk much about him dying."

"You're right there, Tone. There's a lot of memories you don't want to dwell on."

"I know you. You're not going off after midnight. You'll be staying put."

"Nah, I'm off. To somewhere abroad. Oh, get that look off your face. I don't mean right now. It's just that things are going to change now, maybe very quickly, starting at midnight, and I haven't got . . . I haven't got the protection no more. When everyone realizes that . . . well, all I'll have then to protect me is loyalty and tradition."

"Maybe sometimes loyalty and tradition actually count. They do between me and you, anyway. You know I've always watched your back." *Just go out front, get in the car, and go. I'll say you tricked me. I'm going down, anyway.*

"You have indeed, Tone, and I'll see you lot right. I'll distribute a shitload of working cash to the soldiers, and use the rest to leg it."

Maybe give me something I can give them. Just tell me about the freelancers. About the supply.

"Anyway, it'll all go to hell." He threw aside the empty can of lager and grabbed another. "I caused chaos in this town on my way up, but that's nothing compared to when they'll start fighting over what I've left behind. And they don't have the advantages I

20

had. It'll be back to the old days, to shootings on the doorsteps. It's meant to be the end of the world soon, innit?"

"Always is."

"I thought tonight I might manage to keep my edge, that I might get someone I know to extend a deal, but . . ."

Costain inclined his head, waiting.

"Now I might be on the wrong end of it. Someone might make a better offer. And then—"

Costain looked up just then and saw Sefton in the doorway, making out that he was heading for the bog. He held his hand up: five minutes until they arrive.

Okay.

He actually found he was smiling now that they'd got to it. He was the star of this picture—inside, at least—and he'd either pull this off or it'd kill him. "Rob . . . you know what you mean to me. And that's real, that's solid, but this comes from the same place, okay? No reason for me to even say it, otherwise. You see . . . Blake isn't my real name."

"What?"

"Rob, mate, I'm an undercover copper."

Sefton was out of the doorway like a shot, a horrified expression on his face, away and down the stairs without a sound. *Yeah, you just scuttle off.* Costain's gaze flicked quickly back to Rob.

The king of London, his expression now a mask of horror, was getting slowly to his feet. "I could have known," he said. "I could have asked."

Oh, Christ, where did that come from?! Why did he have to go and say that?!

"I didn't, though," Rob continued, " 'cos it didn't seem like there was anything you lot could do."

Costain stayed sitting. "None of what you've built up can protect you from the other gangs. Or from your freelancers if they've been turned. All it would cost you is those fuckers. The dark side of

21

your network. The ones who let you down." *The ones you could have "asked" about UCs!*

Toshack held his gaze for a moment. Then he went for his gun.

Sefton went into the front room, where he ignored the soldiers drinking in front of the telly. He looked at his watch. Three minutes.

No, Costain, the stupid bloody sod, didn't even have that much time.

So, which window? That one. He went over to a lamp, and checked nobody was looking at him. He quickly moved the table the lamp was sitting on by couple of feet, and switched it on. He stood between it and the window, but was smiling and watching the telly again when Mick looked round at him. Then, when Mick turned away, Sefton raised one arm in a loop right up against the window, and touched the top of his head.

Costain was staring at the tiny O-shaped cavity of the end of the gun. Toshack's hands were shaking, but he was aiming at Costain's stomach: the certain shot, the lingering death. "You bastard," he said. "Did *you* take it away from me? Can coppers do that?"

"I don't know anything about that." Costain tried to make his expression convey to the other man that he hadn't wanted it to go this way, that they were now being overheard, and that he had no choice. At any second, the Nagra tape would run out with a loud click, the stuff of UC nightmares, perhaps be the cause of his death now, if Toshack was startled by it. The wall clock said he had three minutes.

"You say you want to help me?"

"I want to. I so bloody want to. You've given me a home here, Rob—first proper home I ever had. I haven't told them nothing, so far. I was planted here, and then I saw what sort of house you kept. So they was waiting for tonight. But if I can save you with what we talk about here, if I can use the resources these coppers have got, and get you into hiding—"

"Grass, you mean?"

Costain got to his feet. "You're the only boss left who cares about that honor shit! You see how London's going, how the world's going! The rest of them use grasses as just another weapon against each other. What's the point of being noble, when nobody else is?"

" 'Noble!' The trouble is, you shite, that your mates would never believe me!"

"They would if it came from me."

"What, they trust you, do they? Do they know about some of the stuff you've done while you were on my books?"

No, and you don't know all of it either. But there was something in Rob's look that said he was desperate enough to listen, that if Costain could find a way through in the next two minutes . . . "Listen—!"

Just then, from downstairs, there came the slam of a door bursting open under the impact of a battering ram.

Rob stood there stock-still, horrified. The sounds of shouting and scuffling rose from downstairs. But no gunshots, which meant that the soldiers, who had never had to fight, were folding.

"Give me something!" shouted Costain. "Something that shows them you were willing to talk before you got nicked. For Martha's sake!"

But now there were boots running up the stairs. All hope dropped instantly from Rob's face. Costain leaped for him. Rob's shot went wild. Costain hit the big man, and they both went down. As they fell he could hear "Gun, gun!" from the Armed Response coppers thundering upward through the house. When they got there, could he trust them? And who at Gipsy Hill was he going to be able to trust with that tape? It said that the nick had been breached; that there was someone who could give out info on UCs.

Rob fought to keep the gun. He slammed Costain to one side and then the other, but Costain managed to keep a grip on the hand holding the weapon. As they burst in through the doorway, Costain realized that Rob wasn't trying to twist it round to aim at him, but was keeping his arm straight as if hoping to get a shot off at—

Costain rolled him aside and that shot went through the window. "Don't you fucking shoot him!" he bellowed.

Many hands grabbed for the pair's wrists and suddenly the gun was gone, and they were being hauled to their feet, and Costain struggled, spat and swore at them as they heaved first him and then Rob toward the door. There were sounds, cries from the next floor, as more officers pounded up into the house. He could hear Martha starting to scream insults.

On the landing, they smashed his face against the wall. His wrists were hauled behind him before the cuffs bit into them. He was pushed back toward the stairs, Rob passing him, but not looking at him. Below, he could see Sefton, cuffed also, being shoved out of the door, in a line with all the soldiers.

Suddenly, at the foot of the stairs, Rob made his move. With a great cry, he surged forward, out of the grasp of so many hands, his own still pinned behind his back, and propelled a uniformed copper into the wall, his forehead connecting brutally with the man's throat and bringing him down. He bounced off the man, bellowing incoherently at all the others, his red face like that of an animal roaring at its fate, defiant to the last. "For you!" he shouted. "For you, if you want, you sow!" Costain didn't know if he was talking about luck or about Martha or what, but it was magnificent to witness. He let out a bellow of coke-fueled laughter, thrashing out again against the uniforms around him.

A kind of ecstatic yell of triumph rose from the rest of the uniforms gathered downstairs. They piled into Rob, some bursting in through the front door, or rushing back down the stairs, pushing past Costain. Rob was lost in the sea of them, crying out loudly under the blows.

Resisting arrest. All the abuse coppers took, people spitting in your face . . .

Resisting arrest. Set off that powder keg.

Though, while in cuffs, it shouldn't. Not these days.

Costain thought—as they heaved him down the stairs soon after, as he still heard the sound of blows and Rob's cries of protest—of the four years he'd been involved in this. Of the six times during that period he'd been stopped and searched. A patrol officer in Kilburn, just a kid, had called him "nigger" and slapped him on the cheek. The one time, too, that he'd had his warrant card on him, and they hadn't bloody found it. He still had the young man's shoulder number scribbled on a piece of paper in his wallet, and he thought of it at times like this.

Quill was fighting his way into the throng now, physically pulling coppers off Rob's back. "Robert . . . Stephen . . . Toshack," he had begun yelling, ". . . you do not have to say anything, but it may harm your defense if . . ."

From the television nearby, Costain heard the New Year's Day celebrations beginning. A moment later there sounded, from the small of his back, a single loud click.

He was dragged out through the door, without any eye contact from Quill, and across the huge dark coldness of the morning, and thrown into the back of one of a string of police vans, like all the other soldiers in their beery suits.

And he let out a breath and closed his eyes, and felt a rush of fear at what was still only in his head and on that tape.

The police helicopter hovered above Bermondsey, every stroke of its blades swallowing the last available money out of its last operation, the coppers inside it watching not just the raid on the Toshack home but simultaneous assaults on the garages and front-room distribution centers and suburban brothels. They were fully intent on their last duties before they'd be on their way into oblivion. *Like the rest of London*, they felt—from on high tonight—

bitterly. They were too intent, in fact, to notice that, through what seemed to be coincidence, every prisoner taken out of every building was being removed in a southwesterly direction.

The wheel that was London had started, ever so slowly, to turn once again.

THREE

In the early hours, Quill watched as the uniforms opened the back doors of each van in turn and led each prisoner into Gipsy Hill police station. Not everyone who'd been discovered at the house was here, because he'd had the prisoners divided up between the secure custody suites at Gipsy Hill, Streatham, Brixton and Kennington, partly to speed up the entire process, partly so that every major player was kept in a cell corridor on his own, and couldn't get his story straight by shouting to his mates. Harry would be ready to do a bit of sleight of hand so that Costain could slip him the Nagra when he surrendered his personal items to the custody sergeant. Getting that part sorted might have been hellish had Quill not played snooker with said sergeant on a regular basis. Thank God they'd now moved on from Nagras, as a rule. Unless the current cuts meant they were now stuck with them again on a regular basis.

Quill hoped they had something more to work with here than possession of firearms and a few class-A drugs found at Rob's house. The gun should be enough to put Toshack away, but Quill wouldn't bet on it, given the prisoner's way with juries. There was nothing found so far that said that the house itself was an OCN drug-distribution center. Neither was there anything that might let them get their hands on Toshack's freelancers. The situation in the house had confirmed his suspicion of a certain desperation on Toshack's part, but, so far, nothing had fallen out as a result of that desperation. Quill had only the sketchiest picture of what had been going on from the uniforms that had arrested Costain upstairs. He wouldn't know more until they extracted the pair of UCs and listened to that tape.

There went Costain and Sefton now, both in handcuffs but apart: one yelling too theatrically and the other acting stoic. The corrupt egotist and the professional: the latter having seemingly called in the cavalry to save the former. Having watched those two go past, he made sure to watch all the others equally. Toshack came out last. As Quill made eye contact with him, the gang leader dropped his gaze to the ground. Quill perked up at that: maybe something was going to fall out of this after all.

Quill waited until they were all brought inside, and then followed, heading toward the Ops Room. Uniforms coming off the night shift stopped to offer him congratulations as he passed. "Fucking Toshack! Kick arse!"

Quill acknowledged the praise, then pushed his way through the double doors that led into the Ops Room. The Operation Goodfellow coppers who hadn't been out in the field that morning applauded him too. He waved this attention aside, getting irritated with it now. Instead he looked at the room beyond them. For the last four years he'd been living with that familiar smell of soup and aftershave. The room was the usual mess: ancient desktop computers, their drives wheezing; family photos; cut-out headlines and dark copper jokes. A sink that was never cleaned because the first thing Quill had done when he'd got here was to lock out the cleaners, whether vetted or not. The wall was used as a screen for the PowerPoint projector, and had biro marks on it to indicate the picture size for best focus. The Operations Board, covered in Toshack photos and organizational diagrams, with "Goodfellow" written across the top, now had a big black X taped over Rob

Toshack's face. Quill went and gazed at it, and felt distantly annoyed that they hadn't left that privilege to him. But would he even have bothered to do it? The X still felt like more of a vague possibility than a fact. In the past, Toshack had got out of worse.

Quill located Mark Salter, the DS who ran the room, who looked, deliberately, only appropriately happy. "Congratulations, Jimmy."

"Yeah, yeah. Tell Ben I want a blood test done on Toshack, and in case he's flying over Moscow right now, I want half-hourly tests until he's at a point where the Force medical examiner will agree he's sober again. We'll strike while the iron is hot, and won't wait for the analyst's report on the tape. Though, knowing her, she'll get it done in time. I want the brief in *now*, so call their night desk, get them to wake someone up. And make sure said brief gets a cup of tea and a biscuit. I want every single detail of this," he raised his voice so the room shut up and paid attention, "done by the book, so at the very least we once again get that king of shit hauled *into* a courtroom for *something*."

"Yes, Jimmy," responded the room in a mix of tired voices.

He gave a nod back to them, then went to fetch his own cuppa: tea bag left in to stew, six sweeteners, milk if it wasn't already on the turn.

He fell asleep at his desk with the cup beside him, just for ten minutes, but it was a sleep so deep that he woke wondering where he was, feeling that he'd been wrestling with something in his dream. He drank his lukewarm tea and wondered what he'd ever find to do instead of this operation—especially if it came to nothing.

Nothingness, that was his enemy. Meaning: lack of.

He had hours of paperwork still in front of him, and maybe no emotional pay-off at the end of it. Not after four bloody years of it. But he started on it now anyway.

Harry came in looking angry, but kept his voice down to a whisper. "Jimmy," he murmured, "first UC didn't give it up."

"What?"

"I gave him a clear and secure opportunity."

Quill rubbed his brow. "He might have decided it wasn't secure enough." But the look they shared said that they both knew there was something more to this. Something dodgy. "He's doubtless got a back-up plan, but if he doesn't go for it, I'm marching uniforms in there and ending his career."

Costain listened to Mick, the inhabitant of the cell next door, snoring. Until relative silence had settled over the corridor, he'd been waiting for there to be a shout that he was filth. But none came, and finally he relaxed over that. They'd put Toshack straight into the back of a car, and obviously he hadn't had a chance to tell his soldiers anything. Food, under a metal cover, had been brought in an hour after they'd been booked in. He'd eaten it all. The back-up plan concerning the Nagra was, as always, for Costain to wait until 2 a.m., then put it under the same cover and slide it back through the hatch, into the corridor. Someone with the right level of operational knowledge would be there to collect it. Now it was 1:57 a.m., and he didn't know what he was going to do.

He'd already balked at giving the Nagra up at the planned handover. There was a traitor inside SCD 10, maybe inside Gipsy Hill itself, but the traitors wouldn't know he knew about that until he had handed over that tape. Then, if the wrong person got to hear it, his life wouldn't be worth shit. He should get rid of it. Unspool it. Wrap it in enough toilet paper and flush it. But then he wouldn't get the chance to deliberately give it to the *right* people, and save his career. Not to Quill, certainly! He wouldn't let him keep the credit. Costain ran a hand over his face, trying to calm down, aware of his heart racing. At least they hadn't taken a sample or a blood test. On that basis alone he'd be fucked. If he'd known the raid would be going down that same night, he'd have stayed off the sniff.

He decided he would wait until he saw who . . . but who might show up that he trusted? The light in the corridor increased slightly, meaning a door had been opened. This was it. A tall figure came and opened the observation slit to look into his cell. Costain felt a jolt of surprise, even of fear. It was Lofthouse, the detective superintendent in charge of Goodfellow. She had the same questioning look on her face as she had displayed when he'd first met her. He had thought it weird at the time. Even being looked closely at by a super was weird for a UC in his position. But this now! This was so far from standard operating procedures.

Lofthouse made eye contact with him, then looked down again toward the food slot. Since she was Quill's superior . . . God, maybe this was all about Quill! Maybe there was nobody else here she could trust. And Costain had to trust someone if he was going to save himself. He reached behind his back for the tape recorder.

At 2:01 a.m., Quill lowered his head to his desk in relief after Harry told him that Lofthouse had taken possession of the Nagra.

He went off for a few hours of proper sleep in the accommodation block, and returned to Ops, blinking in the light of morning, to find that Harry had the intelligence analyst's report ready for him. He read the report, balled it up, threw it across the room, then had to go and fetch it and smooth it out again. He put in a call to Lofthouse, but was told she wasn't in yet. Then he turned back to Harry, and lowered his voice.

"Fuck," he said. "Someone inside here. No wonder the first UC got freaked out."

"Even by my delightful visage? But, no, he didn't know me from Adam."

"We need to get the CCTV record from the custody suite."

"Already done. What would you do without me? But, yeah, this sort of thing is why Lofthouse has been so hands-on. And it's worked, because Toshack didn't know about the first UC. Which means, by the way, that Costain's clean—in terms of working for Toshack, anyway."

"I doubt they'll hold a parade in his honor, after he's provided a tape on which he actually tells Toshack he's a copper. Crown Prosecution Service might not even go for a trial now."

"He only told him at the very last moment, and it's all there on the tape, start to finish, alongside a good dollop of testimony in which he mentions issues pertaining to a prosecution."

"Yeah, yeah."

Harry let Quill calm down for a moment, as he always did. "First and second UCs have been vanished from custody into safe houses, told to stay handy for debriefing. Again, Lofthouse sorted that."

Quill frowned. "I'd have kept first UC in custody."

"Take it up with her."

"How's Toshack by now?"

"Sober, says the FME."

"Right, let's be having him." As Harry departed to organize that, Quill went over to a cupboard, where he found and then opened a box of ancient cassette tapes wrapped in cellophane. "We," he addressed the room, a room he no longer trusted and was now playing a bloody role to, "are the last people in the world still using cassettes. They stick, they jam and, whenever they do, we have to bloody seal them up like they're radioactive and start the interview all over again."

"Your point being, Jimmy?" said Salter, a questioning look on his face. Quill wondered at the extent to which the tension level in this room had increased now that a handful of people in Gipsy Hill knew they had a bad apple in their midst.

"I like the smell of this stationery cupboard." He slammed open the doors on his way out, before bellowing at them from the safety of the corridor. "I feel my new career may be in stationery."

Quill took along a uniform on shift, PC Watterson, who looked about twelve, and had him sit in with him in the interview room, where two other uniforms led Toshack in, his brief beside him, and then left them to it. The brief had a look in his eye that Quill hadn't seen before in any case associated with Toshack. He looked as if he was on the losing side and didn't like it. It was a promising expression, he reckoned, but it didn't add up to much against what was on the other side of the scales. Quill adopted a poker face as he proceeded through the usual lengthy introductions and cautions.

Costain had been placed in a West Indian gang called the Toil just as it and Toshack's gang had started competing for street corners where they could sell smack. He'd spent months in the shebeens of Peckham, those illegal drinking dens where Pa Toil's guys hung out, socializing, becoming part of the furniture, inviting guys back to his place on a regular basis, helping out on the particular night when one of the shebeens got raided by the police and was shut down. As Quill had predicted, Toshack had eventually made an approach to Pa, and had subsequently taken over the much smaller Toil in that miraculous way of his. Those of Pa's soldiers who liked the prospect—Costain included—had thus become part of the Toshack gang. In the two years following that, Costain had risen to a position where Toshack trusted him enough to let him bring Sefton into the gang.

After today's raid, Costain was meant to have been left with his cover intact, letting him maintain a relationship with Toshack. They could subsequently meet "coincidentally" in the back of a prison van, during some transfer between facilities. Costain would tell Toshack who he thought the informer who had brought down the gang had been, naming Sefton as the culprit (because Toshack might have a genuine reason for trusting another gang member), and then apologize for his own bad judgment in bringing Sefton into the gang, and thus get loads of extra juice in return. Quill had played that one often in order to get access to the sort of intelligence that remained locked in prisoners' heads after their gangs had exploded. It had always worked. His UCs still had useful "correspondences" going on with loads of those behind bars, the letters all written and sent from the right postcodes by the staff of SCD 10, who received the replies too.

But Costain had now put an end to the possibility of any of that, having blown his own cover with what was, at the very least, a stupid piece of grandstanding. Having put this unreliable UC into that situation could look pretty bad on Quill's CV—maybe bad enough to create real trouble for him if there were elements inside the operation who might try to get him chucked out before they themselves got fingered.

But that expression on the brief's face had suggested that the gang leader hadn't just been happily telling him about the undercover cop who'd given them some leverage. Toshack looked like a man who'd made his mind up. Very sober now, in fact.

Quill didn't bother greeting Toshack. His old dad had been friends with some of the gangsters he'd nicked, but Quill didn't feel the modern world gave him space for such romantic illusions. He used his house key to unwrap the cellophane slowly and carefully from the fresh cassettes, in clear view of the prisoner. He placed both tapes in the double-deck recorder and pressed the Record button. "This interview is being recorded," he said into the machine. "I am Detective Inspector James Quill, and also present is Constable Joseph Watterson. Will the suspect and his solicitor please identify themselves?"

"Robert Toshack." He sounded very precise this morning.

"Philip Jones, from Austell Probert Mackinley," said the brief.

"This interview takes place at eleven-oh-eight hours on 1 January in Interview Room 2 of Gipsy Hill police station. Mr. Toshack will be given a notice as to the circumstances in which these tapes are used, and the master tape will be sealed in his presence at the end of the interview. Mr. Toshack, your right to free and independent legal advice is ongoing. Although your solicitor is with you, you may ask for the tape to be stopped and have a private consultation with him at any time. Mr. Toshack, I warn you that you do not have to say anything, but it may harm your defense if you do not mention, when questioned, something which you later rely on in court, and that anything you do say may be given in evidence."

He could see the brief hoping he'd slip up. Juries only ever pursued that route if they really liked the bloke in the dock, and defendants' briefs only went for it out of desperation. Quill knew one old lag who'd been successfully cautioned with "Get in the fucking van, you're nicked," but that one had heard the full standard caution on forty-three previous occasions, and was thus claimed to have got the idea by now. And Toshack had enjoyed a charmed life with juries. "You are now under caution. Allow me to explain that further—"

Toshack spoke up. "I understand the caution. I've heard enough of them, so let's get this over with."

"Look at you, the good man in the hands of the barbarians." Quill said it deliberately, to see how much lip the brief was willing to take. And there was his second good sign: not a glimmer of a reaction. "Mr. Toshack, the two tapes that are running will record everything we say here today, and that recording can also be used as evidence. If you're charged with any offenses, a copy of the interview tape will be provided to your chosen legal adviser. We're about to ask you your whereabouts at the time of a series of major crimes, including but not limited to the armed raid on the Barclays Bank security van on the Fulham Road, during which the guard, Mr. Carl Lassiter, was murdered; about leases actually *in your name* on a number of houses of ill repute; about the operation of a number of car-theft rings—"

"I did it all," said Toshack.

Quill forced himself not to swear in sheer astonishment. "Would you . . . repeat that, please, Mr. Toshack?"

The brief spoke before Toshack could reply, clearly not having been prewarned about this. "My client is suffering from—"

"I'm not one of these modern fuckwits who *suffer* from things. I said I did it *all*. Everything you're charging me with. Everything you're thinking of charging me with—"

"If I may have a moment with my client—"

"Get him out of here!" yelled Toshack.

"Are you declining legal representation, Mr. Toshack?" Because, if he was, that was just the old bastard being awkward. Then Quill would have to summon an inspector unconnected to the case in here, who would then have to make a written record of the whole procedure. Quill knew a DS who'd gone ahead without remembering that, and ended up with an inadmissible interview.

"He can stay if he keeps his gob shut!"

So it hadn't been a ploy. Quill suppressed a grin, thinking it was a week late for Christmas. He carefully finished his list of charges, watching Toshack's face as he read them out.

Toshack sat back in the chair heavily, listening carefully, nodding along. "You're not going to believe this," he said, when Quill had finished, "but this is my only way out now. I think I've made a big mistake." Quill kept his expression neutral. "I think . . . someone'll come for me, and I don't know how long that might take. The first thing I have to say is . . ." He seemed to have to make an effort in saying it. "I'm sorry."

Quill blinked. "You're *sorry?*"

"I'd . . . like you to get the chaplain in here, actually, Quill. I'm going to clear my conscience, tell you everything I've done. I am begging forgiveness."

"We'll get the clergy involved further down the line. If you want forgiveness from *me*, you'll need to name names. *Every* name."

Toshack took a deep breath, then he nodded. "All right," he said, "but not here and now. I'm going to need certain things doing . . ."

Quill was thinking how Toshack must reckon he was born yesterday if he thought he was going to put him in a van, to be rescued by his freelancers. Quill later remembered that thought very clearly; it was frozen inside his head. He would recall it every time he remembered what happened next.

Toshack suddenly stopped talking, his lips tightly pursed. Then he jerked his hands up in the air, waved them around violently as if trying to push something away from him. There was a look in his eye which it took Quill a second to register: a look of recognition, as if someone he knew had just walked into the room. He leaped up out of his seat and staggered around. His face was going purple, and it looked as he was having some kind of seizure.

Of all the bloody times!

"Get the doctor!" Quill shouted to Watterson, who was already running for the door. Then he remembered the tape. It was otherwise just him and the brief in here now, but at least the security camera would be getting this. "Mr. Toshack seems to be suffering from some sort of medical . . . event!"

Which was when Toshack became suddenly hard to look at.

Quill wondered if he himself was suffering his first migraine. He felt he was suddenly viewing Toshack from the far end of a long lens; as if, impossibly, Quill was far below and the other man was flying. But, when he blinked and told his brain to get a grip, there the man was again, up against the wall . . . yeah, of course, that was the wall. He was staring at Quill, not playing some trick with him, but terrified—terrified because that look in his eyes was terrified. It was more than terror at what was happening to him, because his eyes were moving so swiftly, as if he was dreaming, as if there was some new horror in every direction he looked. He looked to be trying to scream without even being able to open his mouth. His face had gone purple, and he looked completely full of blood. Quill imagined cartoon steam coming off him and, just for a moment, he swore he actually saw it. The brief was frantically questioning Toshack, asking if he was fit to continue.

Quill tried to reach toward the stricken man, to usher him back down into his seat, to tell him medical help was on the way, because he wouldn't be getting out of it that easily—

The blood exploded into Quill's face.

He fell with the force of it, hit the desk and then fell. Great gouts of blood, far too much, flew around him, covering the furniture, the tape recorder, the room, as if a bucket of it had been thrown over him. Quill managed to heave himself upright, and found blood still showering like rain. He was covered in it. So was the brief, who was yelling hysterically. Toshack, or what was left of Toshack—no, whole Toshack, for there he was, all of him—was just a mass of blood which had come from that mouth, that had burst from him, from his lolling dead head.

The doctor came running in, and there were cries and shouts along the corridors outside. Quill tried to get up, but he slipped in the blood. The doctor was stumbling toward him, as if something could still be done, getting the blood on the soles of her shoes. The brief was now just staring. Quill started to shout that maybe . . . maybe this was a crime scene. Maybe poison! Gipsy Hill needed to be shut down. Now! Now! Lofthouse rushed in, along with a lot of uniforms. She started yelling at him, all the questions Quill couldn't answer. Quill stood away, by the wall, his hands held away from his body, his suit covered in blood, feeling that he would at any moment wake up.

FOUR

Lisa Ross sat in the dark in her tiny anonymous office at the trading estate in Norwood, listening to the Nagra tape for the third time. She didn't want to think about what they'd just called to tell her, about what had just happened. It was too big to comprehend. She had ready in front of her, on the ancient laptop the Met let her have the use of, her report forms where she'd been annotating the background and any possible follow-ups to everything Toshack had said. She invariably found new elements to add on every listen. She'd always felt privileged that DI Quill wanted her to listen to these tapes before he did, that he'd recognized her specialist knowledge in that way. She liked to work straight from the tape, and only look afterward at the transcripts prepared by SCD 10's blind audio typist, Stacey, who was presumably up as late as she was.

But that would be in preparation for a trial. And now there wasn't going to be a trial. Not of Toshack, at least. Someone might have got to him, they were saying, but it wasn't clear how, since he'd been kept well isolated and hadn't eaten anything since his arrest.

She wanted to hit something. She wanted to rip the throat from something. But the only thing she really wanted to do that to was Toshack himself.

The universe had made her the butt of an enormous joke, and she could hear it laughing.

They'd said he'd started to confess. Maybe that was something, at least. For the longest time now, as intelligence on the Toshack organization had always failed, as every avenue of inquiry had shut down, as jury after jury had failed to convict, she'd felt that nothing she had been trying to do would ever work.

Now she knew it certainly never would.

But Toshack was dead. Wasn't that revenge on him of a kind? So why didn't she feel anything? God, she hoped she eventually would, or what was left to her?

Detective Superintendent Lofthouse herself, to Ross's astonishment, had brought over the tape and transcripts in the early hours. "I'm up anyway," she'd said, "so I thought let's cut out one more courier." Ross had felt weird, receiving them from this smart woman at the door of her office unit, with herself dressed in sweatshirt and leggings. Ross had been told her appearance could put the fear of God into people at the best of times. Her right eye was blue, but her left one was gray, and her nose was askew, like a boxer's. For a boxer's reason, too. But Lofthouse, who amazingly had seemed to know who she was, had turned out to be all right. She'd said she hoped someday Ross could come into the Ops Room, get to meet the team. Like other intelligence analysts did, was what she hadn't added.

Ross had yelled out loud when she listened to the tape for the first time, and heard Toshack talk about Alf—insulting his own brother, belittling him. She didn't know the name of the first UC, other than that Toshack referred to him as "Blakey," but she'd grown to recognize his voice and had, for years now, ground her teeth at his gleeful laughter, and how he seemed to appreciate every shitty little thing Toshack said.

Then, toward the end of the tape, when the sod seemed to get some idea of urgency and had started to get some good stuff, but then ended up telling Toshack he was a UC . . . she'd leaped out of her chair. She'd taken the knife she always kept in her pocket, and she'd slammed it into her desk, and then had hated the sight of it there, the idea that now there'd always be a mark.

And now they'd just told her . . . she was never going to read those court transcripts while her news—her intel—was presented to Toshack, and hammered at him back and forth, and all those revelations brought him down. Now the truth would never out.

It was too big to think about. She felt like crying. But she couldn't.

Quill had changed into a spare shirt and trousers as fast as he could, the forensics people taking his own clothes off him and bagging them, right down to his Y-fronts, which he'd tossed over to them from inside a toilet cubicle. The incredible loss of Toshack, the copper mourning for such a huge, juicy target which had been the center of all their lives—he could feel it all within the station. Their prey had been taken from them. From right in the heart of their place.

Lofthouse met him as soon as he was looking decent, and they walked away together quickly to find some privacy. She immediately put a hand on his shoulder. She did that occasionally, not like any other female copper Quill knew. It wasn't just a willingness to touch other human beings: she would run her hands along walls, tapping them as a builder would, as if it was the only way she could ground herself in those horrible places where she ended up standing around at five in the morning. She was one of those higher-rank types from academia, with a slew of letters to her name, but that had never bothered Quill. Her tendency was to cut through things, to make use of the bureaucracy she had on her side. They'd been good comrades these last four years, himself and this always-tired-looking middle-aged woman. She'd saved his operation from all manner of deleterious penny-pinching Met shit.

"It's not your fault, James," she said now.

41

"Was he poisoned? If so, some of our lot will be wondering if it was me who did it, 'cos *I'd* think it was if—"

"We're running toxicology, but the doctor gave an opinion back in the room itself that it was some sort of seizure." She was plucking at a charm bracelet she wore, something she often did when she was thinking hard. On it were attached a tiny horse, an anchor and a worn-down key. "Having pumped himself full of drugs tonight for the very first time, then picked a fight with a roomful of uniforms, I'm not that surprised. This is you we're talking about, and, unless the bloods come up saying you used an Amazonian dart toxin, I'll do my best to get everyone to piss up another tree."

"Thank you, ma'am."

"Besides, Toshack, rather brilliantly, said he was 'guilty of everything,' which could certainly be said to include the charges in front of him. With that, and what is on the Nagra tape, we get everyone else—and can start digging hard for more. Whatever it was that happened to matey, the firm still goes down."

"But not the mysterious freelancers? And now we won't get anything out of him about . . . issues inside this nick."

It was getting dark when Quill finally left the Hill. The lights were on at the Black Sheep along the road, but that was a copper pub, and he didn't want to be among his fellows right now. Not with all the failure and futility that they'd already be starting to make jokes about. They'd lost Toshack. *Quill* had lost him. He now headed for the back gate, intending to go down to the Postal Order, where nobody knew who he was. He'd called Sarah but found that, when he started to talk to her, he couldn't find much to tell her about what had happened, either. "I'm okay," he'd said finally. "Despite the fountain of blood."

He passed a roughed-up pile of soil in one of the flowerbeds, a circular mass; apparently someone had decided to plant something and then just abandoned it. Even the surrounding garden was falling apart now. He had no idea who had employed the gardeners here, but they'd probably gone the way of everyone else.

Quill found Harry already standing at the bar in the Postal Order. He sighed and slumped up beside him. "Fucking detective," he said. "You knew I'd be here."

"I had one in the Sheep first."

"As the bishop said to the bishop."

Harry got them in, and they sat at a table way back in the corner, where the bloody music drowned out any eavesdroppers. "Nothing you could have done, Jimmy. You'll be fine after counseling."

"You what?"

"Six or seven pints of counseling. At least now you've got a story to match your dad's." Quill's dad, Marty, had been a great and terrible rozzer, a Flying Squad detective in the days of lunchtime drinking. "Suspect misplaced all of his blood in custody? He'd have appreciated that. You always were a chip off the old block."

"Yeah?" Quill wasn't keen on the idea of his own pet death in custody being associated with his dad's theatrical punch-ups and dangling suspects off Waterloo Bridge by their socks. "I know people like to think of me as old guard, Harry, but to be this rule-breaker cop I'd need to break some bloody rules. You can't get away with that these days. I put an end to that rough stuff between Toshack and the uniforms as soon as I could. We could've lost everything with that."

"Well, at least you talk the talk . . . usually."

"'Blige! You're trying hard to make me feel better, aren't you? I tell you what—I'll bet that's how the first UC thinks of himself, and all. Only he doesn't know where the line is, while I do."

"You just nudge that line along a few feet sometimes."

Quill put his pint down solidly and looked at Harry challengingly. Nudging Quill to be more like his father Marty was one of Harry's favorite pastimes, while he himself remained the most anonymous bloody copper in existence. But tonight it was all getting a bit much for Quill. "I am this bloke you see, Harry. I don't really know who that is, and I don't know how much is under the bonnet sometimes, but I'm not my dad and I don't do requests."

"Fair enough."

"Great, sorted. My round, then, is it?"

And that became, as predicted, another six pints of therapy.

Quill was surprised by the next thing he really paid attention to, which was his wife Sarah standing beside him. A welcome sight, obviously. He realized he was sitting in the back garden of his house, and this was the geographical location from which he had been examining a completely blank neon-tinged London sky. His arse was getting wet because of the frost. She had a look on her face that said he might have woken her up while coming out here.

"What," he asked her, "should I be like?"

"Oh God, Quill, funny you should ask. I've been up all night worrying about that, too."

She always called him by his surname; it was a fond little habit of hers. "I can't seem to find any meaning in anything, not now." She was a member of the press, he reminded himself, so he couldn't tell her all the details. "Goodfellow, it's done and . . . I don't think we did any good. Someone else'll just move in on Toshack's territory, and the new guy'll amp up the violence again." He spun his finger in illustration. "It's just getting worse and worse, round and round. What am I for? What can I find to do that's . . . ?" He was sure it was to have been a really profound question, but he couldn't find the end of that sentence. "That's . . . ?"

She took his hand and managed to haul him to his feet. "Your meaning is right here," she said, and Quill got the feeling she was probably angry. At any rate, between them they managed to get him into bed.

FIVE

Sefton stayed at the safe house in Wanstead for a week. He slept a lot. He watched daytime telly. He had some terrible dreams. Stupid stuff, easy to forget in the daylight. He was back on his school bus, being tormented by those little shits. Batty boy, that was their favorite. As if they knew. *Posh boy*. In that accent of theirs that he himself did offhandedly now, and still hated. The white kids called him black, and the black kids called him everything else.

"That," he explained to a bloke called Tom, from Norfolk, in the right sort of pub, "is how I realized I had a talent for my line of work."

"What's that?" Tom hadn't really been listening to Sefton's tales of woe, just looking at the other man's chest.

Which was great. But maybe not for tonight, 'cos he was in a safe house, and out for an innocent pint. "Underwear model," he said, and at least the bloke laughed.

So, loads of time alone in his room, lots of time to let the tension flood out, but that only seemed to let the memories flood in. Fucking Costain! He wished he could put it all in the past, but Costain blowing him that kiss had connected. Even now. Even here. No racism or homophobia in the Met. Not these days, sir, no, I've never seen any. I'm one of the good ones.

He had found a gym with a boxing ring, sparred a bit. His partner, a cocky bloke, thinking he saw something vulnerable in Sefton's passive expression, said, "No, come on, two rounds proper like." Sefton dropped his guard twenty seconds in, stepped past the haymaker, and hit him—body, jaw, body—and the kid staggered back, waving his gloves in the air, laughing awkwardly. "Okay, okay!"

Sefton had inclined his head to him. "Yeah. I get that a lot."

That night he had thought about going on Grindr and setting up a random encounter with some bloke who wouldn't give a fuck about all his angst. Yeah, but no.

Then a phone call had come, saying Toshack had died in custody. Sefton had just nodded, because he felt so numb. Then he wanted to hit something. But he kept it all in.

After that he went out for more runs, got himself ready for the debriefing, ready to become his public self again. He wanted to tell them about Costain, about that moment, about the fucking months of bullying, both in and out of character. But he wouldn't. That wasn't who he was. He didn't want to be an adult who was bullied, so he rose above it by not talking. *Or that's what you tell yourself.*

Debriefing took him to anonymous meeting rooms in anonymous hotels. He found some relief in being led through the last few weeks of the operation, giving the required details, establishing a narrative. He'd expected Quill to be there, but he wasn't. His DS led the meetings and, when asked, said Quill was on leave. That didn't bloody bode well.

Sefton wanted, he realized after the first session, to at least be *asked* about Costain. He wanted to be asked so he could . . . well, maybe mention the drugs. Yeah, that.

But he wasn't asked. And was left frustrated. But perhaps that was for the best. It wasn't as if he'd *seen* him take anything, damn it.

That night, in a different right sort of pub, he declared, again without having given the context: "It's as if I haven't got a voice."

"Talk a lot, don't you?" said the other bloke this time.

Sefton gave him a long look that made him take a step back. Then he broke into a cheerful smile. "Sorry," he said, "long day." And he went back to the safe house alone.

And then it was over. He was told he should expect a meeting with SCD 10 for reassignment, considered damaged goods along with the rest of Goodfellow. But then he got another call: this time Lofthouse's office, which was on his approved list but not a number he'd ever used. A new meeting to be held at a Radisson hotel out near Heathrow. This must be a post-mortem, something on the way to holding an inquiry. Dirt was going to be dished and Sefton resolved that, just for once, he'd do the dishing. Against all his experience of the copper lifestyle, he was hoping for some sort of closure.

He stepped out of the lift, walked into the anonymous meeting room without knocking, closed the door behind him and found himself facing someone he didn't know. A young woman in her twenties, who had the strangest eyes he'd ever seen. She looked out of place in a suit, didn't stand like police did—she wasn't balanced squarely on both feet so as to be braced against whatever was about to happen, the way he'd had to train himself not to stand. She thus looked vulnerable, and vulnerable was worrying. Lofthouse, Quill and Costain were there, too. Apart from the detective superintendent, they all looked equally uncomfortable. "Ma'am," he nodded, "Sir." Just a nod to Costain. "Who's this?"

"This is our intelligence analyst, Lisa Ross," began Lofthouse. "Lisa, this is DC—"

What the fuck? "Ma'am, I'm not comfortable with—!"

"You were told at the start of Goodfellow that Lisa was indoctrinated in the operation, but cut out from it for security reasons. And you're now reacting like any UC would, but

Goodfellow is over, Detective Constable. And I've put together a juicy little spin-off."

Sefton felt like walking straight out again. This was the last thing he'd expected. And it was not bloody closure. A spin-off with Costain? But . . . he wasn't being sent home either. He controlled himself. He kept it all in. He nodded to Ross. "DC Kevin Sefton, second UC."

She looked back at him, apparently as fearful of hearing his name as he was of giving it. Then she looked over to Costain. "*You're* 'Blakey,' then?" she said.

"Guilty as charged." At least he hadn't smiled.

Ross actually snorted, which made Sefton hide a smile. Oh, he liked her.

Quill had meanwhile been lost in paperwork and waiting. Waiting far too long for those bloody test results to come in. He'd also been anticipating a post-mortem in which they'd doubtless try to establish exactly what Costain had been guilty of. His own reports to Lofthouse had leaned heavily in that direction. But it seemed he'd been ignored.

"A spin-off?" he inquired.

"Just you four, reporting directly to me."

Quill looked round at the others, and saw they were as boggled as he was. "Two UCs, an analyst and a DI?"

"Yes."

"Well, apart from anything else, I'll need my DS, Harry Dobson—"

"I'm sorry, no."

Quill felt himself getting angry. "Is the possibility of corruption in Gipsy Hill so widespread," he said, "that *we* are the only four definitely exempt?" And he couldn't help but look straight at Costain as he said it.

Lofthouse just raised a warning eyebrow.

*

Costain had only narrowly persuaded himself to come here. His memory darted back now to the night when Lofthouse herself, incredibly, had arrived outside his cell. She'd taken away the Nagra tape. But then she'd come back, the key to the cell in her hand. "Only take phone calls from me," she'd instructed, walking him out to a waiting car. "I'll take care of you. All right?"

He'd felt ridiculously glad to hear that. He remembered the night when she'd called him about the death that occurred in custody. He'd heard about Rob breaking, of him being about to tell it all, against everything he stood for, and then he heard that Quill had been the only officer in the room. Costain had hung up and gone to a door in his safe house and started slamming it. As if that would bring down punishment.

"Just us four?" he echoed, glaring back at Quill in the same way the man was glaring at him. "How are we going to do this without a traffic warden and a dog handler?"

Since that death in custody, Ross had continued examining the evidence from Goodfellow in her exile in Norwood. She'd kept at it ferociously, focused on it, because she couldn't see a life beyond it. She'd kept telling herself she needed to get past how she felt about Toshack. She'd kept trying to find satisfaction in his death. But she couldn't.

And now this new operation was going to demand that she actually *lived* in this world that was not—but was supposed to have been—a happy-ever-after one. It was mad. It was irrelevant. She focused her attention back on the man they were calling Costain, and set about memorizing him as if one day she'd have to profile him.

Lofthouse pointed to the round table in the middle of the room. "Please, sit."

Quill, aware that he was eyeing her interrogatively, even a bit desperately, made to do so but she held up a hand. "Ah, no. Wait."

They all halted. She toyed with her charm bracelet for a moment, lost in thought, then pointed from each person to a chair. "Jimmy, you go there. Tony there. Kevin there, Lisa there, please."

They moved around to their assigned places, feeling rather amazed. None of them had witnessed a detective superintendent having a nervous breakdown before.

"I'm leaving the name of this new operation," she said, passing out the documents, "to you."

Quill gaped at that too. There was a reason that job and subject names were picked from lists of randomly chosen words. What if he suffered a fit of madness and called it after the target? Speaking of which: "What's the objective?"

"Investigate what happened in that interview room. Find out who killed Robert Toshack."

Quill's heart sank.

"And *how*, because the pathologist's tests found no evidence of poisoning or physical assault."

"So . . ." he couldn't quite find the words for a moment. "How are you so sure he didn't die of natural causes, ma'am?" He wanted her to confirm he was in the clear.

"Because, according to the many experts I've spent a long time talking to, there are no natural causes able to do *that*."

He looked to his insanely small team. They looked back, equally flabbergasted. They had, as the old joke about the stolen toilets went, nothing to go on.

"You'll stay at Gipsy Hill." She finally managed a smile. "Lisa, you'll finally be able to join them. But I've found you a nice new Ops Room, to keep you out of the general population."

Two days later, Quill staggered into the Portakabin, carrying an ancient overhead projector he'd found in the stores at Gipsy Hill, and had heaved the quarter-mile back to the trading estate across the way. The inside of this new "Ops Room" looked as unpromising as the outside. An Ops Board that had been improvised from a cork board found at the market, but empty except for a single photo of Toshack. Some desks. A stack of chairs. One desktop PC, perhaps even more ancient than those in Gipsy Hill. A new kettle. He looked out of the window toward the building in which he'd previously worked. He could smell the distrust even from here. "Gone all Professional Standards on us, have you?" That had been Mark Salter when Quill had popped into the canteen this morning. He'd said it with a smile, but it hadn't extended to his eyes.

They're sure we're looking for a mole. And Lofthouse has bloody kept us here on the Hill to do it. When he'd stopped Lofthouse on the way out of that insane meeting, she'd firmly told him there was nothing further to discuss. And that tone in her voice was one he'd learned to pay attention to.

Ross entered and nodded to him, still wearing that face of hers that looked like it might one day end up on a wanted poster or a stamp. Understandable. The only change for her was that now her anonymous building had slightly more people in it. He made tea as first one car and then another stopped outside, and first Sefton, then Costain, entered, having both taken the shortest possible route from vehicle to door. At least Lofthouse had realized how neither of those two would be eager to show his warrant card at the gate of Gipsy Hill, especially since now there was a strong possibility that someone might write down the name on it, so that a visit to friends and family could be arranged. Not that they weren't still vulnerable out here. Not just politically but physically.

"So," he said to his unlikely unit now it had been assembled, "what have we got?"

"A nagging fear that this is all bollocks, Jimmy," replied Costain.

They went over every detail. Quill then called the pathologist to hear it for himself, but it was open and shut. No known toxin. No known medical condition. An impossibility.

There were only a few avenues of investigation that he could even think of as places to begin with. He next set his team to the task of checking out the records of everyone who'd been in and out of Gipsy Hill on the day Toshack died.

"Okay," said Sefton, but with an enormous internal sigh written on his face. And this was just the first day.

"This," said Costain, "is why we became UCs: to share a computer in a Portakabin, processing data."

"Well," said Quill, limiting himself to a knowing look at Costain, "just think—it could have been *so* much worse."

And that was the first week, with the sound of the rain pounding on the roof of the Portakabin, and the slow sensation of false trail after false trail coming to an end. Since the time frame to be checked was the early hours of New Year's Day until the following morning, no civilians had visited, except Toshack's brief. "So it's either a copper or he 'ingested the poison' before he arrived at Gipsy Hill," said Costain.

"You reckon that's likely?" asked Quill.

"No," said Costain casually, as if it was none of his concern anyway.

This felt like internal exile, as if somehow Lofthouse expected Quill to accuse himself of something. The week lasted forever, and Quill underwent several pints of therapy, on his own, each night.

It was early on a Monday morning, before the other two had come in, that Ross looked up from the wheezing PC and caught his eye. She, in her quiet way, had dug in, had become the one who was too busy to make tea. Quill realized that, for her, doing something that still even tangentially involved Toshack must be some sort of lifeline. And he wondered if it would actually be a mercy to her to cut that line and to let her get on with life.

"I've found something in the Goodfellow case notes," she said.

He went over, and she pointed out the entry: "Lassiter, the driver of the Fulham Road security van. He lost a lot of blood, too. It was assumed that he'd been beaten, but I think someone was a bit quick to jump to that conclusion, 'cos the injuries I've got here aren't entirely consistent with that explanation."

"You're saying getting people's blood to explode in all directions might be someone's modus operandi?"

"It's just one data point, so I'm not, not yet."

Quill sighed. "Listen, do you want to go and check out the scene of the crime over at the Hill? The other two bloody can't, but while it's just you and me here . . ."

"I think that's a reasonable risk."

"You think Tony's dodgy," said Ross, as they crossed the road and headed toward the rear gate of Gipsy Hill.

Quill neither confirmed nor denied it. "I do sometimes think there might be some other reason for this weird unit assignment. Maybe to shake something out."

"So why us too?"

Quill shrugged. He saw that it was Josh Stuart stationed at the back gate, and actually got a smile out of him as he showed him his warrant card and then Ross's ID. Ross seemed to be trying to make herself invisible, and she was doing a good job. They headed down the garden path and out of earshot.

"I need this op to be real," she said. "Is it?"

Quill stopped. They were by that strange pile of earth, and still nobody had planted that bloody tree or whatever it was going to be. "You know as much as I do."

"Only, you three already have that look on your faces . . ."

"What look?"

"That copper look. That British look. The 'Oh well, it's all going to fall apart, so might as well get on with it, even though we're going to fail.' "

"Do you have a point, Lisa?"

"Because if this is a real op, and if you all treat it as a real op, we can make real progress. If you make proper use of me; if you let me do what I do. And I'm going to need you too, because otherwise I don't know what I'm going to do. And because . . . we're standing on top of something huge."

Quill realized that her expression had become urgent—amazed, even. And that she kept looking between his eyes . . . and then at the ground by his feet.

He turned and examined the pile of soil closely for the first time. There was a pattern there, preserved by the frost, not washed out too much by the rain. It was as if someone had inscribed it in the disturbed earth with a spade. Or maybe it had needed a tool more precise. It was a fine spiral.

"Literally," continued Ross. "I've seen that symbol before."

With joy bursting in his heart, Quill looked up and around. He pointed up at the CCTV camera that was looking straight down at them. "Bingo," he said.

Quill headed into Gipsy Hill to get the CCTV tapes sent over, while Ross rushed back to the Portakabin to grab her camera. "We've got a new intelligence analyst," said Harry, falling into step beside him. "Since you took away ours." Many more arrests were being made, extending to the outlying reaches of the Toshack firm. Harry waited until the corridor was clear, then dropped his voice to a whisper. "What are you doing out there, Jimmy?"

"Your guess is as good as mine. I asked to get you over straight away—"

" 'Course you did: you knowing which side your bread is buttered. But Lofthouse said no, didn't she?"

"Harry—"

"No no, it's not your fault. But, I tell you what: you have not seen the depth of ill feeling here." He leaned closer and locked that sleepless gaze of his on Quill. "You have no idea."

Costain and Sefton had arrived by the time he got back to the Portakabin, and had obviously been told by Ross that something was finally happening. She looked up from a huge pile of what looked like school exercise books that she'd brought in. "Okay," she said, "where can I display some images?"

Quill had to use a biro to mark a new square of best focus on the wall.

"The spiral tag." Ross's first image, from a PC projector she'd brought in herself, was a photo of the design that had been etched in the soil, the real thing now having been covered in plastic and fenced off—if Quill's orders had been complied with. "A pile of soil, bit wet for London average, in a spiral pattern that seems to have been formed with some sort of vacuum tool. Nobody's ever come up with any more than that, concerning its formation. One of the first things that Rob Toshack got into, when he took over the family firm, was fixing football matches. He needed to make and launder cash very quickly, and a series of big certs would have done that for him."

She clicked the mouse and the next image appeared: a picture of another such symbol, this one slightly different. "The reason we know about this is because this approach immediately clashed with how clean football had become at the time. Players didn't automatically cave in when threatened, so a number of them started to have the spiral tag appear in their gardens. Some of their managers, and a DI called Sam Booney—"

"Sam Booney," interjected Quill, "out of Kensal Rise, shot in the knee in the course of his duties. Could burst an apple with his hand, goes the story."

"—knew what the tag meant," she continued. "It's a legend that was purely associated with West Ham Football Club, before it became a more general threat."

"Is this," asked Sefton, "that same urban myth about anyone who scores a hat-trick against West Ham dying?"

Quill saw Costain glance sidelong at the other UC. "Didn't think you'd be into football."

Sefton gave him a dangerous look, but his tone remained neutral. "Why?"

Costain just shook his head, with a smile on his lips.

"Right," said Ross, "Toshack always was a West Ham fan. That myth of dying after scoring a hat-trick was the myth that he, or rather someone working for him, was using to try to scare these footballers into cooperating with him. This tag was also associated with some of those deaths."

"There really were some deaths," nodded Sefton.

"Who do you support?" asked Costain.

"Chelsea," said Sefton, again in that oh-so-reasonable tone.

"I sometimes get . . . feelings about sidelines, so I do stuff like this on my own time," Ross persisted. "Last night, I ran the numbers. Footballers who score hat-tricks against West Ham do *not* always die in suspicious circumstances, but—"

She clicked to the next image, which showed a series of graphs.

"—they *often* do. More often, statistically, than they should. The shape of the graph here, the extent that it deviates from the norm, is very close to what you get if you look back through records of previously unlinked deaths while looking for serial-killer traits after it's been proved there has been a serial killer operating."

"Bloody hell," murmured Quill, aware of Sefton and Costain also leaning forward.

"So," Costain pointed to the image, "that's saying that there's probably a genuine effect? That someone *was* killing players that scored hat-tricks against West Ham?"

"Thanks for providing subtitles," said Quill.

"Yeah," confirmed Ross, "and if we match players who died after having scored hat-tricks against West Ham with people who have had the spiral tag show up in their garden . . ."

Two circles came together on the screen, one representing the unfortunate scorers, and one for the people with the tag appearing in their garden, and a number whirled in the space where they intersected. It settled at 78%.

"*Fuck*," chorused all three members of Ross's audience, simultaneously.

"So," said Quill, when he'd got his breath back. "That means a seventy-eight percent success rate on the part of a very specific serial killer. Which would just be a brilliant new cold-case lead . . ."

"Apart from the fact that the tag showed up when Toshack died, too. Presumably a statement on the killer's part, rather than a warning, this time. And, erm . . . thanks," she looked awkwardly away, "but there's more. Most, though not all, of these murders were committed with what was assumed at the time to have been poison. Investigators were obviously a lot more comfortable with the idea of unknown toxins back in the day. Also—and this is the big one—the data that doesn't overlap here is uneven. One of those circles on that diagram contains more items than the other. Eighteen percent of the other cases are hat-trick scorers, over the years, who probably died of natural causes. The four percent in the other circle represent people who got the tag planted in their gardens, but hadn't scored hat-tricks against West Ham. Indeed, none of those people is a footballer. They're a range of organized crime network bosses, bankers and made men—many of them with connections to Toshack. I've prepared a list. And how many of those also died?"

She clicked on to another image. This time, the two circles slid together and the numbers gradually spun . . . to reach 100%.

Quill couldn't help it, he started to applaud. To his delight, Costain and Sefton joined in. Ross nodded, looked away again, unable to deal with this reaction. "Shut up," she said, finally. "Let me finish. What we see here, then, is strongly indicative of Toshack hiring a serial killer who specialized in football-related poisonings, using a still unknown delivery system, a killer who also presumably has a love for West Ham—"

"You could see how that would mess you up," said Quill.

"—who, after Toshack abandoned his plans for fixing matches, was kept on, and remained an enforcer, killing on Toshack's orders.

The number of deaths slows down across the decade, perhaps as the reputation of Toshack by itself starts to do the job without the threat having to be carried through. And when Toshack is killed, subject to what we're going to see on the CCTV footage to establish a time frame, that killer—or someone who knows of them—plants their usual marker near the scene of the crime."

"I didn't see any of this," said Costain. "No, I mean, I do believe it, this really is the first sight we've had of one of Toshack's freelancers, but this was kept from his ordinary soldiers."

Quill got to his feet. "Lisa, can you take us back to that first Venn diagram?" She did so. "Ta." He went to the wall and used the shadow of his hand to point at the intersection between the two circles. "That's a *person* there on that screen. That's bloody fantastic police work, that is."

Ross was shaking her head, as if she didn't deserve all this praise. "But the trouble is," she said, "apart from the non-footballers, the people on that list . . ."

"What?"

"The data goes . . . back a long way," she said. "To when West Ham first played under that name, in 1900."

Quill paused only for a moment. "Then it's a gang tradition. We've got an angle now—so let's not look it in the mouth."

SIX

When it was examined, the soil from the spiral was indeed revealed as being different to that of the Hill's gardens, and the same in consistency as any that had been used for the other spiral tags, similar to soils from areas along the river Thames, and extending north of it around underground rivers. Weirdly, it seemed to have been specially conveyed to the site. The CCTV tape, when it finally arrived, had to be taken back into Gipsy Hill so that Quill could find a machine to play it on, but Quill managed to get an IT spod to copy it to a disc that the ancient PC in the Portakabin could then read.

The four of them stood round the monitor and watched. "Oh," said Ross, "so that delay in getting us the footage wasn't just the Goodfellow team sulking."

On what the time code confirmed was the morning of New Year's Day, two and a half minutes before Toshack's death, the video showed the pile of soil not to be there one second . . . and to be there the next. Ross got the IT staff on the line, and they sounded as if they'd been expecting her call. With their help, she narrowed it down to two individual frames. "No soil . . . then soil. It just appeared. And the time code hasn't been messed with. To do this so seamlessly would need serious expertise."

"Then we're dealing with someone who's got it," said Quill. "It's Occam's thingamabob, innit?"

Sefton spent a fun afternoon that Saturday in the Boleyn pub on the corner of Green Street, close to the West Ham ground. It wasn't quite UC work—all he was pretending to be was a West Ham fan—but it was close enough for him to feel more comfortable than he had been lately. It got him away from Costain and that bloody Portakabin, where Sefton found himself swallowing more and more frustration every day. The pub contained a vast display of Irons memorabilia, and a reputation for being peaceful, but committed enough to ask away fans to refrain from coming in on match days. Ideal.

"The curse?" said a bloke with the castle and crossed hammers tattooed on his neck. "Sometimes I think that's all we've got left to make the opposition fear us."

"That's why Ryan Scotley put two in against us—this is twenty years back—and then got himself taken off the field," agreed his mate. Sefton bought a few pints and heard lots of names that tallied with his mental list of those Ross had already discovered. The most recent, a decade ago, right at the start of Rob Toshack's reign, was a Liverpool player called Matt Howarth.

"It's a long time for them to have remembered this stuff," he said, on his return to the Portakabin, "but that means it was always a big deal. There's a few anecdotes worth checking out, and a specific threat of a surreal nature directed at Howarth by a West Ham season-ticket holder. The bloke who told me remembers it 'cos it was on the same day that Howarth died."

"Who made this threat?" asked Quill.

"She's commemorated in the following terrace chant." He cleared his throat, then spread his hands theatrically. "We went one up for Mor-a! She's going to shag the scor-er! Come on you Irons, come on you Irons!"

He waited for the applause. None was forthcoming.

"Her name's Mora Losley," he said. "Bit of a terrace legend."

"Description?" said Ross, already scribbling in one of her notebooks.

"Little old lady . . . but nobody agrees on the details."

"How long ago was she a season-ticket holder?"

"She's still attending."

Ross ran the name "Mora Losley"—as well as all the others—through CRIMINT, the Police National Computer, the Police National Database and the Met's own systems. She found that the same name, Mora Losley, kept popping up regarding quite a few formal warnings but nothing beyond that: no arrests. This was what made something inside Ross relax, that feeling of uncovering something hidden, and of showing it to the world. It was all that could make her feel okay these days. It was as if she was feeling a message forming out of noise.

"She's got a history of abusive behavior," she told Quill, "a lot of complaints against her by fellow fans. But what I'm getting from the West Ham fan chatter online is that, as she's a terrace icon, a lot of them are willing to forgive her anything."

"That's the feeling I got from the lads," agreed Sefton. "She's everyone's barmy auntie."

Costain looked uneasy. "Who heaves the soil about, then? Maybe she's got some big nephews?"

Ross was surprised to hear Costain express a useful thought. "Maybe she's got a son, some relatives, some followers. She's been a West Ham season-ticket holder since 1955." Ross handed Quill the ticket records and the only image she had discovered: a copy of a passport photo, the latest of those submitted every year to get the season ticket renewed. A little old lady who indeed appeared bland enough to be described in many different ways. Ross had found herself looking back to it several times, trying to fix the nonexistent details in her mind and failing.

Quill pinned the photo to the Ops Board that was slowly developing. "List of complaints is interesting," he said. "Abuse of fellow fans, a lot of her upsetting children. And even small instances of violence . . ."

"Against *animals*," said Ross. "She kicks dogs. That's a serial-killer marker."

"Moves around a bit, too," said Quill. "You need an address for the season ticket, and those tally with the ones given at her formal warnings. Loads of different places in the Wembley and Neasden area."

"Where?" said Costain. He got to his feet and took the sheet of paper from Quill. Then a smile spread all over his face. "I know these houses," he said. "In fact, I've been to a lot of them."

Sefton looked over his shoulder, and started to laugh.

"These," said Costain, "are the houses Toshack went to search on New Year's Eve! All except this one in Willesden. That could be the one he went to on his own, before he called us out. Toshack was looking for Mora Losley!"

Quill leaped up, and Ross thought he was about to hug her, but, seeing the look on her face, he awkwardly turned it into a high-five that became a hearty handshake. Then he grabbed his phone. "That," he said, "is enough to merit a search warrant!"

Costain looked around him, as he waited in the unmarked car. The house Toshack had visited on his own had turned out to be situated on a suburban T-junction, with an Irish pub at one end and a West Indian pub at the other, in a row of houses running along a curved street near the park. At lunchtime, in winter sunshine, Quill's tiny team had parked just around the corner from it, where they could hear the sounds of the school playing field. The unmarked van sat at a decent interval along the curve of the road itself. At Quill's request, approved through Lofthouse's office, personnel from the local nick had been folded into an operation that was registered as still being called "name to follow."

That indicated a certain lack of confidence, as if Quill still thought this might be about something other than the obvious. Like catching out Costain? Costain himself didn't really think this could still be about that situation in reverse. This wasn't about Lofthouse suspecting Quill. He'd been wondering if she would pop up again, reassure him again, give him something else to go on as to why she wanted him involved in this. There was one particular thing which could still have him—have him badly. It was what he'd thought of as his exit strategy. But here he was, hanging on, even getting interested in how the pieces were coming together.

Costain had grown up in Willesden, and it hadn't bloody changed much. There were a lot of FOR SALE signs, a lot of boarded-up shopfronts, chain stores that now hid behind sheets of wood instead of bullet-damaged windows. All these neat little houses with individual gardens were from when this had been a posh suburb, decades before he was born. They'd also driven past one of those marooned churches, with a big sunny graveyard, from when this had been a separate village. At one point there had actually been pilgrimages that led people here. Costain remembered deciphering the shopping street at the end of this very road when he'd first walked along it as a copper, his new training considered sufficiently in place. It included honest greengrocer with West Indian produce outside, paying protection; a furtive newsagent with something that looked like a pillbox on his roof . . . That remained there from when that same corner shop had been the entrance hall to an art-deco club where the Charleston was played, back when it took an adventurous train ride to get you to this fashionable suburb. There had been kids on mountain bikes riding up to catch the baggies of coke as they were thrown from that vantage point above. The only difference now would be that they'd ride scooters, and the set of guys chucking the bags would have changed about twenty times in the meantime. Back then he'd actually wondered if there was anything he could do there on his own, and reported this activity when he got back to his nick. There had been posters up for black comedy nights, representing traces of community. There had been black grannies who kept those sociable gardens nice, and owned their own houses. A few doorsteps where people sat outside in the evening. There had been life in the ruins then, green shoots that were signs that the place might resist the creeping gentrification of nearby Hampstead.

From what he'd seen this morning, though, in the last decade the character of the place had tottered from being rotten black and Irish to theme-pub black and Irish, and then reverted to rotten again, without ever having quite been decent black and Irish at any moment in between. God, it was as if the future was dead. As if nobody could imagine now what might come next. He seemed to have fallen into being a copper again, as if someone had handed him a different hat. And that took some getting used to.

They'd met the local uniforms last Friday, and had received a briefing from a sergeant. The place was a typical house in a typical residential street. Nothing on the books, but a couple of incidents nearby this year: a mugging and a pub fight, neither connected. They'd driven just once past the house before they'd parked, Costain being the one allowed to glance idly at it. Bare garden, a little snow still melting in the shade. In fact, it looked a lot like the everyday houses Toshack had dragged them round. Except this one had very dark windows. Heavy black curtains, maybe? But not so much as a West Ham pennant on display.

Mora Losley didn't show up in any official records, other than police ones. It seemed that she didn't use any local services, didn't answer to any landlord; the ground plans were mysteriously absent, and she'd somehow avoided taxation. The council had said, embarrassed, that she must be in the system somewhere, but they hadn't yet come back with anything. It was actually an unprofessional level of secrecy; even international terrorists paid their council-tax bills. The strangeness was astonishing. Not the sort of thing Toshack usually did.

Quill now got on the radio to the sergeant in charge of the

uniforms. That same morning, he'd given a briefing about looking out for traps. Maybe there was going to be a scene, and spitting, and that weird taboo thing of an elderly woman swearing at you.

They got out of the car at exactly the same moment as the four uniforms got out of the van: two women, two men. There were two more already round at the back door. Quill opened the gate and led them up the garden path. He pulled the warrant and search notice out of his pocket, along with his warrant card. He knocked heavily on the door. If there was no reply, they'd move in the squad with the breaking device.

The door suddenly seemed to give way under Quill's knocking, as if it had been standing open, resting against the frame. It swung open an inch or two. Only darkness was visible beyond. Quill looked ill at ease. Costain hadn't heard anyone moving inside. He found himself taking a step back, the UC part of him already anticipating gunfire blasting through that door.

"Police officers," Quill called into the darkened gap. "I am Detective Inspector James Quill. Ms. Losley, we are here with a warrant to search your premises in connection with the death of Matthew Howarth."

No reply.

Quill pushed the door gently with his foot until it was fully open. He stepped inside, the uniforms quickly following him, then came Costain and the others.

Costain found himself taking a deep breath as he went in. This was different from the others: the inside of the house was pitch black. That thin carpet again, though. That bare granny's house feeling. The little window panel beside the door had been painted on the inside with something that looked black and sticky. That was different too.

And on the newel post at the top of the banister there sat something that couldn't quite be made out, but that looked organic, animal origin and long dead. It could only have been fixed there.

Ross's voice sounded tremendously calm. "Is that the skull of a baby?"

Costain stepped forward and now saw what she meant. And, at that moment, the smell hit him. And the others, too, if the coughing was anything to go by.

Quill immediately called for back-up, containment and an Armed Response Unit.

Costain felt the sense of triumph from the coppers around him, and something inside him finally started to relax. This was why Toshack had come to this house on his own. "Serial killer house," he said. "Excellent."

It took them several hours to move into the house properly. First the Armed Response Unit had swept it thoroughly. Then Forensics and Explosives had gone through in turn. Costain hadn't known what to do with himself in the meantime. When he'd been a UC, scene-of-crime had been more of a *before* routine for him than an *after*. More and more police vans arrived outside, a lot of uniforms needed for crowd control as locals and the press started massing. Finally, the house was declared clear, and Quill's team were allowed in.

They found some West Ham paraphernalia, and a scarf left over a chair in the kitchen. Quill got hold of a magistrate, and put out a new warrant for Losley's arrest in connection with the Howarth murder. Even assuming that someone else was doing the killing, such as a family member she kept under the same roof, finding her should eventually lead to them. He also gave orders that all the other houses Losley had inhabited were to be searched.

The tiny skull on the newel post turned out to be fixed in place by purple wax. "No," corrected Sefton, "*claret*-colored wax." A West Ham serial killer—how huge was this? Costain found himself smiling. He was now part of a successful operation and, for a bonus, not as a UC. The guys back home would have a fucking fit. This justified everything Lofthouse had done. She was right to have put him here, if this was the pay-off. This was the *juice.*

"I would hate," he said, "to be doing PR for that football club tonight."

"Obvious she'd have to be West Ham," remarked Quill. "Just one stop away from Barking."

They gradually explored every room. Upstairs was worse than down below. The bedroom was just a soiled mattress, the stink of ammonia so strong that none of them could linger there. Every inch of the walls of the upper floor was daubed with patterns, symbols and writing. Costain found player lists of what the Internet confirmed were old West Ham squads, and what seemed to be maps of geographical features with labels in Latin. The smile was now constantly fixed to his face: he was a detective again. He saw Sefton glance in his direction, so he made sure to smile wider. Yeah, he'd made it all right, no thanks to posh boy over there. Ross brought up a translation on her phone. "The Latin looks like it might be a legal paragraph, a very old one, about the right, or otherwise, of the monarch to enter a private citizen's dwelling."

"And they called her eccentric," said Quill.

Nothing they found there suggested to Costain that the place had been inhabited by anyone other than an old lady.

There was a trapdoor leading to a loft. The armed officers and forensics people had closed it again after they'd done a search up there. As Quill reopened it with a hook on a pole, a puff of stale air from inside made everyone cough. Quill insisted on going first, and who was Costain to deny him that? He climbed up the stepladder that the uniforms had brought with them, and cautiously stuck his head through the gap. A moment later, he called for the others to follow. He sounded excited once again.

The loft had been converted into one big room. It had been

roughly boarded-out at some stage, and over the boards had been thrown a variety of dirty rugs. They'd been drawn on, too, in sticky black: lines, diagrams and tiny writing. It was even colder up here. The room was filled with West Ham memorabilia: scarves, hats, really old posters that were more like theater bills, annuals and a copy of a team sing-along album sitting beside an ancient gramophone to play it on. There was one huge central feature: a wooden tub about six feet across. It didn't have an original purpose in the loft, and it couldn't have fitted through the trapdoor. It must have been assembled up here.

It contained only a huge pile of soil, the surface shaped into a familiar spiral. The room smelt of it, and it looked fresh and uncontaminated.

"What's the betting," said Quill, "that this soil's the same type used to form the other spirals?"

"Jimmy." Sefton was holding up a plastic sack gleefully. On it was written: *Original West Ham Turf. Take the Irons spirit into your garden!* There was a tightly folded roll of other such sacks stashed under a bench.

"Here's what Forensics were talking about." Ross's voice sounded different. She was leaning over an iron cauldron.

They all went over to see. In the cauldron lay three small human skeletons, arranged in a rough circle, head to toe. There were still the tiniest fragments of meat on the bones. Smaller bones lay scattered across the bottom of the vessel.

Costain felt himself relax completely. Thanks to Lofthouse's mad hunch and some good police work, he was once again on the up. "Yeah," he repeated, "serial killer house."

Ross made sure she kept working, knowing the coppers were more used to this. They had a work culture to support them. She'd been quite surprised that Quill had asked her to come along, but, as he'd said, this operation was bizarre to start with, and "she'd pine away if left all alone in that Portakabin." Which was, she guessed, the result of him noting the desperation she'd been trying to hide. From now on she'd have to get used to being operational, he'd said, too. And that had certainly felt better than the alternative. *Until this.* If she even stopped to think about what had happened here . . . so she wouldn't. Had Toshack known about the child murders? Maybe, yeah. He'd have been the kind willing to turn a blind eye, all right.

"As long as it wasn't on his own doorstep," said Costain, catching the expression on her face. She looked away. She didn't like people being so close to her old world—or making guesses at what she was thinking.

And there was . . . the other thing. The thing that, incredibly, this house was making her think about for the first time in years. She could do that if she had to, deliberately not think about stuff. It was . . . just a coincidental thing, just an association. Children in a pot: that just made your mind go to a certain place, and that was a place she shouldn't go. She got out her laptop and carried out a Full Business Objects Search, on the Crime Recording System. She could find only two unsolved missing-children cases for this part of London in the last three years, and both of those turned out to involve older individuals.

"Has it really gone that far?" said Quill, when she told him. "Bloody *three* children go missing, and nobody calls it in?"

"These two modes are really different. Possible poison that leaves no trace . . . and kids cooked in a pot. What sort of narrative has she put together for herself that connects those? She kills the former away, and these at home, probably." She slapped her hand on the wall, over and over, feeling more alive than she had since Toshack had been killed, and also feeling a little alarmed at the intensity of it. "It's as if we're seeing the outlying features of something more complicated. As if there are different killers with different MOs . . . or something. We're in this house, but we're still not seeing . . . what's in the middle."

"If anyone finds a ripe, rosy apple," said Quill, "don't touch."

"You reckon those three are Dopey, Grumpy and Sneezy?" said Costain, indicating the cauldron.

Ross put it out of her mind again. She understood the context of these copper jokes: it was what people who dealt with horrors did. She'd once been shown round the paramedic control center in High Barnet, and they'd put *cartoons* up of their call-outs—what they called their "shouts"—with the highest body count. She wished she had it in herself to join in. For her there was even a little jolt now as she looked at Losley's photo, even though she did it to reassure herself. This Losley woman was a complete stranger to her. But what had previously been bland had now certainly become sinister. No dead-eyed Myra Hindley, this one, that calm look on her face maybe saying: Ooh yes, if you had any to spare, she might be persuaded to snap up just one or two of your children.

The Scene of Crime Officers of SCD 4 had extracted a very new-looking piece of paper from where it had been found folded up and wedged between two floorboards, and handed it to them, properly bagged, for inspection.

Quill laughed out loud when, at the bottom of the same letter, he saw Rob Toshack's signature. Putting all modesty aside, he called Ross over—with her younger eyes—to read it aloud.

"Dear Mora," she read out, increasing pleasure in her voice. "You're not here, and I can't find that door of yours. If it sweetens the deal, I'm bringing a few of my lot over to your safe houses. You can have any of them you want, all of them if you like. Just talk to me, all right? Yours sincerely—"

"Formal, in the circumstances," commented Sefton.

"That's him, all right," said Costain. "Proper, like." There was a horrified look on his face, as if he couldn't believe what he was hearing. "Was he offering her . . . us?"

"She might have had a bit of trouble with Mick and the boys," said Sefton. "Bloody hell, it's like a backwoods-cabin horror movie.

There must have been a whole family of them for him to say that: loads of them across all these houses, if he thought they'd be able to ambush us. And he didn't even bother telling us not to bring guns!"

That thought made the others pause, even as it settled down in Quill's head and made itself at home. What the fuck were they dealing with here? "Hi ho," he said, "it's off to work we go."

Costain took himself aside for a few minutes, and thought about what he'd heard read aloud, and found that a little bit of bile had now entered his lovely day. But, what the fuck, that was history now. Rob had been willing to sell him out to who knows what: well, that was how the world worked, and he'd got in his retaliation without knowing it. And now he didn't have to feel bad about anything. He shook his head and carried on.

Quill called a conference of all those still inside the house, and told them to concentrate on finding a hidden door. But none was found. The next time he looked up, it was dark outside. The noises from out there suggested a major press presence and a crowd of onlookers on the other side of the police cordon, big television lights now heating the air. He phoned Sarah, left a message just saying, yes, he was in the middle of what she was seeing on telly, and so, obviously, he'd be home late. She called back to say there was nothing bloody obvious about it—then clicked off before he could reply.

Lofthouse arrived, relief showing on her face. She went around, touching walls and windows, as if she was considering buying the place. "Brilliant stuff, James. You reckon we'll nick her?"

"I'm amazed someone out there hasn't found her already."

"Quite a few say they've sighted her, but so far it's just the nutters. We've put a watch on the West Ham pubs, and so on. The club are being . . . *fulsomely* cooperative."

"I'll bet."

"I should think they'll burn her regular seat and salt the ground beneath it."

Quill stopped her just before she went outside to conduct her press conference. "Ma'am, is this what . . . ? I mean, you put such a . . . strange unit together. This has the ring of insane genius."

"Flattery is always welcome."

"But I'm waiting for the other shoe to drop. Is this really about . . ." he chose his words carefully. ". . . corruption in Gipsy Hill?"

She looked for a moment to be choosing her words carefully. "I don't know," she said. "Let's find out. At least you're thoroughly off the hook." And her expression now urged him to leave it at that.

Lofthouse delivered her press conference out on the doorstep, the light drizzle reflecting the television lights. She didn't speculate, but asked for the public's help, particularly from those who were West Ham supporters. She was asked about the matter of the child victims' identity, and said that she couldn't add anything on that subject, as yet. Nor could she, for operational reasons (that was, protecting the UCs), offer a narrative that led from the Toshack investigation to this doorstep.

Quill watched it all from an upstairs window. He wondered how iconic that bare doorway was going to become. This was going to be a famous London murder house, like 10 Rillington Place or 39 Hilldrop Crescent. The neighbors, who'd been moved out and were currently being interviewed, hadn't, thankfully, done the usual by saying that Losley was a pleasant neighbor who'd kept herself to herself. (Always delivered in a tone of voice that suggested that, since keeping oneself to oneself was the single greatest thing one English person could do for another, the suspect ought to be excused whatever psychopathic shit they'd visited on other people.) They just hadn't seen her at all. A few of them had even thought that the house was empty, which meant Losley had probably been absent for some considerable time. According to the Internet, on the other hand, the holders of season tickets in seats near Losley, plus the supporters' club, were now queuing up to say she was a bloody pedo and to distance themselves from anything she'd done, from goal celebrations to using harsh language. Quill called up West Ham and arranged to be sent a list of names and contact details for those season-ticket holders seated near to Losley, so he could call them in for interview.

"We've heard from West Ham supporters," said a reporter with the BBC logo on her microphone, "that Mora Losley expressed particular hatred for those who scored hat-tricks against the club. And there's an urban legend about such players being murdered. Is there anything to suggest—?"

And the crowd goes wild, thought Quill, who'd been hoping nobody would make that connection. Lofthouse let the noise die down and started to do her best to quench that particular fire. Sefton tapped Quill on the shoulder, and handed him the late-edition *Evening Standard*. That Losley season-ticket photo featured in it. *The Witch of West Ham*, said the headline.

Bang, that was what she was now.

"Anything in there?" Quill asked the SOCO with the magnetic resonance device, who was running it over the tub of soil. For the third time, because he'd requested her to.

"Soil," she said.

"Yeah," said Quill. "Have a biscuit. Anything else?"

"No," sighed the woman, "as I *said*: a shaped pile of the West Ham soil, wet as you'd expect that club's soil to be, and matching that found at Gipsy Hill, with a layer of what looks to be local soil underneath. We've also sifted it and looked under the tub. Which is bloody heavy."

"Small bones? Needles? You've *completely* forensicated it?"

The SOCO just glowered at him and walked away.

*

At the end of their shift, the forensics team left the loft, heading off for a cuppa, and, in the gap before the next shift came on, Quill looked around and saw that it was just the four of them in here now. Which felt kind of weird. For a while, there, they'd been back in the mainstream of police work. And with luck it was going to be like that from now on. It would surely be the only sane thing for Lofthouse to draw some more personnel into her now highly successful spin-off. Yeah, the sane thing—so how likely was that really?

He called down to the outgoing SOCOs. "Here," he yelled, "can I touch that soil now? I mean touch touch, with no evidence gloves?" Having examined every inch of the cauldron in sight before Quill's team had entered, they'd just taken it—and the skeletons contained therein—off to the lab.

"You're not the first," a female voice came back. "I've already had a feel. But, if for some reason you want to, you may."

Quill took off his gloves, which felt a blessed relief. He reached out to the soil. His fingertips touched it—

Just as he suddenly realized that all the others should be shouting at him not to, warning that a giant and ridiculous potential had risen out of nothing in the very second he'd moved his fingers toward the soil—

And he registered that he did actually hear them shouting, in a sudden concerted yell of fear.

Something gave a snap, between Quill's flesh and the soil. Something shorted out. And everything changed.

SEVEN

Quill immediately knew that something was wrong, but he wasn't sure what. He looked to the others. They appeared to be wondering what they'd just been so worried about. "Did you say something?" he asked.

"No," said Ross, "I just, kind of . . ."

". . . got worried about you doing that," said Costain hesitantly, as if he was suspicious of his own statement.

Quill looked around. Everything looked the same, except—

He'd suddenly thought how the walls looked different. Just for a moment, out of the corner of his eye. But, no, they were just the same. No, over there—was that a door? It was, with a handle and . . .

No, it was just a shadow cast across the wall. Bloody hell, this was like the migraine or whatever that had mucked about with his vision in the interview room. He took a step back toward the trapdoor. And he realized that all the others had retreated a step that way too. He wanted to ask them if they could see anything funny, but there was plainly nothing the matter. "We're way past our shift now," he announced. "We're knackered and our eyes are playing up. Let's get back to this in the morning." The others looked relieved, and there was a slight alacrity about how they went for the ladder. Quill was last to move. That shadow where he'd thought a door had been . . . did he see something moving over there? Something small, like a cat?

No, there was nothing there.

He went over to the ladder and headed down into the main body of the house, where lights and other people waited. He kept his eye on the shadow as he went.

The other three found a car able to take them back to the Hill. Quill briefed DI Farrar, from the local nick, who was going to be supervising the crime scene overnight, then walked quickly out onto the street, past the huddled TV crews. He really was knackered, and his head was feeling weird. His head and his eyes. But he was too wound up to go home. Also he had some unfinished business. He hit a button on his phone and waited until the familiar voice answered.

"Harry," he said, "you fancy a pint?"

He had a couple in the rough Irish pub at the end of the street, while Harry drove over from the Hill. It was a relief that his colleague was willing to come at all. There was a hurling match or something on the telly, torn-up seats and drinkers to match. Some of them looked as if they went home to the sort of rooms that were only one step up from sleeping rough, but still they obviously liked a real pub rather than some shebeen. Quill occupied a snug on his own. This lot would have heard about what was going on down the way, and he no doubt smelt of copper. Meanwhile, the shiny things in here were starting to hurt his eyes: washed glasses; whatever brass was displayed out of reach of grubby hands; the stone floor under the carpet polished smooth by generations of leather. Did he maybe need glasses? Would that not explain a lot?

But there, to his relief, was Harry. Quill stood up, and was surprised to see another man, an older man, enter behind Harry, close enough that they looked to be together. He looked very like

Harry, actually: that same dourness round the eyes. Quill went to join him, and was pleased to see that familiar wry expression.

"You've done all right tonight, haven't you, Jimmy? Sodding serial killer, honey for tea."

"Can't complain," said Quill. He looked to the older man. "And this is . . . ?"

"Because you left the rest of us to do the donkey work on Goodfellow, don't rub it in."

Quill wondered if the older man wasn't with Harry after all. "What are you having?" He addressed the question so that both could answer.

"Mine's a pint," said Harry. There was silence from the other, who didn't go to get one of his own, but just stood there beside Harry, now looking as quizzically at Quill, even as Quill was looking at him. Was this some homeless bloke who'd followed Harry in, and who Harry was now tactically ignoring?

Quill got the drinks in and headed back over to the snug with Harry. The older man came too, and sat down beside Harry. He was well dressed, elderly and looked as if he was retired. Didn't have the face of a loony. In fact a bit out of place in here. The landlady, who looked to be the kind who might, hadn't objected to him not buying anything to drink.

Quill waited for a moment for some cue from Harry, found none forthcoming, and looked between them. "So . . . ?"

"He's bloody enjoying this," said the older man to Harry, leaning over for a stage whisper into his ear, glancing at Quill as he did so. "Look at him. He's called you all the way over here just to gloat."

"Who the fuck are you?" said Quill.

"What?" Harry looked startled.

"Who's your mate?"

Harry glanced over his shoulder, then back at Quill. And now he had a smile on his face. "Oh, have you finally got through to Lofthouse, and got me seconded to your lovely spin-off operation?"

"That's not what he means, son," said the man. "Don't *ask* him about that. Don't be so bloody *weak*."

Quill couldn't help it. After all, he'd had a long day. Maybe this bloke was old, but he was only going to grab him by the cardy and—

His hand went straight through. He fell forward, and had to catch himself on the table with his other hand. His arm was still, right now, sticking through the old man's head. He could feel what it was like inside. It was very cold. The man eyed him mockingly. Quill snatched his hand back.

"Here," said Harry, "how many have you had?"

Sefton had felt too strung out to sleep, so when he got back to the Hill, he went on into London. He weighed the risks: no, it wasn't being part of a non-undercover operation now making him careless. The vast majority of those who'd known him in Toshack's gang were behind bars, and any who weren't wouldn't be seen dead in the kind of place he was going. Just a couple of pints, though. His head felt weird: flashes in the corners of his eyes, sudden colors appearing in the darkness outside the tube train and gone before he got a good look at them. But, what he'd seen in that second . . . nah, that was his brain making something up out of shapes.

He went into Soho, tried the Admiral Duncan, was put off by how loud and crowded it was. He found a smaller pub, still with blacked-out windows, which always made him roll his eyes. They should only have those on a copper pub catering for UCs. He wished there was someone he could share the sense of triumph with. In the car, Costain being Costain and the fact that Ross was preoccupied as always, had put paid to any thought of shared celebrations, though the driver had been congratulating them. Triumph . . . and, yeah, something heavy got into your brain if you didn't make jokes about it. Something else that made him silent and made him need to talk was that bloody cauldron . . .

He had to stop and put a hand out to steady himself as he got a sudden mental image of . . . real children inside it . . . screaming. Oh, God, don't let yourself go there, mate. He went up to the bar and got a pint.

"Haven't see you before. Where're you from, then?" The voice with the nice London accent, a bit south of the river, had come from behind him. He turned to see who it was, and found himself looking at a bloke with a straggly beard as if he was a hipster mountain man, in a suit as if he was something in PR, and with interesting eyes.

"Kensington." Sefton used his original accent even as he said it. Why, Ambassador, you're spoiling your son. He felt immediately embarrassed. He hadn't used that voice in years.

"Really?"

"Nah," and there he was again, lying, "just having you on, mate."

"But you haven't been out round here before? Right, so, this place is bollocks. Let me give you the tour."

His name was Joe. They had a couple of pints at a couple of different places. Sefton was too knackered to really care about which pub he was in, but he liked the company. And he was on for whatever the evening brought because—come on, skeletons in a cauldron—he was off duty now, thank you. And he always loved the sort of offhand friendliness you got when you met a bloke like this. I mean, yeah, they were both thinking about a shag, but that was also kind of a doorway to the sort of hanging out with near strangers that Americans did so well, and the British didn't. Exactly right for him tonight. To be nobody in particular.

"So what do you do, then?"

"Stuff."

"What does that mean?"

"It means I don't want to get into that."

Joe got a resigned look on his face that said, fine, keep me at arm's length, why are we bothering with the social bit if that's all you're after? So Sefton put an arm round his shoulder. "I mean it's been a long day and it's a dull job and I don't want to talk about it. Sorry."

"Okay, taking that onboard. Intense, you are."

"Tell me about it."

It was crowded on the pavements tonight as they wandered along: encountering unlicensed cab offer, *Big Issue* seller, old man in white gloves, beery students; gay, gay, not sure, gay, straight, straight, straight; hen night, Japanese couple, religious ranter; stall selling something that looked like shite and smelt like toffee . . .

And, suddenly, who they all were and what they all wanted hit Sefton like a punch and he wanted to hide hide hide go undercover be someone else quickly before they know you before they get you because you can feel how they might hate you if they saw the real you and if they turned on you with this gaze and this power and his vision went weird and he had to fall back against the window of a Turkish convenience store and the man behind the counter inside started tapping the window saying what are you doing because he was bumping the back of his head regularly against the glass and he was quite conscious thank you absolutely together but he couldn't stop and Joe was staring at him not yet completely freaked out and the force of it was because there was something nearby . . .

He took a breath, closed his eyes.

The fucker must have put something in my beer. Oh God, is this Ketamine or some shit? Is this a sex thing, or was I followed and targeted, and is that the guy whose house I've been in? My warrant card's in my sock. Get to a taxi, show the warrant, go to Paddington Green or somewhere—

But Joe wasn't looking dangerous; he seemed really worried now. So he didn't do this. What did this?

Something was approaching. Something was heading toward him, and that was what had sent him slamming back against the window. Because his body was afraid of what was coming. The owner was coming out now. People inside, buying samosas, were looking out at him. Mad guy. But something was coming. That was what had sent him slamming back away from it. He hadn't realized. Something was coming and this lot were all in danger. Never mind that they were all terrifying, the force of all of them combined that he wanted to hide from. They were all in danger.

The owner of the shop grabbed his shoulder to push him away into the crowd, toward the thing that was coming. Joe started to get in the way, to rail loudly at him: it's not drugs, look at him, he's ill—

Sefton pushed himself away from the shop owner, away from the window, with Joe rushing after him. Get away from this thing. If it was only after him, then get it away from them.

And then he realized that it had changed the direction it was coming from.

It was coming straight through the crowd in front of him. It was here!

It walked through the crowd. It walked right through them, their bodies passing through it, mostly, for there was one old man stepping round it . . . but enough of that, just look at it—look at this mother, it's ten feet tall and it's a plant, it's like a tree but with a mass of green on top, and are those human arms? That's a bloke in a costume, no it isn't, it's bringing with it—

Smell of park, not just grass, not countryside, park. More than smell. Something got park into my head, beyond the smell. There's money and servitude and that anger, all that anger, all that anger at doffing your cap and lowering your eyes as the bastards go past and they're throwing a coin for you and this is you at their houses, Jack in your green Jack after their maids Jack your only day hidden in here Jack get up to all sorts in here, and Sefton thought, *Not me mate, I'm like you whatever you are, money thing, servant thing, old lady remembering thing, city remembering thing—*

He'd locked up again, his hands shaking in front of him like he was having a fit, and it was rushing at him, aiming to go through him—

A moment of smelling, or seeing, all those things at once, in the many corners of his eyes, as if his eyes were suddenly stars and pricked with corners, and it was all those things at once and terrifying! And so cold, made out of cold—

And it was into the crowd again, part of them again, and it hadn't been after him at all, and he staggered.

Joe caught him.

"He still thinks you're bent," said the man whispering in Harry's ear. "All those years you've been kissing his arse, and this is how he repays you."

Quill had stumbled back to his seat, saying, yeah, he had been in the pub a while. He'd been so freaked out he couldn't deal with it. But he wasn't about to run out screaming yet. He sat there and listened to what Harry was saying, numbly nodding along, checking out his surroundings all the time. If he was hallucinating, if he'd got something in his bloodstream, perhaps scratched himself on a nail or something inside that house, breathed something in . . . but he didn't feel woozy, apart from the beer, and he knew what beer felt like, so it gave him something to compare this to. Quill gradually became certain that he was in his right mind.

So what was this fucker he couldn't touch? Who kept on spouting this shit? And Quill was sure now that Harry was hearing it, too, as he could see tiny reactions to it on his face. But it was very subtle. He got the feeling that, even if the man suddenly shouted, Harry wouldn't have leaped up. This seemed to be something Harry was deeply used to. Quill decided that he'd do what he always did whenever he didn't understand certain aspects of a situation. He'd plow right on through. Which meant, for a start, not putting up with this any longer.

"Listen, Harry," he said, "nobody thinks you're a bent copper. *Nobody*. And especially not me, all right?"

Harry looked surprised, they'd been talking about something else. "Thought never crossed my mind, Jimmy," he said.

"Oh, look at you, lapping up the scraps from his table," said the old man. "You're ten times the copper he'll ever be. Look at him, playing the role, saying all the right things. He's just copying his dad. He gets all the attention because he looks right and he sounds right, never mind the fact that you're more talented. He gets promoted just because of how he acts, not for what he does."

Quill realized that he'd only just restrained himself from yelling at the strange man, letting out his fear and anger. But that wouldn't get him anywhere, because this . . . this ghost, or whatever it was . . . it wasn't trying to bait him. Its attention was entirely concentrated on Harry.

"But you're the one who does all the hard work and, you're the one they don't notice. It's always him they talk about, while you stand in his shadow. What's he doing in charge of you? How is that fair? And this new operation—you should be in on that!"

It dawned on Quill that he himself had come to expect that Harry would never say thanks after he'd paid him a compliment or reassured him like that. Maybe now he knew the reason, and he felt like he should hold it against him. But this wasn't *Harry*, was it? It was . . . whatever this thing was. "Like I said, I asked for you," he began, taking care to talk to Harry rather than to the older man. "But we're being kept apart from you lot, like we're contagious, and . . . well, you know who I think the bad apple is. I think maybe that's the reason. Or maybe . . . now I'm thinking that maybe there's something more to it, and that Lofthouse had a plan."

No reaction from the stranger. He was listening, his face set exactly like Harry's. He was kind of one-track, wasn't he?

"But that's no comment on you, either. We're both the sons of coppers, Harry. We know the form. Here, remind me—when did your old dad pass on?"

The man turned to look at him, a snarl on his face. And Quill felt the slight relief of having made him do that.

Got you.

In the car heading back from the Losley house to the Hill, Ross had realized there was something wrong. It was as if something was moving inside her head, and she couldn't push it down. She'd understood the stress of her chosen path, but the trouble was that she'd always expected catharsis at the end. She'd been running for the line, while now she was just working—and then working at home too—until she fell asleep. This couldn't last. This had to end badly. Maybe this was the start of that ending.

She had first felt it when the car turned into Kilburn High Road. It had felt somehow that gravity had changed, that there was something pressing her down into her seat. She had looked to the others, and then out of the window, and became aware that she was starting to see . . . fleeting things moving along and among the shopfronts . . . odd things that the car was going too quickly for her to see, and she felt suddenly glad about that. And the shopfronts themselves, most of them with just overnight lights on now, there were . . . like all sorts of them all laid on top of each other, at different levels, even, as if suddenly her eyes were offering her options. She had wanted to close her eyes, but she also didn't want to because, if this was a form of mental illness, it was as frightening as she expected, but also really interesting. Her hand had gone instinctively to the knife she always kept in her pocket, but then she had let it go again. Best not play with that right now.

She had felt cars and buses pass that somehow felt more *weighted* than others. The underneath of the Marylebone flyover had been, in the looming darkness, exploding fireworks of tracks, of traces . . . of cars crashing, she realized; as if every accident, over decades, had left some sort of record. That must be the delusion she was experiencing, that everything mattered, that everything was recorded, so guilt could never escape, so it was cared about still.

Unlike in the real world. She hadn't wanted to say anything to the others because, if her mind was disintegrating, she wanted to have it happen in private. It came as a relief, almost.

She had felt huge things passing high over the roof of the car. She had felt joys among the fears, even, but it had mostly been just fear. There had been motion between the trees of Hyde Park, and strange lights manifesting, in colors she wasn't able to put a name to. Things moved between the trees faster than was possible. There had been unexpected structures in silhouette. Shadows lurking under shadows.

And then there had been a feeling of some huge, doom-laden presence somewhere distantly on their left, just as the car took them down Grosvenor Place. The car had felt to be teetering on the edge of it, affected by its gravity, sling-shotting around in that whirlpool—

"What's that over there?" she'd managed to say, hoping that some part of the distant light she could see was real.

"Buckingham Palace," said Costain.

She had kept herself a little apart from all she was experiencing, as if recording and reporting on her own fascinating breakdown. This familiar stance had calmed her a little. Never mind that all this reminded her of . . . well, it would, wouldn't it? She had imagined *that*, and she was now imagining *this*. It had probably been set off by those bodies in the cauldron. That had been the knife that had severed something she had herself stretched very tight.

The car had proceeded through Victoria, full of tourists, full of unknown shapes moving among the sightseers. And then up onto Vauxhall Bridge Road. Maybe if she went to sleep and woke up again, her brain would reset and it would all then be gone . . .

No, it wouldn't. She knew it wouldn't. She glanced at Costain and Sefton. Sefton looked calm enough, playing with his phone. Costain had fallen asleep.

She had known, rather than saw, that up ahead stood a building:

a house with stark angular walls and five chimneys. A bad place. The weight and impending sight of it had told her so. Then the car had gone through what felt like a gate, but there was no gate here in . . . in the real world.

And then there had been hands. Hands of air, snatching at them!

She had reacted, of course, she hadn't been able to stop herself, but she'd contained it enough so the other two hadn't noticed, because they really couldn't see.

The hands had let go, too weak to hold on against the speed of the car. But Ross had seen the five coffins that contained the five perfect corpses, their breath rising in dust, the same dust that killed—

And then the car had taken her out of that vision too, and they were now passing over Vauxhall Bridge. The Thames stretched underneath: such a huge new weight, she'd felt it writhing in her stomach. It hadn't given her time to stop breathing hard, to stop reacting to those clutching hands taking her back to when she was a child, to a point where she was almost expecting the blows to fall across her face. It was as if she could hear—the vague sound, but not the details of—distant songs, as if all the associations and memories in London ran down to here, collected here. There were churning shapes down there, yet more shadows in the water. Everything she was seeing, she had understood with that detached part of her, was all part of the same thing. These were the symptoms of one big thing. Maybe that big thing was her mind falling apart. Or maybe this was her looking at something to do with what lay at the center of the enigma she'd described at the crime scene. This was what they'd been missing. Or maybe what she was seeing here was all just a metaphor for the problem she was working on, as if she was a genius in a detective series. Only—she had found she was smiling, her awkward-shaped tooth biting at her lip, her image reflected in the horrible lights from outside—only she was no genius.

Then a ship, an old sailing ship with three masts, was speeding down the river, faster than any ship should be able to move. Its masts were too tall to pass under the bridge. It was going to reach the bridge at the same time they passed over. She had looked in the other direction. Another ship was speeding toward them. This was a steamship with a funnel, smoke coming from it, and a single mast. It looked like a warship but old, primitive. It was moving as if it was in an old film, speeded up, chuffing, impossible—

She'd looked back. From the other direction, the sailing ship was flashing forward now. She'd made herself not yell, not grab her head and hide like a frightened animal, but just look, keep looking, be ready to tell someone else what she was witnessing—

The ships passed straight through each other, and through the bridge and right through the car and through her and the others. Something contradictory rushed through them. It felt old and despairing, like British rain. She'd heard once, she absurdly remembered, that London rain was the sweat of Londoners. It looked like silver, like sprue from model kits, like ancient glue. Ross now felt invaded by something horrible and familiar.

The complex cloud of two ships that shouldn't be one had zoomed out of the back of the car. She'd looked in one direction, then the other, noting the details on those ships, as if she could report the incident. HMS *London* was the sailing ship, HMS *Victoria* was the other. The car had come to a stop outside the Portakabin. Ross got out and numbly, quickly, headed for her own car, without even a nod to the others.

She'd driven home to her flat in Catford, having to stop several times: sometimes because her hands were shaking so much, sometimes because of something she'd just passed and quickly driven on from. She finally got out of her car to unlock her garage, still shaking, looking slowly around the housing-block car park, expecting to see something horrifying from out of her own head, and this time for it to be up close, just it and her. And she knew what it would be. She knew she was going to see it again sometime. It would so obviously be coming for her. It seemed that all the time in between, the period of her becoming a serious adult and a police intelligence analyst, was just a dream, and now she was waking up again.

She'd looked up at the tower block itself: a patchwork of lights, balconies with flowerpots, satellite dishes, dead rugs on the rails, painted Jamaican flags. Even this late at night, there was the distant noise of televisions, children and overlapping music. There were . . . things . . . up there, too. Nothing . . . huge . . . like she'd felt in the distance while in the car. Nothing . . . that bad. Nothing near her own flat. She'd felt worse. She'd been present at worse.

She'd had worse done to her. Maybe that had been real. *Shit, maybe that had been real!* No, no, this wasn't real. This now wasn't real. It had to be that way round.

She shoved the fear down inside her, unlocked the door of the garage, relying on sheer routine to stop her peering fearfully inside it, like a little child, and then drove the car in. She didn't know how she was going to get through the rest of the night. Or the rest of her life.

She'd sat in her flat with her laptop open, every light fully on. She'd made sure there was nothing bad in her home. She had a sanctuary here. But that didn't make sense: how could any place be a sanctuary from what was inside her head? Especially when, last time . . . she killed the thought. She looked up details on voluntary admission to a psychiatric hospital. There were so many in London. There was a phone number listed. It would provide a rest: no constant wondering about how she was. *They* would tell her how she was. She'd called the number.

Quill found what he needed in the man's furious expression. That meant he wasn't going crackers. This seemed impossible, but he was experiencing it, so it couldn't be. This was something that was happening, and he'd got a reaction out of the . . . yeah, the suspect . . . in front of him. He was obviously a wanker, so he might as well be a suspect. Harry was talking about his dad, but not quite as if he was here in the room with them. Because Harry didn't realize that he was, did he? Not entirely. This was like one of those cartoons where a bad angel is whispering in your ear. But Harry didn't think it was real.

"You ever think he's still watching over you?" asked Quill, with a glance toward the old man.

"Yeah, my old mum keeps saying that. She goes along to a . . . whatchacallit, a Spiritualist meeting. She says she talks to him every week."

"So he owns a semi in the afterlife and still does the pools?"

"The fucker," said Harry's dad, "the arrogant asshole always with the glib line. He never takes the time to understand anything properly—it's always about the comedy! Are you going to let him talk about me like that?"

Quill kept his expression unresponsive.

"Yeah," smiled Harry, "they've all got pets and everything, too. She says he's always around, looking after me and wanting me to get on. Load of bollocks." But Harry didn't entirely believe that, obviously.

Costain woke up suddenly in the car park outside the Portakabin, and realized something was wrong before he could figure out exactly what. The driver had said something to wake him up, and was now holding the back door open for him. He saw that the other two had bloody gone off and left him there. He got quickly out of the car, and thanked the bemused-looking driver. He watched the vehicle head off. He was feeling vulnerable, cover-blown vulnerable, for no reason. Weird. It made him look over at his own car and hesitate before heading toward it, look around first before he got in, then get out again and have a look underneath before he turned the engine on.

What the fuck was this? Everything was going great now. He'd even found that he'd been justified in betraying Rob. Was he just anticipating the world shitting on him again, or was this about something real? Was he being set up, getting followed by Professional Standards or something? Was this to do with his instincts trying to get the attention of his brain? 'Cos, hello, listening now, conscious mind in gear, thank you . . . But, no, he couldn't find anything sensible to be afraid of.

He drove randomly, looking behind him every now and then, even stopping a few times, making sudden turns down streets to make it more obvious if someone was following him. Whenever he stopped he would look upward, expecting a police helicopter. He didn't see or hear one, but there was *something* up there, he started to realize. It felt as if there were loads of things up there, looking down at him, meaning him harm.

What the fuck? Was he on something and didn't know it?

He finally stopped the car in a lay-by somewhere near Croydon, his hands still on the wheel, and tried to control this feeling. Yeah, there was something of the effect of cocaine to it, but he hadn't had any of the stuff since that night with Toshack. Trying to get hold of some over the last couple of weeks would have been suicidal, and he was pretty sure that, having worked so hard to keep all his options open, he wasn't trying to be self-destructive here. That was the exact opposite of the kind of person he was. So what was this about? It seemed to be deliberately driving him away from London. Or, no, it didn't care about anything: *he* was driving himself away from London because he had serious opinions on the subject of putting himself in danger, and London now felt . . . dangerous.

But how could London *feel* like anything to him? There wasn't any intel to base that reaction on. What . . . had he developed his own Spidey sense?

But, yeah, that was where it was definitely taking him. Every new turn he had taken in this car had taken him further out into commuter land, heading through all the lost suburban byways and rat-runs. If he kept going, he'd soon hit the M25, and then he could just keep on going, right down to the coast, maybe get a ferry—

No, no, no! *Why?*

Did someone's unconsciousness really function like this? He'd seen movies where someone found themselves acting kind of weird, and it turned out to be about some psychological tic they hadn't recognized in themselves. That sort of stuff had always seemed like bullshit to him; he knew himself too well, but maybe there was something he could point to underneath this urge. It was as if he was now directly feeling something that had always been out there somewhere, but always previously as an abstract entity, a crushing weight of judgment and prejudice and arrogance. Except it was in a specific place now, here in London instead of all around him.

Was this a moment he'd talk about in the future, saying, "And then a little voice said to me . . . ?" Because this thing was pretty bloody concrete, more of a big foghorn than a little voice.

He had wanted to talk to someone, he realized. He'd wanted, ever since Quill appeared in the service station, to convince someone of . . . of what? His innocence? But he *wasn't* innocent. He wanted to tell his story . . . only, since he'd woken up in that car, it had felt as if the thing was already starting to be left behind him now, was instead . . . enormous, implacable, not to be bargained with.

Okay, so, let's get this straight: leaving London *now* would be tantamount to running away. It would make him look guilty of something. It would deprive him of the kudos derived from the successful op. And it would also stop him cashing in on his endgame. He'd prepared that for an emergency exit, and then left it hidden, back in London. He would be leaving all that behind if he ran now. And, though his training and his inclination made running very much part of his world, he fucking hated doing it.

He forced himself to breathe more easily. *None of this is either/or, Tone.* How about a middle way? Call in sick tomorrow, maybe go to see a doctor, figure out if this feeling was . . . fuck . . . brain damage or something. Or maybe an optician thing? He looked around carefully, and then stared into the dark distance. Nothing out there struck him as weird . . . but how could you tell?

So, okay, Tony, how about you get some more data and then make a genuine decision? He started the engine and set off again, making deliberate decisions about which turns he took now, watching himself, undercover, in his own head. At every turn he took, he still felt that urge to head away from London. He went east instead and started feeling it more precisely, now he was looking for it, almost as an actual pressure on his left shoulder. He passed through increasingly rural countryside, forests and parks. He was now in what used to be called Truncheon Valley, where the needs of the Met, house prices and salaries all conspired to produce a belt of police officers' homes. He saw a sign saying *Biggin Hill*, and turned right on a whim . . . and there it went, London was right behind him now, making him relax more with every mile.

This was a pretty bloody clear message, wasn't it? The sense of threat would recede completely if he went in this direction for a while. So maybe this was just himself letting go of the tension, simply relaxing with the therapy of a long drive? Because, come on, he'd seen enough shit *outside* London, too; it wasn't as if the city had a monopoly on oppression. He pulled the car to a halt, made a three-point turn, and headed back the other way.

He felt it coming, ahead of him, after only a minute.

Fuck.

So he turned again, fled again. He passed a sign beside a bit of parkland that said *Westerham Heights: Greater London's Highest Point.* He turned at the junction, parked up, the only car on the gravel, and cautiously made his way on foot along a path between the trees, the only sound nearby being the night wind sighing through the branches. He had to get his eyeballs on to this thing, find out if he could see it as well as feel it, once he was looking at it directly.

He felt it hidden now by the rise ahead of him. Something demanding. Something threatening. Like an enormous . . . audience. He went through a gate and crested the hill, and the wind was suddenly buffeting him directly, the sound of it turbulent in his ears. He was on the side of downlands, facing north toward London. To the northwest there lay Biggin Hill airport, the lit-up lines of the runway, and to the north the lights of London itself illuminated the clouds. But that was just what his eyes were telling him. Underneath that there was much more. So much that he dropped onto the grass, although it was wet with dew that would soon become frost.

There was something in the sky above Biggin Hill. Something he could see that transcended mere sight.

He stared at it, shocked. It was right on the edge of vision and . . . and of *hearing* . . . a dream of vapor trails and the bursts of ack-ack guns firing—he could hear them clearly—and beautiful parachutes and aircraft shapes spinning and interlacing in airborne fights that meant . . . everything.

It meant everything to that great weight out there. But not to him. It—this force he'd been feeling—was trying to tell him how he should feel the importance of whatever was up there. That was a familiar feeling, he suddenly realized, and something he always felt being forced on him. It was something he didn't quite own naturally, but was meant to. Something he was missing. It was especially beautiful when seen like this, a feeling of longing and purity and of enjoying sadness. It was stamped in the sky, and it wouldn't fade. Or, at least, not for a long time. A shared thing that he didn't share. And then he found he hated it, even though he also wanted terribly to have it. Or something instead of it that was his very own. That would be the best thing; it would be so easy to lie back and join in with it. He felt that the great weight beyond it was made up of that particular sensation. There was something real underneath it all that made him ache even more. He stared ahead, amazed at these specific thoughts, which were being put in his head by what he was now seeing. He wasn't in control of his emotions right now, he realized. This power in London, whatever it was, was doing this to him somehow.

He himself was so nearly nothing, compared to the size of that power. He looked away from the ache in the sky, and toward London beyond. He could see strange things there, too. Or feel rather than see. He felt he had an extra sense hovering between all the others, which he didn't yet understand enough, which needed fine tuning. He saw, or felt, lots of tiny individual meanings there in London. They added up to that enormous feeling emanating from the city itself. And it was just from the metropolis, and nowhere else. Costain looked to his left and right. There were other towns nearby, including Sevenoaks and Tunbridge Wells somewhere behind him. But from them there came nothing, not even faintly. This was purely a London thing.

Costain considered it for a while, this London thing: this British thing that had been poured into London and solidified there. He found he wanted to apologize to it. But he also wanted it to apologize to him.

He would never before have imagined a London thing. If he was experiencing a psychotic episode, something the drugs had done to his brain over the years . . . that'd be about *everything* he saw and felt, wouldn't it? Not this one, precise thing. Yeah, he knew a threat when he saw one. And this was *real*.

He sat there for a while longer, letting himself relax, feeling no threat in the woods around him, only beauty in the downlands beyond, but he looked every now and then at where the bad stuff—if it was bad stuff—was. And it was only there. What was over Biggin Hill was like a question posed in the sky. It was a constellation in a suddenly genuine astrology, perhaps significant to him, perhaps not—not good or bad, just real.

For a while, he'd thought he was in on a successful operation, that finally he had something to celebrate. Instead he'd found this.

It was what it was. And he had to face it.

Okay, then.

After a while, he got to his feet, went back to his car, and headed back into London.

Quill had three more pints with Harry. He gradually started to tune out the running commentary from Harry's dad. The more he drank, the more he accepted what was in front of him. Maybe he could even use it. "Harry," he said finally, "are you jealous of me?"

"Don't give him the satisfaction," said Dad.

"What?" laughed Harry. "You've done so well 'cos you're a better copper, Jimmy. I know that. When it comes to getting on, I'm a lazy sod. But I see you putting the work in."

"He made you say that! You do all this to hurt yourself! And he loves it when you do, you pathetic little twat!"

Quill steeled himself. "To some extent, that's true, but it's also just because of how the dice rolled. You're a fucking amazing DS, Harry. If you went off to do something else, using those same skills, you'd be way ahead of me."

"Patronizing bastard." That had been Harry himself, with just the tiniest twitch of a smile—which his dad didn't share.

"But the dice did roll that way, and you're my mate. You're going to be my DS again at some point. I don't want to think of you gnashing your teeth."

Dad burst forth with a tirade of insults, but Quill wasn't listening. He was watching Harry instead. He wanted to see if his laying down the law could make Harry rebel against this thing, if Harry's disciplined side could make this other bastard vanish.

"That's good to hear, Jimmy," Harry said. "Don't worry your pretty little head about it." But, though he gave Quill his most sardonic grin . . . his dad remained.

Quill finally left the pub at closing time, and fended off Harry's suggestion of finding a cab with him. This encounter was going to be just a weird drunk ghost story, wasn't it? Something he'd tell people after he'd retired: "There was this one odd night when . . ."

He staggered a bit as he headed back round the corner, stepping on and off the suburban pavement, going back toward the blaze of lights outside the Losley house. He should call home: *Love, it turns out ghosts are real. Don't have nightmares. It'll never happen again.* But he was still feeling weird and, now he was out in the open, he could still feel the sort of sensation he'd had with Harry's dad sitting there. That coldness, it was everywhere. As if there was a dead dad lurking in a lot of these houses. And . . . above him, and under him. That was too worrying to think about. And that feeling was especially strong, hugely strong . . . right ahead of him.

He had to stop as soon as he saw the Losley house.

He stared at it. He had to look away, and then look back. But he knew what he was seeing was real.

EIGHT

Quill was surprised that Costain was the first to arrive at the all-night cafe on Willesden High Road. "I hadn't gone home," Quill admitted.

"Why?"

Quill just shook his head. This was going to be the hardest bit. He had been drinking black coffee ferociously, and now he couldn't quite tell the difference between drunk, buzzed, and this new weird stuff. But he knew what he was after. He remembered that feeling that had passed among them when he'd touched the soil, and now he needed to find out if the other three were seeing stuff, too, and get them to admit it. They might think they'd been drugged or something, and maybe they had been, but if they were all seeing the same thing . . .

"Listen—" he began.

"You can frigging see it too!" a voice interrupted. They looked up to see Sefton marching in. He dropped into a chair beside them, and stared at them challengingly. "Don't tell me you frigging can't, because I've had my head full of this frigging stuff!"

"Who are you talking to?" Quill reprimanded him, quickly and gently.

"Sorry, guv . . . sir." Sefton looked so suddenly lost again that

Quill almost felt sorry he'd said it. He'd quite liked that sudden show of fierceness from the quiet one.

Costain looked between them, and gave in. "All right, I can see it, too. What *is* it?"

They looked up at the sound of someone else entering, very quietly. Ross walked unsteadily toward them, and sat down beside them. She looked as if she didn't know what to say.

"We're seeing it, too," said Costain quickly.

Ross bit her lip and looked away. "I went to the psychiatric hospital," she confessed. "There was . . . a lot of . . ."

They sat there awkwardly, as she kept a distance between herself and them. They waited for her to finish that sentence. But she didn't.

"You're not going mad," said Quill. "This is real."

"Oh, that makes it so much better," said Ross sarcastically.

"I'll ignore that remark, but I don't want to hear anything like that again—from any of you."

Ross looked up, shocked, as if she'd been slapped. But the others were looking almost relieved. And now so was she. There was a time for informality, which was most of the time, and there was a time for this.

"Guv," they all concurred, grateful to him while resenting it too. He didn't want to keep handling them like that, but it'd do for right now.

"I've got something to show you," he began.

They stood in front of the Losley house, but Sefton couldn't make himself look at it for too long. His thoughts flicked back to Joe in the pub where he'd quickly led him after the incident in the street.

"What was that?" Joe had said. "What happened to you there?"

"Just . . . some kind of fit, I suppose. I ought to get myself checked out . . ."

"Is it still going on?"

Sefton had glanced over to where there was something spindly standing at the bottom of the stairs. And then he'd known he had to get away. Away from things like that, and from where there were so many people, all of whom seemed to be contributing to the weirdness. It had been like the way he felt normally about the general public, but pumped up to eleven. They made him want to hide. He had asked for Joe's number, written it on a beermat, and got out of there. He'd still been able to feel huge things moving about outside that relatively modern bar. So this wasn't all about ancient stuff. He'd edged his way through the people on the pavement, feeling all their expectations and fears, not individually as in telepathy or something, but as one great terrifying mass; feeling what might be looming in the distance. He hadn't questioned this feeling, because he wasn't able to. This wasn't some medical condition; he was in the middle of a new reality. The phone call from Quill had come as a relief. He'd known from the DI's tone of voice that he was feeling it too.

The crime scene didn't look like a normal house any longer. It was a haunted negative of a building, with black windows that were looking into Sefton, challenging him, making him think that, at any second, he'd glimpse something terrible up there. It was entirely different from the buildings on either side of it. "The witch's house," he said. And this time he wasn't making jokes about fairytales.

"Right," said Quill, "so let's—"

But Ross had already set off across the road, heading straight for the front door.

Ross hardly registered showing her pass to the uniform on the doorstep. She had to be first in, had to be in control of this. But, as she walked into the hall of the Losley house, her courage failed her. Rich tapestries hung where the windows should be. The thin carpet was replaced by fur rugs. The writing and the diagrams were still on the walls, but now they shone. There was something chitinous about the colors of the walls, the filthy carapace of a giant insect. As they came in behind her, Ross saw the other three stop and react to it, too. The new forensics shift was making its way through all this, none the wiser, not seeing what was all around them.

Ross felt her comrades draw closer. They had unconsciously formed a square now, their backs to each other, each of them looking in one of the directions trouble might come from, braced like coppers, with legs apart and weight tilted backward; Ross found that she was doing the same, while the room swirled with horror around them.

The stairs, right in front of her, were particularly challenging. It was as if you could see underneath the stairwell and yet up it at the same time. The up-and-down pattern of the stairs seemed to be overlaid on the surface of your eyes. But it was still contained within a discrete space. It was like a Picasso painting of a stairway.

It took her a moment to see what was now perched on top of the newel post at the far end of the banister. Not a skull any more, but an entire child's head. Its neck was like an automaton's, skin hanging around a spinal column which looked to have been screwed into the wood. It had golden curls like a cherub, and bright blue eyes looking straight at them. It blinked, as if *it* was surprised.

"Oh," it said, "you can see me." And then it started to yell, louder and louder. "Strangers! Strangers!"

Ross didn't want to acknowledge it. She didn't want it to be real. She looked back at the others. They didn't seem to want it to be real either. It was as if they were still in a dream. The forensics team had already started looking at them questioningly. They obviously couldn't hear the child shouting. Ross took the lead again, and headed up the stairs. She had to do it through sheer physical memory because, if she looked, she couldn't see where her feet were going. It occurred to her that getting down again would be even harder.

Sefton was looking all around him as they went, letting it soak in. This felt different to what he'd encountered in the street, and had been aware of ever since. The green thing . . . Jack . . . just . . . was . . . *grown* out of something naturally. And that way had felt the same for just about everything he'd felt the distant presence of. This was more like that old bloke who'd stepped out of Jack's way. This was . . . deliberate, something that someone had *made*. It was like his mum had always said, that there was another world underneath ours. Someone—the suspect Mora Losley—seemed to have been taking advantage of it.

They carefully made it onto the upper landing, and stared around them at what was now a polluted palace, medievally regal, adorned with deep furs and tapestries. There was nobody up here, or in the loft either, from the sound of it. The ladder that led up was now glowing in a low light coming from above. Ross made to go up it, but Quill stopped her, and he went up first.

The loft was even more extraordinary. The beams of the ceiling overhead were brilliantly polished, but also stained with time. They now looked like ancient ribs of wood. The roof was alive with a suffused light, like the sparks in a bonfire, as if the smoke of generations was up here. The room was now lined with previously unperceived chests and chairs and other pieces of furniture. The pile of soil was glittering, twitching with stringy golden light, like scribbled lines of writing or of music. Sefton couldn't look at it, because it confused his eyes. But he still found himself wanting to get to grips with it, for that would be the only way you could cope. It was only frightening because he didn't know enough. This stuff had been . . . hiding. It was a language of hidden things and of people . . . people like Mora Losley.

Costain was also gazing around, sizing the place up. Too much to cope with. He'd made a deal with himself about that as he'd headed back into the city and only seen more and more mad shit. He knew what the boundaries were, and what the way out was, so he was in. It was more the case that there was just too much

evidence here, meaning it was the opposite of Goodfellow . . . *oh!*
"This is where all the Goodfellow juice was," he said. "We couldn't
see certain things about Rob's life, 'cos they were . . . hidden from
us, literally."

"And now we're wallowing in it," muttered Quill.

"Trouble is, we can't show it to anyone else."

"Maybe we should get other coppers to touch that soil?"

"That Scene of Crime Officer said she had, and she was her
usual cynical self. I don't think she was seeing this."

"So what's so special about us?"

Costain saw that Ross reacted to that, with a sharp little look
of fear. But she kept her silence. He turned, as they all did, at a
sudden noise from the darkness over against the far wall. A noise
and a movement in the shadows, only a small movement. A rat?
No . . .

A black cat came stepping cautiously toward them. It had rough,
matted hair, stained with something sticky and dark. Its eyes were
green, and they seemed bigger than a cat's eyes ever should be.
It was also looking at them in a way which didn't seem to be how
cats normally looked at things.

"What's happened?" it said. It had an extraordinarily upper-class
accent, like some radio announcer from the past.

They stared at it.

"What are you doing here?" it went on.

They continued to stare at it. Costain couldn't think of a single
thing to say. He was struggling just to stop himself from running.
What was stopping him was the thought that that would be seen
as a terrified rout, a shaming of himself, and putting a target on
his back as he went. And the fact that what had sent him running
was merely a cat.

"Wait here," said the cat. "I'll get her." It scampered back
through the hole it had emerged from.

Costain heard what sounded like enormous, distant doors
opening, the sound echoing down impossible corridors. Where

had it gone anyway? To the house next door? No, they'd seen who lived next door. There was nothing beyond this attic. But there'd been nothing inside this attic either, the first time.

And then there was a different kind of distant echo. It was the sound of something moving. Something disturbing the air. Something moving back along that hole toward them. And the smell that started coming out of the hole, before it—

It was coming. Costain realized, and he sensed the others recognize with him the horrible, terminal mistake they had all made. The end of the horror movie was here now, and they were the victims. They had assumed this house was empty, when all the time . . . *she* was still at home.

Fast footsteps now, marching along, echoing from out of that small darkness. The darkness got bigger, changed shape . . . unfolded itself until it fitted neatly into the entire corner.

Costain took a step back, as he looked to Quill for guidance. The others were doing the same. There were fellow coppers downstairs, loads of them to provide a world of back-up. But they wouldn't be able to see this.

Quill knew he was hesitating, and hesitating terribly. He was thinking that, actually, no matter what this was, he wanted to see it, he wanted to get line of sight on a suspect, make a positive identification. But that was just copper arrogance, wasn't it, that whatever you knew about you could deal with? Was he about to get his team killed? Through lack of intel . . . a staggering lack of intel. Through him getting pissed. They should get out of here now, 'cos they were blown, exposed. He started to say that—

But suddenly there was a door there. A real door forming out of nothing. It glistened red. The door that he had spotted over there only as a transitory glimpse before. It now stayed there, silent, for a moment, then it swung slowly open.

And something impossible yet also obviously the woman called Mora Losley stepped into the room. But she didn't look like that photo of her. She wasn't like anything Quill had ever seen. She was wearing her *real* face now.

They all cried out. Just like that. They cried out like children at the sight of her.

Quill thought she looked older than it was possible for anyone to be. The skin of her face and arms was blackened as if she was bruised all over, where blotches of blood had flowed together. She was almost bald, with only tiny wisps of hair. Her skin was wrinkled as much as any human skin could be. Every angle of her jutted, every bone seemed mis-set. Her lips were cracked. Her teeth were pointed. Animating all that was simple power. Muscles like pistons. Fingers that looked strong enough to pull flesh from bone. Fingers that pinched together in the air. And yet there was something sickly sweet about her, too, a sense of . . . familiarity. She was like something terrible found in a comfortable old library, and it felt like a horrible lure, that sense of comfort—the rosy apple of the past. Her eyes were milky and bitter, but also sullen and hurt like a teenager's.

The cat had come back out too, staying behind her.

She took two precise steps toward them, like a dinosaur in an old film. She didn't seem to be in any pain from all those lesions and sores. Instead, she pushed the pain outward all around her, so as to make everyone else feel it. Her shadow, Quill realized, made the floor steam, killed something in the rugs with every step, contributed to the fug rising to the ceiling. The smell hit him then: cut grass made into compost, polish and sewerage, wine on the edge of becoming vinegar.

She was eyeing at them, considering them. They had surprised her, he understood, for she wasn't used to being seen.

To his own surprise, he found his voice. "Are you Mora Losley?"

She looked at him as if it was astonishing and humiliating to hear her name coming from him. She laughed, and it was a witch's laugh. Not like witches did in children's television. That was only a distant, safe memory of this. Her laugh sounded like small bones caught in an old throat. As if she was on the verge of choking, only she wasn't feeling the threat of that—only you were. "You touched the soil," she said, as if she'd just worked it out. "My mistress's blessed soil. I will now have to clean it. And you have a 'protocol' on you. It's reacted." She sounded like a profoundly deaf person, and the shape of her mouth was doing violence to the words. Whatever "protocol" meant, she was holding it at arm's length, as if the word was as unfamiliar to her as it was to Quill. Her accent was strange. It sounded very London, but not from anywhere that Quill could pin down. There was something almost American about it, except America was new, and this was . . . old beyond old. "You have the Sight now." Quill was about to try to frame a question about what that meant in terms of them seeing stuff, when her eyes narrowed. "I know you."

Quill looked over his shoulder to see who she was looking at.

Lisa Ross had met her gaze, seeming extraordinarily calm now. Calm because she looked to have finally encountered the thing she most feared. "Yeah," she said. "We've met."

NINE

TEN YEARS AGO

Mike the chauffeur would always drop Lisa Toshack home from school. They were friends. He took the responsibility of looking after her seriously. He was always standing by the car at the school gates, glancing around as if trouble might arrive from any direction. He seemed more worried about that possibility every day. He then drove her what would be less than a twenty-minute walk back to her dad Alfred's house on the corner of a tree-lined street in Bermondsey. On the way, Mike would tell her which, if either, of her parents was at home. Mum was often out socializing with the girls, and Dad's job as head of the family textile-import business meant he kept varying hours, spending a lot of time at Uncle Rob's. Uncle Rob was his right-hand man, and his house was where most of the serious work seemed to get done. Lisa had long ago got the idea that there was something different about their business. There would be sudden laughter at family dinners about people doing favors for them, not because they were looking for a favor back but because of who the family were. They were powerful, it seemed: Lisa's friends didn't have families like that, she'd started to realize, but she was offhandedly okay with it. Quite proud of it, really. She was the girl with the weird eye, but her friends liked that, and nobody got at her for it, though maybe they would have done if it wasn't for her family. Its members seemed to do good things. The staff seemed happy to work for them.

Today Mike had told her that her dad was currently at home, but when she went inside the house, there was a weird silence. "Dad?" she called. "Astrella?" No reply. She went upstairs to change, looking forward to afternoon telly.

On the landing she heard a noise. A groan of floorboards and straining rope. There it was again: a noise in her home she'd never heard before. She followed it to the door of Dad's office.

The door was standing open just a little. Sunshine fell as a square of light across it, from the big green and orange window along the hall. There was a smell of old carpet in the air. She saw, as she approached, an odd shape standing inside the office—a too-tall shape. She got close enough to see through the gap—

—and then she was running into the room, toward her dad, who was hanging from the light fitting, his neck in a noose, his head framed in a halo provided by the ceiling rose. She needed to get up there, to get him down as soon as possible. She had the urge to pull on his body, but she mustn't. She looked round and round the room for something to stand on, to reach up to him, but there was nothing that didn't seem a mile away.

There had been no chair under him.

She finally spotted his office chair, tucked in under his desk; she grabbed it, rushed it over, leaped on top of it. There was no expression on his face, but he had a livid bruise on his temple. He was making no sound. His head was tilted to the right. His mouth was a little open.

She ripped her fingers undoing the knot. She ripped them but she got it open. The nearest knife was in the kitchen, and there was no time, no time . . . oh God, had she made the right decision, or had she killed him? "Dad, I'll call a doctor. Dad, talk to me, say something. Dad, say something. Dad, I'm getting you down. Dad—!"

His body tumbled to the ground in a way which nothing with life in it could ever fall. Blood pooled around him and she saw, for the first time, that he had a wound in his side.

She fell down beside him and put her hands on his face, with some idea about doing first aid, but he was cold, and she shook him, trying to make him wake up and he wouldn't, and she started to scream.

"Suicide," said Uncle Rob. "I'd never have expected that of Alfred. Leaving a wife and child, too. What sort of a bastard runs away like that?"

In the next few weeks, one of the great surprises for Lisa Toshack, as she was still called then, was the anger directed at her father. Even her mum, amidst her grief, railed against him. Lisa felt shocked, didn't know where to look when people started on like that. Everybody seemed to join in with it, but she herself couldn't. Though she was doing the big gestures, though she was dressing in black all the time now, she still felt that she wasn't grieving properly, because now that seemed to involve getting angry at her dad, and she couldn't be. She felt angry, yes, but not at him.

She was angry because of what she kept saying, and nobody was listening to.

"It wasn't a suicide."

"That's lovely of you to say, but . . . he had a couple of goes before he hanged himself." There had been a wound between his ribs, a bloody knife found in an office drawer. A knife she could have used on the rope. He also seemed to have slammed his head against the wall, where there was now a dent.

"It wasn't a suicide."

"Love, please . . . don't."

"It wasn't a suicide."

Silence as the rest of the family all looked at each other.

*

She asked to be allowed to say a few words at the funeral. She stood there under the gaze of all those hard-faced friends of the family in their dry-cleaned, big-shouldered suits. Now she dressed in black lace and gloves, just a touch beyond conventional mourning wear. The vicar let her come forward to the coffin while several of the wives, blonde and orange, too many cigarettes, wearing short skirts even here, wailed as if in competition.

She looked at the massed ranks of the family, and saw the hierarchical web of responsibility and fear that had placed everyone in every pew exactly where they should be, involving no work for the ushers. The weight of that web led directly to Rob Toshack, sitting there at the innermost end of the front right-hand pew, with now no awkward counterweight of a senior brother positioned beside him. He certainly looked as if he had something extra on his mind now, but she was sure it was the extra power he had assumed.

She looked him in the eye. "It wasn't a suicide," she said again.

She left it at that and walked back to sit beside her terrified mother.

Rob caught her on the landing, during the wake. It was an expensive affair, with an Irish folk band, and everyone from Bermondsey and beyond coming in to pay their respects. It was an all-day drinking binge, and Lisa had intended to spend most of it in what had become her room now that Rob had insisted her mother move into what had become the new home and headquarters of the firm. Her dad's house had been sold.

His outstretched palm slapped onto the wallpaper just by her face. There was the continuous roar of the party below, but here they were alone. He carried a glass of whiskey, but hadn't drunk from it.

She looked carefully back at him.

"Alfred," he said, "wouldn't have wanted you doing this."

"Yes, he—"

"Shut up. Just for once . . . Oh, no!" He grabbed her as she shifted, swung her against the wall, and stuck his knuckles into her throat. He put the glass down on the top rail of the stairs. "Alf and Maureen always kept you apart from the details. Even though, by the end, there wasn't fucking much to keep you from. Apart maybe from any one of the big bastards who might have come after us. But *now* we're safe. *Now* we have a chance to make this better. *Now* we're going to grow. And you're part of this family, so you're part of that, too."

She shook her head, pulled herself away from him.

He punched her in the stomach.

He hauled her upright while she was still coughing.

"From now on you will be silent, and you will be polite, and you will do what you're told. And you will shut up about my brother's *suicide.*"

She slid down the wall as he retrieved his whiskey. She couldn't remain silent, looking at his face, because she knew for certain now. She was brave in the way only a teenager could be. Brave and stupid and immortal: she knew all those things about herself. And still she said it, "What if I don't?"

He looked hard at her, and she was ready for him to attack her again. But then that hard look became calculating, as if a new idea had occurred to him. "Then you'll see," he said. "You'll be the first to see."

She'd half expected him to come back that night—to come back later, when he was drunk. So she built a mountain of furniture against her bedroom door. Stupid teenage reaction. She felt a terrible weight attached to that word now. She had to behave older now. For Dad. To make things right about Dad. Her lace gloves and shawls and the make-up had become her special thing, her way of protesting within the family, so that the very sight of her would remind them.

She stepped back from the mountain she'd built, wondering

110

what sort of "older" she had to be now, asking herself what she could *actually* do.

She went to bed thinking about it. She fell asleep. And then, sometime in the early hours, she was awake again. Or she thought she was. An extraordinary smell had suffused the room. It smelt like some kind of memory. Like old books and spilled beer and dead flowers left in churches.

Someone was standing at the end of the bed. "There she is," said a high, strange voice, "the disobedient child."

She tried to react, tried to cry out or slam herself back against the wall, but the woman made a simple gesture, and she found she couldn't. She could only look at what was in front of her. The woman looked as if she'd been cut out of the picture Lisa was seeing through her eyes, then stuck back awkwardly into the same space again. There seemed to be special effects around her. The room behind her looked oddly unreal, as if it was just a photograph.

The woman remained in shadow. But she had in her hands held in front of her . . . a copy of a London telephone directory.

Lisa tried to move but she couldn't. If she tried really hard . . . her hand moved really slowly . . . and the woman was coming toward her in a blur.

She smacked Lisa across the face with the telephone directory— so fast it was like a bat on a ball. The back of Lisa's head hit the wall.

She collapsed, oh so slowly, forward, the blood bursting from her newly broken nose. Her head was ringing, slowly; she was feeling different to any way she'd ever felt before. To be hit that hard; it felt it could change her. She didn't know if she was going to be able to even suck in a breath—

The woman hit her again, as her head was sagging, and the blow was just as hard.

Lisa fell in and out of consciousness during the next half-hour, but her body never fell and she never managed to make a sound.

She woke again, her vision a blur, to find the woman standing at a distance again. "This is your master's mercy," she said, "so be thankful."

And then she left. Right through the wall.

Lisa found that she could make noises now. So she did. But nobody came. She'd locked herself in her room. So that couldn't have happened. She finally fell over on one side.

The bruises had almost faded by the next morning. It hurt her to move, but there wasn't a lot to show anyone. Her nose was at an angle, and it hurt to touch it, but somehow it had already set.

Lisa stared into the bathroom mirror. It was as if she'd done this damage to herself.

She started to sob, leaning on the sink and giving way to it, but then she remembered her dad's face again, and how it looked as if he'd done it to himself too, and she made this about him again, and she heaved herself upright, though it hurt like hell, and through her loosened teeth she turned the sobs into a roar.

Mum never saw anything that could have convinced her. So Lisa didn't even try. Mum remained silent at all meals where Lisa was around. Rob kept his distance for a few days, but when he finally looked at her, he looked interrogatively. Lesson learned?

Lisa put away her very particular type of fashions and make-up and music.

For the next three years, she was silent but she was polite. She wore very clean jeans; a crisp shirt; the hair that the hairdresser suggested, every time. She looked just like "a teenager" in a soap opera.

When she started to think about that terrible night, she thought about Dad instead. To the point where she wasn't sure how it could ever have happened. How something impossible could have happened. It wasn't supported by anything in her everyday world. Sometimes she wondered if it was a story she'd written, or if she'd dreamed it. But what had happened to Dad was real. At least she hung on to that.

She made sure her mother never got worried. She hid the allergies she now developed to everything existing in the family home, her eyes streaming at the smell of that carpet, at the polish, even at the air in her own bedroom. She threw back one-a-day antihistamines six times a day.

She had her mantra.

It wasn't a suicide.

Nine GCSEs: seven As and two Bs. She met older blokes through the family, and lost her virginity to one of Rob's soldiers after a party. Afterward, sore and curled up into a little ball, she goaded him with what her mum could make Rob do to him, if she found out. He was having a punt, wasn't he? Thought she was a bit of a tart, didn't he? She got him out of there in five minutes.

They planned a big party for her sixteenth birthday. Lisa Toshack let them.

Now Rob would ruffle her hair whenever he passed. His organization had grown at high speed since Alf's death. In consequence everyone was dressing better. From the distance of history, it now looked as if a weak man had been holding them all back. Mum found a new man, one of Rob's lieutenants, and he was decent enough, neutral to Lisa. She could feel the prohibitions issued about her, the threats said in her name, the anticipation of her future somewhere in the bookkeeping of the organization. They had even decided on her A levels: statistics, computers, finance.

But she was kept out of the heart of it, even though she tried to get closer. Her mum was kept out too. A lot of people were. Now, more than ever, even more than under her dad, there was the firm and there was whatever made it work, and between those things there were locked doors and Rob taking himself off, away from any of the lieutenants Lisa knew.

Three months before her birthday, she made contact with the

Crown Prosecution Service in Bethnal Green. In the weeks leading up to her party, she put several large packages in the post. On the night before her birthday, she kissed her mum goodnight, then she went to the cupboard under the stairs. The knife that Dad had supposedly used to stab himself in the ribs had been returned to the family with the rest of the evidence, years ago. Rob had actually kept it, put it back in the toolkit it had come from. That was typical of him. Lisa had made sure, every week since, that she knew where it was. It was clean, free of incrimination, but she wanted it. She put it in her pocket.

She left the house at midnight, a legal adult now, carrying only a small suitcase and a wad of cash, the loss of which could never be reported to the police.

Her lawyer got in touch with the Toshack family at ten the next morning, before, as it turned out, anyone had even realized she was gone. He indicated that all communication in future would be solely between him and the family. He also told them that Lisa intended to change her name.

She made sure she could not be found. She knew exactly what that would take, and how far the Toshack soldiers would go. Then she thought of what had happened in her room that night, and went many steps beyond. She chose the name Ross, which she'd seen on the side of a refrigerated lorry lying overturned in a ditch. Lisa Ross subsequently worked in a supermarket in Durham, where she was happy and helpful. She was promoted twice. She studied sociology of crime, sports science and criminology part-time at college. She'd been meaning to become a police officer, but the more she read, the more she realized how difficult it would be, if she did so, to carry out what she needed to do.

She walked into a police recruitment van at the careers fair, talked for ten minutes about what her ambitions were, and in response they suggested exactly what she'd already started training herself for. She therefore applied, and was asked to attend an interview a few weeks later and, on the same day, to make a presentation, with half an hour's preparation, about an organizational system she was familiar with.

Dressed properly and efficiently, she stood up in front of the panel, and began her presentation with a chart she'd drawn from memory during that half-hour. "This," she said, "shows the flow of money within the Toshack crime family."

The exclamations of astonishment from the panel didn't manage to make her smile, though she'd thought they might.

The big guys didn't express an interest in her at first, not even an awareness. She was told many times that she had to do what anyone else would do, that her heritage actually made it harder for her. She agreed, she nodded, she knew, but she didn't waver. She went through psychometric testing and, to her surprise, everyone seemed to think she was sane. She didn't mention anything which would convince them otherwise.

She took the three-week basic training course, learning about the intelligence cycle, the national intelligence model, handling five by fives and assigning codes. She was told she was lucky the training center had moved up north, since she'd thus missed a particular grim building in Putney. She hadn't mentioned that, if the course had been located there, she wouldn't have gone. At the same time, she started studying for her criminology degree in the evenings.

Her first assignment as an intelligence analyst was in Bishop Auckland. She watched the patterns of small-scale drug sales, learned how to use I2 link charts to get to know who knew who, where they met, where the money went. She learned how the best intelligence was predictive intelligence, and that it only became intel once an analyst had processed it. How only the phone call logs of criminal organizations formed a closed circuit, without any random calls made to 118 or pizza delivery or girlfriends.

Patterns like that started saying things to her. It was like discerning the hidden contours in a map. She loved it so much, it was nearly enough in itself.

But it wasn't.

Her boss was a senior analyst called Andrea Stretfield, a ferociously calm lady in her sixties, the last, she said, of some previous generation who possessed wisdom that had since been lost. "Don't just crunch the numbers," she advised. "Don't ever be afraid of the responsibility of offering an opinion. There is an art to report-writing, young lady, and it's not about cutting and pasting. This is how we find the naughty men, by applying the craft." At the time, Ross had wondered if this was genuine wisdom, or just the past attempting to claim that it had been better, that the new boys and girls were naive fools. Andrea seemed so sure of everything, but was obviously now a bit out of touch. Gradually, though, Ross came to see how she could pick and choose from the tension between past and present, that having the old guard assert themselves let her take the best from what they knew and then she could apply it to going forward.

She'd imagined that that phone call from her lawyer, a few years ago, would have caused the gravity to shift in Bermondsey, made the drugs and the prostitutes and the gambling and the chop shops vanish. For a while, at least. Maybe for a year. That only then would they start to poke their heads out again, and finally not be able to resist continuing as usual. But, during her time up north, she learned that nothing of the kind had actually happened, and that Toshack had continued business as usual.

That had been a bad night. That night she had again heavy objects up against the door of the bedroom of her flat—and then taken them away again because of how doing that had scared her.

But again she'd thought of her dad, and had kept going.

She had waited, learning her skills in operations that were nothing to do with her. She learned devil's advocacy, brainstorming and analysis of competing hypotheses. She went on a course with the army Intelligence Corps, and loved what she saw of that way of life. Some part of her wanted to be a real soldier, not in the way that Toshack used the word. She made the rank of higher analyst, which was supposed to put her on equal terms with a DI—though she'd never met a copper who saw it that way—and she started to get roped in by senior detectives on completely different operations, to help them with presentations when the money stuff got difficult. She got the reputation she was after: direct and straightforward and *thorough*.

And finally, finally, they came to see her.

A Met detective superintendent called Rebecca Lofthouse showed up at her nick. She looked as if she had no time for any bullshit from Ross, which was good, because Ross had none to give her. She spent a good long time looking at her before she even said a word. She toyed with her charm bracelet instead, then finally she seemed to decide. "Your uncle," she declared, "is a thoroughgoing bastard."

"Yes, ma'am," said Ross.

"If you're working undercover for him, it's the deepest I've seen. And he doesn't need it, not these days. So . . . We've currently got nothing and you might give us something. There are also factors involved about which you may never hear. At any rate, I've decided to take you up on the generous offer which you haven't yet made to us." It transpired that she had an operation in mind, down in the smoke, which would require Ross to be transferred, a request which had already been granted in principle. Lofthouse had already pulled a DI from SCD 7(2), the special projects team, to lead it, and Lambeth Operational Command Unit were letting them use a station that was a significant distance from the subjects, and would keep the op out of the organized crime mainstream, in case Toshack's intelligence-gathering was all it was cracked up to be. Ross, with the possibility of name and face recognition, would even be kept out of that. They were going to play a long game, putting in some UCs using her knowledge. It was to be called Operation Goodfellow.

"Have you got anything else to tell me?" Lofthouse asked, at the end of the final briefing. "Anything you haven't put on the record?" She seemed genuinely interested, eager to hear, even. "Anything you . . . couldn't?"

Ross had thought about it for a moment. "No, ma'am," she said.

TEN

"You are Alfred Toshack's daughter," said Mora Losley. She pointed to Ross's nose. "I made that. It could have been any accident, across the course of your life, but it was me. I am the mother of your face."

The fear gripped Ross now. That smell! It had taken her back to when she'd been terribly hurt. It made her feel very small. This was what she had always imagined she would sometime see again.

As she studied Ross, Losley inclined her head sideways, like a predatory bird, moving her hands in a strangely elegant gesture as she did so. "The disobedient child, a policeman and two blackamoors, one of them a sodomite."

Ross couldn't begin to process that.

"And yet somehow they have a 'protocol' on them. What is it?" The woman took a step toward her. It took an effort, but Ross made herself stay where she was. "Did you make sacrifice and then touch my mistress's blessed soil deliberately, so as to gain the Sight? *You*? Or is this an accident?"

Ross could feel the power of her. Even the force of her shadow on the floor was making the air between them ripple with heat. The fact she had questions was the only thing now saving them. There were so many people downstairs: all she had to do was yell and they'd come running. But they wouldn't see the old woman. They'd be blind to the danger.

"Are you *privileged*?" Losley barked. "Do you make sacrifice, or are you remembered?" Her accent had slid suddenly upward, into something resonating with privilege. Even as Ross distantly wondered what any of those words meant, her mind obeying her training even as it reeled in shock, she was ridiculously reminded of Keith Richards. "Answer me!"

"How . . . how did my uncle employ you?"

Losley stopped. She looked suspicious again, as if this question had revealed some hint of worrying knowledge. "I am not employed. He merely knew of me from the football club." She put a hand to her heart and then to her brow, a kind of benediction. She had said "football club" very precisely, as if she'd learned those words once and kept them carefully enunciated like that. "He made a good sacrifice. My lord of the pleasant face assigned me to his service."

Ross felt very small again. Toshack hadn't even bothered to send this thing after her when she'd run. She couldn't quite believe that. But she'd discovered it now, out of some horrible accident or of some destiny that was going to destroy her. She managed to make herself speak again. "So why did you kill Toshack?" She was aware of Quill looking toward her, still in shock but urging her on.

"When my service ended, my lord of the pleasant face would not hear his pleas, so he offered me sacrifice to continue!" She shook her head, looking at Ross with a terrible aloofness, as if all this were her fault by association. "Modern rubbish. The rules are not *written down*! When I ignored that fucking cunt of a criminal, he tried to tell this watchman"—she pointed at Quill—"my *name*!"

Quill stepped forward until he was alongside Ross, breathing heavily. She realized he was going to do it, this absurd, futile thing. She felt admiration and fear for him. "Mora Losley," he said, and he clearly had to pause and gather himself together before he continued quickly, "you are under arrest for the murder of Robert

Toshack and several others. You do not have to say anything, but it may harm your defense—"

She raised a hand and screamed.

The sound made them stagger. They fell to the ground. And still it continued, battering them from every angle of the attic. Ross put her hands over her ears, and she was properly back there now, sobbing in the dark, with the hugeness looming over her and blow after blow . . . But no. No. She would not go back there. She would *not*.

She hauled herself to her feet. The room swayed in front of her, all in red. Blood in her eyes. Blows still reflecting off the walls. But there was the witch, her mouth slowly closing around the mere sound that had beaten them all to their knees, looking so hugely affronted, so vastly above any of their lives that for them to try to bring her down to their level had made her bellow thus in horror at the insult.

Ross would not go through this again. She had to fight. It was more important than staying alive. She ran at Losley, her hands reaching in front of her face. She got further than her feet expected to, swinging her balance at the last second to throw a punch straight at—

Losley made another gesture.

Ross felt something precious drop out of her head. And then she was looking upward as her body flew away from her, like some aircraft she was falling from, and was soaring up toward the ceiling, impossibly. She twisted frantically, to see what was below her. Hot black entwined darkness was hurtling up at her from out of the floor.

Quill had seen what Ross was about to do and had staggered to his feet, a second ahead of the other two. He was having trouble controlling his bladder, which made him feel like a child in the face of this thing. He had been about to shout something. To yell that they should get out . . . that they had walked into a situation they weren't expecting . . .

He had no idea what he had been about to shout.

But then his brain had fallen through his shoes, and his body was blasted up out of him like a rocket, and he was a falling ghost with no visible self, nothing to him but his own awareness of himself.

He remembered, as he fell and fell an impossible distance, beyond the height of the room, that look on Toshack's face in the interview room. He remembered how his own eyes had hurt at what had been happening, how his brain had failed to understand it. And he realized that Toshack hadn't been slammed up against the wall, as he'd thought at the time. It had been the ceiling he'd been staring down from. And he imagined Losley standing there, invisible, doing to Toshack then what she was doing to them now. With that terrible ancient nurse's face, revealing her sad certainty of pain.

Sefton saw his body flying away from him, and was rigid with fury in the nothingness that was now himself. It had all been taken from him with such ease, like something stolen and thrown over his head. She had all power over him. The word she'd used: "sodomite" indeed! The distaste in her voice as she looked at him and judged him. There was power all around him, and he couldn't get his hands on it. He couldn't speak. Just as always, he couldn't change anything. Just as always, he needed to understand it in order to use it, but for now he had to hide from it, and there wasn't time, because it had him in its grasp.

Costain turned as he fell, and saw what he was falling toward, and he started scrabbling to grab purchase on air and, when he couldn't, he started to scream.

Quill looked down, too, when he heard the screaming, and saw the nothingness below him. It was a void that seemed to stretch in impossible directions, beyond the ability of his eyes to encompass it. The floor warped into it at its outer fringes. Something that felt hot and dangerous, like an invisible fire, streamed up from this void, and he was aware of a terrible gravity to it, as if he was in a nightmare and this was the mouth that would finally eat him, no matter what he did.

He looked up again, and was startled to realize that he was seeing his own body now as it bumped up against the ceiling; that he really was outside that body; that there was somehow more to him than had been contained in that same body.

It was so far away from him now. He didn't know how he could get back to it. He desperately needed to.

He remembered Toshack heating up in that interview room, and he felt himself heating up now—saw his body up there starting to glow with it. What had happened to Toshack then, what he hadn't been able to comprehend properly back then: that was what was happening to him now.

But that was weird, wasn't it? He was still feeling the heat, though it was his body way up there that was being heated up. The same thing was happening to both entities, and he now doubted that some sort of hole in the floor had really opened up underneath him, whatever "really" meant in these circumstances. No, this was all inside his brain: this was him sort of seeing what was going on, him being pulled out of his body. And that extraction wasn't over yet, because there was the heat thing going on for both of them, so there must still be some sort of connection between the two.

He did it without thinking: shifted mentally from one foot to the other, a copper trying to quickly find his balance—

And he was back inside his body, with a sickening feeling of his heart or his guts now stretching away below him, and an immediate horrifyingly painful sensation that he really was about to explode. And that nearly made him step out again, but—

He could see with his real eyes now, the real room below him, and he remembered what she'd said about having to clean the soil, and he wasn't going to be able to hold it in much longer, anyway, and he knew nothing about how any of this worked, but—

He reached down, his fingers feeling huge, inflamed. He could hear the screams of the members of his unit around him. There were only seconds left before they hit whatever it was way down there, and then their blood would erupt from them volcanically, as it had erupted out of Toshack. That thing that was Losley had turned its back on them, was walking back toward her red door, the cat following at her feet, as if they didn't matter any more, not even the exultation in killing them. He managed to grab his zip and pull. He managed to tug his dick out of his trousers. "Here, Mora!" he bellowed, with every ounce of London in him. "I piss on your West Ham!"

And he let fly onto the soil.

Ross cried out as she flew back into her body. She had a second to grab hopelessly for a ceiling joist, and then she fell again, and had a moment to gauge how far it was before she landed, managing to take the brunt of it on her legs. The others dropped like fruit around her, shouting wildly as they landed, bouncing and rolling on the thick furs. She lay there in pain, but adrenalin was already shouting at her to get up. For a moment she wondered if this nightmare was over, if they'd look around now to find that that thing was gone.

But, no, there she was, turned to look at them, her mouth open, staring at them in horror. Ross roared inside to see it. The bitch was *surprised*.

Meanwhile, thunderclouds were boiling their way out of that pile of soil, like special effects in forties Technicolor.

Quill hauled himself to his feet, and zipped himself up. "Mora Losley . . ." he began again, and this time he was yelling it.

He had to yell it because now, rising from all around them,

there came an enormous rumbling noise. Was this her power falling apart?

"Modern . . . children!" she bellowed. "Who allows you this? You have no privilege! You have no idea! This is not how things are *done*!"

"Fuck you!" yelled Costain.

She made a gesture and they all flinched, and just for a second Quill was sure that something had hit him, but then he saw that all her gesture had done was to grab the cat up into her arms. "I am not *limited* by such as *you*!" she shouted above the noise. "I have more soil! I will live as I have always lived. I will do as I have always done. In the past it has been my pleasure sometimes to show mercy, but now you must be taught! I will continue to support my football club! I will kill any player who scores three against them! Try to find me, try to change the way things have always been, and my lord *will* have you!"

She and the cat somehow folded together . . .

And vanished on a dark wing that roared away through Quill's head. And rushed out though that impossible door.

He looked round at the others. They'd all felt it. They were looking around them desperately, afraid of their own fear, not quite believing they'd escaped, still aware of that enormous noise around them. A shout from Sefton made Quill look up again. Something odd had started to happen to the walls: they were buckling inward. The pieces of furniture were shoving themselves up against each other. It was all starting to fall toward that red door, which still lay open, like the plughole which the room was starting to revolve around, as it began to suck everything inside it, downward into . . .

Quill looked to the trapdoor.

Even as he looked, it warped and slowly started to spin its way up the wall.

"Well, don't just stand there!" he yelled to the others. "Leg it!"

To Quill's enormous relief, they did.

They threw themselves down through the trapdoor, and landed hard on the floor below. "Out!" shouted Quill to the forensics shift. "Out!" So now others were running with them, uniforms and forensics in crime scene suits, like a bomb was about to go off. They ran for the stairs, which were folding in on themselves, and were even harder to see and understand now, and they fell down them and rolled, and the uniforms helped them up and rushed down around them, nimbly navigating all the impossibilities.

The child's head fixed on the top of the banister was screaming, and the shape of it was starting to peel off into a long ribbon of flesh that led back up into the twisting, knotting building. Up ahead there was the front door . . .

. . . racing away from them. Receding into the far distance at the end of an impossible corridor, as space stretched under this strange new gravity. Uniforms were running out through it, receding with it. This trap was intended just for the four of them.

Quill turned on his heel, grabbed a fur from the floor, wrapped it around him. He made sure the other three saw what he intended, then he flung himself at the nearest window.

The crashing glass expanded slowly outward. They were escaping something dreamlike and hugely gravitational which was trying to haul them back inside. They burst out of the house as if it was a dying universe, slowly, slowly, reaching the limit of where it could hold on to them . . .

And they were in the frosty night air, above the passage running along one side of the house, and everything was real again.

They heard the distant slam of that impossible door. The entire contents of the house had now fled through it.

And they fell and hit the ground hard, again, and lay there together, gasping, and the window threw itself back together, and the house vanished toward a point that hurt their eyes.

And then it was gone, heading somewhere into the fine structure of the night.

As they lay there, Quill realized he was still holding a scrap of dirty carpet. It evaporated a moment later into a billow of dust.

Slowly, they picked themselves up. A uniform peered around the corner of a wall. "The evacuation's complete, sir. How far back should I set the perimeter, sir?" Urgency and disbelief were fighting on his face. Behind him, Quill could see the big lights of the TV crews coming back on.

Quill turned round to look at what they had just escaped from.

Where a moment before there had been a sort of vacuum, an ordinary house had reappeared. Ordinary to his eyes now, too.

From which all the weight and horror had vanished.

ELEVEN

Quill led them back into the house. The skull was still there on the newel post, but it wasn't a head any more. It looked perversely dull in comparison, simply mundane. So did the soil upstairs. Perhaps this "Sight" had now left them all? He hoped that was the case.

She had been in this house all the while it was searched, hiding behind a door that existed only for her. They had then made her retreat, through mere instinct and accident.

He shut down all these questions and allowed the forensics shift immediately back into the house. Emergency over. His mistake. He was aware of the forensics shift and the uniforms looking startled to the point of laughter: what had all that been about? He couldn't satisfactorily answer them, so he bundled his team into a marked car and they got the hell out of there.

An hour later, Quill stood again outside the Portakabin, and listened on his mobile to his home phone ringing. He thought he could see dawn approaching, or maybe that was just something weird over there toward the east. Because the drive here had shown them that they most definitely all still had the Sight, whatever that meant. His hands were shaking.

The world was much more terrifying than anyone had known— and it had been pretty terrifying before. He had called Sarah intending to . . . what? Warn her? Tell her not just ghosts actually, love, witches too? Nobody would believe them. She wouldn't believe him either.

Just in the moment before he switched off the connection, he thought maybe he heard the phone being picked up, but she didn't call him back.

The others were sitting in the Portakabin, drinking strong sweet tea, not speaking, not looking at each other. In the car they'd kept their eyes closed, pretending they were trying to sleep. Quill felt the same great tiredness, but knew no sleep would come. He'd suffered from shock before. He sat down alongside them.

" 'Sodomite?' " said Costain, as if it had just occurred to him, looking at Sefton.

Sefton looked long and hard at him. "You didn't know?"

Costain shook his head. Sefton kept the look going.

"I didn't."

"Okay," said Sefton finally and looked away.

Quill had known it, actually, but he didn't think now would be a great time to chime in. He went over to a cupboard and found some blankets, and put them round everyone's shoulders. He pulled a blanket around himself as well. They all fell silent again.

After a while, Quill realized that he could see something from across the room. See something with the Sight he still possessed. The realization made him tense again, in a horrible way. But no . . . no, it was just something inside here, not her walking through the wall. It was something on the Ops Board. He got up, feeling cold inside his stomach, and went to see. It was Losley's photo, passport-sized. It now showed her as she . . . he hesitated to think the word, but no . . . as she *really* was. He made himself examine that face. Good to be able to do that, with the real Mora Losley. She didn't actually administer poison or have burly nephews. He went to get a file from the table serving as his desk, and he pulled out the season-ticket records. The date of her first registration, 1955, now glowed dully, completely obscuring another date beneath it. It suddenly came to him that there might be a similar type of glowing covering all those missing council tax and utility bills. This was a woman who could edit the world.

He went back to look at the Ops Board. He hated the way it looked now, not just that it had her real face on it. It was lying to him. "*This* is what's true," he said, without really knowing who he was talking to. Maybe to the board itself. He picked up a spool of black thread, and tacked a solid association line between Losley and a photo of Rob Toshack. And then he added a red victim thread as well, because she had also admitted to being his killer. Everything else, all the bullshit that they'd thought might have something to do with this case, he unpinned. He was left with just the prime suspect and those two strands of relationship. He looked up to find that the other three had stood up and joined him, also staring at the board as if it had betrayed them.

"That's not all we know," ventured Ross.

Quill nodded to her to go ahead.

Her hands shaking, she drew three wobbly stick figures in red on a piece of paper, inside a sketch of a cauldron. She pinned that below Losley, and connected them to her with a red victim thread. She wrote a heading "footballers and others," and attached those to Losley as victims too, ready for the further detail to be filled in.

"She said that Toshack made a sacrifice." Quill attached a victim thread from Toshack to a blank piece of card, and wrote a question mark on it. "More kids, like in the cauldron?"

Ross stopped for a moment, taking that onboard. "Yeah," she said, "he was capable of that."

Costain stepped forward, too. He was looking the most stricken of any of them, and his whole body was shaking. He took the black thread, wrote "cat" on a piece of paper, and connected Losley to that also. Then he did the same for "mistress," and placed it above her. He looked as if he was doing this on autopilot.

"'My mistress's blessed soil,'" noted Quill, doing his best to sound approving.

"Who owns West Ham?" asked Ross.

Quill looked it up. Mostly a bank in Iceland. No women on the list.

"What about that . . . head . . . on the stairs?" said Sefton.

"We're listing pets," said Quill, "so why not furniture?" He pinned up another heading and threaded the connection. Just seeing the board filling up like this, he realized, was making him feel slightly better. Mora Losley was the missing element that connected all the outlying oddities of their investigation, as Ross had perceived it. Losley had been all the "freelancers" Rob Toshack required to make his firm function. She was the suspect that all those murders stretching way back spoke of.

Costain took a deep breath. "Okay," he said, then used another black thread to connect Losley to yet another card above her. "Lord," he wrote on it. And on the card beneath it, he added "pleasant face" as a description.

"'My lord will have you,'" said Quill.

"I reckon that's what she was trying to do at the house," said Costain. "To sacrifice us. Give us to her lord. What did you lot see below you, when our bodies were . . . ?" He gestured, seeming to have reached the end of his ability to talk about it.

"Like . . . something out of *The Sky at Night*," suggested Quill. "My own personal black hole." He looked to the others, and they nodded.

"I saw . . . a lot more than that. I think I might have even got a sight of her lord. There was a bloke looking . . . happy. And she'd just 'given' me to him. And . . ." Costain stopped again. Then he walked quickly for the door, went out and closed it behind him. Through the window, Quill could see his silhouette still standing outside.

"We need to know," said Ross.

"He knows that. But nobody bloody ask him, clear?" They both affirmed agreement.

"Why," inquired Ross, "was it just him?"

"I think he's now asking himself that."

"Fuck me," said Sefton, "who do witches have as their lord? Is that what he's wondering?"

Quill sighed. "I'm way ahead of you two right now, aren't I? Makes a bloody change." He banged his fist on the table, making them both start, and regretted doing it instantly. He felt the terrible chill as much as either of them. "But we don't know, do we? It could just as well be some sort of . . . bigger version of one of those things out there."

"Right," said Sefton, looking almost angry at the idea it could be anything else.

He gave it five minutes, during which he made them another cup of tea, then marched over to the door and opened it, to find Costain leaning against the wall of the Portakabin. "In," he said firmly.

He turned to all three of them, gathered in front of an Ops Board that was now looking healthier, all with cuppas in their hands. "We don't speculate," he said. "We don't do theology. All there is," he pointed to the board, "is that."

They all turned back to the board again. "Listen—" he said. And he started to tell them about what had happened in the interview room, and about Harry and everything else.

They all told their stories in turn. Ross about the drive across London, and then, haltingly, about her first meeting with Losley. Sefton saw all that pain concealed behind her poker face, and held himself back from taking her hands in his. He himself—with several meaningful omissions, because he wasn't going to mention Joe to this lot—talked about his encounter with "Jack," and about the man that had stepped aside from it. Costain seemed to consider what the others had said, and then quickly filled them in on his journey away from London, about how he saw that the effect was limited to the metropolis. They waited for him to say more but, for the moment, that was obviously it.

"Just London?" said Sefton. "So we can get away from this shit by just getting on the train to Brighton?" And then he felt immediately guilty at having been the one to say it.

"I'm amazed you ever came back," said Quill to Costain. The man looked suddenly furious at him, and Quill raised his hands, quickly explaining himself. "I mean 'cos *any* of us here would have thought about doing a runner. I'll bet Ross is thinking right now about going back to her old nick."

"Old Nick?" said Sefton, "I wouldn't use that expression."

Which made Ross burst out into an enormous, awkward laugh, and then she put a hand over her mouth, her eyes gleaming with tears as if she'd done the most terrible thing. Sefton found himself weirdly pleased, in the midst of how shocked he'd been feeling. He never told jokes; it had just slipped out and made a change in the world.

Costain managed a sad smile. "We could all easily hop it," he said. "We could put in for transfers, take any family we have with us. We could leave all this behind. Except . . . I think I now have to consider so carefully every . . . decision I make. And I think that getting out of it now . . . doing anything but my best to help nick her . . . would be wrong."

The tone of his voice was so alien to him, so beaten down, that Sefton almost wanted the bully in him back. Almost.

Quill nodded, giving that statement its due. "We *all* have to decide," he said. "A highly dangerous suspect has admitted to several murders, and has threatened to carry out more. She's going to kill any player that scores a hat-trick against West Ham Football Club. Their next match is tomorrow night. We know her MO, and we've already worked her background. We have that tiny advantage: we can do proper police work on her. While we were working on that board, it felt as if we were also working to stop her—and that made me feel better. What about you two?"

Sefton nodded. There wasn't really a choice, as far as he could see. "You're right about going after her, but it benefits us too, doesn't it? I don't want to have to stay away from London all my life, and who knows what else is waiting out there? If we can find some way to nick her, maybe then we can force her to take away the Sight from us and all."

And that got a gratifying reaction too. That hope he'd found had touched a chord in all of them.

Quill looked to Ross, who was deep in thought. "She almost certainly didn't kill my dad," she said. "Wrong MO. But she's a serial killer, and only we can have her. And," she pointed to her nose, "I fucking owe her."

Quill held up a finger as if to mark this moment. He went over to the pile of paper and card, and took out a long strip of cardboard upon which he wrote something, then pinned it at the top of the board, having finally decided the name of the investigation. Just for once, he didn't feel he was taking a risk by making it relevant, though the witch from *The Wizard of Oz* looked positively benign compared to this one.

"Operation Toto," he said.

TWELVE

"Just nobody ask which of us is missing a brain. Operational objectives." Quill began writing them down on the right-hand side of the Ops Board:

> 1. *Ensure the safety of the public.*
> 2. *Gather evidence of offenses.*
> 3. *Find subject Mora Losley.*
> 4. *Find means to arrest subject.*
> 5. *Arrest subject.*
> 6. *Forcibly negotiate removal of the Sight.*
> 7. *Bring to trial/destroy.*

It took Quill a moment to add that last word, Sefton realized. But they all nodded when they saw it. "Yeah," he concurred.

Quill shrugged. "We don't want to turn this into some sort of witch hunt." Which was the point at which Sefton understood what the man had done. He'd turned their personal nightmare into something approaching business as usual. It wasn't bloody sustainable, but it at least gave them solid ground to put their feet on. The blankets had been left behind, hanging on the backs of their chairs. It was now starting to get light outside the Portakabin.

"I'm going to put in requests for bill records from . . . sod it, all the thirty-three boroughs, going back . . . well, as far as they go, which'll only be ten years or so, but it's a start," declared Ross, going to the computer. "There'll be a pile of them, but if her alterations, her edits, stand out that clearly, just skimming them will do."

"It'll take weeks of grunt work and potentially lead nowhere," said Quill. "Excellent: that sounds like police work to me. Anyone got anything else?"

Sefton found one of the new police pocket books he'd been given when he'd suddenly stopped being a UC, and leafed quickly through it. There wasn't much there that related to anything that was true—not now they knew what the truth was. He put it aside, went to the cupboard and found four plain notepads. "Special pocket books," he said. "*Not* as issued by the IBO. For our sort of stuff. Like Ross here has always used for her speciality. Maybe one day a court will be prepared to believe us. We can't put this stuff in the regular pocket books, but we'll need to remember things."

"And now paperwork," Quill nodded. "I'm feeling more at home all the time."

Sefton felt weird at doing so much speaking up now. His skills had been, up until now, basically hiding, pretending and observing. It must be the observing part of that which was giving him all these ideas. "Yeah, well, that's what this is about: *remembering*. We have to . . . remember better than she does. Starting with . . ." He grabbed a marker pen and a sheaf of paper, and started urgently writing out big headings. "Protocol." "The Sight." "Privileged." "Make Sacrifice." "Remembered." He held up those last two. "That's an either/or," he explained, his brain moving so fast that he just hoped he was making sense. "She asked us if we 'made sacrifice' *or* if we were 'remembered.'" He put them up as headings down the lefthand side of the Ops Board. "And . . . this is a new area on the board, where the concepts go." He stared at it for a moment. He'd just created a new area on an Ops Board. An innovation in policing, just like that. It was only a matter of time before someone stopped him from doing stuff like this.

"So what does 'remembered' actually mean?" asked Quill. "How is that the other choice, instead of just making sacrifice?"

"Maybe that's what I felt about the difference between stuff that's sort of . . . grown . . . like Jack the green man was, and . . . *made*, like Losley's stuff is."

"So long as we don't properly know things like that, we're going to be living on assumptions," said Ross, looking up from the computer. "We need to get used to that, using working assumptions but bearing in mind that they are just that."

"And feelings as well as assumptions," said Sefton. "Copper instinct. Like when the guv . . ." he hesitated, but then had to say it anyway, ". . . got his cock out."

"If you write that down," insisted Quill, "do make the context clear. How do we limit what we record? Ghost ships, Harry's dad, your Jack creature . . . it's like claiming every crime in London is relevant to a murder case."

"If we didn't know what murder was," said Ross, "they would be." She came over and looked at Sefton's new side of the board with an expert eye. "Everything we see with the Sight is part of . . . a hidden culture of London. Like an OCN could be divided into chop shops, robberies, toms and drugs, and each of those have their own subculture involving loads of signifiers and definitions that interact with each other. But it's all still the one thing, and quite often we encounter a small part of it and, given time, pull at that one thread to find a way to nick the whole thing. There are new factors appearing in normal police work all the time: new security behaviors, tech use, drugs. But maybe this special culture is a bit easier because, unlike with organized crime, there might be only two ways for someone to get into this business . . ." She pointed at Sefton's signs. "I mean *sacrifice* or be *remembered*. We have some idea what one of those involves: from seeing the kids in the cauldron." She now linked those pieces of paper with white thread. "We need to find out what this other concept means."

" 'Protocol,' that's the word that applied to us," said Costain, pointing at the other sign. "That's the important one for us lot. She mentioned it as if it wasn't something she was used to, either."

"Yeah," said Quill, "I noticed that, too. So that's someone else's technical term, not one she'd use normally herself."

"It's called 'a Protocol,' and we 'had it on us,' as if it's something physical—that's what she said—and it 'reacted with the soil.' "

"But of the four of us in that attic, only *I* touched that soil," said Quill. "This must involve some sort of area effect, like a hand grenade going off."

"Whatever, that's how she thinks we got the Sight, why we're seeing all this shit. So what *is* it?"

Nobody had any answers to that one. "We need to use these new eyes of ours," said Ross, "and check out the evidence again."

"Well," said Quill, "there's one piece for which we can do that immediately."

They stood at the fence at the back of Gipsy Hill police station. Sefton could now see the mound of soil shining from here. "If we touched that," said Quill, "would it give us more of the Sight, or would it maybe switch it off?"

"Neither," said Sefton, to himself. He looked up when he realized the others were wondering why he sounded so certain. "She left it there. It's not precious any more, so it must be kind of . . . used up." Quill popped inside the fence to take a quick look. It took a few moments for it to dawn on Sefton that he wasn't worried, standing here, that the uniforms might get a look at him. The possibility that any remnants of the Toshack organization might learn his identity was nowhere near as threatening as what he now knew lay under reality itself. "It's better in the day," he said, "don't you reckon?"

Costain glanced across to London. "Yeah, maybe."

Quill returned to tell them that this mound of soil, when seen with the Sight, looked like a pale reflection of the pile they'd seen inside the house, before Quill had pissed on it. "And, yeah, I touched it, but no joy to be had."

"I don't think it's a symbol of anything," said Ross, "not like we thought. These things are invisible to most people. When that soil got pissed on, suspect wasn't psychologically traumatized, but she got so worried she actually *legged it*! No, this is *practical*. A system we don't know much about, but still a system. I think, for some reason, she *needs* the West Ham soil. She told us she needs to keep it clean, and I don't think that's a psychological tic on her part, either. I think she *needs* to bring it with her when she's killing, to put it in that heap, in that pattern, otherwise she just wouldn't do that."

" 'I have more soil,' that's what she said," recalled Costain, "as if it was valuable to her. As if it's her stash. Maybe that's why she's got so many houses."

"Like with a heroin-distribution network," said Ross, "you don't keep all the eggs in the same basket."

"We know Toshack tried to find her at her main home first, on his own. Then he went round all her other houses, her safe houses. He went up into every loft, maybe because he was checking to see if she'd left some soil there, which would mean she still used the place."

"While he was getting the rest of us to make as much noise as possible downstairs," said Sefton, suddenly sounding shocked again.

"The fucker was using *us* as bait! He was trying to make her come out and grab us! We were to be his sacrifices, like he said in that note!"

"He tried to do that again when the raid went down," said Quill, "calling her a sow and all."

"Why West Ham soil?" said Ross. "Just 'cos she's a fan?"

Nobody had an answer to that either. Quill called the nicks in all the areas where the other Losley houses were located. They'd already been sealed off by Goodfellow, but now he asked to hear from them about what had been found in their lofts.

"Get them to piss on it, too," suggested Costain.

Quill declined that recommendation. He swiftly heard that largely empty tubs had been found in all the houses, with just a layer of local soil left at the bottom. "Right you are: she hauled in her stash."

Quill felt the new energy of his team, and liked it. But now they needed to do something positive with it rapidly. They needed an aim to work toward, or all this new hope was going to fall apart again. They went back into the Portakabin. There had been a lot of e-mails forwarded to them concerning possible Losley sightings by members of the public but, given that she could make herself invisible, Quill had the team give them only a quick once-over, and they found nothing that caught their eyes. He got copies of the Goodfellow files e-mailed over, but he was deeply familiar with their contents, and there was nothing that leaped out at him now that he had this new way of seeing. "She said she met Toshack at the football . . ." he reminded them.

Ross found on the PC the list of season-ticket holders in seats close to Losley that West Ham had sent over to Quill. "I was going to get to this today," she said. She ran her finger down the list of names. Then stopped at a particular one. The seat next to Losley's was occupied by one Robert Toshack.

"Get in," said Quill triumphantly.

He found the disc with the CCTV tape on it and played it again. That familiar corner of the building, and that flower bed. One moment there was nothing there, and then there was Losley, who'd literally appeared out of thin air. Quill again found himself startled, fearful even at the sight of a moving image of her. "It works through video as well as still photos," he said, with a cough to conceal his reaction. On screen, Losley took a small bag from her pocket, and poured the contents out on the ground, tracing a spiral with her hand, the other turning in the air. A pile of soil far too large to be contained in the bag was deposited there, arranged in the familiar pattern, shining with power.

"Maybe it's like Wi-Fi," said Ross, "she can only operate so far from a base station."

"Why do it out there?" said Sefton. "Why not just arrive in the interview room itself?"

Quill clapped his hands together in realization. "Because she needs to put soil on soil! To put her earth on top of what was there before. Like with those containers in her houses."

They watched as Losley walked directly toward Gipsy Hill police station and straight through the wall, moving her hands before her as if she was performing an intricate dance. "Those gestures, all the time," observed Sefton. "That's not habit, that's meaningful. That's how she does what she does, using words and gestures as weapons."

Quill liked how much he was speaking up now. And now he had a sudden idea himself. He called up the nick, then headed over there to pick up a much less controversial CCTV camera recording. He played that back in front of his team, and they all saw the next part of the action: Losley in the interview room, sending Toshack flying up to the roof; Quill looking on awkwardly, his expression and body language saying he was trying to look in all directions at once; the expression on the brief's face also saying that he didn't quite know what he was looking at.

"It's as if we scratched the lottery card of reality," he said, "and this is what was bloody underneath. Not a big win, really."

"The eighteen percent!" said Ross suddenly.

"What?" said Quill.

"The eighteen percent of the other cases, the hat-trick scorers over the years who we thought probably died of natural causes . . ." Ross went to the computer and busied herself for half an hour, then gathered them round a display on the screen. "They're almost all from teams *outside London*. So sometimes she'd get them when they came back to town, sometimes she'd forget or give up, sometimes they never came back at all. But she never followed them home!"

"That means she's got an operational range," said Sefton. "Soil in her pockets will only take her so far. Only London provides power. And she only has power inside London."

"Fuck," said Ross, "that's why Toshack didn't send her after me. I was up north." She added a note to that effect to the board, under Losley's name.

They mulled that over for a few moments.

"I'll see if she's caught on camera anywhere else inside the nick," said Quill. "Though I don't know if we'll learn anything more from it. Meanwhile . . ." he turned to the others and realized that, with two UCs and an analyst, he had no sensible way of picking who should do the legwork. "Toss a coin for who calls up West Ham again. See if they have a list of people who they sold their soil to. Then tell them to stop."

They actually did the coin toss, and it turned out to be Costain whose job it was to cajole and intimidate the West Ham hierarchy. Quill listened to him doing it, impressed but also a bit freaked out. There was something in the man's voice that sounded as if it was his first day on the job now, too eager to impress. He felt that Losley had already taken a piece out of one of his team by making Costain behave like that. The football club turned out only to have a mailing list of people who'd bought soil over the Internet. Getting that sent over was no problem, and indeed it arrived by immediate e-mail. But they were selling a lot of soil right now, because they were in the process of moving to their new home, and every fan wanted a piece of the old Boleyn Ground at Upton Park, and those in charge couldn't see any reason why the police would want them to cease trading. All Costain could say was, "it's an operational matter."

When Quill waved to him to give the phone over to him and have a superior officer yell at them, Costain held up a hand and went into overdrive. "You know what you get when you Google 'West Ham' now? Serial killer, serial killer, serial killer . . . oh, look, there's also some news about your FA Cup run, there on the third page. Only saving grace is, you're helping to catch this killer by cooperating so fully. Yeah, I will speak to your chairman, that'd be nice." When he eventually put down the phone, job done, Quill slapped him on the back.

Costain nodded solemnly. "Yeah," he said.

That afternoon, Quill led his small team into Gipsy Hill, causing a raised eyebrow from the station reception officer on shift when she saw Costain and Sefton. Everyone would now be gossiping, Quill knew, about the huge pay-off from what had originally looked like a weird and intimidating spin-off. And everyone would be wondering why they themselves hadn't been considered good enough or straight enough to go after the real juice behind the Toshack organization. Seeing the four of them march in right now, including the UCs, half of the operational team would assume they were here to nick someone, and the other half that just showing them those two UCs was some sort of demonstration of trust.

Plus, of course, Quill's lot hadn't slept and they all looked like tramps.

Nods and smiles of appreciation greeted Quill when he entered the Ops Room, but he could feel the dutiful nature of it, the fear and irony at the edge of it. Goodfellow was busy to overflowing with paperwork and personnel, but it was all post-raid stuff eclipsed now by his serial killer. Quill felt glad to be back in his real world. Except here came Harry, with his dad beside him. Quill looked over his shoulder and saw the other three checking out this new vision. Well, at least nobody else in the nick seemed to be carting dead relatives around with them.

Harry held out his wrists. "It's a fair cop, Jimmy."

"Don't kow-tow to him," said his dad. "You little shit, you're worth ten of him."

Quill wished desperately that he could talk to Harry alone. That they could go for a pint again, be proper mates again. "Harry," he said, "come on now—"

"What," said Harry, suddenly serious, "you're not *really* here for me, are you?"

"Don't be fucking scared of him! What sort of a friend is he, to lord it over you?! He's just a pretend copper, an actor playing a part!"

Quill clapped his hands together to get the room's attention. "All right," he said, "you lot, listen. I came over from my Siberian exile to say that Operation Toto has found conclusive proof of what I always suspected: there isn't and never has been a security leak in Operation Goodfellow. More than that I can't tell you, only that . . . I never bloody believed it, okay? I never sat there looking down at you lot, thinking any single one of you, Harry here included, were anything but the best bloody coppers in the world, all right? And to be put at this distance from you like that . . ." He found he had a catch in his throat, and let it stop him. To his amazement, Harry came over and put a hand on his shoulder, which made his dad scowl. And the applause slowly started up again from the whole room. Only this time it was genuine.

Quill raised a hand in acknowledgment, then clapped an arm around Harry's shoulder, and hauled him away from his dad. "And, erm, also we popped over 'cos we're after the keys to the evidence room. And any chance of a cup of sugar?" Behind him, he saw Sefton putting his hand right through Harry's dad, and getting a glare in return.

"Jimmy, mate," said Harry, "I'll open it up for you myself." Quill followed him through the door, looking over his shoulder to where the other three were all backing out of the room quickly, embarrassed by and not used to dealing with the appreciation of their comrades. He was glad they'd got to see that, though.

Ross had hoped that the door of the evidence room would be heaved open to reveal a glittering mass of objects: like the contents of that locked study in the Toshack house that she'd had such expectations of, but that had contained no juice at all when the UCs had searched it. She'd hoped that this look back into Goodfellow would be more fruitful than Quill's examination of the operation's files. But at first glance that was not to be. The shelves contained rows of tagged evidence, and a pile of Toshack's favorite cardboard boxes at the back, but nothing at all leaped out. Their Sight counted for nothing here. She'd delivered some brave words about Losley, but it was now slowly sinking in that her revenge was still going to count for nothing. More than that, something worse had taken Toshack's place, and she hadn't prepared herself for it, hadn't focused herself in the right way. The death of her father was now sidelined. It felt horribly selfish to make the pursuit of Losley all about her own teenage injuries. But what else could give her the stimulus she needed to get through this?

"So we look through it all again," announced Quill. "We untag, process, seal and record."

"I'll give you a hand if you like," said Harry. "Be good for me to catch up."

So they worked their way through all the stuff.

"Why," said Sefton, "did this bloke keep eighty-three stationery boxes with nothing in them?" He glanced over to where Harry was busy opening boxes, Quill being forced to look over his shoulder continually, because Harry wouldn't be able to see what they were looking for. Harry's dad kept berating him, both of them getting increasingly worked up.

"There was nothing like this when my dad was in charge of the gang," remarked Ross. She was starting to feel the effects of fatigue, seeing things out of the corner of her eye which scared her awake again, but which weren't real, just memories, the symptoms of sleep trying to force its way into her.

"He kept his local branch of Staples busy," said Sefton. "That'd be good for his epitaph."

"Though it does fail," observed Ross, "to tell the whole story."

"Listen to you, with the copper jokes."

"Why is he looking over your shoulder?" Harry's father prodded. "Look at him, he'd much rather have just his new friends here. He doesn't trust you. You're not quite the thing, are you? Not any more."

"You may have wondered why I'm looking over your shoulder," said Quill to Harry. "It's 'cos I'm looking for a particular piece of evidence, and you wouldn't recognize what you were looking at."

"What is it, exactly?"

"Can't tell you. Due to the usual operational bollocks. But—tell you what—you find *anything* unusual," he looked meaningfully toward Harry's dad, "and it'll be pay dirt. Then I'll use it to try and get you recruited for Toto. And how often do you get to use that sentence?"

Harry nodded appreciatively, and took another box down from the shelf.

Quill waited for a moment to see if Harry's dad was going to react to anything, then, when he didn't, wandered over to the others, glancing back to see the ghost looking at him angrily. "He's a bit one-note," he remarked quietly. "I was hoping, 'cos he was his dad, he'd want to help Harry a bit and so he'd whizz about like a genie and find what we're looking for. But he's all about delivering the abuse." He sighed. "I can be a bit of a bastard, you may have noticed."

Quill felt the energy draining from his team as it became clear they weren't going to find anything new. He said a fond goodbye to

Harry, glowered at his dad, and forced on himself another burst of enthusiasm. He drove them out to the Toshack house, so they could keep talking in the car, and, apart from a couple of near misses, found that nothing of the Sight jumped out to stop him from driving safely. Maybe, he said, the wonders were still concealed in the place itself. But the house, emptied for purposes of evidence, was completely normal. Even that regularly locked office the UCs had had such high hopes of turned out to be utterly mundane. As night came on, they returned to the Hill and the Portakabin, and managed, slumped together, to watch CCTV footage from the nick that merely showed Losley, as expected, impossibly approaching and walking through the wall of the interview room. All that they'd recently added to the board was a list of notes in the Concepts section, beneath a new heading about "Soil."

"I think we've worked off a bit of that original shock," said Quill, "so you'll be ready for what comes next." They all looked up at him at once, those defeated faces again expectant. "We know where she's going to be. She might have only one bolt-hole left to run to. And we know she's got a limited fuel supply. She's a big monster, but so's the Met. Normal police methods have got us a long way, so let's use them to see how much of her is merely front. Go home and get some kip, because tomorrow we're going to nick her."

"You look terrible," said Lofthouse. "Will a drop of gin help with that?"

Quill waved that suggestion aside, settling heavily into the comfort of the chair facing her desk. "It's only ten o'clock at night, so a bit early for me." He noticed that she wasn't wearing her charm bracelet, and then felt a little uncomfortable about noticing it.

"Bit of a blip in the media coverage last night. They went away again through lack of fresh material, thank God. What's this about a broken window and a hoo-hah at the crime scene?"

Quill didn't want to lie to her. "Just . . . one of those things," he replied.

"Have you got everything you need for tomorrow?"

"Yeah, I think so. Ta for getting that sorted so fast."

"A lot of it involved persuading Brian Finch, the Stoke City chairman, that his players might have anything to fear from a mad old woman—even one who poisons people."

Quill suddenly thought of something. Did the bemusement they'd all felt at the super putting this incredibly weird team together mean she knew something extra about this situation he'd found himself in? "Does . . . the word 'protocol' mean anything to you, ma'am?"

"Are you saying that operational protocol is getting in the way of—?"

Quill shook his head, dismissing it. "Thanks for all you've done, ma'am," he said. "Let's hope it pays off tomorrow."

THIRTEEN

Quill drove himself home to his semi in Enfield. A journey which seemed to take a day. He had to keep the radio turned way up to keep himself awake. Every now and then, outside the car, some weird sight shouted into his eyeballs. "Yeah, yeah," he responded.

The lounge floor was covered in bizarre novelties. The kitchen floor was messy and the house smelt of . . . must be some problem with the plumbing. But the Sight told him nothing disturbing about any of the rooms he looked in, thank God. Outside, his street had looked normal too. He heard music from upstairs, so Sarah was home.

He looked round the door of her office, trying to project sobriety before he remembered that he was actually sober. She didn't look up from her computer, therefore he knew she was angry with him. He watched the back of her head, the defensive hunch of her shoulders. He'd been thinking about this all the way home. He wanted to tell her everything, but she just wouldn't believe him. They weren't . . . close enough, he felt, for him to tell her something impossible and for her just to accept it. Maybe they had been close enough once. The more he'd thought about it, the more he'd found there was now this . . . hole in the middle of their relationship. It was as if it had taken him witnessing the impossible to make him realize that. But he had no idea what the vacuum between them was, or how to start fixing it. Sorting stuff like that out was something he wasn't naturally equipped for. He and Sarah had always just got on with it, and neither of them liked the deep and meaningful. Which was awkward now that life had got deep and meaningful.

"Love," he began, "listen, I've been thinking about us moving out of the city, Reading or somewhere, me commuting in—"

"Have you?" She was thinking that his suggestion was way beside the point.

"Yeah, look, I've been trying to call you. That was me in the middle of the night—"

She looked round at him. "Yeah, I guessed that because it was your number on the phone. Me being a brilliant detective."

"You've seen the case we're working, how big it is—"

"And it's just you, is it? There aren't other shifts who could take over from you?" She had worked up to full-on anger now. And she was so beautiful. And he wanted to cry. They'd always fought a lot. And, until very recently, he'd thought that was good somehow. Again, he didn't know why that had changed, and it felt like the reason had fallen down the hole.

They continued the row into the early hours. It exhausted them. They were silent for a while, but the row erupted again in fits and starts, and then died. They made a really late supper together. She tried to tell him about how the delivery firm for the local paper she worked for had started to throw bundles of copies away rather than bothering to distribute them. How that made her wonder why she herself was bothering. Her newspaper, she said, like everything else, was going the way of the dinosaur, but it didn't mean they should just run away out of London. "We've got a life here, haven't we, Quill?" Quill couldn't answer.

"What's wrong?" he said to her in bed, near dawn, when he woke from a terrible nightmare and realized that loads of it had been true. But he said it so quietly that he almost wondered if he was talking to himself.

In the anonymous safe house that had become his home, Costain lay awake listening to the traffic outside. He'd fallen asleep, but woken and dozed again in fits and starts. He didn't want to sleep, because sleep felt like death. He kept thinking back to that house, and what he'd seen beneath him. That man, just a man in a suit, smiling up at him. But what was fixed in his mind was different to what the others had described. It was something particular. Something personal.

He could try to do the right thing as much as he could—the right thing as others described it—and it lost him his freedom, it cut his bloody balls off, but okay. What he couldn't do was make up for the endgame he'd prepared as insurance, his escape route from both the Met and the Toshack mob. It was too risky to go and unearth it right now and, even if he did, just having arranged it counted as a strike against him. Only, every day he kept it would weigh more and more heavily at . . . at the moment of his death, he guessed. The others had seen speculation. They were being fed to a void. He'd seen a prediction: something already prepared for him.

At 4 a.m. he got up and shaved, then he drove out to Gipsy Hill, looking calmly at the horrors of the night that appeared to him. They were nothing now, compared to what was in his head.

Quill stood in the director's lounge at the Boleyn Ground, Upton Park, looking at the assembled directors and chairpersons and hangers-on, including Brian Finch, from visiting Stoke City, and Peter Brockway, chairman of West Ham itself. From a great window behind them, he heard and now felt the gathering force of a Premiership football crowd assembling. On the table lay the morning papers. The headline of the *Metro* read: *Mora: Score a Hat-Trick and Die.* "They're already on first-name terms," he observed, picking it up. "I know what you're thinking: why couldn't she be like most Londoners and support Man U?"

"So, let me get this straight," said Brockway. "She kills criminals, coppers, kids and footballers who score hat-tricks. She uses poison . . . or a bloody cauldron. Is there *anything* you've ruled out?"

Quill thought for a moment. "Not a lot," he said. "But we do know her behavior pattern indicates she'll very much want to be here. And we think she might try to access the pitch. Which is why we've had uniforms watching it since the early hours, and why we've now canceled all leave and got more bodies in the ground than in Highgate Cemetery."

Brockway didn't look particularly satisfied. "May I remind you, we had to *ask* you to bring in sniffer dogs. I should think she won't get further than the turnstile. Still, me and Brian have come to a gentleman's agreement."

"I've told my players that if any of them puts two in, they're to hang back and not go for a third. That's all you're getting. It's against the FA code of practice, as it is. And it's giving in to terrorism."

Quill managed a smile. He took the bottle of water from his pocket, drained it in one swallow, and handed it to a PA for a refill. "Got any more of that coffee?"

"You'll be going all through the match," remarked Finch.

"I hope," said Quill, "I won't have to."

Ross, with Sefton beside her, watched the hordes pouring in through the home supporters' entrance, just inside the tower-like gates on Green Street. They stood with their backs to a wire fence, watching the warm bodies pass them, in their claret and blue. "Dad was always Arsenal," she said, feeling the need to say something. It was hard not to push herself back into the fence. The sheer . . . weight that this mass of people brought with them, now that she was seeing them with the Sight . . . it was sort of like an expectation, a shape that demanded a response from you. It felt terrible, like the raging of a mob, the sort of thing that could push you toward the kind of cynicism that coppers felt about the general public all the time. But when you looked at any of these individual faces, they were just people looking all the different ways people looked. There were also uniforms everywhere, a density of them she'd never seen before.

The plan was to defend the pitch if there wasn't a hat-trick, to grab Losley if she tried to get more soil, to take her down by sheer numbers. If she was invisible when she did that, there would be one of them watching the match at all times, and they'd send in the army of uniforms at any sign of pitch disturbance, and the stewards had also been told to pile in. If there somehow was a hat-trick, and thank God that was very unlikely now, that defensive pattern would be altered to form an army around a much smaller target. The four of them with the Sight would be watching every aspect of the audience in the stadium, hoping to pick out Losley.

Ross felt pleased at the size of the organization. It was a warm feeling of being in the Met mainstream. At the end of all this, though—and it felt like a risk to even hope there was an end in sight—she was still going to have to deal with having been denied her revenge. But she had at least found a new depth to the world. And she would have helped rid it of something terrible.

"Well, duh," said Sefton, "I'm surprised your uncle got away with being an Irons fan in Bermondsey. I kept wanting to say something about how odd that was, when I was acting as one of his lads, but, you know . . . guns."

"Listen to you," she said, "sounding more camp." Then she remembered she didn't know him at all well enough to say stuff like that. "Sorry."

"No," he managed a smile, "depends who I'm with, yeah? I definitely stand straight among this lot. Not like the way police do, not like I'm in a club, just . . ." He indicated his own stance, which just looked normal to her.

"You've thought about this a lot."

"Done it more than thought about it." He inclined his head toward the crowd. "One o'clock."

It was a man who was trying to laugh along with his mates, but on his shoulders he carried a dead child, the boy's legs beating against his chest with every step, his hands clasping his hair tightly at the scalp.

"Fuck," whispered Ross. Just a moment of random chat, and then it had all come crashing back.

They'd seen a few such things among the crowd, but not everything leaped out at them this way. The variety of things the Sight showed them included some quite subtle effects—stuff that your eye could miss. Or maybe they were just starting to process it as they would through normal vision. As a test, they'd popped into the club shop and asked to buy some soil. It wasn't on sale now, they'd been told, because of health and safety. "True, that," Sefton had remarked. But they'd glimpsed a few sacks of it behind the counter, and it didn't seem to have any power associated with it.

"If it did have power in itself," Ross had then said, "this stadium would be like a giant searchlight. It has to be something specific about the soil and her."

Costain had meanwhile been patrolling the concrete caverns of the stadium, and now he headed up the steps to the Bobby Moore Stand. He looked out over the enormous crowd that had now filled the stadium, just as the tannoy announced that the minute's silence for Losley's victims was about to begin. The huge sound of so many people swiftly quietened, became an almost unnatural emptiness of distant coughs and shuffles. People looked at the ground or closed their eyes, appearing pious to show they could be, not knowing—because nobody knew—who those child victims had been. There was something defiant in the completeness of it. This lot were determined that Losley wasn't part of them. It wasn't that he could feel that same emotion inside them as individuals,

154

not quite. He could almost . . . see it. But it didn't feel great. It felt like a vacuum, a *need* to feel. The whistle blew for the end of the silence, and a vast roar rose all around him, another empty assertion of togetherness.

Costain had grown up as an Arsenal fan, and his dad had often expressed a hatred of West Ham. These days he could just about name the squad, and he watched it on TV if it was on, but he'd still been kind of dreading this moment. The crowd all started to sing, all at the same moment, as the club song came on the tannoy: *I'm forever blowing bubbles* . . . They had one attitude, one purpose. They were one thing. And Costain, standing among them, felt his undercover hackles rise as never before. Here he was, an away fan, secretly one of the great enemy, possessed of the Sight. It was like being in the mouth of some giant animal. He could feel the vast potential hatred for yet another facet of what he was, though it was deeply buried inside him. It hit him like thousands of tiny blows, beating against his skin. He was the enemy: *the other*. Well, it was what he was used to. He now did what he always did. He took a deep breath and joined in with the song.

The Sight didn't like that. He could feel something huge and unknown, something beyond what these thousands of small people knew, reacting to it. Or maybe that was just the feeling of gears slipping inside his head, as he pushed against the tide.

The song came to an end, and there was an enormous, explosive cheer. Costain walked to the end of a row, to look over to where Losley's season-ticket seat had previously been. They'd taken it out, and every seat beside it or behind it, including Toshack's and all those to the distance of one seat away. As if even where she'd sat was infectious. Now a steward stood to one side of the gap, in case anyone . . . well, who could guess? He wondered how pleased those other seven season-ticket holders had felt to be relocated. The authorities must have made a decision as to how far to take that dislocation. It suggested a sort of rough instinct about the kind of thing the Sight revealed, that everyone had an inner knowledge about evil that didn't reflect science at all. Nobody in that meeting of directors would have said "Leave it, it can't do any harm, it's just a seat." That viewpoint could only reassert itself a few seats further out. They knew, but also they didn't.

There was a well-dressed, powerfully built man walking purposefully along the same row of seats. He was keeping his head down, therefore Costain couldn't see his face. He was walking in a way that was out of the ordinary, something coppers always noticed, but it took Costain a moment to work out what exactly was odd. He didn't seem to be having to edge around people's feet, or get them to lift up their plastic beer glasses out of his way. He was heading for the little square emptied of seats, and nobody seemed to be paying him particular attention. And surely they would be. Maybe they knew him, as a director or something. But, no, then they'd be shaking his hand. But there was nothing of the Sight about him. It was as if he was . . . beyond all that. Costain started to get a terrible feeling about the body language of this figure. He didn't want to see that concealed face. Sod that. He himself started to move along the row, toward the group of missing seats, but in his case that meant doing all that awkward stepping and looking down that the other figure had somehow avoided.

He took a glance up. The figure was now standing in the middle of the empty square where those seats had been, looking away from him, into the main body of the stadium, seeming pleased with himself. The steward clearly wasn't seeing him. The crowd wasn't berating or applauding him, so they weren't seeing him either. Costain increased his own pace, determined to get his hands on him.

And then the man turned and looked straight at him. And he smiled an enormous smile. It was a smile of recognition.

Costain collapsed. He fell among the feet of fans who started bellowing at him. He felt as if the entire stadium was suddenly tilting on its side. He had a vision of it rolling downhill. The sky was spinning overhead. Costain couldn't allow this. This fucker was goading him now, challenging him. *Just because of where I saw him last, he thinks I'm his bitch, to knock over with a bloody smile? Fuck gravity!* He launched himself forward, hauling himself from seat to seat, having to push his way past every intervening foot, making the people he was getting past yell at him, the force of the crowd around him turning against him in an outraged roar as they saw where he was heading. And, all the while, that bugger kept smiling at him, and the force of that smile was like a gale in itself.

Costain finally burst out at the end of the row. He was about to yell at the man, and land a hand on his collar.

Only suddenly he wasn't there.

He collapsed again, this time inside the empty area. He was dragged to his feet by the steward, who was yelling something at him. And the crowd all around were yelling too, booing and starting to throw things, coins and wrappers, now he'd ventured in to the place of taboo. Costain grabbed his warrant card and brandished it at the steward, who backed off, his hands in the air. He felt like turning in a circle, holding it up to all of them. *See? See? I'm actually one of the good guys!* The catcalls and yells subsided, but only a little.

Quill eventually found him leaning against a concrete wall, somewhere in the depths of the building. The match had started, and Costain could hear and feel it ebbing and flowing above them, the sound and sensation resonating through the stone. Costain reported his encounter in the correct manner, like a good copper, but he couldn't help mentioning the thought that had slammed into him through that gale of public opinion caused just by an invisible smile. "Listen, what if what we've discovered . . . what if this is the reason everything's so shit?"

"What?"

"This evil shit that nobody knows about, this is *real* reality, isn't it? We do our best, we give to charity, we put in our shifts, we fucking recycle. But all the time this is what the world's *about*. That bastard was in charge of that stadium, and his . . . gang—Losley and people like her—are the ones with the power to run reality, the way drug gangs run countries. Maybe they're the reason why the banks got fucked up, and politics is corrupt, and there's war all the time, and frigging global warming, and every year a new epidemic. If the boss then decides really to put the screws on, in a few years' time everyone is just going to be fighting each other over the last few fucking *scraps* left!"

Quill held up a hand to stop him. "I have thought about this," he said. "And I think that if it's all true, which it won't be, 'cos everything's got a bit of front to it, then it's a *good* thing."

Costain stared at him.

"If this *is* why the world is shit, then . . . don't you get it? We've been given the greatest opportunity any coppers have ever had. We've seen the cause of all human evil. And we can nick him."

"You're saying, we could *nick*—?"

"Best not name him. It might be like in Harry Potter. No, I reckon that's why he showed up now. We met his enforcer, but we didn't run away and hide. He's wondering if he's got a game on."

Costain couldn't help it: he started to laugh. "Bloody hell, Jimmy—"

"It's a way to go, anyway, right? Thinking that? Trying that? Tell me that's not a way to go."

They both jumped at the sudden noise erupting above them. The slam of a thousand boots, and a horrified pulse of group emotion that had stabbed straight downward toward them. And then they heard and felt the rumble that came afterward: the yell of anger, the collective fire of being hurt. Costain closed his eyes, now the moment of release was over. "One–nil to Stoke," he said.

Ross was on the other side of the stadium, with Sefton, watching the crowd and not the match. They'd quartered up the audience, and through binoculars studied every occupant of every seat. But while there'd been a few things noticeable from the world of the Sight, none of them was Losley. They turned as the goal went in. The celebrations among the away fans were muted, and Ross watched as the player, Linus McGuire, ran quickly back to the center spot, keeping his head down. The display on the big screen showed laughter from his team mates, however. *Careful you don't get two more, mate!*

She realized that she hadn't just intuited that emotion, but she'd felt it from the crowd. She glanced over to Sefton, who nodded. "I can feel this kind of . . . raw group desire," he said. "We've got senses other people don't have, now. I think this is how Losley knew . . . about my private life. I don't think she actually read my mind, or any shit like that. One of those gestures she made kind of read my barcode. Excellent gaydar. We've just had the first hints for ourselves of what it must be like to see things as she does, like big crowd emotions we'd probably get anyway, or how we could have gone up to that guy and already known he was a grieving dad. God, I'm just talking and talking—"

"You're doing analysis, is what you're doing. We should work out how she does it. Or maybe you have to be . . . I don't know, special like her.

"No," Sefton shook his head; this was really important to him, "it's the opposite of special. Losley's not the queen of the entire world, is she? She's hiding herself in . . . well, okay, several . . . council houses. When I felt this power up close in the street, when I felt it inside that Jack thing, it was sort of . . . angry, dispossessed. It didn't feel that it was in charge. It felt like what you might be left with if you had nothing else in the world, and if you were desperate enough to turn to it. I think I can just start to see how you could approach the idea of using it, and feel how you might if you weren't . . . overwhelmed by it. But I think I would still be overwhelmed by it every time one of those sodding monsters or some shit—"

Ross both felt and heard the noise rise from the field and crash through the crowd around them. She and Sefton turned at the same moment . . . and on the big screen saw Linus McGuire again trotting back to the center spot, his team mates rushing around him. He looked actually burdened now, the laugh he was sharing with them was awkward.

The crowd felt complicated. It hated feeling complicated.

"Take him off," muttered Sefton. "You're two–nil up at fucking West Ham, so sub him!"

"That'd be visibly giving in to threats," said Ross. "It's okay. He won't try to score again." But she knew she was just telling herself that.

They became aware of the chants rising around them. West Ham songs, but also tunes that referred to the current situation—creating waves of horrified, relieved, cathartic laughter. "We'll see you on *Crimewatch*, we will . . ." To the tune of "Que Sera Sera." Ross saw Sefton start to laugh at that, and then he put a hand to his mouth, altogether too tense to let it out.

"Anything from the uniforms?" That was Quill arriving, with Costain beside him.

"No sightings so far," said Sefton, looking up from his Airwave radio.

"If she is here," said Ross, "she's either invisible, or looking different from how the fans normally see her."

"At least we've forced her to change her habits even that much," said Costain.

Ross was struck by a sudden thought. "I wonder if she *can* actually still hide from us now? You know, can she shift up another level, past what the Sight can see?"

"I've, erm, been thinking about that," said Sefton.

They all looked to him, and he seemed again to regret having spoken up. To him, it was as if there was something shameful about the nature of the speciality he was developing. After all, he'd been the one to say it was the language of the dispossessed, and Ross wondered now how much he included himself in that group. "These are all just assumptions, but we said we were doing assumptions, so . . . I don't think she'll have done that. Not yet. This is rough stuff, big-button stuff, either one thing or the other. We've got the Sight, so we can . . . *see*. It feels as if, to take it up a level, she'd need to counteract that with something else, something bigger, and that would be going out of her way, which she doesn't want to, you know . . ." He looked between them, suddenly seeming to realize that they didn't know, really. "Like I said, just assumptions."

"I don't know if she *is* in here somewhere," said Quill. "But someone else *has* made their presence felt." Costain then described his encounter.

Ross got out her laptop, awkwardly held it up with one hand, and ran the PRO-FIT facial description software. "Go on," she said, "let's be having him for the Ops Board." And she quickly selected facial composite items as Costain described the man to her. They'd just about finished when a vast, terrible, scared sound burst from the crowd.

They slowly turned. On the pitch, Stoke players were again milling around Linus McGuire, celebrating—but celebrating *at* the crowd, defiant almost, as if violence was going to come and strike down their mate any moment now. McGuire himself stopped moving. He held the others back.

"Don't," Quill whispered. "Don't provoke her."

The footballer kissed the badge on his shirt, then raised three fingers. The subdued West Ham supporters' reaction turned instantly to jeers.

On the big screen above them the replay was running. McGuire was in a scramble on the goal line, a lot of feet and heads sticking out among a lot of defenders, as the ball curved down toward them. Anyone could score. And indeed it was hard to see how McGuire could have, while staying out of it at the back of that mass of bodies. But then the picture flickered, and Ross realized that it was changing just for their benefit, as McGuire was shunted forward a few feet from where he'd been, his body being flung at the ball like a projectile. His head caught it precisely, and sent it into the top corner. He looked astonished as he landed again, the force that had propelled him sending him skidding along the ground.

Ross felt something looking at them and knew the others were feeling it too. Something enormous was saying hello. Her hand reflexively went to the knife in her pocket.

Among all the swaying, yelling, chanting thousands, there he stood, the man Costain had described, just below the screen as it reverted to being a normal scoreboard. He was smiling broadly.

"She isn't here. She was never going to be here," declared Costain. "This isn't our trap. It's his."

The look on Quill's face was terrible to see.

Sefton's Airwave radio hissed with urgent communication from the uniforms. Ross let go of her knife and looked away quickly from that horrifying face, back to her laptop, determined to fix all its details in her memory so they could have him.

She saw that the composite face on the screen was now smiling too.

When she looked up again, the man was gone.

And then all hell broke loose.

FOURTEEN

The crowd rose from their seats amid a vast, jeering roar, Irons fans surging toward the lines of the Stoke fans, as if it was their fault that McGuire had scored. He was immediately substituted, and ran for the tunnel to the away changing rooms as abuse and objects were hurled at him. The uniforms and stewards rushed forward, to get between them, and just about managed to keep them apart. The fans fell back like an ebb tide, bellowing at each other across the lines.

"Come on," Quill shouted, and led his team running for the steps.

Quill burst in through the door of the away changing room, a bunch of uniforms with him and his team, having shoved their way past all the idiots that tried to get in the way. The enormous noise of the jeering echoed all around them. It didn't seem to be just one opinion of what had happened, but many, all interfering with each other like waves crashing around the stadium. Physios and assistants and players came toward them, all yelling in different languages. "Change of bloody plan!" Quill yelled. "Get your trousers on, Linus. You're going on a long journey."

And there he was, the player himself, with a grim look on his face, already buttoning his shiny suit. "I don't know . . . Nobody's said . . ."

"That's what we're here for. Let's be having you." Quill grabbed hold of the man and hauled him to the door, just as Finch, the Stoke City chairman, arrived to get in the way.

"Now, hold on. We offered you our complete cooperation but—"

"Brilliant. Try to keep up." And they were off and out of there.

Quill spoke quickly into his Airwave radio, as Finch tried to argue in his ear, Costain having to actually grab the star player away from the trailing mass of people who followed them. He could hear Ross behind him, keeping Lofthouse in the loop on her mobile. With the uniforms kept so busy on crowd control, the original plan was shot, and there was no chance of keeping McGuire safe on the team coach. Their only chance now was speed and surprise.

They came out into the fading light at the players' entrance to the stadium, just as two cars pulled up. They were CID unmarked cars, driven by DCs from the local main office who'd been handy when Quill had started yelling. They'd have to do. Outside the gates, Quill could see the media forming up on the pavements. He found a CID officer, threw a towel over his head, and got the uniforms to form a cordon as the man was bundled over to the first car and shoved in the back. "Fast as you can, go visit lovely Swindon," he told the driver, then thumped the roof and stepped back. The car headed off out through the enormous gates, the media moving in but then giving way in the face of a blaring of the horn. Costain meanwhile held McGuire back in the tunnel, out of sight.

"She might buy it," said Ross, "if she keeps herself separate from the world, hiding away in that room of hers."

"Yeah, yeah."

Finch was looking increasingly worried at seeing all these precautions. A growing phalanx of people was gathering around McGuire, looking as if they might lure him away at any moment—

agents, trainers, who knew what. "Detective Inspector," the chairman began, "come on, surely there's no need for—"

"Shut it," said Quill. He pointed at McGuire and gestured for him to come over. "This isn't down to any of that lot. This is just down to you. You want to do all you can to help us catch a child killer?"

"Absolutely." He meant it too. He had a serious look about him, this boy.

"Then come with me." Quill had the uniforms hold everyone else back, as his group led the footballer away from further protests.

They pulled the car into line with a couple of police vans from the regular match turn-out, and walked McGuire out to it, wearing a police uniform, the cap pulled well down over his head. Quill looked at the alert young face of the driver, and realized just how much danger he was going to ask him to walk into, without this officer having been adequately briefed. Or maybe he just felt a need to do this himself, to show that smiling bastard—that even if they'd had their roles reversed, even if the operation was falling apart, even if the tiny hope he'd provided his team with was going to be dashed—someone was still willing to take him on. He felt his hands shaking, and grabbed hold of the door to hide that. "Out you get, son, I'll take it from here."

Ross stepped forward as he was exchanging places with the officer. "This isn't a good idea. What if she's after *you*?"

"Then she gets me." He slammed the door behind him, and nodded to Costain. "And then you're in charge." Then he turned the car in six cramped points, and drove out of those gates in company with the two vans, past a media crush that didn't register his passing. As soon as the traffic opened up, motivated by the fear of a witch on his tail, and with the confidence that the traffic cops would let him pass, Quill floored the accelerator.

He took the car up onto the North Circular, where he made a nuisance of himself in the winter dark, weaving in and out of the match-day traffic, yelling abuse and hitting the horn, his lights on full beam. A lot of it was bravado; a lot of it was him knowing they had nothing to feel sure of. She could either see him or she couldn't, and only speed was on his side. Or maybe she didn't have enough of whatever this power was to do it this time. Maybe her boss had set her a challenge too? Just get this bloke out of range of Losley's power, to the point where if she came to visit him up north, it'd just be a little old lady arriving on his doorstep, without her soil all glowing with energy, and they'd have broken her, immediately showing her that she was not going to get to do what she'd always done. Then *they* would have won. *He* would have won. A victory over her, over this strange nothingness that seemed to have leaped out of the corners of his depression and exploded a hole in the middle of his life. Winning this now would make his team feel they could win the entire war, realizing that this was a war, not a nightmare, which would finally engulf them. That was the battle going on in his head, too, every moment since he'd acquired the Sight.

"You're taking this really seriously," said McGuire.

Quill liked his concern. "There is," he said, "a lot we can't reveal."

"But you're on top of it, right? You're going to get her?"

"Yeah." Quill said it determinedly, as if she herself could hear. For all he knew, she could, though he hoped not. "Meanwhile, I'm taking you up the M1. Once we get north of Watford, the local uniforms can get you back home to Stoke."

"Can I call my girlfriend?"

"When we get there." Because who knew whether Losley could listen in to phone calls? In fact, who knew *anything*?

As he passed Brent Cross, all lit up on his right, Quill started to really deeply *hope*. He was in a modern city, *his* city, in a modern car and, once he just got past this interchange and hit the motorway, he would be up and out and past the M25 in fifteen minutes. And the M25 bloody well should be as far as Losley could use the

166

power of London. His Airwave radio told him the decoy car was already past the M25, going west. He hadn't lost any lives tonight, either. He glanced at McGuire in the mirror. He was young enough, just about, to be Quill's own lad. He felt the ache of something missing there. Not that he had a kid, and why not? It suddenly felt terrible that he and Sarah had never gone for it. Between them, they'd have had a wonderful kid—

He realized that McGuire was suddenly staring ahead. "What's that?!"

Quill looked back to the road. Something was shining in the dual carriageway in front of them. And, coming right at them faster than any car, right in his headlights, there was a figure—

He threw the car sideways. Too late.

She rushed through the front of the car. She didn't break the vehicle as she passed through it. She was going fast and slow at the same time. She trailed lattices of gold and silver that struck sparks off the metal as she passed through it. She brought the stinking beauty of the executioner's sword. Her hands danced in an intricate pattern. Quill had time to see her fingers pulling at the air, spinning more gold from it. Old books invaded his car, turning it inside out. She turned to look at him, as she moved past at eighty miles per hour, her head cocked to one side again.

"Do you know how I do this?" she said.

Quill didn't answer. He was trying hard to move, desperately to put himself between her and the boy. But he was caught in a different sort of time, a slower sort. He was impotent. He was deeply, deeply a fool. His pride had now brought him and an innocent to slaughter. He was almost, horribly so, pleased for himself. To get to the end. He was anticipating the car crash that was about to happen to him, that was already happening to his body.

"I make sacrifice to my lord of the pleasant face, that is how things work. Three more children went in the pot so I could do this. If you keep attempting to limit me, I will have to make more sacrifices. And therefore many children will die because of you.

My lord of the pleasant face told me how this would be tonight. He appeared to me—in so rare a visit. He told me not to return to the football matches."

Quill tried to say something. He wanted to yell at McGuire to get himself out of it.

But then time was gone again in a flash and McGuire's body was hitting the roof of the car and hot darkness had burst up from the ground and a scream fell away into the depths. The boy exploded with blood. The liquid splattered onto the window, passing Quill. He had lost control dreamlike ages ago. And he wondered, at the last moment, why he hadn't been taken too.

Losley vanished through the back of the car, her laugh staying as an echo that fluttered as the metal burst open around it.

The car spun back into complete time, hit the pile of soil that stood in the road, slewed across it, and plowed into the crash barrier.

Costain got out of the marked car in which he'd been a passenger, Sefton and Ross walking quickly beside him. They showed their warrant cards and were allowed through the cordon. The dual carriageway had been shut down on the northbound side, and cars were backing up on the southbound, to get a look. It had started to sleet, the drops of ice in the air reflecting the bright lights. Ahead of them a spent pile of Losley's soil shone dully.

"He won't move from there, sir," said a uniform. "He could . . . I mean he's . . . not hurt, somehow."

Forensics were already swarming around the car, with an ambulance standing uselessly nearby. The crashed vehicle had compacted, and the remains of McGuire were being picked out of a back-seat deceleration area where he would surely have been killed anyway. The windscreen had collapsed into daisy chains of cellular glass spreading out across the road, reflecting light in all directions, like Christmas. The front seats were crushed, airbags inflated. And impossibly, beside the car sat Quill in the cold and wet, with no expression on his face.

They helped him up. Costain let Quill push him away, starting to stumble away on his own. "I felt it hit," he said suddenly. "I knew I was going to die. But she didn't let me. Because she wanted me to know about the children."

FIFTEEN

Dr. Piara Singh Deb, DMJ, was a forensic pathologist working out of Lambeth, and he knew about coppers. He knew they reacted only slightly to the dead. That they rarely expressed anger at the perpetrators, whom they seemed to view as a sailor would view sharks. That their dark sense of humor concerning corpses always sought out new depths to plumb. And that, despite being so unlike how they were portrayed on television, they always expected *him* to have coffee and sandwiches handy.

Singh had never before been part of an investigation that had received such media attention. The free tabloid that had been thrust into his hand at the tube station this morning had carried that photo of Mora Losley on its front cover, and so did every other newspaper he saw as he headed for St. Pancras Mortuary. Singh supposed that this represented the mother lode for any editor: a serial killer who murdered children, gangsters and footballers. His daughter had asked him earlier about Linus McGuire. The canteen here was full of gossip. For this hour, and probably just this hour, the bulletins were leading with a story on one West Ham supporter who was claiming, dubiously, that Losley had offered to babysit.

Singh found the team from Toto quite surprising. He could see they were tired, and so he expected the usual crudity and impatience, the usual blank reaction to bodies unless he showed them injuries done to testes or breasts. But these four . . . for a start they looked like junkies. As if they'd slept regularly in those suits. Their eyes were red and they stood looking about to fall over at any moment. They'd reacted hugely when he wheeled out the corpses of the three children. That wasn't odd in itself. Police officers, in Singh's experience, tended to be "lookers-after," meaning the oldest sibling in their family, or the sort of only child who takes on the responsibilities of its parents. The woman here, though she wasn't a police officer, had some of that about her, too. More than anyone, they didn't like harm done to children, because they always felt that something could have been done, and therefore they sought— and he'd heard this feeling expressed in the most extraordinary ways—to blame themselves for it. But this time the reaction was different. They were horrified, yes, but it was as if they'd expected to see something more than what he was actually showing them, and were angrily frustrated at the mere sight of the bodies. One of the two young black men stayed absolutely silent. He looked lost, as if he desperately wanted to help but didn't know whether anything he could say might prove worthwhile. The other was very proper, addressing Singh by his full title, all please and thank you. But there was something odd about that, as if he'd been ordered to do so, and resented it. The analyst did most of the talking, and she seemed to be the one with the greatest command of the situation, but even she spoke in a clipped monotone. The DI looked completely out of it, seemingly forcing himself to listen, putting a hand to his brow, appearing stressed to the point of distraction. Singh wondered if he was grieving privately, and persisting at work despite that burden.

He had to make himself stop paying such watchful attention to these strange coppers, and more to the work confronting them. He felt a little worried as to how they might react to his conclusions, which were so grim that they'd laid a considerable weight on his own shoulders. The three victims, he announced, were two boys and a girl, aged from four to seven years old. Their teeth featured dental work that looked British to Singh, including a filling that was less than a year old. He hadn't found any unique skeletal markers, dental implants, diseases that affected the bones— the sort of thing that would help with identification. They were all Caucasians (he pointed out the smooth nasal sills and the U-shaped palates), and the remaining strands of hair indicated that all three were redheads (he'd found enough of it to harvest mitochondrial DNA). He'd pulled teeth from the bodies and found—and it had been a bit of a lottery whether or not he would, considering that there was none left anywhere else—nuclear DNA in the pulp, so he was certain in stating these three children were siblings. If they found a candidate for a mother, he'd be able to make a positive identification from a mouth swab. His office was already checking the DNA against the NDNAD database, and would let them have the results as soon as possible.

"What were the circumstances of their deaths?" That was from the analyst.

"There are traces of flesh, so the skeletons weren't picked clean, and there are no indications of sharp-force trauma, no knife or tool or tooth marks."

"So not cannibalism?"

"I'd be inclined to say no, despite the media speculation. Were any internal organs found separately? We didn't receive any."

The analyst shook her head.

"Yes, I was afraid that might be the case. And I think I know the reason. The bones show signs of pot polish, meaning they've been softened by heat and then collided repeatedly with the walls of the cauldron in which they were found. Look at the pale coloration of the bone, which is a sign of exposure to steady heat. And look at this, too." He indicated the small bones of the fingers and toes, some of which had been found in the cauldron alongside the skeletons. "There are small fractures on several of these. This is perimortem damage. Living bone breaks like this, in splinters or fairly straight lines. And among the small bones we found a lot of shredded and split fingernails. He held one up with tweezers. "This is evidence of a struggle, in close conditions, where the victims were so concerned about escape that they were willing to harm themselves. I think it's possible that these three may have been . . . boiled alive."

By the way they reacted, he had indeed added to their burden— a burden which he was sure he didn't fully understand. They clearly knew horrors beyond even what he had just described. He felt for them.

The one young black detective thanked him very properly, the other stayed silent. The analyst merely nodded to him, and then they were on their way. The DI didn't look back.

Singh found himself wondering if this investigation really should be left in such trembling hands.

Sarah Quill sat at her desk in the newspaper office, thinking about Saturday night.

She had heard about what had happened to Linus McGuire, but she'd had no idea that Quill had also been in that car, until he got home, supported by two uniformed police officers. She'd wanted to yell at him, and felt horribly guilty at such an impulse. How dare he risk . . . himself. Them. And what they were. That had suddenly felt like so little; it should be more. He'd just waved the coppers away, and they went off, and he'd been left there looking lost. Again he looked as if he'd been drinking, without actually having been drinking. Not a word had come to his lips, none of the usual bollocks. He'd finally let her hold him, and they'd stood like that for ages.

"Talk to me," she said. "Tell me."

"I can't. I don't want to lie to you."

"Why do you feel you'd have to lie to me?" But he'd been silent, then, and nothing she could say would make him change his attitude. She'd heard what his mates at Gipsy Hill sometimes said about being married to a member of the press: *rather you than me*. But she could tell there was more to it than that, and it scared her. This was going to eat away at him.

It had been the next morning when he'd tried to say a few funny things, but kept coming up short. It had been the next night when he just seemed lost again. She missed that act he put on, and was horrified that there was something big enough to make it fall away from him. She didn't want to keep asking, but she knew she would persist, because it was all she could do.

She could feel it in herself too. It seemed that Quill was trying to be honest, but she'd meanwhile managed to bury something inside her. The way they stared at each other as if they were angry and scared by each other, by what was missing between them. It felt now that the Quill she knew might go missing forever.

Sefton stumbled out into the mortuary car park, the other three beside him. The rain lashed down on them. "The noises in there," remarked Costain.

"That was what it was like at the psychiatric hospital," said Ross.

"Boiled alive," Quill whispered. And that made Sefton feel it again, the horror of those bare skeletons. He saw the others reacting as well. They'd had their sense of distance taken away. It felt as if they were all rookies again. "If that's what she does every time . . . think of all those kids." He remained absolutely still for a moment, as if he had lost everything, every hope. They'd been running on empty, and they'd known they were. It had been Quill who'd kept them going. Now that he was like this . . . they seemed to be carrying on only because they had no other hope. At least now they had a few days' grace. The next West Ham fixture was an away game against Liverpool. Which meant that even if a player did score a hat-trick against them, it might take a while for him to next come to London. If the Losley case had been big in the media before, now it was huge, the sheer impossibility of the killing of Linus McGuire slamming it to the top of every Web site, every news bulletin. And the bullshit they were coming out with—about hurled grenades, mines planted in the road. Sefton wondered how far Losley would have to go before the media just caved in and started saying she could walk through walls and destroy cars with her body. Finch had given a couple of interviews that had started to suggest Quill was at fault, that the death of his player was down to dangerous driving, but Lofthouse, without prompting from the investigation team, had got the mayor of London to call the chairman at home, and that had put an end to that. It had been Ross's idea to visit the mortuary and look at the skeletons again, though none of them had any thought as to what the Sight might reveal about them. Again it turned out that they'd been pinning their hopes on nothing.

Now she looked up from where she was checking the e-mails on her phone. "You were right," she said. "It *is* what she does every time."

They stood outside the Losley house that Costain and Sefton had visited in Wembley, under a vast polyurethane tent that had been put up to obscure the site, the rain pooling in its canopy. Forensics workers had uncovered a pit in what had been the garden. The sides of the pit revealed strata of bones, including small skulls. It was like an archaeological dig of a battle that had only involved children. Working to a pattern as they did so, the forensics teams had found a similar collection of skeletons at all of Losley's houses, almost simultaneously.

"That would have taken . . . centuries," said Costain, "she's that old. She's been doing this all that time and . . . nobody's noticed."

"Sod starting with 1900, I'll pull all the parameters off my searches, start them at the year dot," said Ross. Now she sounded to Sefton to be deliberately trying to energize the rest of them. "I haven't found anything odd in the list of bills from the councils yet, apart from for all the houses we know about, but I will. We'll have loads of nuclear DNA by now. Those kids in the cauldron were taken during the last year—"

"And we'd find three new ones," said Quill, "if we could locate her new house."

"So bells will start ringing on the NDNAD, and we've put out the word for open cases featuring missing kids."

"No," he sighed, as if Ross was a fool. "She's fixing this. We'd have heard something straight away. Three from the same family? Who can lose three kids and not report it?"

"Jimmy," said Ross, raising her voice, and that was the first time Sefton had heard her use Quill's name, "we'll *have* her."

Quill seemed to be on the verge of bellowing something, as he stared at the bones, but when he actually spoke his voice was again just an urgent whisper. "How?"

Sefton decided that now was the time for him to speak up. He'd been sitting on what he'd been working on, expecting that any moment a lead would come up through traditional police work. Talking about what he'd been doing seemed . . . obscene in comparison to what they'd just witnessed, but he couldn't see another way forward. He didn't know if what he was going to offer was just a distraction, but even that might do some good right now. So he made himself speak. "While we're waiting for more evidence," he said, "maybe we can . . . work the background?"

He didn't feel any more confident as he showed them, back at the Portakabin, what he'd found. He felt that he was risking something again, showing them the part of all this that, for some reason, felt most personal. But this was all for those kids. Everything they did now had to be for them. The Ops Board had only changed in that it now had that photofit picture under the heading for Losley's lord, and a much bigger piece of card ready for a list of her victims.

"Jack," he said, showing them a picture on a London folklore Web site. "That thing I met, its full name is Jack in the Green. Sort of like a big tree."

"Those are legs sticking out," said Ross, studying the photo. "You're not saying it was a bloke in a costume?"

" 'Course not, not what I ran into, but it can be. People dressed like this still lead May Day parades. They have since the sixties, a revival of what used to go on in London every year, centuries back. He's something the old trade guilds put together, as a big showpiece. They went from house to house, all of them in different sorts of costume—dames, princes—to collect a kind of tip, their only extra for the year. Happened a lot around Soho, so he's still in the right place. They used to stop at the end of the circuit and all dance around Jack, as if he was a kind of mobile maypole."

"And someone got sacrificed at the end of it?" said Quill. "Is that what you're saying?"

Sefton paused. "Everybody *says* stuff like that . . . that this must go back to before the Romans, but . . . you don't often find any evidence. I looked up those ships of yours as well," he looked to Ross, "HMS *London* and HMS *Victoria*. The first," he found the photo of what looked like a computer simulation of the ship on the bottom of the river and read from the text, "escorted King Charles II back from Holland at the Restoration, then it blew up in 1665, and sank in the Thames Estuary." He went to the next image. "The second, on the other hand, was the most powerful ironclad afloat, specially named after the Queen on the occasion of her Golden Jubilee . . . but it sank in a collision with another British ship, in the Mediterranean even, in 1893."

"So these are ships haunting the Thames?" suggested Quill. He sounded impatient, but he was at least waiting for Sefton to get to the point.

"It's more complicated than that." Sefton looked hopefully around at their bemused faces. "I think I've got a good example we can look at. And it runs on a timetable."

But why did it have to be here?

As he led the other three along the tree-lined avenues of Kensington in the rain, Sefton wondered if there was anything more than coincidence to this. The winter rain was pissing it down on houses that had flights of steps leading up to their front doors, and three different kinds of compost bin in their forecourts. Exactly the sort of place he'd grown up in. Just round the corner, in fact, was the building where his dad had used to rent the upper-floor flat with the roof garden. Sefton had regularly stood in his school uniform at a bus stop a couple of streets away, and been literally spat at by the kids walking past as they headed for the local comprehensive. That London accent they used, it was the same one his tormentors at school had used—and he'd ended up using it, too, as a way of life.

A bus stop. Waiting for a school bus. That connected to something very particular in his head. And now this case had brought him back here. It seemed that coincidence definitely should be part of this stuff. But if you started paying attention to all possible coincidence, finding meaning in everything, then you'd be fit for the loony bin. And that would be worse for them now than for anyone else.

The others were all checking their phones, every other minute, for news from the DNA databases. Sefton found the bus stop he was after and checked it against the Web site on his phone. Yeah, this was the one. The four of them managed to cram into the shelter beside two nannies talking in what sounded like Russian, and an elderly man in a dufflecoat that smelt of beer. The display showed nine minutes till the next scheduled service. But what they were after, if the Internet was to be believed, would come along a couple of minutes earlier than that. There was no reason why they couldn't try to see it at a whole variety of places, but here was special somehow. It was only here that he'd read about it actually appearing to other people. Who knew if having this "Sight" would make it different for them? This would be a first experiment . . . if this stuff could be experimented on at all.

On the bus itself was where everything had been worst for him. A small bunch of kids, who'd all found their different reasons to pick on the posh little black child, had built up complex narratives of abuse, rhymes, stories and things they'd make him do that were repeated many times a week for five years. Many different drivers had all ignored it. Hell is other people. That bus was the cauldron he himself had been boiled in, and that had made the UC.

He forced those thoughts out of his head and concentrated on the job at hand. He looked again at his watch. "One minute."

They all craned their heads to look out of the shelter and along the suburban street.

"It's not due yet," said the man in the dufflecoat.

Sefton nodded in reply. Through the rain that was bouncing off the trees and floating across the street, there appeared shining ancient lights, shining too brightly while yelling about what was approaching . . . and a gray shape, red faded to dust-colored, was emerging, approaching faster than any vehicle should.

Coming out of the rain, a bus roared into sight. The number 7 with its final destination, Russell Square, indicated on the front, and adverts for Ovaltine and Guinness along its side. There were the silhouettes of a driver and his passengers. It was only the age of the vehicle which made it seem like a "ghost." But it was obviously something to do with the Sight. Sefton took a quick look at the other people at the bus stop. The Russian nannies were looking straight through the bus and past it, as they continued talking, but the old man . . . no, he wasn't like that side-stepping bloke in Soho, because he wasn't so certain, but nevertheless he had turned his head quickly as if to follow the movement, as if he'd just glimpsed something but wasn't sure. Then he'd looked away again.

Not giving anything away, Sefton let his gaze follow the departing bus, glimpsing only shadows inside, through the entrance leading to the stairway at the back. And suddenly he shuddered at what he felt there. He'd had a sudden flashback to that dark warm void below him. Not that he believed in Hell—he was sure Costain had come to the wrong conclusion about what he'd seen—but he knew what it would be like for himself: a bigger bus, with more people inside to contrive torments for him. What would have happened if he'd raised his hand just now and requested it to stop? Where would it have taken him? Probably not to Russell Square.

He watched the bus vanish into the rain again, the cloud of water that had parted for it dropping like a curtain and filling the space where it had been. He had to grab hold of the bus shelter to stop himself shaking.

They found a Starbucks. "In June 1934," Sefton read from his laptop, "London Transport held an inquest into the death of a bus driver who'd been killed at the junction of Cambridge Gardens and St. Mark's Road, after he swerved violently for no apparent reason. Other drivers testified at that inquest that they had also had to swerve at that spot, to avoid a double-decker bus, a number 7 to be precise, in the livery of the General Omnibus Company— which had become part of London Transport the year before— which 'whizzed out at them,' and then disappeared. These appearances happened at two particular times of day, there being a morning service and an afternoon one."

"So the bus driver that got killed didn't stick around to become a ghost," said Costain, "but we just saw the ghost bus that killed him."

"My point," said Sefton, "is this. You hear stories like that all your life and think: cool, a ghost bus. But now we have to look at this stuff analytically . . . a *ghost bus*?! The 'ghost' of a *motor vehicle*? A public conveyance, presumably, which didn't head toward the light, move on to join the choir invisible in . . . bus heaven, the great terminus in the sky, where all good buses go when they . . . I don't know, break down, but instead is doomed to . . . drive eternally the streets of Earth! How can there be a ghost *bus*?!" He looked between them, hoping they were getting this. "There isn't even any record of a number 7 crashing."

"There very probably would have been at least one death occurring on any particular bus route—" began Ross.

"So one death onboard is all it takes to make an entire bus into a ghost? Why not ghost houses where people died, or ghost hospitals? Every bit of London would be full of them. Listen, what about those ships you saw?" He felt the risk of pursuing this, the risk of losing them with theory rather than the sort of factual detail coppers worked with. But Ross had said they should allow assumptions. And more than mere assumption, he was certain, he was starting to put together a working hypothesis. "They must have had lots of passengers on them but, in their case, as in the case of that particular bus, we don't see any of those people sticking around to become ghosts. We see the vehicles themselves. Even if we agree that vehicles can 'die' and come back to 'haunt' places, one of those ships was sunk somewhere else! So what's it doing on the Thames? We could find, if we wanted to search the bottom of the sea, what remained of the actual hull of one of those ghost ships of yours, haul it up, restore it to full working order and launch it here, and then there'd be the real ship and its ghost floating on the same river! How does that work? And what about that Jack thing I met? He's not even a real . . . person, or vehicle or anything that you might even think could die and haunt somewhere, he's just an . . . idea!"

"You're saying it's not always about something that's died and stays on here afterward," said Costain.

"But sometimes it is," said Quill, "like with Harry's dad, or the kid that bloke at the football match was carrying."

There was silence as they considered that.

"That old fellow at the bus stop saw it," said Costain.

"Yeah, he did," Sefton found himself pointing at Costain as if he'd got an answer right in a quiz game, and realized how patronizing that looked and lowered his hand. "But only for a second . . . and that's another thing. I don't think this is about who's got the Sight and who hasn't. I think it's a . . . spectrum of who can see what, when and where. That place, for some reason, is where it's easier for people without the Sight to see the thing. And then it vanished for us too. But maybe we could follow it and see it elsewhere. Or maybe we could see it all the time if we used some of those hand gestures."

Ross managed one of her awkward smiles. "You've got something going here," she acknowledged. "Go on, establish the narrative."

Sefton shared that look with her, feeling relieved.

He took them to Charterhouse Square near the Barbican and, as the rain battered down on them, they bent down to hear more clearly the agonized, continual screaming under the carefully mown grass. Quill got quickly to his feet and walked away a few paces. "A plague pit," explained Sefton. "Some of them are meant to have been buried alive."

"Ghosts again," said Costain.

"Yeah, sort of. It's meant to be the ones who *were* still alive doing the screaming."

Quill sighed. "Fuck me. I wish there was some point at which this team of ours could decide to go off duty, 'cos I need a pint."

Sefton nodded obligingly. "We can do that, too, and continue the demonstration."

They ended up drinking at a pub called the Sutton Arms. And Sefton felt an awkwardness as they had a pint without having officially come off duty. But Quill was right. With just the four of them in the only unit pursuing this, they could never really go off duty, so they had to cut themselves some slack. There still hadn't been further word from the database searches. He asked the pub regulars what their ghost "Charley" was like, and then led the other three as they looked around the place, finally finding a shimmering man with a ruddy face sitting on his own in a corner, staring wide-eyed at every woman. He looked part funny and part scary, in a ratio which changed, Sefton thought, almost every second.

"Definitely scary," said Ross when he asked her. And, in that same moment, Sefton watched as the man's leer became less a thing of seaside postcards and more like something you'd imagine on the face of a rapist. "I wouldn't mind interviewing him, mind. What could one of those things tell us, if they've been hanging round for centuries?"

"Harry's dad wasn't much use."

"That might not always be the case, though. Maybe I should work out a questionnaire."

They sipped a careful two pints each. Quill hesitated a moment when Sefton said they'd get a better look now it was dark. But finally he followed them. Sefton took them to the Charterhouse itself, off the square of the same name.

"I looked up some of the most historical places," he explained, "by which I mean places where terrible shit happened. Places that are meant to have ghosts. This was originally a priory, like a monastery, and it's been used for all sorts of stuff since." They entered the complex of cobblestone courtyards and old buildings, with signs pointing to restaurants and toilets, and still a few hardy tourists. Immediately Sefton pointed out the wraithlike figure of a monk drifting through the grounds. They watched for a minute as it repeated the same pattern of movements. Quite a few tourists seemed to look round as it passed them, but none of them stopped and stared. Conditions, whatever they were, obviously weren't right for them to see it entirely.

"Now that," said Costain, "is a ghost."

Sefton consulted the Web site map, and walked them over to a specific stairwell inside the main building. He leaped back as a man dressed like something out of Shakespeare walked out of it, with his head tucked underneath one arm.

"Even better," said Ross.

"That," Sefton said, "is Thomas Howard, the fourth Duke of Norfolk."

"And he is—?"

"Some dead posh bloke. I could read you his Wiki."

"What he is now is a well proper ghost," said Costain. He sounded to be putting some hope in the simplicity of the statement. Sefton looked to the others. They didn't look quite so burdened. He hadn't yet got to the point of this exercise but, along the way, the familiar nature of some of these "hauntings" seemed to be doing the team good. That was kind of awkward, given what he'd particularly wanted to tell them. Even Quill was now looking more engaged.

"Okay," he said, "maybe there are categories we could sort this stuff into . . ."

"Ghosts, witches, objects, like the ships . . ." suggested Ross.

Sefton hesitated. Right now he didn't want to tell them that he thought it was more complicated than that. But he had to reach the end of his demonstration. "Let's get to the final stop on my list," he said.

It was getting close to 7 p.m. by the time Sefton led them into Berkeley Square. The pavements were still busy with office workers going off to the pub, tourists heading between sandwich bars and coffee shops. The little park in the middle had a few remaining parents with pushchairs and owners of small dogs, or the homeless combing the bins that by now were full of the remains of the day.

"Number 50, Berkeley Square," said Sefton, as they arrived at the address. The ground floor contained the shopfront of Clanfields, a dealer in rare books, with a window that looked warm and inviting and modern. They all looked up together. The upper floor radiated darkness. "According to all the books, this is the most haunted building in London."

Costain watched Quill summon the manager of the shop and, albeit with a bit of initial weariness, manage to summon up his usual rough-diamond character to talk to her. He looked relieved to be throwing his weight around again. Costain knew how that went, but these days he wondered if merely pretending to be someone other than the cringing savage that was surely inside everyone was bad in itself, yet another contribution to whatever complex of burdens was taking him to Hell. Everything for him was now about that. Everything had to be.

The manager had been about to close up for the evening, and was understandably concerned at having a detective inspector on the premises. "It's the sort of thing I hope we can do without a warrant," explained Quill. "Nobody in your firm is under suspicion of anything. But, unfortunately, I can't tell you much beyond that."

He asked her if they'd heard anything strange from the upstairs floor, and it was immediately obvious he'd touched a nerve.

"You're interested in . . . all that?"

Costain felt stupidly offended by her tone. The weight he felt on his shoulders, that they all did—to these ordinary people it was merely "all that." But he recognized the direction his thoughts were going, and made himself stop thinking badly of her. Every thought, every moment . . . how much would it take to scrub him clean? Or would he one day be able to put a bullet through the head of that smiling man and get out of jail free? Or was that a bad thought, too?

"Purely professionally, ma'am."

She made a sour face. "Every few days, someone comes in asking about it. We're a bit fed up with it, to be honest, and none of us believes in it. Except, you know, whenever we hear a bang or a crash from the stockroom or the office, we say 'That's just the ghosts.'"

She led them up a narrow unpainted flight of stairs, a sudden contrast to the shop below. It got quickly colder as they climbed, and Costain found himself thinking of the warm comfort of that pub. He put that unworthy idea out of his head, too. Every thought, every moment . . . But it was going to take more than that, wasn't it? Some holy ceremony, some great deed of repentance—or just making right everything he'd done. But how could he do that, when so much of it was lost in the past, beyond altering? He wasn't used to shit like this slopping around inside his head. He hoped that it wasn't showing on his face. That was the last bit of front he had left.

They came out onto a landing with bare boards, an open door that showed a tiny office beyond, two closed doors leading to the stockrooms further back. "This is where it's all supposed to happen," she said. Even with all of them up here beside her, she looked eager to retreat. Their vague interest was making her believe far more than she normally liked.

"We'll take it from here," said Costain, carefully doing another good deed.

They waited until she'd gone back downstairs, then they took a quick look round the small office, waiting for Sefton to give them some cue about what to expect, but he remained silent, as if he was waiting to play a gag on them. There was a faint sense of unworldliness about this place, and Costain wouldn't have wanted to work up here alone. Especially with the desk facing the grubby window and your back to the door. But there was a confidence about the team now, and Costain had to admit this had been a good idea of Sefton's, whatever his eventual plan was. They'd become a little more familiar with the enemy, and all they were going to find here was another floating specter, or probably a whole bunch of them. But that would be okay, for it looked like "ghosts" were the shallow end, and a long way from Losley.

Sefton headed over to the door into the stockroom. He gently opened it, then looked inside. "I think it's worse in here," he called back. Costain went in along with the others.

They were standing in what had once been a bedroom: plaster curlicues in the corners of the ceiling; an elegant bare window, now dingy, and dark outside. Bare boards. Another door led to what might still be a bathroom. This room was full of boxes, carefully stacked piles of them arranged in rows, with delivery forms in cellophane attached. There was a tall glass-fronted bookcase that contained what must be duplicate stock or books too precious to be displayed downstairs. Also there was a side table on which sat still more books, paperwork lying beside them, a Stanley knife having just hacked open a new delivery.

"All dark and brooding on the outside," said Quill, "but nothing evident in here."

"Just the potential for something," said Sefton. "That makes sense, too. The building itself has a reputation, so from outside it's kind of a 'ghost' too."

"Oh, my God," said Ross.

They all turned to look, and Costain was the first to realize what the woman was seeing. The room had got significantly darker, but without the lights dimming. It was as if the darkness had moved in from every corner. He felt his pulse increase, his breathing grow faster. *Bit of a white-knuckle ride coming up, then. Okay.* It was as if he'd stepped into an open doorway with light behind him, and was, for some reason, pausing there. He wanted to run. *I will not run.* He controlled himself. His fear suddenly seemed as artificial as this darkness was. It wasn't coming from inside . . . *Oh fuck.*

He could feel it. Something enormous was approaching from all directions at once. Its shadow had fallen across the house. The Sight seemed to be turning a dial in his head, up and up and up. "This is not the shallow end," he said. "This isn't like what we saw before. This is bigger than Losley, than anything else we've yet seen . . ." *Bigger than what that smiling bastard lets us see of him. Or maybe this is him!*

"No," said Sefton. "Wait a sec. This isn't what it looks like."

Costain looked to Quill, who nodded back at him, visibly sweating. So now Costain had his orders: now he had to stay if he was going to keep on being the good little boy. The four of them, as one, took a step closer to each other.

"An experiment," said Sefton. "This might make it a bit easier." He went over to the table, grabbed a marker pen, and on the polished floorboards drew a wobbly circle surrounding the others. Then he stepped back inside it.

"What's that about?" said Quill.

"In what I've read online, any sort of circle is protection."

"Oh," said Costain. "Great."

"I think . . . you might have to be prepared to believe in it."

"Now you tell us."

There was a sudden noise from around their feet. They all looked down. The ink circle was sparking and hissing. And now Costain became aware that it was significantly lighter inside it. They shuffled closer together. "Now I believe in it," he said.

"As long as it isn't broken," said Sefton.

The darkness became solid around them. It became a warm, close thing, like being pressed up against some enormous animal. Costain slowly lost the ability to see anything elsewhere in the room. He had to look at the others to check he hadn't gone blind. Normal evening was contained only in this circle. A smell wafted through the air. He'd smelt it before, he realized, and now he really started to feel afraid. He looked over to where the door to the stairs should be. All he would have to do now was run six paces—

He stopped himself. *No!*

The smell was the same one he had smelt during those moments of horror and falling in Losley's attic. It was like the most terrible nostalgia, something that connected your brain to somewhere outside time; as if something inside you knew an awful truth that your memory didn't. It was that place you sometimes went in dreams, when you then awoke thankful to be back in . . . he now hesitated to think of it as the real world. Because, somewhere inside him, he was desperately hoping there was a real world elsewhere that he might one day get back to. "So," he said to Sefton, "you knew that ghosts were real . . . and you led us to the 'most haunted building in London.' What's up with that?"

"I didn't . . . I don't think it's—!" What Costain most of all didn't like was that Sefton seemed completely wrong-footed by this experience now. Whatever he'd expected to happen, this was obviously a long way from it.

There was a low noise from the ink circle, a static hiss that was slowly rising in pitch.

"I think the circle's melting," said Ross. "Do you think it's melting?"

"Experiment over," said Quill. "Can you get us out of here?"

Sefton seemed to panic for a second, then he bent back to the floor. "Okay," he said, "I'm going to draw a circle intersecting this one, and then another, and we'll slowly head toward the door—" And then he shouted in surprise and jumped back—as the pen rolled away into the dark and was lost. He held up his hands and Costain could see the burns on the tips of his fingers. "Oh fuck. Oh fuck, I'm sorry. I'm sorry. I didn't expect this."

"What was the plan?" asked Quill, whose voice had become very precise. All pretense had left him. That realization chilled Costain too.

"I thought it'd be hard to take, a lot more so than the tourist ghosts. Because that's what all the books say about it, that there's a terrible sense of fear. But the most important thing about this place is . . . it's not true."

"What?"

"It's like that bus that had never crashed, like one of Ross's ships that actually sank in the bloody Mediterranean! I followed everything back. I looked up all the details. This place is just a chain of people making up stories, all of them based on what the last one said. And some of them are actually, you know, just stories! Fiction set in other places, then retold about here, made up by writers! From 1871, there was one about a maid having suffered a fit here, and so a bloke stayed in the room and saw the same stuff, only that was the plot of a story in a magazine three years earlier. This is where a new bride was going to live, but she left her husband at the altar, and he was left mad and wandering. Or a rich man kept this place empty only so that he could visit it, lock up the caretakers, and do something evil. Or this was where a lunatic brother was kept, and fed just through a hole. And none of it— *none* of this shit—is true! The 'most haunted house in London' doesn't present a single item of evidence." He sounded to be arguing with the darkness itself. "And, absolutely, there's no proof that anyone ever conducted a sacrifice here. So, if it's one thing or another—"

"This," interjected Ross, "is what Losley meant by *remembered*."

"Exactly . . . and so are the tourist ghosts. But this is the extreme case, the one I was leading you to to show you, the one case that tests the rule. 'Cos it's *not true*."

"Stop believing it's real, then," said Quill. "Wish it away."

For a moment, Costain was sure he could. He visualized the darkness as not being there. When he went undercover, he always felt he was absolutely in charge of what he believed about himself, could project that persona to other people, acting a part and making them believe it. But . . . now it felt that he wasn't in charge of every part of himself, because part of him—the part that he knew had done bad shit in the past—had been judged and found wanting. He kept scrambling to make up for that flaw. And that flaw put a hole in everything he tried to do through exuding confidence alone. Every time he said something funny, there was now that thought undercutting it: am I hurting anybody? It felt as if he couldn't take a single step without hurting someone. Or, at least, the person he was right now couldn't. And he didn't yet know how to be anyone else. That flaw meant that . . . he found he couldn't project anything of *himself*, couldn't make the world around him believe anything. So he couldn't make this darkness go.

None of them could.

"We didn't believe it when we came in here," he said. "Or we thought it'd be easy. If it was as easy as that, we'd be fine."

They heard a noise in the darkness, and they all fell silent. And there it was again. A footstep on the stairs.

"Sometime in the 1870s," said Sefton, "and this is just what a short story from the 1930s says, there were these . . . these two penniless sailors who'd heard all the previous stories, only they were too poor to care, and they—"

The footstep again, closer now. That door they couldn't see would soon open.

"—they broke in here, 'cos it was empty, and they stayed the night. They lit a fire. They fell asleep. And one of them woke up and he heard—"

Another step.

"That's what he heard: something on the stairs. But, of us, it was just me that knew that. So you don't need to know about this to experience it, so apparitions aren't about what the people who see them believe—"

"You should have told us all this," said Quill, "before we entered."

"Would that have made a difference?" whispered Ross.

The sound of the door opening. Something stepped slowly toward them. It felt huge, but not focused in one place. Instead, it seemed to be all around them. Costain could sense it trying the air around the circle, pushing at it, trying his eyes too at the same time, testing his skin, trying to find any way in. Costain's eyes strained to discern it in the absolute darkness. But it felt like it was all darkness at once, unknown and unknowable. Was this the smiling man? How would he react if it was him? Was the man coming for him now?

"As long as the circle isn't broken," said Sefton, "we're fine. Believe that, 'cos it's true. We can stand here all night if we have—"

Their phone text alerts all went off.

They all jumped simultaneously at the sudden noise. Costain let out a relieved breath. The tension was broken. Whoever that was was from *their* world, from the world of forms to fill out and warrant cards and cups of tea. It was probably the news about the DNA searches they'd been waiting for. It was like a torch they could hold up against the dark. Something *modern*. He took out his phone and defiantly hit the text from an unfamiliar number. He expected to see a proud announcement of success, of hope he could use to hold off this dark, even to hold up the screen and yell at whatever it was that they were closing in on it.

He stared at what the text actually said:

Any communication breaks the circle.

Costain looked down on hearing a sudden noise, and the others looked too. The circle had roared into a sudden, consuming flame.

"Oh fuck," said Sefton.

The circle evaporated. The darkness rushed in.

Costain ran.

Behind him, he could hear shouting. He didn't make it to the door.

As the darkness swept over him, Sefton bellowed in despair and threw himself flat. And then there was silence . . .

He waited. He raised his head slightly. He saw that his hand had landed across what remained of the circle. An ache in his palm told him that he'd snuffed out the fire on a small section of the ink line. And so he was still connected to it. Careful to keep his hand where it was, he looked around. Beside him, still as statues, caught in the act of shouting, stood Ross and Quill. Halfway across the room was Costain, frozen in mid-sprint. That was what had happened to the two sailors. One had run, the other had stayed, and been driven out of his mind to the point where he'd thrown himself out of the window.

As Sefton watched, he saw a tiny movement of Costain's arm. Time was still going, then. Sefton was just experiencing it a lot more quickly than the others. *Nothing special about me. Must be because I'm still touching the circle. They've been caught by whatever this is.* He moved his hand a little, and saw the edge of it. He slid his knee up, until it was touching the line too. Then he lifted his hand quickly, ready to slam it down again. *Still fine.* He put one

foot down on the ink by his knee, and managed to stand. *Okay.*
He looked out into the darkness that had infested every inch of
the space, like a darkened theater around a bare stage set. The
most haunted house in London. And he himself had led them
here. Costain had been right about that: *Arrogance. You start to
take a bit of charge of your life, and you go mad with it. You're not
used to it.* The Sight was now worked up to a pitch inside his head,
pulsing out of everything around him. The darkness had bloody
texted them! Had that been his fault, had him saying it made it
happen? No, otherwise they could have *believed* their way out of
it. It was the mass of opinion that mattered, he was sure of that
now, unless you were one of those people who could surf that
with words and gestures—or something like Losley's lord, whose
opinion seemed to matter more than other people's. Oh, very
British.

But not many people in London right now would know about
the details concerning this place . . . *Oh. It must be the memories of
the dead, too.* Somehow. That would suggest they were somehow
still around, lingering in an . . . afterlife. But he didn't want to
credit that, because it went against everything he believed in, and
what he believed was even more important now. Perhaps the dead
also existed only as some sort of reservoir of memory held around
London. He remembered the rising fear among his team as he'd
told his story. It was as if they'd summoned something here, by
using the Sight, in a chain reaction between what they expected
and what collective opinion said about this place, and what they
could see, which had then reached a moment when it went off
the scale and kind of . . . shorted them out. If he hadn't been
touching the last bit of the circle, what would have happened to
all of them? *People vanish in London all the time.* With his fumbling
"experiment," he'd brought them to the edge of that. So he had
to get them out of it. *How?*

He stared out into the dark, let himself get a flavor of it.

The roar of the engine underneath . . . a school bus. His school bus.

Children, pressed all around, holding him down, his face against the floor, singing taunts round and round, batty boy posh boy homo, all in that accent he hated that was also him that time they'd made him eat fag ends, the walls of the bus locked around him, and the doors will never open—!

He stumbled, nearly fell off balance from where he was standing on the line, so had to take a mental leap back. He found his feet again, breathing hard. Okay, so when he looked into it, it was about himself. That was probably what the others were experiencing too. Costain would be getting another taste of what he'd decided was Hell. One way to muller a copper: take them off the grid. This was just fear pushed to the maximum. It was like being trapped under the surface of a frozen lake. It was what he'd felt inside Jack, but far worse. This was the perfection of the weight and terror of the crowd. *Just as well I've got freedom of thought, it'd really be hell if I couldn't step out of it. The kind of stress that'd give you a heart attack. The others haven't got long. I can't walk into that, so what can I do?* At least it could only kill him. He didn't think there was anything beyond death to be threatened with, and he felt that conviction was a strength here.

So this was *remembering.* The force of it was huge, like continents. It was older than everything. It flowed through everything. He wanted to utter something brave at it, to make a joke at it. He couldn't, not just now. *What would it take to make it forget instead of remember?* He felt the answer emerge: to make something *forgotten* would take an enormous effort, a continuous effort during every moment. To do that was way beyond him. But instead of forgetting . . . what about trying to create a different version of what was remembered here, to remember not this horror but some of the other things this place had been or was meant to have been? Those memories wouldn't be as powerful as the fear, for fear was always so strong, but . . . his research had also said this house was a den of criminals, counterfeiters, who used that fear as a cover. Okay, so they wouldn't still be here as "ghosts," because there was

194

no legend, no memory of that; besides, he had to get rid of even the idea that there were ghosts here. He imagined instead the remains of coins discovered in the gaps in the floorboards, an exhibit commemorating it, maybe, a plaque on the wall outside, this place as a historical building, the infamous counterfeiter gang, with modern actors playing the roles, that manager downstairs laughing about how they get the crime tours coming through here . . . He made himself see the details—

And, for the first time, he felt the Sight pushing back against this world he'd found himself in. He could see these fragile things in his eyes now. Light had expanded from where he was, making a vulnerable space on the stage set. Knowledge was power, literally, in this city. He stopped himself from celebrating, because he knew this would last only seconds. He dared to step off the marker line. He grabbed Quill and Ross by one hand each. He started to drag them toward the door, pushing against the nightmares that confined them. Their faces were looking at things beyond him, their feet dragging along like reluctant toddlers. He pushed them into Costain, sent him, also, stumbling toward the door.

Four of them? They could have made their own circle, he realized, with a part of his mind he associated with deduction—with UC thoughts about what OCN shape was like. Only five would be better than four, the shape of the organization of five would be strong. Thoughts like these were being formed inside him by the sheer pressure around him, he suddenly understood: natural defenses in operation, his persona finding a way.

But the fear was strong. The fear had more force. The fear had been thrown back and now was . . . going to come crashing in on them again!

He gathered them all with him, and *shoved* them at the door. They rushed through it together. They got over onto the other side. They fell in a heap. The door swung shut with a bang.

And suddenly the light in the corridor was again provided by a bulb. The four of them were just lying there, staring up at the bulb in its dusty lampshade. Sefton thought they must look like something from an old painting, with their clothes and their hands flung out in glorious abandon. He started to laugh, but then he bit down on it. He didn't like the feel of where that reaction might take him. He was panting too hard, so he put a hand over his mouth and took smaller breaths. He felt aware of his own failure that had led him to this knowledge.

The others started to sit up, to look at him and each other. They were shaken to the core. Costain had his hands covering his face. Footsteps approached. *Footsteps on the stairs.* But no, no . . . not now.

The startled manager was peering at them. Slowly they got to their feet. Quill just nodded to her, no funny line appearing on his lips. Sefton just about managed to get himself down the stairs. The others stumbled down around him.

Costain found he could hardly put one foot in front of the other. He reached out to Ross for support, and appreciated that strong shoulder. He felt as if he was going to burst into tears or else throw up. Doing either would feel like death. He had seen it again. It had nearly had him again.

They went back to the pub. Costain put his hands on his pint but didn't trust himself to lift it. He didn't feel able to look at Sefton, even though the man had saved him. That was wrong. He looked at the other two, who were shaking as much as he was. "Headless fucking ghosts. As if!" he said. "We had no idea. We're not even rookies. We're just . . . kids!"

"We . . . we learned something." That was Sefton, looking angry and defensive. "It doesn't matter if it's true or not; it's what people believe, and—"

"Shut the fuck up." And then the crushing limitations descended again. "Sorry, sorry!"

"It's okay—" Quill began.

"It's *not* okay! We're playing . . . cops and robbers because it *comforts* us. That's all there is to it!"

Ross took Costain's hands in hers. "What did we all see?" she said. "I saw . . . my dad, over and over."

"I saw a lot . . . of fuckwittery concerning myself," said Quill, "about which I feel like suing someone. Pity, then, that it was all true."

"Complicated." Sefton shook his head. "I need to think about it."

Ross looked back to Costain. "So what about you?"

He didn't want to answer, but . . . this was still going to come out. It was beyond his control, and he hated that too. "I saw it again . . . what I saw in Losley's attic. The place I'm . . . I'm going to."

"Hell," suggested Sefton, sounding like he wanted to say it out loud, but also sounding like he didn't bloody believe it.

"Back in the attic, you lot were being *sent* there, so maybe it appeared differently for you. I was just . . . getting there early, so I saw all the details. And I saw them again just now."

"No," said Quill, "we don't do theology—"

"Jimmy, we have to," said Ross.

"That smiling bastard was there, too. And down there he felt like . . . like one of those gang enforcers who have done the really bad shit, the ones where you can see it in their faces that they can't surprise themselves with how far they'd go, because there *is* no limit to . . ." He had to stop. He was shaking so hard, it took him a moment to continue. "The sort that put blowtorches to informers' feet. Every UC . . . we *think* about those guys, about ending up in the hands of one of them."

"Yeah," whispered Sefton.

"He's the biggest version going of one of those terrifying sods. He knew all about me, so I had no secrets I could give up to spare myself anything. He's waiting for me when I die. I know he is, it's just obvious. Does nobody get that?"

Sefton again nodded, grudgingly. "Yeah."

"And with him . . . there was this informer. Sammy Cliff, his name was." They were silent now, listening carefully. "He kept pretending he didn't want my money. This is years before Goodfellow. He kept saying he was 'on the side of the police'; that's the catchphrase we joked about with him. Fucking little bike boy, user, dirty fucking hair, burns . . . that smell on his skin." He saw from their faces that they'd all known similar. "He kept saying how he was nothing, a pile of shit on the pavement; that's what he once told me he was. When it became clear we weren't going to get his boss, best we could do for him was not nick him. And it was bloody obvious to the gang, by the end, who the informer was. They can't run anywhere, not kids like that. Their idea of running is going to a different mattress. He ended up with one of *those* blokes. They burned his feet off, worked upward from there. They made a party of it, there were cans and condoms all over the warehouse. We heard all the details. So there he was, Sammy Cliff, waiting for me. He didn't even look pleased. All he was there for was to wait his chance to see what had been done to him also being done to me. Forever."

"So," said Sefton, oh so gently, as if he was talking to a lunatic, "you think that now you have to be good."

"It's my only chance, yeah? And it's so bloody hard to think of every single thing, all the time—"

Sefton was shaking his head. "Can I say something?"

"More of your theories," said Costain, "'cos *that* worked so well! Sorry!"

"There's no God, so there's no Heaven—"

"How do you *know*?"

"—and this 'Hell' might well be like that, might well have the ghost or the memory or whatever these things are of this informer of yours in it, but it is just the place where the big boss of whatever we've found—"

"How do you *know*?!"

"If you'd listen! I've found out—"

And suddenly Costain was up out of his seat, and had thrown himself at him.

Ross leaped up just as Quill did. She managed to grab Sefton so that a punch that would have taken Costain's head off went wide. They hauled the pair apart. They fell on the floor as one mass.

Bar staff were running over, shouting. Among all the confusion, as they were being hauled to their feet, Quill's phone beeped. As he stumbled out onto the street, looking angry as he did so, as he made himself do it—he looked at the screen. "The DNA database results are in," he said, his voice incredulous. "They found nothing."

SIXTEEN

"A vicar, a rabbi and an imam walk into a Portakabin," said Quill. He was looking up at just that. Sefton and Costain looked over in surprise too.

Ross raised her head from her endless scrolling through computerized bills records from various London boroughs. They'd all got back to that, letting their eyes cover page after page to see if they noticed one of Losley's edits in the records of a borough where she wasn't known to have lived. The same effect, frustratingly, didn't hold for the DNA records. There were no matches with the DNA from any of the child skeletons, or from the skull on the newel post, in the files for any still-open cases. That is to say, none of these victims was listed as a missing child. Having heard that staggering verdict, they'd expected the files to have been edited, and had got copies sent over, but they showed no sign of tampering. It wasn't that Losley had altered the records of who these children were; it was that the world seemed to have forgotten them. There came with the results a great mass of descriptions, details of hair color and teeth and ethnic origin (increasingly diverse as the strata approached modern times) and how, on several occasions, there seemed to be groups of three siblings taken together. The West Ham away game against Liverpool had finished in a nil–nil draw. The next home game would be on Wednesday. Costain and Sefton were doing their best to avoid each other, and Sefton hadn't raised the matter of looking into the background materials again, though Ross saw him poring through pages on the Internet.

Quill had been in conference with Lofthouse a great deal, trying to find some resource or clue in the evidence coming out of any of the searched houses, Toshack's included, but so far there had been nothing. They had so many alerts for missing children in place it wasn't true, and also a public that was keen to cooperate to the point of being terrorized. Consequently, playgrounds were empty and school runs were packed. The unit had asked to be sent reports of Losley, and now had way too many of them to sort through, from places as far afield as Inverness and Guernsey. An elderly woman in Aldershot had even been forced to leave her house after persistent attacks on her by youths identifying her as Losley. Ross had decided on some filters for sorting these reports, notably instantly chucking away all those from outside London. Still, working through them was another thing each of them could be doing when whatever else they did was proving fruitless and they felt they had to be doing something.

And behind it all was the specter of that smiling man, Losley's lord—the shape in the dark whose existence, every now and then, suggested to Ross, on the edge of sleep, that all they were doing was futile.

The Ops Board had only a couple of new things added to it: an explanation of "remembered" by Sefton, and the phone number from which the darkness had texted them. It comprised a string of numbers which appeared in no searches, and which Quill had scribbled at the bottom left of the board. Ross had pinned up a sheet to cover the board a few minutes ago, and it was a bad sign that her workmates hadn't mentioned that.

"Detective Inspector Quill," she said now, "these are my guests."

Yesterday morning she'd realized what might bring together Costain's needs and Sefton's needs, and had arranged it without bothering to ask the increasingly distant Quill if it was a good idea. She got to her feet. "This is the Met chaplain, the Reverend Toby Franklin," who looked as if he'd come straight from being kicked around on the rugger pitch, "Rabbi Peter Shulman," who looked as if he'd walked into the wrong room, "and Dr. Firdos Irfan, who's an imam," and who also looked to be regretting this already. "These last two gentlemen work in the prison service in London."

"What's this about?" said Sefton, standing up. Costain was looking kind of thankful and awkward at the same time. He'd clearly got it straight away.

Quill eyed her questioningly, then nodded. "Let's call it showing initiative."

"I was expecting to meet someone with a spiritual crisis . . ." began Franklin.

"You might well call it that," said Quill. "A dirty great spiritual crisis. Tea, Reverend?"

The three clerics started to look concerned as they realized that this was about an operation. Sefton kept his distance as he watched Costain fussing over them. He felt almost betrayed, though Ross kept looking at him encouragingly. It seemed that his colleagues hadn't heard a word he'd said. If these three men had any power, then the churches and mosques and synagogues of London would be aglow with it. This counted as a wholesale adoption of what the other two probably saw as Costain's agenda, and if this had been a regular squad . . . well, he supposed he could have complained to somebody. Not that he ever would have.

Sefton had spent every waking moment since the bookshop incident researching the world in which they now found themselves. He'd come up with a lot of theories, only he was sure now that this lot wouldn't want to hear them. Not after he'd led the group into danger. Not after they'd pulled him off Costain—who'd come at him, not the other bloody way round, but who'd nearly got what was coming to him. Only, because of the situation they were in, there couldn't be any talk of disciplinary action. It was as if they were all waiting, instead, for some regular police-work-shaped clue to come along, rather than bothering to deal with his stuff. When he'd spoken to Ross about this stuff being for the lost and downtrodden . . . well, maybe he'd got it more right than he'd imagined. For he was the specialist here, slight as his expertise was. These three priests simply didn't know what the world they'd found themselves in was like. Getting them in here was like getting a bloody psychic into a normal investigation. He pushed the anger down inside, folded his arms across his chest.

"Reverend—" Quill began, turning to Franklin.

"Or Toby," said the priest.

"Yeah . . . Reverend, Rabbi, Imam, we brought you here to ask you . . ." He looked to Ross.

"For point four or seven on the Objectives list," she said, nodding to the concealed Ops Board, "I think we could do with some holy water."

The clerics stared at her.

"No," said Ross, "seriously."

"What do you want that for?" asked Shulman.

"That would be an operational matter," said Quill.

"Okay . . ." said Franklin, "what exactly do you *mean* by—?"

Sefton couldn't take it any longer. If they were going to do this, they were going to do it. If he'd known this was what Ross had been after, he'd have been able to provide her with all the details. And, as long as this was all there was going to be to it, he had to admit she had a point. He located on his phone the Web site he'd bookmarked. 'Holy water,' he read out. 'A sacramental, as used in baptism, having been blessed by a priest.' We'd need at least several large bottles of it." He looked challengingly at Ross. "For testing."

"Or," said Ross, "you could just . . . *do* the water supply of this building, so we can get it out of the tap when required." She looked hopefully between them.

The clerics stared at each other. They then stood up. "All right," said Irfan, "I've had it. Your analyst got us to come all the way over here because it sounded urgent—"

"No," Quill said, "listen, this isn't a joke—"

"You know," said Franklin, "even a couple of years ago, nobody would have dared to do this. Now I get kids knocking on my door, I get prank phone calls—"

"You think we're *making this up?*" snarled Costain.

The clerics fell still.

Sefton watched the three men of faith doing what they did. He saw their body-language skills, their active listening, their voices pulling more and more explanation out of the others, to the point where he had to speak up and remind them of what couldn't be said. They were preying on the group's tiredness, on the stress, seeing their job as merely ameliorating that. They were also obviously aware that this was the team dealing with "the witch of West Ham," and were excited and alarmed by what their being here meant. Whereas in fact they were here, to give Ross some credit, to demonstrate whether what they represented meant *anything* in this new world the team had found. Proof of meaninglessness would help Costain with his issues.

"Holy water," declared Franklin finally, when it became clear the team weren't going to share beyond a certain point, "is the water that's blessed during the Easter vigil, after sunset on the day after Good Friday. Or at least that's the only time it's done."

"And it lasts all that time?" asked Ross. "I mean, if you needed to do a baptism right now?"

"Any water that's added to the blessed water becomes blessed. I think that's the rule."

"Sorry," queried Sefton, "you *think?*"

Franklin shrugged. "It's been a long time since I've run a church. We just performed the one ceremony, and the rest of the year we filled the font up from a bucket. Listen, what can you tell me about the *purpose* this is going to be put to?"

"Saving the lives of children," Costain had said it before Sefton could stop him.

"And this would be saving them from . . . a suspect that's into the occult?" said Shulman. "This 'witch' of yours? And so, because they believe in the power of Toby's 'holy water' . . ?"

Costain looked to Quill, and didn't continue.

Franklin looked frustrated. "It's very hard for me to provide something like this when I don't believe in the system it represents."

"You don't believe in holy water?" said Sefton.

"I believe the power of God can do anything, but He doesn't need any particular thing to do it."

"That's idolatry," agreed Irfan. "I'm not comfortable with any of this."

"Holy water, as you call it," said Shulman, "this means nothing to me and my colleague here. And I think even for Toby this is . . . a metaphor."

Sefton turned away so they wouldn't see him rolling his eyes. "No good to us, then."

"You don't believe in the devil?" That was Costain again.

"I think the 'adversary' in the Bible is a metaphor, too," began Franklin, "for Christ's hunger and fear—"

"Like the Yetzer Hara," said Shulman, "the evil inclination of human beings. It's sometimes personified in art—"

"And in the words of my faith also, but 'shaitan' is also an adjective, absolutely, that can be applied to people too," joined in Irfan.

It sounded as if they were going to go on like this for some time. Sefton sighed, glancing at Ross. "You should have got a Catholic."

"I tried to find a Hindu and a Buddhist too."

"Thank God you didn't."

Franklin spoke up then, and when Sefton turned to look, he saw that all the clerics were giving him a rather offended look. "All we're saying," he said, "is that we believe in evil done by people."

"That is, and I'm sorry this displeases you so much," added Shulman, "because I'm a Reform rabbi. But even an Orthodox rabbi will tell you the time of ghosts and shades and shedim is in the distant past."

"And I," Irfan joined in, "spend my whole life trying to make people see how *my* tradition is a modern, relevant—!"

"Please, Imam . . ." Quill raised a hand, "Rabbi, Reverend, we're working against the clock here."

"I'll provide you with whatever . . . symbols you want," said Franklin.

"As long as you realize—" Shulman raised his hands warningly.

"—that they are just *objects*," finished Irfan.

"Thanks," said Sefton, "but we'll be the judge of that."

Ross produced some large bottles of mineral water. Meanwhile, Sefton watched as Franklin got a book out of his pocket, and found what he needed to say.

"Father," he began, "you give us grace through sacramental signs, which tell us of the wonders of your unseen power. In baptism we use your gift of water, which you have made a rich symbol of the grace you give us in this sacrament . . ." When he'd finished, he took the tops off all the bottles. "And we need salt," he said.

"What for?" said Sefton.

"What's *anything* for? It's what we do in my church."

Quill found some sachets. Franklin blessed that also, and added it to the bottles. "Salt has always been regarded as a protection against evil," he said. "Maybe that's because it preserved meat."

"Oh, that'd be science," said Sefton, failing to keep the triumph out of his voice. He could see what the others were seeing, and what had made Costain look awkward. Like the bastard had half wanted this to be true, because then there'd be rules and something they could fight for, even if it meant he himself was going to Hell. The blessing hadn't made any difference to the water. Adding the salt hadn't changed that.

"Surely, science always applies?"

"Are you Richard Dawkins in disguise?"

"Sorry, Reverend," said Quill quickly, "we really appreciate what you're doing here."

"Perhaps," suggested Ross, "you could say some different words, maybe something a bit older, a bit more . . ."

"Irrational and superstitious?" suggested Shulman.

"Yeah."

"Not from me," Irfan shook his head. "Islam is a blessing upon mankind. Nothing further therefore is needed. Allah will either help you or He won't. His will isn't contained in a bottle of water." He looked to Franklin. "No offense."

"None taken."

Sefton finally gave in to the temptation. He had, for both Costain's sake and his own, to take this as far as it could go. "After our experience the other day," he said, "I've been putting some stuff together." He went and found the holdall. He'd been planning to tell the others about it, at some point. "Okay," he said, "what about these?" He produced four silver crosses attached to chains. Franklin took them in his hands, and blessed them. Doing so made no visible difference to them. He also blessed, rather more reluctantly, the horseshoes intended to be hung upside-down, the crowbars and bits of rusty scrap that the online folklore journal he'd found had called "cold iron," and, with raised eyebrows, the pair of silver-plated handcuffs that had set Sefton back a week's wages and that he'd distantly worried about claiming on expenses. None of these items glowed with a divine light afterward.

Shulman reached into his pocket. "Would you like this?" he asked, showing them his key ring, upon which hung what looked like a tiny, flat hand made of metal. "It's a Chamsa, a Hand of Miriam, a present from my niece in Israel. It's a *symbol* of protection." He took it off the chain and laid it on the table. "If you ask me how far I go before I think the symbolic turns into the practical, it's the Torah scrolls, and anything where God's name is written, like a Mezuzah, which comprises particular verses from the Torah put in a case and fixed on a doorpost. Not apt for a non-Jewish household, of course, or I'd send one over. But as to the supernatural . . ." He shook his head. "The rabbis of the past are meant to have been able to do things like having calves appear or making birds burst into flame with their voices, though why you'd want to do that I have no idea. But that was because of their deep understanding of the *natural* world. Whatever you're facing here, in the end it will turn out to be something that is founded in nature."

"Thank you," said Quill, adding the Chamsa to the other objects.

Sefton noted that there was no reassuring glow there either. He hesitated a moment before placing the final object on the table, in front of the clerics. It was a wooden stake.

"Oh, come on," said Irfan. "You think you're looking for a vampire?"

"No," said Quill.

"Ah, so you're planning to drive that through the chest of a *person?*"

"No." Franklin stepped back from the table. "I draw the line there. And so should you."

There was silence from the coppers. Sefton put the stake back in the holdall. It didn't matter, anyway. Costain had assumed his poker face, as if this was just to be expected.

Shulman sighed. "I wish I knew what it is you're going through, all of you."

"I think," suggested Franklin, "you could do with being blessed, this time as *people*."

Costain, Ross and Quill sat down in turn for Franklin to say some words over them and touch their heads.

Sefton remained standing. He studied again all the various things Franklin had blessed, but still no glow, no weight, no added feeling to them.

The blessings finished, now these futile people were looking to him. The proof of their uselessness was sitting before him. And even that, now they could see it, hadn't convinced Costain to free himself from his fears, hadn't made the other two politely show the clerics out. Sefton almost wanted to laugh. "I . . . just don't believe in God," he declared. And then he wanted to say sorry, damn it.

"Bloody hell," said Quill, "neither do I! Neither does Ross, I should think! But we need all the help we can get, so—"

"Kevin, *please!*" said Ross.

The use of his first name was more moving than he'd expected it to be. As was her appeal. But . . . Sefton only shook his head.

"Well," said Quill, "I don't think I can order you. That's got to be in contravention of something."

"It's important to me," said Sefton, "not to do this. It's . . . who I am." He realized, as he said it, that this was the first such declaration of anything that he'd ever willingly made out loud. Franklin came over and took his hand. Sefton tensed and warned him. "Don't try and do anything against my will."

Franklin sighed. "I myself, just me, Toby Franklin, hope that you find the strength you need. To *misquote* a phrase: though you walk through the valley of the shadow of death, may you fear no evil."

"I hope so too," said Irfan. "Whatever you're going through, it's clearly real to you."

Shulman came over. "You'll like this," he said. "We prefer the term 'benediction,' because, you know, 'blessing' . . . in the end it's about throwing blood on something. It's what the word actually means. But don't worry: it's not something I'm going to do *to* you." He raised his hand. "Praised are you, God, ruler of the universe, who made good people like Kevin here. There you are, it's sort of sidelong."

"I'll send you a crucifix," suggested Franklin. "But all it will mean is that I'll be praying for you."

"I will be too," confirmed Irfan.

"All of us," said Shulman.

Sefton looked to the others, and he realized this was the first supportive thing anyone who wasn't a copper had yet said to them about what they were going through. It had too much of an effect. It was too seductive.

"Thanks," he said. But he didn't fully mean it.

After the clerics had left, Costain sat holding the various objects in his hands, looking for any sense that these were not now what they had been before. There was nothing to detect. He felt as he had when he'd been a kid, and had put his hands out for the communion offering, without knowing he shouldn't, and had munched down quickly on the wafer that was just a wafer, and had felt quite drunk after a sip of wine that was just wine.

"They won't work," said Sefton, addressing him for the first time in days, but with noticeable anger in his voice.

Costain had tried to make himself apologize for the fight, but he couldn't manage that. And he was getting the growing feeling that mere apologies weren't going to cut it, anyway. "If it's about belief, more people believe in *this* than—"

"Maybe all this weird shit we're discovering is for the people who weren't included by the major religions, who got fed up with it not working, who needed something different."

"I think I might . . . have to try to believe." Costain said it honestly, then looked to Sefton, hoping for some fellow feeling.

"Great. What will you think about me, then?"

"What?"

"The gay thing."

Costain wanted to say that wouldn't make a difference, but realized he didn't honestly know what any particular church would expect of him.

"You think you've seen Hell," said Sefton, before he could reply. "So you've got a gun to your head. If I was them I wouldn't take you."

SEVENTEEN

Westminster Hall: an enormous public edifice with a stage at one end; a vaulted ceiling; marble steps; polished doors with metal lock plates that collected fingerprints. The smell of a library, the echoes of a concert hall. It was Saturday morning, and the match would be on Wednesday. Quill stood in the entrance area, forcing himself not to habitually watch the people that passed by, carrying boxes or pushing carts. A poster indicated that there was a New Age fair today but, looking at this lot, he'd have guessed that anyway. He stood out like a sore thumb and he knew it. No UC was he, especially among this lot with their long hair and sandals and tattoos. He was concentrating on his coffee, on not letting his hangover drag him even further down. He was trying to ignore the red hue of the light penetrating every window, the way the building seemed splattered with blood. He wondered what that was about, before he found a bronze plaque describing the building's history. This once high security venue, actually part of the Houses of Parliament, you could now hire out, thanks to this cost-cutting government, for your collectors' fair or your union meeting. The metal detectors had been moved to where it joined with the lobby of Parliament itself. This was where Charles I had been tried, among many others, where they'd demanded his head and signed the death warrant. It had then had Cromwell's severed head sitting on the roof for twenty-five years. It was where coronations had been celebrated, too. The place *smelt* of royalty, of being afraid of something flighty and a bit random when it wanted to be, and a bit too real when it didn't.

It had something of Losley's attractions to it as well, a terrible jollity but with blood infused in its bricks. It was a bit like those ships or the bus, then. This whole building had a bit of ghost about it. That way it suited how he felt right now. Part of him was aware that, maybe even now, and more and more certainly as Monday evening approached, more children would be in Losley's hands. And also that, for some reason, nobody would miss them. And that seemed to be his own fault, no matter what he told himself. The match would see a hat-trick, because that smiling bastard would make it happen, and the hole inside him, he was sure of it, would widen by a notch as if held open with forceps. He was overlooking something terrible.

"Jolly," commented Ross, appearing beside him, and looking around.

Sefton and Costain soon joined them. They, too, were eyeing the white middle-aged crowd trooping past. "Plain clothes, is it?" said Sefton.

"You're sounding a lot more sarky these days," observed Quill, and then regretted it as Sefton clammed up and looked away. This outing was designed, at Ross's suggestion, to keep Sefton's agenda of background research going, but in what they hoped would be a less dangerous way. But Quill wasn't sure the DC had quite understood that, in that he still looked as if he'd thrown his rattle out of the pram. Getting him and Costain together on the same page was going to take some doing.

"We're here on your say-so, you know," he said.

Sefton looked back, blankly. "Yeah. Sorry."

The interior of the hall was also stained red, but thankfully there was no trace of shambling monarchs. Instead, clouds of them floated loftily overhead, mixing with each other like colored oil in water. You might call that art rather than a haunting, since they were hardly to be counted as people. Far below their empty gaze, long rows of tables were covered in occult paraphernalia and lifestyle accoutrements, ranging from crystals to racks of colorful dresses. It was like something from after the apocalypse, this bring-and-buy sale held in the palace that nobody quite knew the meaning of any more. Quill passed a woman with a bowl and a chalice on her table, who was offering, her sign said, "WHOLE SPIRIT THERAPY," and who was, his new senses told him, completely harmless.

She smiled at him, and he felt he should say something. "What do you do?"

"I'm a witch."

Quill couldn't help it. "No you're not," he said, and moved on.

The stage at one end of the hall was occupied by large paintings of dolphins and eclipses, the man trading them presumably having paid a bit more for his pitch. Over the odor of royalty, half jeweler's shop, half butcher's shop, there was that splendid metropolitan smell that Quill had always associated with the civic spaces of London: some sort of polish, obviously, but now it also contained the same force that had made the marble and brass shine with use. It was the smell of people. In a good way. Sensing anything about the masses in a good way was a bit new for a copper. But Quill supposed that, right now, he was willing to take comfort from anything that didn't equate a mass of people with the horrors of the football stadium, and afterward.

He'd ordered the others to enter, observe and report back to him in an hour with any points of interest. Given their experience in the bookshop, he'd added that they were to leg it immediately away from anything seeming remotely dodgy. They were looking for raw evidence, but especially anything that could be used as a weapon against Losley. At first, it seemed to Quill that this was going to be a repeat of the clerics' visit. But then he spotted a little shadow of meaning on one table, a little flash of something being put into a box on another. There wasn't much of it . . . but it was here. He clicked the button on his phone to send a text that said, *We're on.*

Ross let a false smile appear occasionally on her face as she walked through the rows of tables, listening to the chatter of the people tending the stalls and their customers. Her team were grasping at straws, also running out of time. At least the chief's text indicated there was more here than there had been with the visit of the clerics. As she passed, nobody was talking about anything weird: tea, the weather, aches and pains, the way the world was going these days . . . this lot certainly weren't the youngest demographic. Business was bad. Table prices had gone up. Someone was wondering whether or not to start accepting credit cards, only then they'd just go and bloody replace them with something else. Ross found herself distantly enjoying listening to them. They seemed to be an everyday sort of people. There was a restful nostalgia about them, for something she'd never really experienced.

And she was feeling so tired. It was tempting to think of herself sitting one day behind a table like one of these, taking refuge in being part of a community like this, where nobody would look twice at her eyes, her bent nose. It was like she often wished she had a favorite record or movie, in the way other people did, rather than just favoring something that was on the radio or the television when she happened to be paying attention. Other people seemed to have things to belong to or things to be. Other people said they were enthusiasts, fans of, supporters of. But no, she chided herself, *That can't come true until you've finished this. And then, whatever happens, you have to find a way to deal with not getting revenge for Dad.* She couldn't imagine herself going back to being a normal analyst, even if they somehow got rid of the Sight. What she was hoping for, she now understood, was a happy ending. Which right now felt so impossible that it was almost like inviting death.

Every now and then she saw a flash of something interesting, but she didn't react, didn't let them see she'd noticed it. She stopped when she realized she was now feeling a couple of larger presences in the distance, one on each side of the hall. Following orders, she'd didn't head toward them, or even look, just kept on down the middle.

But then she felt something else right in front of her. At this end of the hall, along on the wall furthest from the stage, there sat a young woman: one in a row of three traders, the others uninteresting. A hand of tarot cards were spread out, face down, on a black cloth in front of her. The cards looked heavy and meaningful in her delicate hand. She looked up at Ross and it was obvious she was seeing her as just another potential punter. "Shall I read your fortune, my darling?"

Ross considered her orders for a moment, then she went to sit down.

Costain felt as if he hadn't really slept, only he supposed his head must have dropped for a couple of hours. He was in a world of rules now, when he really just wanted to cut loose and swagger again, and be the star of this picture and, God, maybe get a toot from somewhere. Only, yeah . . . that would be bad. He felt awkward around Sefton.

"What is it between you two?" Ross had asked the previous night, after the DC had left. Costain had shaken his head. "I read his Goodfellow reports," she continued. "He always said good things about you. It was reading between the lines there, and your own stuff, that made me think you were a shit."

Costain had been genuinely surprised. Then had found himself laughing. "What do you think now?"

She'd shrugged. "You're *our* shit."

Sefton hadn't been undermining him. That unfairness had been in his dreams that night. He had bigger things on his conscience list: things he couldn't deal with right now, because it'd be unsafe to do so. But every time he started to think of what words to use to Sefton, he found himself getting angry again. He still wanted to hate him. That entire house of pain was still there in his head, even though now it had no foundations. And that felt, somehow, even more annoying. And now he was standing beside him at the tea stall in the middle of the hall. When Sefton nodded to him, he let himself behave as if they were mates.

"Might as well look as if we're together," said Sefton, under his breath, as he pressed the tea bag against the side of his cup to try and force out a bit of flavor. "Seeing we're the only black guys in here."

"The New Age," agreed Costain, "does not recruit in line with best practice. What have you got?"

Sefton moved alongside him, so they were both facing the same way. "Three and nine, the two big noises in town, behind the rows of stalls on either side."

One of the aims of this expedition had been to find out if anyone who was in any way like Losley would come along to a New Age fair. "Yeah. Bloody hell, I can feel their presence, nowhere near on our witchy friend's level, but . . . yeah, there they are. *People*, though, you reckon, not your . . . spooky *things*?"

"At a guess, more like our old witchy friend."

"Keeping their distance from each other, like bosses would. You reckon they realize we're here?"

"Seven, two here and eight at the back have all checked me out, but I think that's because I is black. As for the level bosses . . . I don't know. All that's different about the four of us is . . . our advantage."

"If you want to call it that."

"I don't know why it'd show up. We don't look . . . particular, to each other."

Costain lowered his voice. "You want to try a walk-up with one? Just stroll in like we own the place? Like in that shebeen in Romford?"

Sefton looked startled. "That was fucking terrifying."

"This will be more so."

"Oh, right, this is 'cos marching straight in would be brave—would be 'the right thing to do?'"

Costain sighed. "Are you going to keep giving me shit about that?"

"If you want me to stop, Tone, you can always order me to do so."

"What's your question, ducks?"

Ross wondered if that was the fortune-teller's real accent. It was like something out of a soap opera—the chirpy cockney sparrow, a bit irritating, a bit false. She looked to be late thirties, ears pierced, with evidence of two earlier piercings, tattoo of some sort top left arm obscured by dress, natural brunette, green eyes, no visible fillings, about five foot two, hundred and ten pounds. That tightness of the skin about her. Thin not because of the gym, but with those biceps. This was the kind of woman Ross often saw in interview rooms.

She tried to affect a gentle, spiritual voice without being too hello-trees-hello-flowers about it. "Hi, I'm Lisa."

"And I am Madame Osiris, at your service." The woman added one of those crazy aitches onto "Osiris," as if she was something out of Dickens. She was dressed a bit like that too. That was a genuinely old dress, the wreck of a real Victorian ball gown. Frayed and stitched up, but not by a tailor. She looked like someone who once might have been seen staggering on stage at a music hall. What, was she actually from that time, keeping herself young? In the way that Losley's record stretched far back enough to accumulate all those bodies? No, this was a modern face. This woman was just trying really hard to seem antiquated. And Ross got the feeling it wasn't pretense just for this moment, but something she did all the time.

"Is that your real name?"

The woman raised an eyebrow. "Is that your question?"

"Oh, sorry." Ross considered her question. She was feeling the power in those cards, but did this woman know how to use it? What if she asked the obvious: *Where is Mora Losley?* That was assuming the cards actually worked to answer questions rather than just doing something else, such as make money vanish from her pocket. And that name would surely draw attention. This was their first encounter with another user, and who knew what alliances existed among them? This woman had been keeping her left hand under the table since Ross had arrived. She might suddenly attack Ross with something she had no defense against. "Okay," she said. "My question is: how can I win?"

"Right. What sort of divination would you prefer?" She made a swirling gesture with her right hand as she indicated the three choices, and Ross imagined for a second that she could feel something moving around her. "Tarot of London? *Book of Changes?* Tube Oracle?" Each gained weight and importance as she indicated it. So it wasn't the objects that were meaningful to the Sight, it was the woman—or rather what she was doing. Ross didn't let the excitement show on her face. This was definitely someone a bit like Losley, the first such they'd met. The *Book of Changes* was a small leather-bound volume, the Oracle seemed to be a cork-backed platter of wood that lay face down on the table, the Tarot were obviously the cards already spread.

"All three."

"That'll cost you."

"Okay." Actually, not so great an idea. They'd have to sign off on any expenses claims for operational budget. That meant the team would soon have to come up with some convincing lies about stuff like this.

"Cross my palm with silver. That'll be a carpet."

Ross had been brought up in London and had never heard that one. "Sorry?"

"Thirty quid. Blimey, you're far from the madding crowd, aintcha?" Good. The woman was used to setting herself above her punters, not afraid to be dismissive of them, and she had taken Ross to be as foolish as any other. She took Ross's money and it was gone into that left hand under the table. "Let's start with the Oracle," she decided, and turned over the piece of wood, which now was revealed to look suspiciously like a decorative place mat. It had a map of the London Underground on it, an old one that didn't have the DLR on it. The woman produced a metal pendulum, and set it twirling on a string right over it. "Ask your question again."

Rather self-consciously, Ross leaned across and spoke into the place mat. "How can I win?"

The woman suddenly let go of the pendulum, jerking it hard toward Ross's face, making her jump back. It hit the wood, rebounded violently and, against all possibility, dropped back into the middle of the map. Its pointed tip was precisely on—

"Baker Street, on the City side of the Hammersmith and City Line. That's the top side, by tradition. And all is tradition . . . tradition is all." She'd said that under her breath, like something she often repeated. "So, love, that's one way you can win. What or who do you most associate with Baker Street?"

Ross realized who that could mean. And probably not the bloke who'd had a hit with the song of that name. But not a great deal of help either. Still, something real seemed to be going on here.

"The line's interesting too. The City Line, that's memory . . ."

"Why is the City Line memory?"

"Tradition. Every line stands for something. Nobody knows why."

"Nobody?"

"So full of questions, and yet she's only paid for the one."

"I'm sorry, I do seem to keep breaking the rules." Ross let a little of her real desperation show on her face, put her hands on the table, as if coming to a big decision. "This is . . . very important to me. Please understand, any help . . . any at all. Look . . ." She put an upper-class note in her voice, suggesting there was the potential for a lot of money here. "I'd really appreciate it."

The woman smiled broadly, but Ross didn't let her satisfaction show on her own face. The bait had been taken. "That's what I'm here for, help and interpretation. You've got the right look about you, my darling: I can tell you'll ask the right questions. And you're bright enough to understand the answers. Bright enough to come to the likes of me, too, rather than any of these hangers-on." She indicated the innocent fortune-tellers to her left and right, busy with their own meaningless consultations.

"Yeah, I sensed you were different," Ross went on. "It's like there's . . . there's something about your voice."

The woman nodded sagely. "I said you was clever. You always sound out how a seer talks, my darling. Not all in whispers that won't break the surface, but with the proper London. Proper London isn't your darkie talk, like the kids do now. It's not your estuary English . . . Gawd, that grates on my ears. It's from *before*."

Not that much before, reckoned Ross. This movie Victoriana wasn't that old, nowhere near as old as London; it was just a gesture in that direction. Maybe that was something to do with degrees of power. This woman didn't sound anything like the insane mixture of tongues Losley had used. Oh, *speaking in tongues*, was that a thing, too? "You seem to know so much about these things."

"I know what my mum used, and her mum before her, and her mum before that, hetceterhah."

"Don't you ever want to change it? Make it more modern?"

The other woman shook her head quickly, her eyes widening. "You don't want change. Change is the enemy of memory, like my mum always said."

"Could . . . could I learn it?"

"Maybe. It's about the way you talk, the way you move. The past is the thing, and that's what the people in the know do, we follow the past."

Ross felt the truth of it in the woman's eyes. Here was someone who had the past always looming over her, wearing a parent's clothes. This lack of a present or a future was suddenly startling, and genuinely sad. She made herself focus on the job again. "You must have had a really hard life." That phrase, said right, at the right moment, always opened a few doors.

The woman paused, searching her face, clearly wondering how much she could trust her. Wanting to talk, though. *Come on, come on.* "Well, that's where you find the power, isn't it? Like my mum said, between the game and the gutter. Most of it works without you knowing what it means, or how it does it. You can sometimes work it out, just a bit, or sometimes it's just obvious, just being how things should be. You try and work one of those out with your school head on, you'll be up all night pondering the complexities of life. That's how the City Line is memory, it's one of those: you can kind of see how it works, but you can't *think* about it. All this stuff is just enough to get by. You don't get no riches out of it, not really. You start thinking you want that, you start asking for more, it quickly gets to be more than you can handle. More than the likes of me can, anyway."

Ross decided to take a risk. "You've obviously made . . . sacrifices."

The woman was silent for a moment, a real, hurt part of her rebelling, her eyes only just keeping faith with Ross, just the promise of money and being listened to keeping her on the hook. "What do you mean by that, now?"

"I've . . . read some old books . . ."

The woman thought for a further moment. Then she raised her left hand from below the table and put it down in front of her. All three middle fingers were missing, and there was scarring up and down the wrist, old wound on old wound, not in an angry, self-harming way, but something more like the endless search of the junkie for a suitable vein. "Of my own flesh and blood."

"I'm sorry," whispered Ross. "So you can't get . . . remembered?"

"What? You've read a bit, I see, but not enough. How would I make a big enough splash to get folk to remember me?"

"Well, Mora Losley seems to be . . ." Ross stopped as she felt the words bounce off some sort of tripwire in the air. She felt the confidence leave her face.

And now the woman was looking at her as if she was the scum of the earth, the promise broken, another betrayal in a whole life of them. "Oh," she said. "Oh, so you're a fucking rozzer."

"I'm not," said Ross quickly, letting the truth that she wasn't actually a police officer be a kind of lie. "If you really can see, you can see I'm not."

"Judas words. As good as." She was getting to her feet. She was about to march away, or maybe start yelling. And here was someone who might be able to find Losley for them directly! By answering just the one question! Ross had to keep her here. She remembered what the woman had said about doing what *seemed* appropriate. Copper gut assumption again: there was one thing that all the stories seemed to insist on.

"I paid you," she said. "We have a bargain. You can't break it."

The woman stopped. She now looked ferocious and, for a moment, Ross thought she was actually going to strike her down with something. But, finally, she sat down again and glared at her. "You cunt," she said.

"Yeah," nodded Ross. "I'll take that as a compliment."

Quill had systematically checked out all of the people of interest in the center of the hall, recording their appearance in his special notebook. There was something particular to them, they were the ones in the old clothes: an ancient waistcoat here, a battered greatcoat there. The fashions of everyone else, while occasionally baroque, didn't incline so much toward the distant past. When he made his way back through the fair, a few of them were no longer about, a couple had left their stalls completely unattended, having taken away with them any items whose presence had been obvious to the Sight. So this lot could detect the law, and not necessarily through extra-sensory means. They'd had that look about them, too, like the ones you hauled in from the pub for an identity parade, and took a quick shufti in the files while they were present. What all those folk also had had in common—and this shouldn't have come as much of a surprise—was that the objects of power he'd glimpsed had all been either of a particularly London character (a chipped coronation mug, a bunch of London Pride flowers) or could have been if only he'd known what he was looking at (a branch, a bracelet of thorns). So much for the silver handcuffs, although he supposed that, since it was blessed by the Met chaplain, they did have in their possession some very London holy water. Pity that Chamsa wasn't local, too. He went to the ticket seller at the door, and was introduced to the organizer, a thin man with a ponytail, in sandals and a business suit. Quill followed him into an office, for a more formal introduction involving his warrant card.

"Oh," the man said. "Oh, now, is this about Mora Losley? What that woman does has nothing to do with these peaceful practices going back to the time of—"

"Yes, sir, I'm sure. This is just a routine check, nothing to worry about. I'd like to be able to say that the . . . what would you call it, the occult community?"

"The New Age community!"

"That you've been offering us brilliant support and a nice cup of tea. So, if I could just take a quick look at your list of who's at what table . . ."

The list showed two big tables, on either side of the hall, each rented to a major dealer. Quill wondered therefore if maybe what he was feeling there was quantity rather than quality, as it were. He gave the list back to the organizer, thanked him for his helpfulness, told him his silence would be appreciated, and headed off to have a quick butcher's at one of the tables identified.

This was indeed where the professionals were based: real swords, glassware, fabrics, paintings in frames, unicorns and dragons. It made Quill sigh a bit: they were among this terrifying weight of people and history, and yet here were vague guesses at it being regurgitated as tourist tat. Oh, so no change there, then. There was nothing specific about most of it, nothing particularly . . . London. The table was staffed by young men and women in T-shirts bearing the dealer's logo, with an older man, a bit of a pot belly on him, in charge. Nothing odd anywhere, and certainly not among the merchandise. So where was the huge sense of unease about this table coming from? It seemed to be located further behind . . . Quill saw that, at the rear of the displays, there was a stack of the boxes this stuff had been transported in. Unnoticed by the staff, someone was rooting through them, not looking as if he had any particular purpose, but more like a tramp searching for food. He was a big lad with broad shoulders on him, wearing a tattered military coat, a garment that looked as if it was from the Boer War. Woolen gloves, so no fingerprints. He had that special sense of meaning about him. The Sight knew him, and he made Quill afraid. But Quill had been up close with Losley, and had also been in the presence of whatever that smiling man was, and he didn't rate this bloke as being in that league. He took a step closer, leaving only a couple of punters between himself and the man who was obviously keeping himself unseen by the traders seated in front of him.

Suddenly the man looked up and sniffed the air. He turned, and Quill felt his gaze sweep the crowd. Any second, he was going to spot him.

Quill felt afraid, but he was more afraid of looking afraid. He didn't want to experience how whatever this man was going to threaten him with might chime in with the emptiness inside him and with the previous impotence he'd suffered at the hands of this lot, further diminishing who he tried to be.

"Hoi!" Quill bellowed. "I want a word with you, sonny Jim!"

That terrible gaze engulfed him, and the fear accompanied it. But, a moment later, with a crash of boxes—

The man was running for the door!

Quill felt an old energy come flooding into him. He sprinted off after him.

Costain had been surprised to find that the dangerous gang boss he'd had in his head when he'd considered this move had turned out to be a gawky young man in a T-shirt advertising an occult shop. He seemed to be in charge of this large stall that had so many punters flocking to it. Sefton had then popped over to check out the other side of the hall, and reported back about the other shop, that what they were actually looking at here was a room seemingly shaped not by occult power but by money.

So where had the power gone? Costain couldn't feel it now they'd got here. It almost seemed as if it was . . .

"Hiding," muttered Sefton under his breath. "It knows we're here."

"How do you know?"

"You get used to this stuff. Just tune into it."

"Do you?"

"It's now under something . . . or someone on that stall's gone dark on us."

Costain summoned all his confidence. And, yeah, that felt like a blanket that had a lot of holes in it now. He straightened up and began walking as if he had a gun on him. He headed straight for the young man, and noted Sefton peeling off behind him to check out the merchandise further along the stall. "Hey," he began, ". . . no, never mind about the queue, I'm talking to you, son. Who's in charge here?"

"*The Book of Changes.*" The woman sat opposite Ross, staring coldly at her, and held up the small volume. "Pick a number between one and three hundred and sixty-eight."

Ross took a while to consider. She was wondering if she should text a message to the others to converge on her position. After their business was concluded, she was going to have to try to apprehend this woman. "Two hundred and . . . seven."

"One to three?"

"Three."

"One to seventy?"

"Three."

"Right," the other woman said tersely, "that's Fives Court. That's the first part of your answer."

"Is that book . . . the *London A–Z*?"

The woman was silent. She clearly wasn't going to offer any more than she had to. "Again." This was even more like the sort of divination which might have found them Losley. Ross gave her three more random numbers. "Four Seasons Close. You'll 'win' by favoring the first over the second. That's your answer. Five is better than four."

"What does that mean: five is better than four?" *Four what? What was five?* "Do the locations have anything to do with it? Does the rest of the address matter?"

The woman remained silent.

"Listen," said Ross, "you know we're after Mora Losley, and you surely can't agree with what she does. You could help save those children—"

"I won't help you. Not your kind. Never."

Ross pursed her lips. "Okay," she said, "let's go for the Tarot of London."

Quill burst out of the hall into the corridor outside. The man he was chasing was just ahead. "Police!" he yelled. The ragged red-faced man spun on his heel and, for a moment, Quill thought he was going to stop. But he was fumbling to get something out of his pocket. He found it and snapped it up to head height, pointing it straight at Quill. Who threw himself into cover behind a pillar

227

adjacent to the wall. He hadn't got a good look at the thing, but it was close enough to a gun to make him move.

"I really do just want a word with you!"

But, as he said it, something enormous rushed at him from behind. Quill was hauled away from the wall and thrown into the middle of the corridor. He reflexively put his arms around his head and staggered, aware that he was being battered left and right by . . . air. Air carrying leaflets and rubbish and cardboard boxes. But what was worse was the anger of it: the air was hot and furious and needed something, was missing something as much as Quill was. It was nothing to do with this man, he realized. The man was just . . . using it. That understanding let him find his feet. He could hardly see the bloke now, just a shape in front of him. He couldn't see how he was producing this effect with whatever he'd grabbed. The beating around Quill's head got worse, and there were stones now, and suddenly one shot through his guard and struck him across the temple.

Quill focused all his anger on the man in front of him, put his head down, gave a roar and charged.

"I don't know what you're talking about!" The young stall manager was looking at Costain fearfully.

"Don't give me that. Where is he? Where's the boss?"

"Barry's back at the shop—"

"Fuck me, do you want me to tell him how you were like this? You know what I'm talking about, 'cos if you didn't, you wouldn't be scared: instead you'd be angry. I'm talking about—"

"London stuff," said Sefton, arriving beside them as if his boss had called him over, looking bigger somehow than Costain was used to seeing him. "London rules, you feel me?"

Costain was sure there was a crowd gathering around them now. But not one of them questioned the basis on which he was verbally abusing this poor kid. This was like a market where the stallholders paid protection money. A lot of people here knew vaguely that there was another class of people who came round here sometimes, and so did this kid. And all Costain had to do now was keep carrying on like one of those.

"We . . . we don't have . . . We're just . . . paraphernalia."

"I've got all the crystal unicorns I want, boy. You know what I'm talking about."

"Are . . . are you the ones who were going to collect the package?"

Costain looked skywards in apparent relief, and bumped fists with Sefton. "Finally!"

The man went to look under the table. He came back a moment later, carrying what looked like a bit of flat red stone wrapped in a sheet of paper. "It's nothing to do with us," he said. "He just left it here and said someone would come asking for it."

Costain nodded as if this was all entirely expected, and took the package. "You can now go about your business, my friend," he said. "Good day to you." He led Sefton away from the stand, and the crowd parted meekly for them.

"Wish we could have asked for a description," remarked Sefton.

Costain just about managed not to snap at him. He was holding the paper-wrapped package between two fingers, hoping that he hadn't messed up any fingerprints left on it. By means of the Sight, he could feel the burden of something notable, the strange weight of it in his hand. "You feel anything?"

"Yeah. It's a tiny bit different to what we felt from across the room, so I reckon we must have felt whoever left that here, and then that feeling changed a bit, without me noticing, 'cos then I was just feeling the presence of this."

"So he got away under cover of it?"

"I think so."

The piece of paper was secured by a small piece of sticky tape. He laid the package on a shelf beside a window, got out his multi-knife, and sliced through it. The stone was revealed to be a fragment of red tile, with faded decoration down one edge. Costain took a step back as the paper flapped open. He saw that Sefton had felt it too. The weight of it had suddenly increased. That was the feeling of something hiding that they'd experienced. On the paper was written a message in a large, scrawled hand:

You smell of modern shit. Leave us alone. We smell
death near you soon. You brought that on yourselves.

"Death near us soon," said Sefton. "Well, there's a shock." He put his hand over the tile, as if trying to gauge the forces involved. "I wonder," he said, "if this would hurt someone who didn't have the Sight?" He lowered his hand closer and closer to the tile. "It's not getting any stronger."

"Just leave it."

"If it can hurt us, maybe it could hurt Losley." He touched his palm to the tile quickly and then raised it again.

"Don't fucking do that! Did I tell you that you could do that?"

"Like you'd know one way or the other." And there was that furious look again, the real Sefton now that they were out of character. "I'm the one who's been looking into this."

"You're not planning on recognizing my rank at all, then?"

Sefton seemed to pause at that. He didn't want to say it out loud—which was just like him. His eyes locked on Costain's, his finger reaching toward the tile again. And suddenly with a yell he withdrew it. Blood went flying from his finger.

A drop of it landed on the tile.

And motion blurred everything as something battered Costain's entire body.

"A Shaft of Light in Paddington Station." The fortune-teller laid down a card that showed a painting of just that, looking like an old advert or something. The light looked summery, with dust motes hanging in it. "Something Glimpsed from the Underground." That was the image of what must have been a tube carriage window, with a brickwork arch outside it, also a green and blue light that spoke of meadows gleaming through it. "The Sacrifice of Tyburn Tree." She slapped the third card down over the first. She'd made a pass of her hands over the cards before they'd begun, and they'd regained the same lustre of importance that they'd had when Ross had first glimpsed them. Now they looked . . . delicious, meaningful like Christmas, a colorful present that had been unwrapped, a terrible pang of nostalgia that was like the prospect of happiness and repose she'd felt from the rest of the fair. But this third card looked terrible, too, and it connected with her. It was a man hanging by his neck, in silhouette, other terrible wounds having been done to him, judging from how the crowd, in faux-medieval dress, all around him were pointing at various parts of his body. The fixture from which he hung sprouted many such nooses, like it was a proper tree, and rooks flew all around it.

"What does it mean?" she asked.

The woman looked angry, but some explanation seemed to be required here to fulfill the bargain. "The first two are indications of different sorts of hope: summer and autumn. The third is what the hope is actually about."

"The hanged man?" She remembered that name from TV shows. It had always made her look up.

"These aren't like normal Tarot cards, which are for the rest of—" She stopped herself, and for a moment Ross thought it was because she'd already said too much, but it seemed that she'd noticed something else about her subject and now she was smiling, revealing gaps where teeth should be—another sacrifice, Ross guessed. "Oh," she said, "this is important to you personally?"

Ross didn't want to show it. "The man being hanged . . . is a sacrifice?"

"Does this cause you pain? Are the details going to make you suffer?"

"Yes."

"Then you listen here, copper, and I'll tell you all about it. The berk on the card, he's had three things done to him. The three-fold death, they call it: he's been sacrificed three times. A death wound to the head. A death wound to the side. A hanging to kill him too." The woman was gleefully examining her face. "Makes his soul like gold, that does—commends him to the fire."

"To the fire?"

"So I'm told. Sends him to Hell as solid currency. You get a lot in return for a three in one."

Ross felt the room swaying around her. She felt the knife in her pocket. She suddenly had in her mind a picture of her dad's face tilted up against the ceiling rose. The bruise on his head. The wound in his side.

Quill's head collided with the ragged man's stomach. With a cry, the other fell back, and whatever was in his hand went flying. The buffeting winds shut off. Quill leaped to grab him. He got his hands clenched among the dirty ancient coat, and slammed the man down onto the marble floor, hauling one hand behind his back, pulling the handcuffs from his own pocket. But then he realized that he was sitting on top of just a dirty old coat with nothing in it. And then on top of nothing at all. He was crouching on bare marble, his arse in the air, handcuffs jingling from one hand. He looked up to see New Age punters walking past him, raising eyebrows.

He got to his feet and looked quickly around the floor. There they were. He grabbed a fold of his own coat to pick them up in. Then, feeling nothing very dangerous from them, though there was definitely power of some kind, he took them in his bare hand. They were two thin paddles . . . or vanes. They were made of very old metal, with ancient decorations, like something from out of a long barrow that should now be in a museum. And in his hands they felt useless.

*

Sefton lay on the hard floor, his head ringing. He felt as if he was back in the playground. He'd just been thrown to the ground by something with that same effortless power over him. It had felt as he imagined being caught in an explosion would feel. But it had left him . . . he made himself breathe deeply . . . with his ribs intact, and . . . he rolled over . . . his hands were just bruised where he'd landed on them. He managed to look over at Costain, who was pushing himself to his feet, looking quickly around him as if he might be attacked again. Sefton himself slowly stood up. The piece of paper was blowing away in shreds, departing too swiftly to catch, too swiftly for normality, and all that had been left of the tile was dust that was vanishing into a red stain on the floor.

The crowd was staring at them, though trying not to. What had they witnessed? Not as much as the two policemen had. That had been an explosion meant only for those with the Sight, a silent warning—something that felt as if it had been put together hastily by an anonymous member of a subculture that didn't want to be policed. "That was my fault," Sefton said.

"Yeah," nodded Costain, looking angry, "it was. Let's get some details on this fucker." And he led them off to find the stall manager.

"I don't know nothing about that," the fortune-teller was saying, but Ross wasn't listening any more. "Our bargain is fulfilled."

Ross got to her feet at the same instant the woman did, intent on apprehending her.

The woman glared at her. "We haven't had the law bothering us for a few years now. We stayed out of sight of them. But then they was got rid of, and so will you be. That's the way the wheel's turning."

Ross gave her a hard stare. "Try and get away, I'll have you." She could hear running feet behind her. The others had finally come to find her. She kept eye contact with the woman, who produced a small knife that was too small to make Ross back off. She felt like reaching into her own pocket and comparing blades.

But, no, she had to keep her authority. "What're you planning on doing with the potato peeler?"

The fortune-teller suddenly drew it across her own palm, and cried out at the pain. Ross took a step forward, to try to stop the woman doing herself any more harm. But then it occurred to her that she hadn't paid proper attention to the floor. It was really interesting, so she got down on to her hands and knees and, dimly aware of the rest of her team arriving, she settled on the perfect spot, a brass line at the edge of where the wood and marble flooring met. She raised her head back, smiled at the others, and—

Costain threw himself at her and sent her rolling into the table before she could dash her brains out. The table flew toward the woman. He was desperately holding Ross down.

"Let go!" she yelled. "I have to—!" And then normal awareness rushed back into her head. "The suspect!" she shouted. "Stop her!"

Costain eased off just enough to see that Quill and Sefton had already pushed the table aside—

To reveal that the woman had gone, like a dove out of a conjuring trick, taking her equipment with her, leaving only a spray of blood across the white cloth. There came cries and shouts from all around, as people who did and didn't know the truth of it gasped.

EIGHTEEN

They sat on the steps outside, the Houses of Parliament looming behind them, the office lights coming on in the afternoon twilight. Big Ben began to strike four, and Quill could swear he heard the echoes reverberating through this new London he was learning about. They sounded to the depths and resonated back off the sky. They rang through people and memory. "The woman at that table turns out to have paid them in cash and provided a false address. Bloody sketchy description you got of that bloke who left the . . . bomb or whatever it was."

"I reckon he disguised himself," said Costain, "like Losley did."

He looked to Ross. He'd have expected her to have got her laptop out by now, but she was just staring into the distance. "All right," he said, "so that woman told Ross that we're going to have to be like Sherlock Holmes to win: hardly a revelation. She also said that five is better than four, whatever that means. We've also discovered that there used to be some form of law enforcement among this community, but that's gone now. And we've found that stuff associated with London, made in London, about London—that stuff seems to have power in London. I got these things too." He took the vanes from his pocket and, meeting Sefton's gaze, handed them over to him.

"And there's going to be a death close to us," muttered Sefton, accepting them. He'd retreated into his shell again.

Quill closed his eyes for a moment, as that statement put a weight in his stomach weirdly beyond what he'd expect to feel at a threat. He felt he should know what it was about, and was feeling vulnerable that he didn't. "Yeah, but . . . later for that. Lisa, what aren't you telling us?"

She composed herself for a moment. "My dad," she said, "he was Toshack's 'good sacrifice.' He was sent to Hell, and Toshack got Losley's services in return."

They were all silent. Quill looked at Sefton, who was silently disapproving of their terminology again.

"Which makes me realize something," she said, making him look back. "Everybody thought my dad committed suicide. Including the coroner. So this stuff can close cases that should have remained open. We've only instructed the databases to look through open cases, so how about we look at closed ones, too?" Quill made to put a hand on her shoulder, but her expression deterred him.

That evening, Quill oversaw the rewriting of the Ops Board. "Speaking in tongues" and the three items Ross had consulted through the fortune-teller were added to the Concepts list, as were "London items," "old law," "five over four," "tile bomb," "vanes" and "someone close." "Remembered" had been expanded to include Sefton's ideas about the memories of the masses and the dead. Photofits for new suspects Fortune-Teller, Windy and Bomber had been put up, unconnected to Losley so far.

"We're going to end up with a whole other board just for speculation," he observed.

But then, with shaking hands, Ross took down the speculative card under Toshack, picked up a piece of card marked "Alf Toshack," and attached it to Rob's picture by a victim thread. Then she stood looking at it for a few minutes, as if she could rip up time and have him at her mercy by sheer fury.

*

236

West Ham were playing at home on Wednesday evening. It took until Monday afternoon for the list of closed cases of missing or murdered children, enormous as it was, to be sent to the Portakabin. It wasn't just a computer file, since Quill had asked for the search parameters to go back to the very start of when records were kept. A van arrived, with two archive clerks from Hendon carrying boxes of papers. The computer file included a lot of cases where the perpetrators were currently serving jail time. Ross, who until then had been obsessively trawling the list of bills again, started there, getting the others to begin on the physical files.

"One thing I'm after," she said, "is Caucasian, red-headed, parents of three siblings. The parents of those kids in the cauldron. With the older files, you're looking to match up the descriptors we've got of the older victims longer ago, particularly the siblings taken in threes. The cases are now closed, so the authorities at the time will have come to a solid conclusion as to what happened to them. We're looking to prise that open, and see Losley."

Quill didn't suggest that it was a meager hope. He made them stop every hour for a cuppa, and they worked on into the night. Until—

"Got one," said Ross. Quill and the others went quickly over to see. "Tereza Horackova was her name, a redhead—look at that photo. She was serving time in Holloway prison for multiple murder of children, before committing suicide a couple of years ago." She went on to the Internet. "She was convicted of killing her own children," she continued, her voice starting to crack. "Three of them, and the ages fit, but she always insisted she didn't have kids." She looked up the DNA swab details and e-mailed them to Dr. Deb before his office closed for the night. "I've got her home address."

Quill didn't want to argue with that look on her face. Instead he went to get his coat.

The house in Acton was now occupied by a Bangladeshi family who spoke little English and were reluctant to let them inside.

They managed to find a translator from the local nick, and that way eventually got granted access. They did only a cursory search, but Quill had got what he needed from the garden, where there were the faintly glowing remains of soil pushed to the side of where a patio had been installed.

"She kept rigorously to her story," said Ross, "insisting that she had no children. She couldn't explain the many signs suggesting the opposite, up to and including the slide and playhouse in her garden. Losley came here all those years ago, she took those children, and she made that woman forget them. That's how she manages to steal kids and nobody notices."

"Bloody excellent," said Quill. "Coppers are bound to remember cases like that. We'll find a few more."

"It's just a pity," said Costain, "that this is close enough to Losley's Willesden house for her to have operated from there, so we don't have a sniff of another base."

Quill put out the call to every nick in London: they were after current or recent cases where parents of missing children claimed not to have any kids. Especially anything that had just come in. Ross had found them something vital with that obsessive determination of hers. It put hope back into him. But, as Quill walked out of the gate of the semi, he was struck by something: a sudden fear that made him look back. He paused, his eyes searching the garden, finding nothing. It was . . . just that feeling of missing something. Again, that echo resonating inside him. Sooner or later he'd figure out what it meant. Maybe all this was just telling him that as a person he was built on nothing. Well, he knew that, and he'd keep going anyway. He headed back to the car and ordered the others to go and get some sleep.

On Tuesday morning they had a reply from the pathologist, stating that the swab record from Horackova was indeed a match for the mitochondrial DNA found in the kids in the cauldron. Quill called up the arresting officer of the time and filled him in, just in case

Horackova had relatives who should be contacted and could be interviewed. But there were none. And, so far, there were no replies from any of the London nicks that had been forwarded his message about anomalous perp statements. "If we don't get a lead by tomorrow night," he told his team, "I've put a plan in place for any footballer that scores a hat-trick." He handed a folder to Ross. "It's not much, but it's all we've got."

"I didn't think you were going to call me," said Joe, eyeing Sefton over his pint. They'd been talking about pretty well nothing for an hour. And Sefton was getting more and more tired, and more and more certain of what he needed. And he was so aware of "*We smell death near you soon*," and he needed to find some way past all of this.

"I've been busy."

"You *look* like . . ."

"Yeah."

"Do you want to tell me anything?"

"Yeah." So he told Joe everything. Copper: he showed him his warrant card, because he wanted to establish a baseline for the shit to follow. UC. Losley. Everything. He was totally breaking the rules, thus leaving himself entirely vulnerable, but, what the fuck? Joe's expression grew worried, then scared. "Walk away if you want to," Sefton said. "I need to tell somebody or I'll go mental. I need someone to talk to about this, to bounce some ideas off, and . . . just to talk to. I'm not being listened to, and we're running out of time. It's match day tomorrow and we might be going to hear about some kids being fucking *boiled alive*."

"So this is why a lot of the news about Losley makes no sense."

"You believe me?"

"I think . . . I'll reserve judgment. Maybe this is . . . a sort of a metaphor for something, but I saw you when you met 'Jack' that time, and you weren't faking that. The least I can do is listen."

Sefton grabbed him by the back of his head and kissed him.

"Okay," he said after, "maybe that's not the least I can do."

On match day, Ross woke to her alarm, aware that she'd had terrible dreams, but not remembering them. She went in to work with her iPod playing loudly in the car. Not using the radio, because then she'd hear about Losley. She didn't want to hear about Losley until she walked into the Portakabin, and then it was all about Losley. Because at that point she could *do* something.

Do something about Losley? It seemed even more deferred now. That discontinuity was sinking deeper and deeper into her, so she felt that it would one day reach her heart and kill her. What did getting Losley matter, if her dad was in Hell? Continual torment. No passing of time. No ending. She had felt it distantly. She had heard Costain describe it. She could imagine it. And imagine it she did, till she stopped herself. She thought instead of the kids they were trying to save. Then she felt guilty. And so that cycle went round and round.

The newspapers were full of anticipation, a pile of them sitting on the table. That Losley face was everywhere, today looking like a badge in the top right-hand corner of the *Star*. The *Sun* had put a green filter over the photo.

"It's as if she's become a cartoon character," said Quill. "Except people are also terrified of her. Families are taking their kids out of school and moving off to the country—"

"The rich ones," said Costain.

"—but the public deal with it by making her into . . . I don't know, Mr. Magoo with murder too. She's bloody *everywhere*." He must have seen the look on Ross's face, because he led her over to where Sefton had placed his holdall on one of the tables.

"If we find her today," said Sefton, stepping forward, "we're as ready as we can be."

"If this was an episode of *CSI*, we could use that single photo of her to find her in databases, crowd scenes, bloody . . ." Quill waved a hand to finish his sentence. He looked as if he'd had a few last night.

"I think that feeling," said Ross, "of not being able to control things is why people started doing stuff like Losley does, way back when. That's why it's *town* stuff. Everyone going back and forth in the city, doing deals, getting one up on each other, when maybe you were used to how it was in the country, just working your land and stuff, same thing happening every year . . . The city makes you want it *now*, makes you want it *easier*. But the bureaucracy of the city also grinds against that, makes you look for a way to get round it."

"Dark satanic mills," said Sefton. "But the city *changes* all the time. And the users we've met dress *old*. It's as if, long ago, a few people worked out some ways to use this stuff, which worked back in the day, and they've been passing those methods on. Maybe this lot are bottom of the food chain. They're just . . . living in the ruins, playing out the same old games."

"They're like junkies," said Costain. "They're not really using it. It's using them."

"Maybe they're still getting used to their new freedom, if someone was previously policing them. I wonder who that was? The bigger dogs? I think Losley's the only one of those we've had a scent of."

"It's a pity," said Ross, "that we can't tell the public about the forgetting, however she manages that."

"Thankfully," said Quill, who had been reflexively checking his e-mails again, "coppers have less imagination than the general public. We've got something here."

Late last night, Terry and Julie Franks, who lived in Brockley, had been arrested on suspicion of murder. Mr. Franks's brother, puzzled, amazed and then outraged when he'd continually asked about his nephew and niece, and been rebutted with increasing vehemence, had finally gone to his local nick. "'Cos the Franks," said Quill, "have insisted they don't have any children!"

"She wouldn't want to keep them for long," said Costain, "so she's taken them ready for tonight."

"I'd say she won't kill them until she knows she needs to," said Ross. "She must know that taking them, even with this forgetting bit, is the most dangerous thing she does. Most of the long boiling process must therefore happen post-mortem. No hat-trick, she hangs on to the kids for next time."

Quill got on the phone and started yelling. "No, tomorrow's not good enough. I want them put in a fucking van and brought over here for interview right now. You read the papers, don't you? Yeah, bit of a hurry on here!"

Sefton was pinning a map of London to the wall. He stuck a red pin in Willesden. Ross realized he was indicating where Losley's houses were, and she looked up the other addresses to add further pins. Sefton finally added a speculative white pin at the Franks' address in Brockley. "Look at how far away that is," he said.

"Indicative of a new base," said Costain. "Fucking A."

Ross brought up the council bill records for Brockley, and started spooling through them, though that was going to take her hours.

Quill suddenly shouted incoherently. "Patterns!" he continued. "Patterns with the victims! This is what I've been missing! Frigging *map*!"

Ross swiftly brought up a list of where every victim with a pile of the soil in their garden had lived. They grabbed yellow-headed pins and, between them, covered the map.

Then they stepped back.

And inclined their heads and squinted, as if they were looking at a particularly difficult piece of modern art.

"It's sort of like a . . . jumping horse," said Sefton. "Maybe?"

"There's a kind of concentration around . . ." began Quill.

"Storks on the roof," said Ross.

"Eh?"

"Is there a genuine correlation between number of children born in Dutch houses and the number of storks that come to nest on the roof, supposedly bringing babies?" said Ross. "The maths says, 'God, yes'; it screams out at you. But that's because bigger houses equals richer families, equals more incentive to breed. At least, that was the case back when rich people did breed more. Here all it means is that, yes, this pattern isn't completely random, there is a concentration here, but that's only because those are upmarket areas where footballers and gang bosses might live. Money is a hidden power too. And everything's within reasonable reach of Losley's known addresses. Correlation does not necessarily equal causation."

Quill slumped, and Ross thought she could see something terrible appear in his face. That wasn't what he'd been missing. And whatever that was, it was getting harder for him all the time.

"Pity," said Costain. "I've always wanted to be working on a case where the dots on a map formed a pattern."

Ross called the Brockley nick, and got photos of the suspects' house sent over. "Look there," she said, for there was that glowing soil shape in their garden.

The match was due to kick off at 8 p.m. And, of course, it was going to be broadcast live on Sky and Radio Five. Purely for the sport, of course. As the hours ticked away, and all four of them continued looking through the council records for the boroughs around and including Brockley, and started pulling out the many sighting reports of Losley from around that area, Ross found that she was developing stomach cramps. It hadn't even occurred to her to eat, and she wondered if any of the others were managing to do so. It took until bloody nineteen-thirty for a van to arrive outside the Portakabin, bringing with it the two suspects, Mr. and Mrs. Franks. Their brief had arrived also, Janice Secombe from Mountjoy's, stepping carefully out of her car and raising an eyebrow at the stretch of mud between her and the cabin itself.

"Ross," said Quill, picking up the tape recorder he'd borrowed from Gipsy Hill that morning, "you're with me in interview room one. By which I mean the far corner here. You two, keep checking those records and loom menacingly in the background."

Quill knew Secombe from many such encounters. She was obviously loving this bizarre lack of the usual form, knowing how it'd play before a jury. But Quill was pretty sure these two weren't destined for a trial. He set the tapes running with all due procedure, then he studied the suspects sitting across the table from Ross and himself.

For a moment, in his mind's eye, he saw blood bursting from their faces.

This was going to be such a long shot. Despite the briefing notes they'd prepared on a few things they could have a go at, there were whole areas which, especially with a brief present, could not be touched on. Not without having these two immediately set loose with one hell of a story to tell the press, one which would snare the team and stop them from having the freedom to do what they had to.

"My clients," began Secombe, "are the victims in a missing persons case—"

"No we're bloody not!" said Terry Franks.

"—who have suffered severe trauma—"

"We haven't!"

"They . . . agree with me, however, that there is no justification therefore for treating them like criminals. And I personally fail to see what they might have to do with the case you're obviously pursuing here."

That aspect must be freaking her out. They'd hidden the Ops Board before this lot had arrived, but Secombe knew which of them was working on what. Terry and Julie Franks looked as if they hadn't slept recently. They were both in their late twenties, him with a number-two haircut that was growing out a bit, earring, white jacket, T-shirt with something pretty on it. If his mobile rang, it'd be something R & B. She was in a gray top that looked as if she'd worn it for three days. Layers in the hair, but no make-up today. She hadn't been bothered. She wasn't trying to put on a front, and hadn't even done the tiny modest stuff that she would have done to attempt to indicate she deliberately wasn't trying to put on a front.

Innocent, both of them. He wouldn't normally have let that supposition mean anything, because you always worked the facts in front of your accumulated experience, and he had in the past met many seemingly innocent fuckers who'd done some terrible shit. But in this case he knew it to be genuine, and—had he a heart to break—it would have done so. They were saying something to him about himself, but in ways he couldn't understand.

"All right," said Terry angrily, "what's going on?"

"They keep saying we've got kids," interrupted his wife, still trying to be reasonable while he was already worked up. There was half a laugh in her voice. "It's bureaucracy gone mad! As if we wouldn't know. But I'm glad we can sort it out now. It's some sort of error in the paperwork."

"I'm sorry, Mrs. Franks," said Quill, "but it isn't."

Terry immediately started to speak, but the brief cut across him. She said, "We're still trying to establish the facts in this case, aren't we?"

Ross put copies on the desk of what the brief and the Franks pair had already seen: birth certificates for Charlie, aged five, Hayley, six, and Joel, seven.

"We keep saying there must be a mistake," Terry continued. "Just the same name . . . maybe they used to live at our address."

Ross, with no expression at all, put the photos on the table. They'd been taken both from what had been found during a search of the Franks' house and from the albums of the children's uncle and other relatives. They showed Terry and Julie with three happy, messy, gurning children at a theme park, by the sea side, on the deck of a cross-Channel ferry, wearing stupid hats.

The couple stared at the photos, as dumbfounded by them now

as they must have been when first they saw them. "That's just it—why would someone go to all that bother," Terry protested, "to Photoshop these? We are obviously being set up for something!"

"If you don't have any children," said Quill, "why is your house full of toys? Why, on several occasions during the last year, did you hire your niece as a babysitter?"

"First Craig, and now you lot!" The man was getting shrill, as if he could fight reality back to what was normal. "We get so worked up, we can't hardly hear what people are saying, because they keep going on and on! You think we might just let these kids you think we have wander off, and forget about them? Forget about them after they went missing? Our own kids? Do you really think anyone would do that? Is that how far you think we've sunk?"

"Everyone is looking at us funny," said Julie, more carefully, "and there's something they're not saying. It's like they think we're . . . pedophiles. And we're not! We're terrified of people like that."

"Why?" said Ross.

The couple were suddenly silent.

"Why would a couple without children be terrified of pedophiles?"

The silence continued, while their mouths worked as if they were trying to find something to say.

Julie finally raised her hands. "I have . . . been thinking about this," she said. "We're not . . . Whatever you may think of us, we're not stupid."

"I didn't say you were," said Quill gently.

"I remember buying the . . . I suppose you'd call them toys. Over, well, years. I remember buying this . . . junior tennis set from the pound shop. Just this pair of yellow plastic rackets and a soft ball. Perfect, I thought. Only now . . . now I can see that seems weird, because we don't use it, do we?"

"It's not a crime," muttered Terry, "whatever this is, it's not a crime."

"And I have to . . . to try really hard to think about that. It's like if I don't think about it, it goes away again. Like my brain doesn't want to think about it, because maybe there's something . . . terrible. Please . . . Please tell us. Are we . . . living wrong? Is there something . . . *wrong* with us?"

"Mrs. Franks—" began the brief.

"There can't be something wrong with *both* of us!" explained Terry. "Everyone thinks we're lying—"

"I don't," said Quill, causing the brief to look startled.

He put a photo of Losley on the table. They'd wondered if making this connection would get some huge and terrible reaction out of the couple, so they'd left it to last.

"Who's that?" said Terry.

"I gather you haven't been paying much attention to the news?"

"We read the paper," said Julie, sounding as if she wondered what they were being accused of *now*. "The *Mirror*, every day, cover to cover. Though Terry starts at the back, don't you?"

"Then you should remember Mora Losley, the witch of West Ham? She's been featured on the front page six or seven times, as the single biggest story."

The couple glanced at each other, and then back at Quill, a look on their face that was half fearful and half wondering if he was joking.

"Never heard of her," said Terry.

Quill and Ross stared at each other. And then at Costain and Sefton, who were coming over to boggle at this incredible news.

They all said it together. "Oh . . ."

They sent the Franks and their brief over to the nick for a cuppa, the uniforms from the van escorting them. The football had started, and Sefton set the PC to stream it, so it became a noise in the background. Ross realized that they'd hear any goals just from the crowd volume going up. It caused sheer stress, but they had to do it.

"She made them forget *her* too," said Quill.

"Which means it wasn't a snatch-off-the-street job," said Ross.

247

"We don't know how it went with Horackova, but the only reason I can see for making people forget Losley herself is that they would have seen or known something important about her, something that could be used to help us."

"Maybe we can hypnotize them or something. Maybe that's exactly what she does."

"Long-term, maybe, but does science even work against this? If hypnotism is even science. No, fuck that . . . fuck that. The shape of the hole can tell us. The hole is what she took from their memories; we have to think about that shape." Ross realized she was pacing back and forth, waving her hands wildly. But sod how she must appear. "*How* does she make them forget?"

There was a sudden roar from the PC. *"And it's one–nil to Norwich City!"* yelled commentator Alan Green. *"Tony Ballackti, that's five goals in three games for him. And, only five minutes in— who'd bet against him doing it again in this match?"* And that sarcastic suggestion in his voice echoed what everyone else in the country was feeling. *"Some people in the crowd are already shouting for them to take him off, but they're being roared down by the Norwich fans. Ballackti himself is shaking his head. He wants more goals! They say any hat-trick player has got a helicopter to take him out of here straight after the match, that Cardiff themselves have hired private security. They say lots of things but they're not telling us which of them is true."*

"Exactly," said Quill.

Ross found that the thoughts in her head had now jammed. A terrible silence reigned.

Then Sefton kept going, and she loved him for that. She sagged against the wall and listened.

"She must use one of her bloody gestures on them," he said. "Nobody's done anything that wasn't line of sight, even if you count text messages. She appeared in their garden, and . . . no, like with Toshack, she couldn't do it through the wall. She needed to get inside—"

Ross let out a little noise from her throat and considered.

Eighty-three more minutes. Two more goals. A prolific scorer. A defense with holes in it. And then three more children to be boiled to death. Charlie, aged five, Hayley, six, and Joel, seven, whose faces they'd seen in those photos. And only them to stop it happening.

"She doesn't need to be invited in," said Quill. "She's not a vampire. She'll just walk through the wall."

"Waste of energy, though," commented Costain, "waste of soil. She's in a war, so she doesn't waste ammunition. If she can get them to open that door, she will."

"And walking through the wall, unseen," said Ross, forcing herself back into this discussion, "would not necessitate her having to get them to forget about her." She paused suddenly, realization dawning. "Maybe they saw part of her MO! Something she doesn't want known, something she wants to be able to do again." Ross had started to shout, and she knew it but she couldn't stop it. "*That's* the shape of the hole. What wouldn't she want us to know? Maybe she's . . . pretending to *be something*?!"

"Not the babysitter," said Costain.

"Don't tell me those two have a cleaner," said Sefton.

Quill grabbed his phone and told the uniforms to get the Franks back over. The four of them actually met them halfway to the Portakabin and marched beside them on the way back inside.

Quill was already firing questions at them. "Who," he said, "has access to your house? Not individual people, but types of people."

The couple looked at each other, feeling increasingly scared. "I suppose . . . the social workers?" suggested Julie.

Quill didn't bother asking why such people would visit a "childless couple." "In the plural? Can you describe them?"

"There are two," said Julie. "One's Maria, who's a . . . colored lady, in her forties, going gray a bit before her time. And the other . . ." She suddenly stopped. They were now standing at the door of the Portakabin, Ross shivering with both the cold and the tension, the sound of that bloody radio washing over them. "It can't be only the one, because Maria was asking me about the other one . . ." She put a hand to her mouth. "Oh God!"

Quill darted into the Portakabin ahead of the others. He'd made sure there were no more details to be had from them, and then sent a screaming Julie and her husband back to the van, back toward a legal process that he would try to make sure didn't hurt them. In his hand he held the business card of social worker Maria Sutton. Her mobile rang six times . . . then she answered. Quill put the conversation on the speaker.

"I only know about it because other people on my list mentioned her," she said. "There was quite a scare about it locally, over the last couple of weeks, what with this old woman showing up and claiming to be a social worker. And I did wonder about Mora Losley, because it was all over the local papers. But this woman looked nothing like her, and it never seemed to come to anything, since no children were taken."

"She was preparing for lots of sacrifices," said Ross, too far away to be heard by the woman on the phone. "She was sorting out where the local kids lived, and she didn't make them all forget. She didn't need to."

"Other people on your list: have you got that list in a document you can e-mail me right now?"

Sefton went to Google Maps on his phone, and zoomed in on the area Maria Sutton now described, two or three of the poorer neighborhoods of Brockley, presently being squeezed out by the continuing gentrification of the area. There were open spaces here: Crofton Park, Telegraph Hill Park, Peckham Rye Park. All Quill could think about, as he finished the call, was how that would give Losley room to lurk—lots of places for her to connect her remaining West Ham soil to the ground.

"She's in there," said Ross. "The bitch is in there somewhere."

Quill looked to his e-mail and found the address list. "There's only about twenty of these." He drew with his finger, on the screen of Sefton's phone, a rough square. "If she kept this close to home—"

"And Tony Ballackti has been brought down in the penalty area! The referee is pointing to the spot!"

They all fell silent. "Don't choose him to take it," said Costain helplessly. *"Don't."*

"And there is despair at the Boleyn Ground now. It feels as if this is going to go on and on, with a parade of goals. The fans here, they've been hit hard by the press stories of the last few weeks. Speaking to some of them, they think they've been tarred with the same brush. And now Norwich are showing no mercy. It's Ballackti to take the penalty, because it would normally be. It has to be, I suppose, if we're not giving in to fear."

"You don't know anything about fear!" yelled Quill. "You don't fucking know about *fear*!"

"Ballackti puts the ball on the spot, brave in the face of all this. And I've never heard such sounds from a football crowd."

Quill could imagine the smiling man somewhere among them, revelling in it.

"There are West Ham supporters, here and there, not barracking Ballackti exactly, but shouting to him. They're trying to tell him not to take it, to miss it deliberately. They're pleading with him."

Ross grabbed the phone from Sefton so quickly that it nearly made him drop it. "We can see what she's done to the records! What about the Internet?! Try Google Street View!"

"But Ballackti steps up, he places the ball . . ."

Ross pinched at the screen, making agonized expressions as each zoom-in took seconds to load. "I think I can see something. In those streets, just a dot." She zoomed in closer. They all craned to look.

"He's taking his run-up—!"

"Where is it?!" asked Costain. "What's the address?"

A roar from the crowd. What sort of roar? They already knew.

"And Ballackti's put it away for his second goal! Surely they must take him off now? Surely, if they don't, he'll score again!"

But now they could all see it, as they'd seen the house in real life. As they'd seen Losley on that camera footage. The obscene light shone out of the screen at them: glistening and slick, an abomination in this world. From one particular suburban street. One particular house.

Sefton grabbed his holdall and the team ran for the door.

NINETEEN

Quill had asked for a BMW 5 Series from the motor pool, and had it parked outside last night. Now they all leaped into it, Sefton throwing his holdall in the boot. It was getting dark.

"I'm the best driver," said Costain, almost pushing Quill out of the way.

"I'll assume you mean you're a level-two driver, cleared to handle this unmarked car." Quill reached up to slam the magnetic blue light on to the roof, and plugged it into the "Kojack" electrical socket in the dashboard. "I'll get us a CAD number so you can jump the lights."

"Whatever." Costain looked over his shoulder and checked that the others were wearing their seatbelts.

"Shall I say ETA twenty minutes?" called Ross, already hitting buttons on her phone.

"Twenty minutes? Sod that." Costain pushed down on the pedal, and mud flew from the wheels as they accelerated toward the gate.

Quill called Lofthouse first. "I want uniforms ready down there, ma'am. I mean a *lot* of uniforms, as suspect is armed and dangerous and has potential victims on the premises. Scene commander to let me know RV point—"

Ross didn't register what he was saying. She was talking to Brockway at West Ham. "So Norwich haven't taken him off?"

"The fuckwits," whispered Sefton beside her.

"We strongly advise . . . we *officially* advise . . . Okay, they know that, okay."

"What's causing that?" said Costain. "They'd never normally do that. Something's influencing them."

"If he does score a third time," Ross continued, "as soon as he comes off the field, he stays put, security detail to surround him. Have you got everything we asked for ready?" The West Ham chaplain was ready to bless the player, the room and the said coppers. Quill had speculated that, while being at the West Ham ground itself would presumably give Losley a great deal of power, she had so far proved unwilling to do anything awful there, and might not want to harm anyone directly connected with the club. Ross had already sold this approach to the club on the basis of what Losley herself believed. She now received assurances, switched off the phone, threw it down—and then grabbed it up again.

Quill switched the radio on, and they all fell silent, listening until it was clear a third goal hadn't been scored. "If there's a hat-trick, I'll send whatever uniforms are at the location straight in, whether we're there yet or not. She'll be able to hold them off, we'll likely lose a few, but I'd rather that than losing the kids." His tone didn't sound to be inviting debate. He was again taking that responsibility on himself.

Sixteen minutes later, they spotted the cluster of unmarked vans ahead, two streets away from the Losley house, as arranged. In zero time, Brockley nick had done them proud.

Quill stepped from the car and shook hands with Inspector Ben Cartwright, who looked as if he'd just won the lottery.

"Losley," he said, "on our patch. Result."

*

"You know what they call Method of Entry teams?" said Sefton to Ross, as they watched Quill briefing some uniforms in the back of one of the vans, their enforcer ram held ready between them. " 'Ghostbusters'—if only they knew." He was trying to keep talking, because she looked all closed in on herself, in a terrible way, now that she had stopped working and was just waiting. He could feel it in himself, too. *We smell death near you soon.* It had been written by someone who probably knew. They were going in now and they had almost nothing to protect them that they hadn't had last time. They had no choice. He found himself again revolted by the thought of what Losley was intending to kill these kids *for.* Not out of madness or anger, but for what must seem to her to be a good, practical reason. To her, the sacrifices were *fuel*: a source of energy for any subsequent attack on the footballer. She lived in a London where that sort of equation must be commonplace. He thought back to holding Joe in his arms, in his hands, and took some comfort from that.

Quill and Costain came over to them, from where they'd been consulting with Cartwright, their breath visible in the street lights. The vans had pulled up beside trees that had cracked the pavement, in front of houses doubtless filled with busybodies already going frantic on Twitter. The radio in the car was still on: the match had reached half time, the restart due in two minutes. No further goals yet, thank God.

Quill turned to address the expectant uniforms, all clad in Metvests, whatever good that would do them. "We're doing this old-school. One van at the back door, two at the front, the Ghostbusters do the door; my squad go in first, taking advantage of the suspect's psych profile"—the same excuse as at the football club—"to attempt an arrest. A unit from Specialized Firearms Command is on the way, but they won't get here for another twenty minutes, and Inspector Cartwright shares my desire for urgency, given the presence of potential victims. Objectives of the operation as follows. One, any of you lot gets hold of one of the kids, you run straight out of that house with them, and keep going all the way to your nick. Do you understand me?"

The uniforms rumbled in assent. They enjoyed being bullied for something this big. Something where they might get home to their families and say, "I saved a kid today."

He continued: "Two, regarding suspect herself. Leave her to *us*. Do *not* attempt to engage her. She comes in your direction, get out of the way. We're talking poison needles in her clothes, hidden weapons, the lot. Objective three: suspect's cat." He didn't pause for them to react. "Information potentially hidden on it. And it's dangerous. Again, don't try and grab it. Leave it to us."

Cartwright raised an eyebrow. "The *cat* is booby-trapped?"

"Welcome to our world," said Quill.

Costain started up the BMW, and looked over his shoulder at the three others sitting in it with him. What that note had said—*We smell death near you soon*—they'd all be thinking about that. In the past he had never thought about death, even when he'd been in really deep and one wrong word could have meant a bullet in the head. He'd been so stupid then, every moment. What would a *good* person do right now?

"Proud to know you," he said. "You're good coppers." He reached over his shoulder, and just Ross and then even Sefton shook hands with him, because that was the thing to do, yet no passion in it. Quill quickly did the same.

And that was it. It didn't make a difference because there was still Hell.

"Fuck it," Costain whispered. And he gunned the BMW forward.

Ross felt almost nothing as they turned the corner, and accelerated toward their target. She was saving any feeling for when she had Losley right in front of her. She hoped that, like a hero in a story, how she felt would make some difference to what then happened to her. She held on to that thought.

"Go go go!" yelled Quill.

Costain launched the car, at high speed, straight at the garden fence, its headlights illuminating the woodwork—

And then they were through it, and slamming to a halt in that empty square of garden, wet soil and grass flying up and spattering the side windows. "Out!" he yelled, though he didn't need to, because they were all leaping out already. Sefton hauled his holdall along with him. The house above them shone brown and chitinous, polluting the air around it in waves, seeming fleshy cold in the night. The exterior looked exactly the same as the Willesden house, down to the type of front door.

He wasn't up to this, was he? He was missing something inside him. He wasn't what he pretended to be.

Fuck that, he'd have to do.

The uniforms were running in around them, the Ghostbusters forming up on the door in their usual reassuring, exhilarating way. The silent gestures, the sudden movement—and together! They swung their "master key." The door burst in. They swung it back again and stepped aside.

Quill ran inside, yelling. His team went in along with him.

He had faith in his team. More than in himself, in fact. And faith in the uniforms behind them, who'd die to get those kids out. The four of them ran into the hallway, and stood looking around at what the exterior of the house should have already told them: it was exactly the same inside too.

"Strangers!" yelled the head perched on the newel post.

The uniforms rushed in behind them, astonished at the filth even they could detect.

Then the smell hit Quill. Could that just be hot water? "Cooking smell!" he bellowed. "Up!"

They sprinted up the stairs that confused their senses, not caring about what they saw or where gravity was, falling and scrambling, while the uniforms made it look easy, in their ignorance, and came thundering up behind them. They rushed to the point where the attic access was directly overhead. There was noise from up there: a radio . . . a radio football commentary.

Quill looked round for the ladder, and realized that, of course, here there wasn't one. He jumped up on to Sefton's shoulders and heaved himself upright. He burst up through the hatch and shoved it aside.

There she was, Losley. Offending the world, and him, with how she looked.

There were three naked children huddled in a cage beside her: Charlie aged five, Hayley, six, and Joel, seven, and they were screaming and sobbing but all alive, still alive. The room was full of information, pent up with it, as if it was all nearly ready, as if it could only be seconds more. And there was the soil, and there was the cauldron, the water in it boiling, on top of an impossible blue fire that crackled and sparked like bright animated paper. The noise of the radio filled the room, sounding perversely normal, and Losley was already turning to start screaming something over its racket—

Quill got one foot onto the floor and he ran at her. He was vaguely aware of the others, his three and the uniforms, clambering up, following. He grabbed the crucifix that Franklin had sent over, the one with the Bishop of London's seal on it, from his throat and bunched it into his fist. He hadn't felt any power in it, but he'd convinced himself that he believed in the power of horror movies and how it would be enough.

She was yelling at him, hurling threats. There was that outraged screech in her voice, as if she was amazed they'd kept trying, that she was *so* much more powerful than them, that—!

"Kiss this!" he bellowed, and smashed her in the teeth. She went back and down. She spun up again. She'd rolled up like a table footballer. The crucifix had done nothing more than his fist and surprise impact would.

But the cage had already been cracked open with bolt cutters, the kids were in coppers' hands now, and they were running for the trapdoor.

Losley spun round to stop them—

"Hoi!" shouted Costain.

He kicked over the cauldron, sending water that smelled like decay roaring across a floor that exploded with dust on contact with it.

She turned to deal with that—

"Losley!"

That was Ross, yelling what she was doing so the witch could hear it, as Ross unloaded the first super-soaker professional-standard water-pistol carbine full of piss and London holy water into her new container of soil.

But it wasn't working! It kept flying off it. Something was protecting it—

The witch had thought of that. She'd changed it.

Losley spun back again to Quill, triumphantly.

But the uniforms were out of there now, the kids were gone.

And now Sefton had thundered up behind Quill, on his run up, throwing something with great weight right past his shoulder. The bagful of Millwall FC soil caught Losley full in the face. She screeched—like nails on a million blackboards. The uniforms must just be seeing an old woman screaming at all the ridiculous things they were doing to her but, for all that, Quill's team were being proved right.

Yelling something incoherent, Ross ran into close quarters and let fly with the second carbine, pumping pure London holy water all over Losley. They had no idea if it would work, but the more the merrier.

Quill took the silver handcuffs from his pocket. "Off her feet!" he yelled.

The four of them grabbed her at once, and they overcame their fear and they lifted her as if she was nothing—a bone frame with special effects attached—and they made for that table with her, keeping her feet from the floor. They had the advantage of surprise this time. They had learned this time. They had conquered their fear.

But the soil was intact, they knew. All the power was still there. They were terrified of her, and only their velocity was saving them, and that might give out any second.

The uniforms were all out of there; they'd got the children safely away.

Costain grabbed her hands and wrenched them over her head, behind her back. She screamed again, the very sound clawing at the air. The silver handcuffs snapped on, and they slammed her flat onto the table again.

Quill felt a huge frightening triumph rise up inside him. "Mora Losley!" he yelled, making himself somehow keep his voice level, because now she was going to have a trial and a brief—she was going to be dragged through one now, like normal people, like scared little people on their level, for wanting to fucking boil *children*, and she was going to cut a deal with them along the way and turn it all back to the way it had been, and this was his tribal cry: the victory that would mean he was the thing he thought he was, "you are under arrest in connection with multiple charges of murder, you do not have to say anything, but it may harm your defense—!"

"You can't stop me," she cried. "History is on my side."

And then they all fell through the floor.

TWENTY

The sensation of falling turned out to be what it was like to be holding tightly on to someone when they vanished with their house all around them.

Ross fell as the wave went through her and over her head. She was aware of the others falling beside her. *Again! She'd done it to them again!* The house was folding up past them this time, separating itself from them, not trying to take them with it. It was rolling back toward that red door into which it had all rushed the last time.

But right in front of her—

Ross dived for the shape she'd glimpsed, seen across a space which she didn't understand. She got her fingers around it and pulled it to her, and held on against a force that was trying desperately to haul it away from her.

Beside her, Quill slid across the floor. He was heading for the door, which was now swinging shut, having stayed open, Ross realized, only because of what she held in her hands. He recklessly jammed his hand into the gap between the door and the frame, then pulled his fingers out at the last second—

—leaving a wedge in place. The door thudded against it and held.

A terrible creaking noise filled the air. The others covered their ears, but Ross wouldn't let go of what she was holding, and the others looked to be in as much pain as she was. It was as if reality itself was cracking. Quill began to stagger toward the doorway. The air in Ross's lungs had got too large, somehow, too hot; it felt as if she was going to burst. Ross sensed the gravity on what she held increase to a point where she was sure it was going to haul her toward the door unless she let go. But she would not.

Something gave way. Something cracked.

The door slammed with a concussion that made them fall over.

They slowly got to their feet. The room had vanished. Ross looked over to where the soil had been. This time, she'd taken it with her. No more supply dumps, now that they were on her case.

Quill hauled himself over to where the door had been and looked down at something steaming on the floor. It was the perfectly flattened remains of a rubber door wedge. "Glad I didn't get my fingers in there," he said.

Ross suddenly remembered what she was holding, something that was struggling and spitting and very real. She suddenly felt perversely furious at it.

"So last time was deliberate," Costain was saying, not having noticed yet what she'd got. "She was trying to take us with her, disorient us, then take us out."

"Or she didn't have the energy this time," said Sefton.

"We saved the kids," said Quill. "We stopped her."

"Hoi," said Ross, "look what I've got." They all turned to see that she was clutching in her arms the mangy black cat.

"Now," the animal began, "wait a moment—"

Costain grabbed a sack from the floor and flung the cat inside. Then he tied the opening in a knot. Inside the bag, the cat hissed and spun around. "We have an accomplice in custody," he declared.

"Tell *that* to a judge," muttered Quill.

Ross swallowed an urge to laugh. She could feel them all giddy with it, the incredible feeling of having saved the kids, of having survived! Then she started to hear the screams from outside.

*

They jumped down from the loft and raced down the stairs, back to normal now.

They got out of the door to where the noise was coming from, aware of the increasing shouts. People were staring out of the windows of their houses, more and more of them. "Get back inside!" Cartwright was yelling. Two uniforms were lying on the pavement, their blood pooling around them. Others were tending to them, too late.

They stopped. They stared. Dead coppers. What they'd done had produced dead coppers.

"She's heading toward the railway!" a woman shouted from a top window. "I can still see her!" She was pointing along the road.

"We stopped her bailing out!" yelled Quill. "She only managed a short hop, and she can't have much power left! Come on!"

Costain shoved the sack into Cartwright's arms. "Get that back to the nick," he said. "Hold on to it."

Then the four of them raced off after Mora Losley.

It felt good to Ross to be in hot pursuit, to feel the pounding of blood inside her. She and Costain and Sefton, who all kept themselves very fit, soon pulled ahead of Quill. Sefton was still running with his holdall, but they were all pushing themselves as hard as they could go. Because there she was! There was a thin shape darting ahead, pausing, hauling herself along again. They nearly had her! She turned the corner. More and more people were coming out of their houses, into their gardens, pointing and shouting. "Get back!" Quill was yelling to them as he ran.

Ross knew Cartwright would have called it in. There'd be cars coming in from all directions. One sped past them now, siren blaring, making Quill yell for it to go on, my son!

Dead coppers.

Ross saw the lights of the vehicle turn left ahead—

And there was some sort of explosion, a ball of purple light that rose up high over the houses, though nobody could see it but them. They got to the end of the street and saw the marked car in pieces, two officers thankfully staggering out of it, because that was all she could manage now, all that was left to her! They were pointing down a road that ran alongside a railway cutting, as a train roared past behind the houses, sounding its horn as if all of London was joining in on this chase, the city alerted to the thing amidst it which claimed to be part of it. Ross felt good about the city: it was on their side, surely it was!

And there she was again, off in the distance, impossibly already at the end of the street. And she'd turned again, right this time, some sort of bridge over the railway—

Quill was on his Airwave radio, yelling a description of where the suspect was heading.

They sprinted after her.

She led them through one suburban street after another, past houses, and garages on the corners with metal shutters, and pet shops and schools. She was loping, slowing down, as were they. The network of cars and coppers on foot must be closing on her now. Ross could almost hear the running footsteps echoing from other streets. She could feel this like some medieval hue and cry. Up ahead there were ever more shouts as people spotted Losley— her off the telly—and they'd be phoning each other now, Tweeting each other to come to the window and see, as Losley became a trending topic, as the whole city converged on her.

Straight above them roared a helicopter without a police logo. "Frigging TV news team!" yelled Quill.

They came to a halt at a corner, and got the TV news displayed on Sefton's phone. There she was: a dark shape, like a target in a foreign war, running past people's gardens. Heading straight for a fence . . . and going right through it, as if it wasn't there, with a flare of white light that Ross was sure only they saw.

"There are some sports pitches, or a school playing field ahead—" began Sefton.

Quill heard from Cartwright on his radio. "She's going straight across the pitch. We've got people coming out of their houses all over. We are attempting an intercept with multiple cars along Ivydale Road. Stay at location. Pick up's on its way."

A marked car arrived a minute later, and took them at high speed, blues and twos blaring, through the crowds of people that now lined the roads, straight to Ivydale Road, where the crowds were even larger. Quill saw that some of them had makeshift weapons now: tools and cricket bats. But they were holding back, leaping aside to let through the multiple police cars that were racing down the road toward an intercept point.

"How's she doing this?" the driver was yelling.

Quill's team jumped out of the car without anyone answering her. They rushed toward where the other vehicles were converging—

Just as Losley burst through, from a gap between houses that shouldn't have been there. She spun and looked round with fury on her face, and with a terrible fear that Ross sensed in that second: the hunted animal who would do anything to escape. The crowd roared at her and heaved forward, except at the front, where the people were pushing back, terrified at the sight of her. Terrified but excited and caught up in it.

Losley looked around at them, at the masses of people and police closing on her from all directions. She looked across the road, from one row of suburban houses to another. She looked at the mob and hissed at them.

The people in her way broke and scattered.

She hurled across the road. She went straight through the uniforms. Screams and explosions of blood, and coppers were shouting, *She's got a gun, she's got a gun.* Coppers fell bloodied and injured and crying out but, again, not dead, as if her power was waning at every moment. The crowd began screaming and some of them started running.

Quill's team followed, slamming their way through and around members of the public. They were right behind her again. She was running toward a house. She rushed into the garden. She leaped at its front windows, with television light flickering behind them. The glass caved in, and there were shouts from inside, and then screams.

Quill got to the door and hammered on it. "Police!" he bellowed. "Police!"

A woman opened it. "She's— she's—!"

He burst past her. The others followed.

She was already through the house, and out a back door, now just seconds ahead of them. They could almost lay hands on her. Ross felt her hands clutching at the thought of it.

Mora ran straight down the thin back garden. They sprinted after her, ducking past a rotary washing line and crazy paving and gnomes and a rotten wooden fence, and at the bottom of the garden there was—

A high stone wall. And beyond it an expanse of trees. Thick, even with only the bare bones of winter, a black mass against very distant lights.

With an impossible leap and two upward scuttles like a spider, hand over hand, Mora was over the wall.

They themselves slammed against it. "Where?" Quill yelled, turning as the family whose house this was came stumbling outside. She hadn't had a chance to hurt them.

"That's Nunhead cemetery," the woman said.

"Tonight, somewhere in this 250-year-old, thirty-acre cemetery, reopened less than a decade ago and still partly a ruin, the police think Mora Losley has gone to ground. Attempts to seal the site have proved futile, as groups of people have formed and ventured into the cemetery, guided by their phones and portable devices, taking along torches and improvised weapons. They say there's safety in numbers, but look at them here, as our helicopter shot captures it: all those lights down there

are ordinary people taking the law into their own hands. More and more of them doing so as our coverage has continued, though the latest to arrive are being turned away by what's now an enormous police presence. Our camera crew is there with one . . . I nearly called him a protestor."

"We're all of us parents, and we've come down here to ensure—"

"Find her! Find her and make sure she doesn't get away with it!"

"You seem to have weapons with you?"

"The police better hope they get to her before we do. I've got kids!"

"Burn the witch! Burn the witch!" Half laughter in the young voices, but half meaning it.

"I wish they'd stop calling her a witch. I'm down here to point out to people that this ancient and peaceful tradition . . ."

"It's absolutely unprecedented. Police have sealed off several roads to stop people from other parts of London heading to the cemetery. Tonight the capital is gripped by anger and fear, and it's all focused on this one woman. I have here a police statement which says she remains only a suspect, she is not to be approached, but I'm hearing . . . is she even still in the cemetery? We're getting reports in . . . Now we can go to a map, as we're getting reports of sightings of Mora Losley in Kentish Town, in Clapham, in Brixton . . ."

Quill and his team looked out over the expanse of the ancient cemetery. Between the trees flickered torches, everywhere they looked. The landscape of graves and vaults and distant buildings rippled with a strange heat amid the cold of winter. The first place they'd headed had been somewhere Sefton had found on his phone in the Wikipedia description of this place: a restored chapel. They weren't the first to have that thought. Quill had to yell at crowds of angry people with torches, some of them literally old-style flaming torches, all of whom felt they had a perfect right to be here, who wanted to tell him that if he did his job better, that if he knew what it was like to raise kids in London, with pedophiles on the streets, and now a frigging witch—!

That was when she'd lunged out at them.

Costain had lashed out, the others had jumped back. But it had just been a sudden vision of her, a hallucination that immediately faded. A trick, Ross had thought, with sudden hope, something she was trying out to put them off the scent. But as they trudged out of the chapel, they started to see that she was everywhere, near every cluster of people. A sudden vision of her here, a glancing visual impact of something like her there. She kept the crowds yelling that there was something over there, in the darkness. All of them, they were chasing shadows and thus . . . making her be here. Ross leaned against a tree, feeling something so hugely despairing lodging in her lungs and head that she felt it could kill her.

"She's become *remembered*," said Sefton. "The masses have got hold of her. These visions aren't really her. These are people's ideas of her. She's—"

"Everywhere," said Quill, looking up from his phone. "She's all over London. There are people in Shoreditch who swear they've seen her . . . coppers on the street there who say they nearly grabbed her. And meanwhile the *real* her . . . she could be anywhere!"

"Do you think she did this deliberately?" said Ross. "Or that she knew it'd happen?"

"I doubt it," said Sefton. "Not the way she was running."

They finally found a pile of glowing soil behind the building. Losley, with the crowd seeing her everywhere, must have laid down some soil she'd carried with her, on top of the local variety, and used it to vanish again.

Ross felt the others slump. There had been victories tonight—rescuing the kids, catching the cat—but at such a cost. *Dead coppers.* She could see it on the faces of the other three. It felt to them that their own selfish problem, their speciality, had reached out and slaughtered their brother officers.

"I think you're right," said Costain to Sefton. Ross saw the accusation evident on his face, about himself as much as them. "This is what being remembered looks like. 'Do you make sacrifice, or are you remembered,' that's what she said. You're either someone who boils your kills in a pot, or you're someone London remembers. Well, now she's made a big enough splash for all of London to do that. Now she's got hold of *both* sources of energy. Now she's got all the power she needs. And we gave it to her!"

"The bloody general public gave it to her!" said Sefton. "They're what we're really fighting."

"No change there for coppers," sighed Quill. His phone rang at that moment. He listened for a few moments, then gave a few curt instructions. "I told them it was okay for them to move Ballackti," he said. "The match finished two–nil."

TWENTY-ONE

By a few mornings later, on his morning drive to work, Quill was seeing Losley *everywhere*. For real, not just in the media. Wherever enough people thought they'd glimpsed her, there was a scarecrow of her fixed in the Sight, jerking and yelling, but making ordinary people who walked past unseeing suddenly look sideways or jump at the fleeting image that had somehow intruded into the corner of their eye. She now seemed to be a fixed and central part of this London that Quill was increasingly feeling separated from.

The forensics people had finished with the house, whereupon Quill and his team searched it themselves. It had turned out to be the same abandoned Losley house as always. "When she's at home, everything's the same, down to the same head stuck on the newel post," said Ross. "She's clearly willing to spend a lot of energy taking it with her, so I think it's safe to assume that she's only got the one actual *home*." She was starting up their continual, endless process of debate again, her tone that of someone who insisted on carrying on marching into the wind. "It all then gets folded up and transported through that red door. If we got through there, maybe we could get into all the houses she can use to . . . put her real home in."

He could feel the same suspicion in her as in himself. It was as if they were fighting all of London now, with a Losley on every corner. "Why wasn't there a hat-trick?"

"The smiling bastard's stringing her along," said Costain. "You keep your soldiers on their toes, always let them know who's boss."

"I think he's getting her wound up," said Sefton, barely looking up. "Pushing her to go even further."

They had turned out for the funerals of the officers from Cartwright's team who'd been killed when Losley made her escape: PC Andy Stinson and PC John Mattheus. It was a dress-uniform event. Sobbing wife and girlfriend and questioning children. A lot of stony coppers throbbing with anger, all directed toward the thing that Quill and his people had not yet caught. There had been a lot of hearty handshakes, a lot of hard-eyed slaps on the back. "You nick her," one DI urged. "You nick her for all of us."

Terry and Julie Franks had been reunited with their three children. Quill hadn't been there to witness that, but he could imagine it. "I've never seen such family stress," the social worker had reported. "They seemed really awkward with their own children."

A phone call made to the family had confirmed it: they still didn't remember. "I feel so guilty," Julie Franks had told him. "I don't know what to say to them, what to do with them. They cling on to us, and we know they . . . deserve to be loved, but it's like they're not really ours. We don't know what to do, and there's nobody we can tell." Quill hadn't felt able to tell the Franks the truth. Something had been said about blaming drugs, but the Franks wouldn't believe that; they'd mention what had been suggested to others, and in the end it wouldn't have helped them cope. The wound Losley had inflicted would fester. He felt for them about what they must be going through.

Ross and the others had started to study Google Earth pictures of all of London, surveying them methodically, in the same way they were still going over the bills and the closed-case records. But the truth of it was that there was too much data in all three areas for four people to handle. All they could hope for was a stroke of luck. Quill had seen Sefton experimenting with the vanes he'd snatched from his attacker, holding them in different positions, moving around the Portakabin with them, but he didn't seem to have had much luck yet with getting them actually to do anything.

And, on Monday night, West Ham were once again playing at home. In an FA Cup quarter-final against bloody Manchester City.

"So she has to get a line of sight on someone to make them forget," said Ross now, again become the force that kept them going. "But then that must kind of . . . spread out. We know it's a bit random, from what happened in the Franks case. Schools forget. The paperwork's still there; it's not like the way she edits people's memories, but loads of teachers just can't see it. We know of social workers who were made to forget, but we know of relatives who weren't."

"Maybe," said Sefton, "it's about what's in someone's head when she makes them forget. Maybe it depends on what they think of in connection with what she's making them forget. It goes out into the world and finds those things and zaps them. If you don't think of Great-Aunt Nora as someone who knows your kids in that second, then Great-Aunt Nora keeps her memories of them. It's another pattern that lies under what we'd normally deal with."

Silence fell again. "All right," said Quill, "it's time we interviewed the suspect." He walked over to Gipsy Hill and fetched the cage containing the cat, which glowered at him silently all the way back. As they entered the Portakabin, it looked up at its own picture on the Ops Board and curled up into an uncommunicative ball once more.

He put the cage on a table and the others gathered round. They'd been putting aside their impatience and made the cat wait for this, giving it time to worry about its situation. "Hoi!" he tapped the cage until the cat uncurled itself and stared at him. "You're not staying in the Hilton now. You're with the bastards who know what they're doing. No food or drink until you start talking, capeesh?"

"Yes, yes, I understand."

"Do you know where Mora Losley is?"

"In general," it sighed, "yes, I suppose I do."

"Can you tell us how to find her?"

"No."

"Does that mean you can't, or that you won't?"

"It means I am simply not made that way. I am unable, because of the way in which I was constructed, to provide any information concerning my mistress's whereabouts, or to tell you anything about her which would allow you to impede her movements in any way." It sounded, thought Quill, as if it was reading that stuff off a card.

"That's an interesting way to put it," said Ross. "She doesn't mind us hearing all sorts of other stuff about her. All she worries about is us getting in the way."

"Are you saying she made you?" asked Sefton. "She actually *made* something with a personality, with a mind?"

"Indeed she did, centuries ago, out of the body of a dead cat. I learned to speak through listening to the wireless, later, when that device was invented and my mistress acquired a set."

"What are you intended for?" asked Quill. "Spying for her? Warning her?"

"Not at all. I was made to agree with her. The head on the stairs is for warning her."

"Did she make that too?"

"Why, yes, obviously." And now Quill felt patronized by a cat. "Only I've been incorporated into this body for simply ages, and the head on the stairs has got a new skull . . . well, it'll be twice now. Every time she has to change residences suddenly. The bodies get left behind, you see, but the information that animates the head goes with the house. Its job is to shout out when there are intruders. Which works well enough, I suppose, if the radio's not on or if she's not halfway to another property. It's a maze back there, moving between all those houses."

"You're a very chatty interviewee," observed Quill.

"I was hoping for some of that food and water you mentioned. And it's not as if I can give anything away. Cut my whiskers off and drown me, if you like, but I'm incapable of actual treachery."

"How many houses does she have?"

"I'm afraid that *would* count as helping you find her."

"How do you feel about her boiling children alive?" asked Costain.

"I enjoy the children petting me and talking to me while they're held captive, and I also enjoy, during the boiling, the smell and the cries of pain. It's *all* rather marvelous."

"But . . . they're innocent children—!"

"But in order for my mistress to have the power to do her lord's will, I'm afraid they simply have to die horribly. I do apologize, but it *is* my nature to agree with her."

"Can you give us descriptions of the children?" asked Quill.

"Human beings all look rather alike to me—and there have been quite a few." They asked it more questions, and its answers continued to be maddeningly polite but, on the matter of how to find their quarry, utterly useless.

"Now, please," said the cat finally. "You promised food and water when I started *talking*, and I've been going on and on."

Quill took one of the cans of cat food he'd bought from the cupboard and spooned some into a saucer, leaving another saucer of water beside it. The cat stepped out of its cage and started eating, pausing only to excuse itself when its stomach made a sudden noise. It looked up when it had finished. "I do believe," it said, "that my mistress would wish you to know more about her. Once you do, you will surely share her point of view and perhaps also, we can but hope, her cause. Allow me," it said, licking a claw, "to tell you her story."

TWENTY-TWO

FOUR HUNDRED AND
SEVENTY-FIVE YEARS AGO

Mora Losley stood at the window of the master bedroom, at the top of what the locals called "the tower." She was sixteen years old, full of fear and foreboding. She could feel London in the distance tonight, she was sure. For the first time, she could see the glamor of it, the light of heaven that flickered between the meadows and the villages and the gardens of the great, all the way to the great palaces along the river, York Place and the Palace of Westminster and the Tower, which radiated importance and threat. The musician had claimed it was the light of heaven. She had heard people at court talk about it as the very opposite: as something one must never see if one was to retain one's soul. Or perhaps it was still only her imagination. Perhaps she wanted too much to be like her mistress Anne, the Queen. She was kinder to Mora than even her mother had been, who had herself served as maid to an earlier Queen. But perhaps this royal kindness would soon result in horror.

Anne Boleyn had been the best wife King Henry ever had. He had split the Church for her, for her mind as well as for having her in his bed, since he had read all the books she'd given him on the evils of Rome. She had borne him a daughter, and that

275

had pleased him, for a while. But he wanted a son, *he wanted a son*, till that desire and those words echoed around every corner of Hampton Court and Greenwich. Mora had watched her mistress's desperate struggles to do as he wished, the care she took when bathing after she had been to his bed, the horrors of her howling in grief at both miscarriages. The sand was trickling through the glass. The King's patience was stretching thin. He now looked at other women in the same way that he looked at fillies of good stock. One day, Mora had entered the Queen's chamber to find her with one of her musicians, and at first she had thought they were practicing some new dance. He was rehearsing gestures with her, over her stomach. Mora had noticed how her mistress had turned every holy icon in the room to face away from them, and she began to fear. Strange smells wafted from a brazier and, to Mora's horror, blood was dripping from the Queen's palms. She had then stepped forward, afraid that he had wounded her.

"Don't be scared," the musician had said. "This is what is called sortilege, the creating of obligations in the world, the weaving of the pressures." She had been shocked then by the coarseness of his accent. She had seen him play instruments at the court, but had never heard him speak. "It is learned in cities. But I hope," he smiled, "that it will be of benefit to the country." Mora's mistress had made eye contact with her then, to assure her that all was well.

Mora had not been able to ask the question in her mind: was this not witchcraft? Back then it was never mentioned at court, but Mora had heard it said in the streets that her mistress was a whore, even that her mistress was a witch. She had changed the peoples' age-old religion, had whispered of change in all sorts of ways into the ear of the good King, and they hated her for it. But Mora could not believe that anything Anne did was wrong, so she instead asked, as she did with every art used around the Queen, if she too might learn it, so she could be of service to her mistress whenever the musician was absent. The Queen agreed, as long as, and Anne managed a scared smile as she said it, it wouldn't make the girl conceive a child. It took some effort, but the Queen then persuaded the musician to begin tutoring her. Mora was angered by how boldly he spoke back to her mistress, but Anne needed him, and he knew it. Mora noticed the coins jangling in his purse.

And that was how she had learned of the other tides surging through London, sweeping down the river and off the hills and round the buildings, and in the minds and hearts of . . . well, women more than men, beggars more than courtiers. That was how desperate the Queen had become. During that time of learning, the whispering started to be heard in the palace too. As Henry grew more distant, everyone became interested in who visited the Queen's apartments, and when, and the maids were warned to be careful who was paying court to them. Even the Queen's brother George, who came and went freely, started to be looked at in the way that Mora started to be afraid of: that look given by dangerous dogs sizing up a weaker member of the litter.

Anne had become desperate, sensing every eye in the palace on her, sensing them acutely now, as she seemed to look through the walls and into a great vault beyond. "A gigantic prison, this London is," she told Mora. She requested that she be allowed to take her retinue to one of the King's houses outside the city, in the village of East Ham. To everyone's surprise, the King agreed. And for the last few weeks, it had been fine, and the weather had become better as winter turned to spring. Anne had brought with her a merry court of musicians, dancers and debaters, though sometimes Mora thought that was more to distract her courtiers than to entertain the Queen herself, who concentrated on her studies with her special musician and with Mora, and for days at a time would stay in her chamber, calling only them to her side. And the things Mora had seen there, the way she started to be able to see, by angling her hand, the weight they were all under all the time; the ocean they were at the bottom of. She dreamed one night of London as an underwater kingdom, itself with pressures and tides and waves, and at the center of it all was the King, the whirlpool itself. Mora wondered, on waking, what the King looked like to informed eyes like the musician's. Did he shine like the sun? Did he reflect the forces of London, like the moon was said to reflect all the lights below it? (That was a dangerous thought.) Or, more dangerous still, was his light the infernal kind that the Queen sometimes talked of seeing, when she grew frightened of what she had taken on, and would desperately ask Mora if what they were doing was a sin?

Now, as Mora looked out toward London one noon, she tried not to think of what had happened during the last few days. The musician had suddenly vanished, could no longer be found anywhere in the house or the village beyond. Then, early this morning, while Anne had been distracting herself from her growing fears by watching a game of tennis, a messenger had arrived from the King at Westminster, ordering the Queen to appear before the Privy Council. The tone of the message itself was at least basically courteous, but it was the attitude of the messenger that spoke loudest to Mora and, judging from the look on her face, to her mistress. His expression was like that of a goodwife in a whorehouse.

Anne promised she would obey, then she rushed back to her chamber, accompanied by Mora, and the two of them had spent the next few hours ripping blood from Anne's palms, desperately seeking a pregnancy through whatever means, crying out for the Queen's womb to bear fruit, even though they neared the end of the time when it could reasonably have been Henry's child. Finally, Anne had sent Mora off for an hour of troubled sleep.

She had been woken by one of the other maids telling her that the Queen's menses had come. Anne didn't summon Mora to her company, so she had come up to this highest window to gaze out in the direction in which they would all depart later that day . . . and to consider a fear that was gathering inside her.

And now she could see—she was sure she could feel as well as see it—that danger was coming. She could feel the tide of the King's will. And then, across the pastures, she saw the first banners approaching. Then the tiny figures that were huge to her with meaning now. The oncoming horsemen.

The escort was led by three members of the Privy Council sent to fetch Anne, and they pounded on the door of Green Street House with all the watching mob, starting to shout, "Get the whore, get the witch." Mora heard the other maids screaming and running, and she feared that her mistress would be dragged outside and killed in the street, and maybe all of them along with her. Mora stood where she was. She looked down at her hands, and she searched everywhere through her eyes, and she felt the pressure of the city around her, and she sought something she could do. And she found it.

She ran down to the kitchen and found a blade, and then went to the pigsty in the courtyard. She could feel in the air what her course of action had to be. It was the only hope for all of them. "Mistress!" she called out, projecting her voice along a path that wound through the battering tides about them, from her mouth to Anne's ear, and she knew her mistress heard her. Mora bent toward the pigs, and slit the throat of three of them, their desperate squeals flying past her. She arranged the bodies in a pattern which seemed to complement and at the same time complain about the London massed around it. It just seemed the right shape. The blood intertwined in a knot at her feet.

And then Anne arrived, all alone. "Mora, what have you done?"

Mora hadn't done it yet, but she did now. She planted her feet into the pool of blood, into the soil directly beneath it, her life locked into that spot, like a tree growing into the earth. She knew now that she could never be moved. "Take my hand now, mistress, and they won't be able to budge you either."

Anne hesitated. And then she put her hand, cool and calm and beautiful, the hand of a mother, into Mora's feverish grip.

"They insist we have babies," declared Mora. "They insist it—and they will realize their error!"

Anne looked uncertain, even fearful. "They are saying our teacher has confessed to . . . to what he did with us, and to more that he certainly did not. But this is more than he ever showed us. Where did you learn it?"

"Out of the air. Or I call it air, at least. We can't breathe it as it is, so we have to change it first."

"Mora, this is going to be bad—for you and for me." And at that moment the soldiers, followed by the mob, burst into the courtyard, and the three Privy Council men strode toward the pigsty, looking astonished. The mob started to call out that this was a fit place to find such a Queen. But one of the councillors yelled for them to be silent, that Anne was to be accused, not convicted. Mora felt the heat of the mob, felt their hunger for blood. It felt as if they hated her mistress, yet loved her at the same time. They loved her for being something they could hate. They might love her entirely if she became a victim, but for now she was still someone who had made them suffer. They had their own tide of opinion which rolled like a sea around them. They started to question why the Queen was clasping the hands of a maid in such a demeaning place. The councillors, standing at the fore, could see, more clearly and were desperately asking for the Queen to let go of Mora's hands. Two of them, Mora decided, had her mistress's genuine interest at heart, but in the face of the third what she saw was only violence. He opened his mouth, pointing at the pigs, and started to bellow about witchcraft.

The shout went up all around them then: *Witch! Witch! Witch!*

"She isn't a witch!" yelled Mora. She was looking straight into Anne's eyes, pleading with her to stay, knowing that as long as she held on to Mora, they couldn't take her. She realized that they thought the pigs were a sign of Anne's witchcraft, not Mora's, so she repeated. "She isn't a witch!"

Anne gave her a look which tried to say sorry and thank you and to bless her to God. That glance was full of worry and fear, like a mother's. She was going to show them her innocence, like pearls cast before swine! Mora screamed at her not to. The Queen muttered a prayer under her breath, then she let go of Mora's hands and turned, and the mob almost fell on her, but the soldiers held them back, and the councillors led her away.

Mora grabbed hold of a post. The mob tried to haul her away too, but their hands simply slipped off every time their fingers tried to clutch at her. Mora could feel the fabric of London itself getting in the way. The Queen vanished into the crowd, the official body escorting her. Mora didn't see her look back. She herself stood there firmly as the mob started to throw things at her, hard objects which all missed her, mud that splattered back at them. She was like a mirror they had fashioned, as she stood there looking back right into their eyes and their yelling mouths.

They even brought instruments to try and prise her away. They dragged her sobbing fellow maids along to plead with her. She watched as some of them suffered instead of her. They brought fire, too, until the remnants of the soldiers warned them that this was the King's property, and burning it would be a hanging offense. Mora stood there steadfast. She was standing for her Queen. She was planting something in this soil, to take root there and boil them—and all the mobs they would later breed. They deserved nothing better, not the mob itself not even the maids with their pleading words that they would just as soon turn against her.

They waited there for days, and even took turns in standing watch. Having heard of it, the King sent several courtiers to observe. They questioned her with words that Mora largely didn't understand, and even asked her if she had given her soul to Satan. Mora then replied, saying she had not, that she didn't know what a soul was, that she thought Satan might possess many faces, and how did they know they themselves didn't serve him? They grew wonderfully, impotently angry at that. They replaced the local guards with soldiers, and gave orders that nobody should feed her. But Mora experienced no need to eat or sleep or shit. Something enormous was happening to her, and she concentrated on it alone, and made an inner joy out of it. She was binding herself to the soil.

Two weeks passed thus. They taunted her with what was happening to the Queen, how she was imprisoned in the Tower and sentenced to die. The musician was dead already. Mora saved her breath to scare them with sudden noises. Her only power over them now was fear. She was stuck here, she knew, but she was stuck here as a demonstration. She and the guards were alone in the great house, apart from the crowds that came to see her, that spoke of her far and wide. Then one day a guard, himself not looking too pleased, told her that Queen Anne was dead, though her sentence had been commuted from burning to beheading. The crowds that came now looked sad for her, for she was something that remained of Anne, who had suddenly become the "good Queen."

Finally, a priest came, and tried to bless her; all the while she yelled at him. She was afraid they were going to burn this place after all, but then they all went, and they locked the gates behind them. They locked every exit that Mora might use, in fact, and bricked up every window, as Mora discovered two days after they had left, when she started to feel confident that this wasn't a trap to get her to move from her vigil, and went to look inside the house. Walking away from that spot where the bodies of the pigs had started to fester, and the blood had become an old stain, was surprisingly difficult. Mora found herself strangely restrained, as if wrapped immobile in sheets. She barely made it to the upper rooms before having to run back, feeling an exhaustion like death about to descend on her.

She sat down, panting, in the pigsty. She wasn't hungry, and felt full. But she realized with horror that her stomach was cramping with the pain of emptiness. Her body wasn't used to this new life that had been forced on her. And now she couldn't see how there would ever be an end to it.

It took her five years to break free, walking slightly further from the pigsty every day. In that sleepless time she came to inhabit the empty rooms of the great house. She sat amid the ruins of nobility. She found nothing of use. She had no windows to look out of, but she was able to feel the world beyond. She felt it in more detail all the time. She could feel what the mob thought of this house now: that it was haunted. But they didn't quite remember Mora. The bigger idea of Queen Anne overshadowed her. Eventually they probably only knew that a woman haunted the place, but didn't know why, and they didn't even consider that she might still be alive inside the haunting she had been sentenced to.

One night, when she was sure of her power, when she had considered and refined it, Mora walked to the great doors . . . and through them.

She stopped once she saw and felt the presence of London outside. It had changed. It had got much bigger, much closer, in just that passage of time. It had changed like she had, twisted up by all her cramps and tensions, becoming old before her time. Walking away from the house proved difficult, so she made a short first expedition, in secret, and then searched her heart for how she could do it more easily. She took soil from the pigsty and put it in her pockets, and now she could walk at least a little way further abroad.

She heard locals still talking about Anne, about how she'd lived here, and Mora would say under her breath, as she passed them, "She wasn't a witch." Some wench was now on the throne. On a couple of occasions, the people she passed happened to be talking of witches, and they looked at her and saw her in some strange way, and started to chase her, terrified but eager.

At some point, without ever really deciding on it, Mora accepted that she now probably was a witch. She had become this thing that her mistress had never been. She had been led to it by her mistress's honest wish for motherhood. Mora had had no choice in the matter. It was like a wheel running downhill.

She took to hurting the people in secret, to going about absolutely unseen, learned by constant experiments with the gestures of her hands, copied from the musician, and flashing a knife from a pocket, hurting them with small cuts, killing their dogs and cats, and pledging them like she had the swine; sending them on somewhere and feeling the tide washing hard into her at the moment of their deaths.

The locals started to talk about her again. And it seemed that someone at court had remembered, because one day when Mora had returned to her sty and was standing there in pain during the night, she heard the gates open again, and soldiers entered.

That night, Mora learned that her power was not as great as she had thought it was. Now that she had stretched the weave to let herself move out and about, so others could move her too. They were here to kill her, ultimately, but first they raped her many times, having to straighten out her curled-up older self to find the soft young girl concealed inside.

They were so pleased with themselves at having conquered the witch that they decided to keep her captive, and made one of the stables into a cage where they could visit her. They put her in chains of cold iron forged in London, and those felt as if they would hold her, at least for a while. The house was opened up again, and the mob came back to see her, too. She seemed to be a gibbering old lady, she realized from inside herself sometimes, whenever her mind came to the surface. The mob handed her food, which she put down beside her. She felt that taking it would lead her back to normality, where she might be destroyed even more, split apart on the rocks of expectation. The mob seemed to like her as a thing they could come and view.

*

One day a child, a little girl, came along to see the witch. Mora smiled at her, and took the bread she offered. She complained that the chains were so rough on her, and she was so weak and would be dead soon, and asked if she could be set free of them, just for a few moments. That wicked, cunning child went and found the key, perhaps off her father, and she took off Mora's chains.

Mora killed her with her bare hands, and dedicated the child's death with the correct gestures, enjoying the feeling of what had been the child's mind being swept off to face punishment. And so much more strength flooded into her then, more than she had ever felt before. She could suddenly see it all, see the tides and the angles, see how buildings and people altered them.

She killed all the soldiers, one by one, dispatching as many of them as she could as sacrifices. She became something even greater with every moment. And now she was able to glimpse who she was sacrificing to, and to hear a distant laughter. Mora didn't care. They deserved it. She raped those who had raped her, and then sentenced them to die forever.

When they were all dead, she closed the gates of this charnel house behind her, and walked out through the wall, invisible and mighty, into the white sepulcher that was London.

With the Sight, she could see that the soil she carried would let her go no further than the bounds of the city. But, by carrying it, she could travel anywhere within it. She was like a great predatory fish being let loose into a large lake. She was master of this expanse and no further.

She turned to look back at the locked gates of the house. "She wasn't a witch," she announced for the last time.

Centuries passed, and Mora experienced too much life. London grew around her too, astonishingly, her small pool becoming full of more and more of "the mob." In a tavern one evening she counted the years of kings and queens, and realized she was seventy. And though she now looked it, and looked back to her youth as a woman of seventy would, she had not a single new ache that had crept up on her, only those that were old friends. The same was true at age one hundred, and then passing through the decades to two hundred, and then she let thoughts of that go too, and forgot she had an age.

She would take three children, and make a good sacrifice, and feel life flooding back into her, and she wanted to laugh at the mob at the same time, knowing that she again had vengeance on them for what they had done to their Queen, and to Mora herself. They claimed they so loved their children. They loved them enough that they would kill innocents like her mistress to have more. So she loved giving them fewer. She would sacrifice adults too now, in a way she had learned when the city burned . . . and she had stayed among the flames, dancing and learning the skill of giving someone whole to the flame, so that the moment of striking and of sacrifice became one, spending and receiving in the same instant. That was like being in love with the destruction, having congress with it.

In order that people would know what she was about when they glimpsed her, she learned what the people most feared from such as her, and made herself into that. She therefore fabricated herself a cat out of so many sacrifices that she lost count, all of them boiled together at once in a cauldron that she stole from the back of a cart, and then infused it into a dead mog she'd found lying in the street. She made it as something that would reflect what she herself was back at her, something that would not argue, not offer her any distraction that might lessen her purpose or stay her hand. It was to provide all the good things about having company, and none of the bad. It was nothing like a child, for it was nothing of her, and yet only her.

In the aftermath of the Great Fire of London, she gradually became aware that, in this small pond, there were starting to be others who did as she did. They came with all the buildings that were now shutting out the sky. Some of them hid in the shadows, as she did, but some walked around in silks and hats. With civilized gestures of the right hand, they described to their servants where they would place such a building, while crafty, secret gestures of the left hand were making sure the angles of that building were right for the unseen tides which only they and Mora knew of. Mora herself did not feel inclined to meet those of either kind, but she feared the latter more, seeing immediately that they worked for kings and had the stuff of kings about them. She hated kings half the week, and the mob for the other half. She recognized the irony that, as people flooded into the small pond she was trapped in, they all seemed to feel the same, thus hating themselves as being part of the thing they hated, or at least all of them did a little. As more of them came, more buildings appeared, and so more of the crafty architects who knew the same secrets as she did arrived, until Mora found herself feeling limited. It was as if they were fencing off more and more of the tiny space she survived in.

So she was on nobody's side, remained just the thing that took away children, and she took steps never to be revealed, which meant the parents seldom realized. Hers were the children that got lost in the cracks of the city. She was on no side until, returning one day, as she often did, to her mistress's house—which had come to be called, to Mora's great pleasure, Boleyn Castle—to take more soil from its grounds, she saw a group of men outside it, kicking a ball. That also gave Mora great pleasure, because it would have angered the King mightily to see the game he had forbidden being played over one of his properties. They weren't playing at archery now! She therefore stayed in shadow and let those men live, and made sure always to seek out her sacrifices far away.

As the years passed, what the men did there grew and grew. One day they stuck in the ground a flag with an image of a castle on it, which was now to be their emblem. The spot where they played became known as "the Boleyn Ground," and when they built a stadium for spectators, it had big towers standing outside it. Mora had long since started to attend these matches, hidden at first, and then later in disguise and having paid money. She was increasingly tempted to support them with her craft, and to ensure they were always victorious, but she managed to resist that urge. In truth, she didn't want to diminish the joy at genuinely winning and, yes, also the sorrow of losing. They became increasingly bound together, occupants of the same soil, and the team's victories were also Mora's. When wireless became commonplace, she saw those around her in the stands listening to it, so she stole a set for herself, and started to listen to the commentaries, and eventually to other things that told her stories about the old world. She switched it off rather than hear of the new. The new was what limited her and bricked her in. The cat even started to talk with the voice of the radio, but still only told her the news she wanted to hear.

She hated witnessing the team's defeats, hated the loud celebrations of the filthy scum that scored against them. So every now and then, but taking care not to do it too often, she would send the worst of those shits to Hell early. She became well known to a few of the spectators, and in time had stories told about her.

It was only a few years ago that Mora started to have a distant feeling that something around her was changing. The secret tides of London were moving almost imperceptibly in some new direction; only one as sensitive as she was might have noticed. One autumn morning she was gathering soil near the stadium when she realized that someone who should not be there was watching her. She turned, ready to send a force slapping against him from her palm, but then realized immediately how little such a tiny reflex would mean to him. He was smartly dressed, having the stuff of kings about him, yes, but he was common too. So he was either both of those things she hated, or neither. But he was smiling all over his face, and that made her choose neither. He was smiling *about* her, which was something Mora was only used to, sometimes, on her beloved terraces. He told her she had made a contribution to what he called his stocks, and that he applauded her. And he did applaud, and every clap of his hands sent joy flooding through her, and she realized who he was. And finally she knew that here was the creature that, with her visions of Hell, she had long suspected existed. He told her there was a possibility that soon, because of all they were doing to contain and limit London, the descendants of those men in fine gloves, who were always meddling, would stop her from being able to reach her beloved ground.

Mora was horrified. He asked her whether she would owe him service if he removed, as he was planning to do, those who might block her from the Boleyn Ground. She told him with certainty she would. He told her that a man who'd made him good sacrifice had just, at his suggestion, bought the season-ticket seat next to hers. She was to work for him for ten years, and then stop, and the work would serve a higher purpose than it seemed to. He licked his palm and held it up; Mora saw a streak of blood there. Hesitantly, but aware that she was in the presence of, for the first time in centuries, a power that could harm her, a power that asked very little and was being civil, Mora kissed the palm offered to her and tasted blood like water and ashes.

And then he was gone, and Mora found herself weeping, shedding black tears that scorched her face and marked her beloved soil. Because she had now met the power of another king, and, just like that, he had reminded her how she was a victim.

But she did what she was told, and she met with the man Rob Toshack. She even told her name to him, so that he might know it. She found that, despite her anger and hatred at her own weakness, they had much in common, that this was easy work indeed, and that she could therefore remain herself. And so she let herself forget that she was merely a victim. Except at somewhere close to her heart, where she always remembered. "She wasn't a witch," she would still insist. But now she didn't know whether she referred to her mistress or herself.

TWENTY-THREE

As the cat came to the end of its story, Ross felt a terrible fury inside her. "That doesn't *excuse* her," she began. "That doesn't . . . !"

But looking at the faces of the listening coppers, she realized that none of them thought so either, and she turned away. The ridiculous voice of that cat, talking so nicely about Toshack and the sacrifice of her dad . . . She wanted to hurt it for how it agreed with her.

While the cat ate a second tin of food, Sefton followed the others to the Ops Board. "It's not just that she's only got special powers in London 'cos of the soil," he said, "but she can't bloody leave!" He amended the board to reflect that, but felt frustrated rather than triumphant. With her everywhere around, it was more like *they* were stuck in here along with her.

"And we heard about the old law again. But they were got rid of not long ago," observed Quill, making a new addition to the list of concepts.

"And . . ." said Costain, reaching out with a marker for the photofit of the smiling man, ready to write a new name underneath.

Sefton grabbed his arm and stopped him. "We don't know if she's right. Putting the name up there would be suggesting we *knew*. We don't do theology."

Costain glared at him, but finally put the pen down.

Ross spoke up then, sounding angry at both of them. "Listen, if we can only manage to nick her, and we can convince a judge that it's against the public interest for her to be kept in the city, and we can then get her sent somewhere else to be detained before trial . . . I'd like to find out what happens to her as that prison van heads up the M1. That'd be one solution to Objective seven on the Ops Board: bring to trial or destroy."

"Maybe," said Quill, "that would be the point at which to start negotiating about a few things. Like Objective six: us getting rid of the Sight. But we have to nick her first. And that cat isn't going to help."

Sefton watched as the others drifted back to their regular tasks. He'd observed some lessons of his own from the cat's story, but wasn't sure they were the kind of things that would mean anything much to the others. He wasn't even sure about them within himself. But now there was somebody else he could tell.

The march held that Saturday headed down one side of Hyde Park, a long column with banners and drums and air horns. In the middle of it walked Kev Sefton, feeling deeply awkward, as Joe strode beside him.

"I wanted," said Sefton, "to talk somewhere private, you know?"

"It's noisy enough for privacy, and I'd promised them I'd come along."

"Who are 'they'?"

"It's against the cuts. This is mostly Occupy, but our section is walking under the pink flag." Uniforms lined the route. Cars sounded their horns as they passed, either supportively or aggressively, it was impossible to know. Sefton tried to find support around him, wondered if this sort of thing contributed to being *remembered*. Maybe. But you needed to mean a lot more, individually, to a lot more people, before you could draw on power like that, even if you knew the right gestures and could make your voice sound the right way. It was like a big but weak force, while sacrifice was for smaller things, but stronger ones. He wondered if Losley, now she'd mastered both, had turned into some sort of higher being, and was no longer concerned with killing. But then he noticed that one of the copies of her was stalking along beside the parade, as everyone else talked about the match on Monday, and just a look at that essence of her told him she still was what she was. She couldn't forget her past, that history of hers they'd heard. She was addicted to that past. It was all he could do to keep himself walking along, as he felt the weight of the crowd around him, the nausea of all these individual desires seething among the single purpose. Thank God he had more control of the Sight now, or he'd have been in real trouble. He'd hoped to be able to talk to Joe about this stuff, but, just looking around now . . .

"I'm already—" The music around them suddenly got even louder, and Sefton had to shout to be heard above it. "I'm already having to try very hard not to see a few things even among this lot."

Joe looked around, interested. "You mean with the Sight?"

"No, I mean like that bloke in a mask, and the couple of canisters being passed back, and I'm not keen on how sharp some of these sign poles look."

"Look, we don't all—"

"You know what I bloody am." *I'm like her, against one thing and also its opposite, like a lot of people now, maybe like a lot of people always are. And that pink flag above me is sort of my West Ham, but so's the warrant card in my pocket. And I don't want either to become my club, like hers is.* "Listen, I've been thinking about what I need to do."

"What?"

"I heard her history, and she went through some extreme shit. She was dedicated. She was passionate. You meet a fighter like that, you've got to step up, you've got to be on their level, yeah? I've just been fumbling around with this shit, I've been experimenting, I've been making mistakes. I can't seem to find my right moment, find my voice. *She* didn't do any of that: she just dived into something she feared, in order to help someone she loved. At least one of us needs to get as deeply into this stuff as she did. And there's only me who's doing it. I've got to learn it the hard way, without a teacher, like she did. Maybe get hurt like she did, dig as deeply into myself as she did."

"If you feel that, then—" But now there were shouts from ahead of them, and the sound of horses charging, and the crowd burst apart in all directions around them, yelling and screaming.

There'd been some violence up ahead, and it exploded back down the column of marchers, splitting it as whole groups tried to turn away from the route, either to get out of the way or because they'd arranged it beforehand. Sefton and Joe stumbled and swayed with the crowd surging around them, as shouts grew louder from every direction. Sefton felt the Sight pushing the violence of the situation into his head, making him want to hide. Then the group were shoved aside as another group came barrelling into them, and they found themselves slammed back against the railings. People started climbing up over them, some of them masked, all of them yelling. Some of them tumbled over the railings into the park, and some of them merely fell back.

"Oh fuck," said Sefton, "we've been kettled." And, just as he said it, in came the smoke, a wave of it directed elsewhere but blown back against them. People nearby started throwing things back in the direction of the attack, their muscles and shouting and sweat all getting into his head now. He looked deep into the swirl of the smoke and saw tantalizing images of proud protest, of ragged peasants and charging soldiers and gunfire and a map unfolding of how that eruption had poured a more lovely and awful England into the world. He felt it like another awful nostalgia, a road he couldn't take, an illusion and a truth both at once. He knew that if he stayed here long enough for the smoke to get into his lungs, he'd be taken by one side and thus lose his place

293

in the other, and end up off his feet, and unable to stand as he needed to now.

He grabbed Joe and kissed him. "We're going now," he said. And then he pulled out his warrant card.

"What do you mean, 'we're going'?" But Joe let himself be dragged forward as the crowd went bulging that way, toward a perimeter on the pavement where people were shouting at and arguing with and attempting to negotiate with a row of uniforms with helmets and riot shields. There was a sudden surge behind them, and Sefton found himself thrown up against one of those shields. His warrant card flew out of his hand. He bent to pick it up—

He was knocked flying, a knee in his head. His hand closed over the card. Beside him, Joe fell, along with a row of others, a baton bouncing back off his head. "Hoi!" shouted Sefton. "Hoi!" He leaped to his feet, hauled Joe up beside him, and saw the waves back away from him, gathering strength: the two sides about to slam down and force him into some screwed-up space he couldn't live in. He held up his warrant card in front of him like a talisman.

"Right you!" bellowed the copper directly in front of him, his shoulder number hidden. Sefton and Joe were grabbed and hauled through the shield line. Sefton was shoved down again and heaved himself up, ready to thump the next uniform that waved a baton at him—

But they were out of it now. The wave of uniforms had moved past them, leaving them both sitting there in the road. More uniforms rushed past, and from this angle Sefton could see a running battle taking place, the uniforms being pelted alongside those railings, and he felt an immediate stupid anger back in the other direction, and the waves inside him and surging across the protest rolled round London again and never broke. Sefton went over to Joe and helped him stand, put his hand to the man's wounded head.

"Thanks for getting me out," Joe said.

"They shouldn't have fucking—!"

"It's okay. I know you're—"

"You know I'm both. Which is why I'm not going to be remembered, since nothing complicated gets remembered, not as it really is." He looked back at the protest and saw the batons rising and falling, and felt the blows echoing off the sky above him, echoing all the way from the suburbs. "That's why I'm going to have to make a sacrifice."

Quill had heard from Sarah that she was spending Saturday working at the office, and he very much didn't want to be at home alone with his brain in its current state. So he'd gone out into the pubs of London. Out of a feeling of duty, he'd texted Harry to come and join him, half hoping he wouldn't be up for it, but he was.

Quill knew his London pubs, enough to diagnose one from a glance at the exterior. There were pubs that defined neighborhoods, in that strange way that London had neighborhoods just because of imaginary lines on the ground. There were pubs that were about the British going out into the world, changing and being changed, and coming back to find the old inn still standing, the old crowd around the fire—apart from those that had died of plague while you were away: the Road to Jerusalem; the Balaclava; the Pillars of Hercules. There were pubs about the trade guilds of the city: the Carpenters' Arms; the Coopers; the Square and Compass. There were pubs for the heads of all the kings and queens, and for the heads of enemies brought back to Blighty.

He wandered down to the pleasant neighborhood around the British Museum, and found a battered leather armchair in a pub which was all enormous windows, like being inside a jewel box, and which, after a quick inspection, had nothing terrifying about it. He opted for a pint of one of their pleasingly filthy real ales, leaned back and tried to relax, tried not to drink quickly enough to distract himself.

Until Harry and his dad arrived . . .

"Now you've got all of the Met working for you at every football match, brilliant!" Harry was sounding his usual self, but these days

Quill didn't need his dad beside him to hear the subtext, to explain the strain in his face.

"One of these days," said his dad, "he might even get around to including you."

"I miss having you about," said Quill, and he meant it.

Harry actually had to pause a second to reply, as his dad laughed mirthlessly. "Well, it must get pretty stuffy in that Portakabin, with the four of you filling the place up."

Quill managed to laugh along. "How's Goodfellow?"

"Oh, limping to the finish line, Jimmy. But there must be an Aladdin's cave of evidence somewhere, and we ain't got it. We don't have Toshack's accounts. They're probably somewhere on the Continent now. We don't have his supply. And we've heard whispers of the top brass saying that, since Toto gets along so well with only the four of you—"

"Oh, don't give me that!"

"No, no, it's all right. You haven't caught her yet, have you? God help us if you do!"

How had Quill ever enjoyed this? Harry had been the furthest thing from his thoughts during most of this investigation, but he'd always thought that somehow they'd get close again. But how was that ever going to work, unless they managed to force Losley to take the Sight away from them?

"So, how's . . . ?"

Quill missed what his friend said, because he was thinking of something else. And now he couldn't even remember what that was. "Sorry, Harry?"

"I said . . ."

His own dad would have loved sitting here among the shininess of these horse brasses. They always had shiny stuff in pubs, like in churches. To take your mind off to relaxing places. And, no, he was missing something, again—he was bloody missing something! He made himself turn back and look Harry in the eye. He now realized he was breathing hard. It was as if his brain was using up his body's energy as it tried to do something. Harry's dad was looking at him as if he was a prize chump. "Harry, you'll have to forgive me . . ."

"What's up, old son? Are you falling asleep on me?"

Quill held himself in place, his arms locked on the chair. "Could you say that again, slowly?"

"Oh, the great detective's had a revelation. It's one of those moments, like on the telly, where it all falls into place. From the top, then . . ."

This time it was like something huge screeching against something else, two massive surfaces in contact, and it made his head hurt so hard. He knew that if he let his attention slip aside from what Harry was saying, it would stop hurting. Such a weight was trying to stop him from hearing Harry, from understanding him—

Quill felt himself on the edge of blacking out. He let his attention slide off into something pleasant: a vision of his dad walking a few paces in front of him, tall in the sunshine. He came back to reality a moment later to see Harry standing over him, looking shocked, Harry's own dad, smiling all over his face, by his shoulder. "Are you all right?" Harry was shaking him. "Jimmy, can you talk? Can you move your face?"

He feared Quill had had a stroke, and Quill wondered for a moment if that was true. He moved the muscles on both sides, put a hand to his brow. "It's all right, it's all right. Harry, there's . . ." There was nothing at all going on here. "I'm just tired." He wondered what all the fuss was about. Harry was overreacting a bit, wasn't he? Quill managed a broad smile. "Look, you get them in, while I go and have a slash."

The toilets were as baroque as the bar itself, all imposing imperial Victoriana and boasting the names of every man who ever invented a sanitation device. Quill splashed some water on his face. He'd . . . what, had he just fallen asleep? What had he missed? What was he missing? It was as if it was just there, just behind his reflection, just inside his idea of who he was, just beyond what his mind could touch.

Through the door, he heard the sound of Harry gasping.

Quill burst out of the Gents to see Harry floating over his chair, his skin red with heat, shaking and sweating, his eyes desperately fixed on a flickering light that was bursting impossibly up through the floor. The smell of it rolled over the thick carpet toward Quill. He didn't look down, though. He was looking to where Harry's dad stood beside their chairs. He was holding on to his son by one hand, almost affectionately, like a balloon. He kept glancing up at him.

Losley had been here. In just those few seconds, Losley had been here, but had left Quill, and taken Harry instead. Had what happened to him earlier been some sort of diversion? Hardly, she wouldn't know he'd react like that. But it wasn't too late, and Quill took a step forward.

"Stop," said Harry's dad, "or I let go of him."

Quill stopped. "You've changed your tune."

"She made me a bit more than I was, didn't she? Now, my boy Harry here's got a message for you. Haven't you, boy? What did the nice lady tell you to say?"

Quill looked round, maybe hoping for some sort of help, but he just saw the looks on the faces of patrons who had probably watched him stagger back into the bar and start talking to some bloke who looked too out of it to reply. He saw them try and glance over, but the looks they gave instantly slid off something that felt too hard on their eyes.

Harry's gaze located Quill, and he seemed to wake from the trance his terror had put him in. "Jimmy! Help me!"

"I will, mate!"

"My dad . . . My dad's holding me . . . right on the edge of it. I can feel it, Jimmy. I can see what's in there. Why is it my dad?! Why's it him doing this?!"

"It's not your dad. It's just . . . just what you think of as your dad. You've always been thinking of him, haven't you?"

"I . . . I 'spose! I never thought . . . I never saw him like this. I always just thought he was looking down at me!"

Harry's dad made a tutting sound. He tugged suddenly at Harry's wrist, like he was warning a dog. "Go on, son!"

"If I tell him the message, you'll let go of me and I'll be off down there anyway!"

"Yeah, but if you don't, I'll do it anyway, and then she'll have to find some other poor sod to do this to."

Harry was sobbing, shaking his head, staring at his dad; he couldn't believe it.

"You keep him there," Quill reached for his mobile. He couldn't hope to get his team here in time, and he had no idea what they could do to help, but he had to try.

"No," said Harry's dad again, letting go of Harry for a moment and then catching him once more.

Harry yelled in terror. "I don't deserve this," he panted. "I haven't deserved any of this. And this now, this now . . . !"

"Of course you don't deserve it!" shouted Quill. "This is something she's doing to you, not something you're doing to yourself! None of us is!" The other punters were openly staring at them now, the two yelling drunks in the corner.

"Come on," urged Harry's dad. "We've got to be off soon, son."

Harry took some deep breaths, and seemed to steady himself. "You'll get her, won't you, Jimmy? You'll nick her?"

"Mate, don't tell me it—"

"You heard him. I don't have a choice." He looked at his dad again, and then looked guilty. "I've failed so much . . . all my life, Jimmy. Now I'll never get to be as good as you."

"That's not true."

"Shut up and listen. I don't have much of a sitrep for you. The woman I take to be your prime suspect was in here . . . looked like an old woman, late seventies . . ."

"She can look like anything, Harry. I should have explained."

". . . and then she looked like . . . something terrible. And I could see nobody else was looking at her, and I got up, I tried to go for . . . No, I tried to run. And she pointed a finger and twisted something in the air, and . . . all of this happened. And then *he* seemed to come out of my head and right into the middle of what I was seeing . . . and she . . . she put my hand in his . . . and it feels just like his real hand, Jimmy. It feels like when . . ."

"Compose yourself, Harry. Take your time." Quill looked dangerously at Harry's dad, wondering if there was any gesture he could make, just a random pass of his hands, that might harm the thing, or might save Harry.

Harry looked around the room, as if savoring the real world for the last time. All he's got, thought Quill, was that bloody awful distance shown by the British when they don't want to relate to something. Maybe, being a copper, the familiarity gave him comfort. Then Harry started speaking again, quickly, as if afraid his courage would fail him. "She said that she's got power to spare now, so she's going to kill anyone who scores even one goal against West Ham. She's going to keep taking the children. Jimmy, you've got to tell my Sal—!"

"And that's your lot," said his dad, and let go of Harry's hand.

Quill shouted something and flung up his arms, expecting an explosion of blood. But Harry was floating on the edge of the cosmic weirdness, light blazing around him, his suit starting to flare at the cuffs and elbows, his arms cartwheeling helplessly, his gaze still finding Quill as if he could hold on through that connection.

"Don't worry, son," said his dad. "I'm coming with you. I'll always be with you now, always there to egg you on." And he vanished.

Harry's face erupted with blood.

Quill stumbled over to the body and sat there, dazed, for quite a while. There were screams and shouts all around him. A barman arrived and was staring at Harry, not knowing what to do. But Harry was dead . . . and the punters were leaning over to look or stumbling back.

Quill made himself stand up, and found that he also was covered in blood. Again. He noticed his friend's blood on his lapel, and looked at it, curiously unaffected by it, everything too big for it to sink in now. Quill saw that, coming round the bar, a couple of paramedics had run in and were moving toward them. He stood up, swaying.

He got home hours later, again having tossed all his clothes into a forensics bag, the last traces of his closest friend with them.

Lofthouse had arrived at the pub and had tried to offer words of support.

"Every goal scorer." He said to her, repeating the words to her, until she realized what he was talking about. "She's escalated her threat. Now she's going to kill *every* player that scores even *once* against West Ham." Lofthouse promised to get on to it immediately. Quill got his phone out, and tried to text the news to his unit, but his fingers couldn't find the keys, and he asked Lofthouse to get that done instead, and if he could leave the scene now, please. People began talking about Losley's poisons again, and he didn't want to hear it.

A marked car took him home. Slumped in the back seat, he managed to get minutes of something which felt a bit like sleep, but never quite left him unaware. He just about fell up against the door of his house, and paused there.

He so wanted to tell Sarah. He wanted to tell her everything. But she wouldn't believe him. That had to be an excuse; surely he could *make* her believe him? But there was still something other than that, shouting at him—an emptiness, something he was missing. He kept using those words to himself, but what did they mean?

He fumbled for his key.

*

He could hear Sarah was in now, typing away upstairs. "I'm home," he called, and there came a muted call back. She obviously hadn't heard about what had happened to him. Right, because he'd asked not to be named. She just thought something big had happened in his case, so would be surprised he was home. He himself was surprised he was here.

He wandered into the kitchen, intending to make tea and then sit down somewhere, try to sleep. Harry . . . bloody Harry . . . after all these years.

Oh!

We smell death near you soon.

That was what whichever small fish had left that note had meant: Harry. They'd felt it coming. Quill felt a stab of guilt over his relief at the thought. It was Harry when it could have been Sarah, could have been . . . who else? No answer to that.

God, the kitchen was a mess. What were all these junk-shop novelties lying everywhere? Was this really what the two of them were making of their lives?

Maybe he should quit. Nobody would blame him. Not now. He could just not go in any more. She could quit too. No future in her job. No future in his. They could get out of London, make a new life, and he wouldn't have to deal with seeing . . .

And let someone else, less able, entirely vulnerable, deal with Losley. Like the way Harry had. Quill leaned against a kitchen unit.

Sarah entered. "Are you making tea?" she was already asking. And then she saw him and stopped. "What's happened?"

He shook his head. He didn't want to come out with the lie version now.

"Oh God, when Losley killed that copper tonight, were you . . . ?" He went over and held her tight. They held on to each other together, and she let him stay silent.

But there was something else in him. Something that needed to be asked. "Why is the house in such a mess?"

"Quill, don't start a row just to—"

"No, I mean . . ." He was aware that the copper part of his head was working at this, working and working, gears still missing each other—not something he was used to when at home. "The two of us, okay, we seem to be living these . . . distanced lives. Around something . . . that was there but now isn't. Was that always how it was? All of those things that might have been you and me together, that might have been . . . exciting or interesting, they seem to have been channeled into . . . something else."

"Our careers, you mean. What are you, a teenager?"

"No, something else. It's like a . . . black hole, like something that's taken loads of our lives, and now we can't see where it's all gone. And it seems to have happened so suddenly, so . . . recently."

"It happens to everybody."

"No, this isn't . . . This isn't something you can talk about with reference to . . . something that *always* happens. This is . . ." He didn't have a word for it. He gently let go of her, then he led her by the hand—as if they were two stumbling children—back into the lounge. He pointed at the piles of DVDs with colorful cases, the bizarre nick-knacks and odd books that were everywhere. "Why do we have all that stuff?" She frowned at him, her own brain working. And all he could think of were the gaps in what Harry had said. The things he hadn't been allowed to hear. There were the same sort of gaps here too.

He led her to the rear of the house, toward the door leading to their little back garden, but beside which was another door. He couldn't even remember what was in there, he realized, but it seemed to be the center of what he didn't feel like he should be looking at. That's why he'd brought her here, so he could see it again, so he could . . . He didn't know why he was doing this, just letting the deductive part of his brain make it happen. Feeling its way. And it was like bloody crawling uphill.

He pushed the door and, as it swung open, he suddenly understood, without knowing why, in some feral, desperately caring part of his mind, that what he was about to do would hurt not just him but Sarah, terribly.

Inside the room, there was more weird and colorful stuff. Piles of it. He didn't know why this was here, but he realized that he knew the word for this sort of room. The feeling of that moment was like something hard falling into his stomach.

"Why," he said, "do we have a *nursery?*"

TWENTY-FOUR

Ross had been woken in the early hours by a text message from Quill that called for her and the others to assemble at the Portakabin right now. She'd hardly got off to sleep. Until then she'd been following the news coverage of the attack on the pub, with her special notebook out on her lap, wondering why the team hadn't been called to the site.

She entered the Portakabin to find every light switched on and Quill, Sefton and Costain standing in front of the Ops Board. Quill turned to glance at her, and the look on his face scared her. On the corkboard behind him, a thread connected the photo of Mora to a small picture of a tiny baby. "She took my daughter," he said.

Ross stepped closer, trying not to let the horror of it overwhelm her. It was the lack of any writing underneath the photo that made her ask. She sensed the other two feeling as lost as she was. And she realized, in that second, what must have been done to them all. "What's she called?" she asked.

Quill took a moment to control himself enough to answer. "Jessica, apparently."

Ross looked for the gap in her memory and couldn't find it. She wondered if she'd ever known that name. She wrote it under the photo.

*

305

He told them about Losley's threat concerning the footballers. That meant they had forty-two hours until the next home match, with Man City.

"How do we know Jessica's not . . ." Costain paused for a moment, then visibly decided it was best to continue, ". . . already dead?"

"Losley would have told me so," said Quill. "She'd want to . . . let me know. It's as if she wanted this to be a surprise, when I figured it out. Because I think she knew I would. This is her down to the ground, and we should have realized that from what the bloody cat told us. It's not just about keeping on with the sacrifices so that she has the huge amounts of power she's going to need to kill every goal-scorer. No, she needed to make this personal. She wanted me to *feel* it." Then he had to stop for a moment. "All right, listen, you lot."

He sat down at the table, and made them all sit down too. "When this aspect of the investigation becomes clear to Lofthouse, as it will when she wakes up this morning and is told that forensics are all over my gaff, then there'll be pressure on me to step aside. I'm not going to and, going on her past eccentric form, I think Lofthouse might let me stay put. If I could, I'd tell her . . ." He went to the board and grabbed the picture of the baby. ". . . that because I don't know who this is, I'm only 'copper' afraid, that it's not in here." He tapped his chest. "Not that I *could* tell her that. But, if I'm being honest, I think knowing fully what I'd lost . . . I think that'd be . . . better somehow, you know? Natural. What I'm feeling now, there's no name for it. The only other people who've ever felt it that we know of are Terry and Julie Franks. I need to *fix* it. Sarah needs to fix it. This morning . . . it wasn't that the veil suddenly dropped from our eyes. We actually had to persuade each other about it. She made me go into the nursery with her, and we looked at the crib. We looked at all the DVDs of *Teletubbies* and *In the Night Garden*. We kept having to force each other back to concentrate on it." He told them about what else they'd found at the house. "Forensics found a pile of soil half-concealed under a hedge in the garden. Sarah might have noticed it if it had been out in the open, since she's been following the story. As you know, I've hardly been home. If I'd just taken one walk out into my own garden . . . or maybe she'd have made it so we couldn't see that either. If I'd asked any of you lot, you wouldn't have known, or I wouldn't have heard you say anything. But if I'd just *thought* for a moment how I myself might be a target! I've constructed this bloke for me to be, out of bits and pieces, and he's the sort of bloke who never *could* become a target. *This* is what I've been missing. The fact that I'm a dad."

"Don't blame yourself," said Costain.

"I think I'll be joining you in Hell," said Quill gently. "I think I might be on the edge of it now." He looked at the photo. "I can't see anything left," he said. "We could stare at Google and the bill lists for days, but with all her new power maybe she can conceal all that from us now. That cat's no bloody use. I'm going to be left with this child I don't know, this little stranger, as my very own bloody ghost standing there in that nursery. I can see it. I can see it. I'll be able to distract myself whenever I'm here; it's not going to be following me around like Harry's dad did. But it'll be there to remind me when I get home, locked into that par-ticular place. And I'm calling it an it. I'm calling my own baby an it." He put a hand to his forehead and grabbed his flesh so hard that Ross was afraid he'd draw blood. "We're helpless. *I'm* helpless."

Ross now found that a horrible feeling was creeping over her. "What if . . . it's not just you?"

They called up every friend and relative they could think of, including some deliberately distant ones they *wouldn't* readily have been thinking of. Ross could see how the shortness of Costain's list was troubling him. But waking up a distant cousin eventually convinced him. "No, Tone, you ain't got no kids that you don't know about. Mate, why are you asking?"

Relief and guilt came with the knowledge that the three others didn't have any children. Nor did anyone close to them here in London have any that weren't safely at home. Ross wanted to joke with Sefton that she hadn't thought kids were likely in his case, but he had such an intense look on his face, as if he was coming to some huge decision.

As dawn came up outside, Ross went back to the board. "How did she do it?" she said.

"I remember her zapping me with something back in her attic, that first time, just after you told her to go fuck herself," Quill glanced ironically at Costain. "I thought, at the time, it was just for her to grab the cat."

"Bitch plans ahead," observed Costain. "Okay, we've got to ask." He went to fetch the cat's cage, put it on the table, tapped it until the animal woke up, and then showed it the baby picture. "Recognize her?"

"Oh," said the cat, "that's the very young one."

"When last you saw her, was she still alive?" asked Quill, all in a rush.

"Yes, I believe so. Mora had quite a business to keep her fed. Oh, the bawling that thing made! That's why she keeps her in one of the tunnels between houses, as with a lot of the younger children."

Quill closed his eyes. Ross went over to him and, against her whole nature and his, took him into her arms.

In the early light, Sarah Quill stood watching the forensics team combing her back garden. She felt that she should be seeming more desperate, more agonized. She saw the police expressions and saw them wondering why she wasn't. She realized she was trying to fake it, trying to look like those people you saw in police appeals to the kidnapper. She felt stupidly guilty, and genuinely guilty, and she had no idea how to describe how she felt. She was angry at Quill, and at herself. She made police officers cups of tea, while trying to look devastated, hating the fact that her hands didn't shake. She kept trying to direct their searches, interferingly, meaninglessly. She kept standing at the door of the nursery as forensics combed it, hoping the details would connect to something. They had used a childminder, apparently, who was struggling to explain why she hadn't visited the house for weeks, why her books, to her own eyes, showed no sign of the Quills. Neither the census, nor the borough records showed any sign of their child to the custodians, yet they did so to investigating officers. One social worker, it seemed, had kept asking all the others what was going on, to the point where it had become an office joke. Sarah kept looking at the photos that Josh, her nephew in Scotland, had sent. Photos of Jessica, aged eighteen months. She knew this must be a terrible wound that she had suffered. She kept hearing from the family liaison officer assigned to her how Losley kept the children safe. But there was an *until* involved there. Quill had told her: two days.

She wanted him to be here, and she wanted him to be out there, along with his unit that these coppers here kept complaining about not being part of, but kept saying was too small to achieve anything further. She overheard these conversations; did they really think she wouldn't?

"How did she make us forget?" she had demanded last night. Quill had then told her: everything had finally come flooding out of him. Every detail made her more angry. "That happened to you, and you didn't tell me? Things like that exist, and you didn't tell me? How could you keep me out in the cold like this? Who am I to you?" But she believed him very readily, because it was the only option. She got scared at what lay outside, dragged him to the window and made him explain what he could see out there in the night. The journalist part of her kept arranging it into tidy questions, but the person she was went deeper than that. Someone who had thought she was married, and hadn't thought twice really about the strength and quality of that relationship kept ripping those questions up in sheer fury. How *dare* he? How dare he not have *told* her about the danger to her *child*? He just stood there and took it from her. He wasn't taking on some sort of noble burden, just accepting the truth of it, rocking slightly on his heels.

She felt the world was against her now. She found it all too easy to see London as Quill described it, as a tentacled monster at the heart of a whirlpool that had snatched away their child. But it was Quill she saw as failing to put a stake into the heart of that monster. It was him whose desperate attacks on the monster had slammed a hole into the ground, who'd caused everything to start whirling around them. He had put an emptiness into the heart of everything, as well as having one inflicted on himself. It was as if something from inside him and his job had spread out into the world and engulfed them.

She stood against a wall, her body propped at an angle it would never normally have assumed, as if she'd been shot, or was a toddler, and she tried in her head to find her way back to a baby called Jessica.

At 10 a.m. Detective Superintendent Rebecca Lofthouse was sitting at a table facing the special committee of the Football Association, which consisted of five white men in their fifties. She took a deep breath. "With respect, Mr. Chairman," she said, "what the *fuck* are you doing?"

The man looked to have faced his fair share of criticism in his time, and he was proud to have done so. But now he was eyeing her with a strange expression, as if he literally didn't know why he was taking this position. He and his fellow committee members, selected from the high and mighty in the game, had occupied this grand meeting room at Wembley Stadium for three days now, and only this afternoon had she been called in to hear personally the extraordinary news that was about to be given to the press. Now that she'd heard it, she still couldn't believe it.

"We are not," declared the chairman, sounding flustered and angry, "giving in to threats." And his glance slid sideways toward an empty seat at the table. Lofthouse glanced at the others, saw they were all looking over there. As if someone else had given the orders, which they didn't necessarily agree with, and then had . . . gone?

She shook her head to clear it. "Mora Losley is now threatening the life of every player that scores even one goal against West Ham."

"We're aware of that fact, but—"

"The Professional Footballers' Association has threatened to strike, the government has already requested you not to continue, and you were agreeing to the point where everyone was sure—"

"We live in a free country, and—"

"All the managers are saying they'll tell their players not to score against West Ham. These games will be a farce. That's giving in to threats, making every match about *her*!"

"We will not—"

"And it's one of my coppers, one of mine now. DI Quill has had his own child taken." She remembered that terrible strain on Quill's face, that utter lack of his usual brave energy. He'd looked so complicated, so knotted, but he'd asked to be allowed to stay on the case and . . . well, she had felt she had to let him. He'd justified every bet she'd made, on such a flimsy basis. Who knew what horrors he'd already faced, beyond those she knew about? She found her hand going to her charm bracelet. "There is a child in Losley's hands whom she will undoubtedly *kill* if a goal is scored!"

"We've considered that, at great length. We feel it's *your* job to prevent that. But we can't give in to every psychopath."

She kept her voice level. She didn't want this lot accusing her of being hysterical. "I'll have your arses for this. I'll fill the pitch with coppers if I have to, and arrest the teams before the match begins."

"Now *that*," said the chairman, "would be illegal."

And he was right. She couldn't make it happen. Lofthouse thought she heard a laugh from somewhere nearby. She turned to look, but there was only that empty chair. When she turned back, she saw that the committee members were all looking over there too. Only they were all bloody smiling.

Ross had listened in disbelief as Quill relayed the news that the matches were going to continue. "It's as if football can somehow soak up death," she had said, after he'd finished. "As if it's immortal; that a club or a league or a match will always carry on. They'll just have a minute's silence and wear a black armband."

She'd gone back to her work, aware once more of that clock still ticking, only thirty-three hours to go; aware that the only thing she had to go on—that endless flow of data crossing her screen—probably now had no more secrets to divulge. She looked up from it an hour later, needing to rest her eyes. The air of tension hadn't ebbed. Sefton was making quick, decisive notes. Quill was pacing before the Ops Board as if something would suddenly leap out at him. Costain had gone to get the cat some more food. Ross watched distantly as he gazed at the animal for a long time, as if pondering something, as if needing something to be fond of and wondering if it could be the cat.

"I thought you'd stop feeding me," said the cat, "once it became clear to you how little help I can be."

"Yeah, well," he said, "I thought it was about time someone showed a bit of fucking decency about something."

"I do appreciate that."

"You don't have much of an ego on you, do you?"

"I am, at heart, a dead cat. My mistress has told me, many times, that I am worthless. I am forced to agree."

"But it's not about what you are, is it?" Costain leaned closer to the cat. "It's about what you could be. Imagine being one of the good guys, one of *us*, fighting the good fight against Losley."

312

Ross thought she heard a certain artificiality in his tone, like something he'd voiced or thought of often.

"I really don't see how. I can only ever agree with her, and thus I believe she should remain at liberty. Though I would . . ." It hesitated. "Well, let's just say you're much kinder than she is."

Costain reached out and stroked it under the chin. "I think it's time I gave you a name, mate. Do you want to choose?"

The cat mewed in delight. Ross was sure it preferred to wait to hear what he'd decided to call it. There was something pathetic about its eagerness.

"I think," said Costain, "I'm going to call you Tiger Feet."

He seemed oddly distant from what he was saying. But perhaps that was just what this man was like, how she didn't feel warmth from him even when he was being kind—or forcing himself to be. She could feel sleep tugging at her again in the afternoon sunlight. They had to find another avenue of inquiry soon, or they'd all break. Well, not her, because she'd do something else instead of break. Or just her body would. Into her mind came the images that kept her going, and the anger about it that she kept trying and failing to project onto Losley, away from its real cause, which was the now unreachable Toshack. There he was again, her dad, hanging from the ceiling. The person that made her, the person she thought of every waking moment, the ghost that—

She actually fell. She fell off her chair. Her chair skidded across the floor. All the others stared at her. She stood up. "I . . . I think I've got a lead, only . . ." She couldn't say it aloud. "Give me a couple of hours." She grabbed her coat and put one foot in front of the other, and then she started to run—before Quill could demand good practice from her—out of the Portakabin, out into the meaningless sunlight, sprinting for her car.

Sefton found that he wanted that to be an excuse. There was something to be done here, so he didn't have to carry out what he'd now come to the conclusion only he could do. No, not good enough. He got to his feet. "Me, too," he said. "I'm sorry." He found that he wanted to say something to Costain too. But he couldn't find the words. He also got to the door before Quill could start to say anything.

Quill didn't know how to feel. He knew that if anything drastic happened to those two, then any knowledge they found would be gone with them. And many other copper rules applied, besides. But he'd been staring at the Ops Board for hours, dealing with calls and e-mails from other operations that offered up useless lead after useless lead. What his team were doing now, he felt, was away from the board. And that honored him.

He looked to Costain. "What about you?"

"Actually," Costain glanced back toward the cat, "yeah."

"Want to tell me about it?"

"No."

"Okay, then." Quill flapped his arms uselessly. "Don't get yourself killed."

Costain picked up the cat's cage, the cat inside it already looking startled, and came over. "Listen," he said to Quill, "you and me, I know—"

"Nah, come on. Is this just you doing the right thing again?"

"Well, yeah. But—"

"But we don't ever know why anyone does what they do, do we? You might have stayed even if you hadn't felt forced into it. You came back that first time, didn't you?"

"And now I need you to trust me."

"I'm watching you heading for the door with something that's halfway between evidence and a witness, so I think I'm there. Is that it, or are we going in for any more of the touchy-feelies?"

Costain nodded to him.

Quill nodded back.

Costain headed out to his car, taking the cat with him.

TWENTY-FIVE

Ross stood in front of what had once been her family home, on that corner of a tree-lined street in Bermondsey. It was raining again on this Sunday afternoon. Only a couple of details of the house had altered: whoever owned it now had changed the garden, and put up different curtains. There was, thank God, nothing that looked special to the Sight.

The door was opened by a middle-aged Asian woman, who eyed her suspiciously. Ross presented her documents, and told the woman she could call the station if she wanted to confirm her identity. The woman kept the door on the chain while she did so, but finally let her in. Ross knew she must look suspicious, her professional politeness hardly concealing the personal urgency of what she was doing here. "It's a routine inquiry, ma'am, to do with an ongoing investigation. Nobody here is in any trouble."

"I should hope not!"

Ross didn't react to that. "I'd like a look around upstairs, please. Alone."

The smell was so nearly the same. New people, new fragrances, same polish. She stepped onto the landing and walked straight past the door leading to what had been her bedroom. She moved on, instead to where Dad's office had been.

315

The door was, once again, open just a bit. She resisted the awful urge to first peer through the gap, and instead just pushed the door open and went in.

What Quill had said about where he'd see the ghost of his daughter—that had been the first seed of it for her. She recognized that in retrospect. He'd been right: like with the ships and the bus, this was about places too. People didn't always carry their ghosts around with them. In her case, she'd suddenly realized, she had very much associated her father with this room. She knew he was now in Hell. She knew that more definitely than any other fact in her head, but without having a solid sense of what that meant, even considering her own experience. But Harry's dad hadn't been just a bundle of Harry's own insecurities. According to Quill, he'd acted with his own volition, right at the end. She hoped that hadn't all been down to Losley. Ross didn't know how it worked, so this was going to be an experiment. A terrible experiment. But she owed it to Quill to find the courage to do this.

She stepped into the room, closed the door behind her, looked around at the unfamiliar furniture of a spare bedroom. She looked up and saw that the ceiling rose was still there. No huge reaction to seeing the ceiling. It was just plaster. She made herself remember again, and now she could see it clearly again: that moment that was stamped into her, that had made her. She focused on every detail of what, if she could see a ghost specific to her, she might expect to see here.

"Dad?" she said.

No answer. But she suddenly noticed something: she could smell something new. Him, his aftershave, the smell of his jacket, the cigars and beer. And something under that, which spoke of vastness and closeness, of Halloween, of things let in on special nights. "Dad, if you can hear me, I need to see you. It's . . . it's not just for me. It's something important. I know you'd always try to look after me . . . no matter where you are. It doesn't matter what you

316

look like now, or what's going on, you can . . . come back. It's okay."

She waited, feeling afraid and vulnerable but waiting. She smelled it before she saw or heard anything, and then a rose of thorns burst from the ceiling above her. And that distant smell burst in along with it. And the room was full of uneasy light. She staggered back but she stayed on her feet, looking up, looking and looking . . . A feeling of potential harm had flooded in all around her. Something formed out of those shapes above.

And there—there he was again. Hanging there, making choking noises, the noose once again around his neck. It was as if the memory she'd fixated on for all these years had been preserved here. There was his wonderful face, alive again, an expression living on it again. She stared and stared as the blood hammered through her body and head. It was him. It was him! He spun and rocked in the awful light, looking at her desperately, one hand outstretched. She could see clearly the signs on his body of what the woman with the Tarot cards had called the threefold death.

But this time she had a knife. She grabbed it from her pocket, dragged the stool from the dressing table across the room and leaped up onto it. She started to saw at the rope. But the rope was like diamond. This was a new nightmare. Her fingers kept slipping off it. The blade kept flying away from it.

"No!" he said. His voice! He could say things! "Lisa, no! Don't touch it! You can't cut it, girl. You can't undo it. Don't you get too close."

She stopped, helpless, staring at his face, loving him. And he looked back at her, and it was the best thing. It was the best thing. But she was still helpless.

He looked quickly upward, over his shoulder. His voice was a gasp, limited by the rope, but not as limited as it should have been, and that was terrible, that implication that this was usual for him now. "I can't stay long or they'll notice."

"You don't deserve to be in there!" She hadn't wanted this to be about her and him, but she couldn't control a single thing she might do or say now.

"I had a bad life, love. We kept it from you."

She wanted to ask him—ridiculously—she realized, if what she was doing now was okay. Or if she had betrayed him as well as the family. But there was no time for that. "Dad, I've been given . . . they call it the Sight?"

He made a strangled cry, took another moment to breathe. "No, not my girl. That means you can see all the things I have to look at every day. This is another punishment they're *doing* to me!" It was terrible to hear him so fearful. A dad shouldn't be afraid.

"This is about . . . There's kids, Dad, okay? She kills *kids*. She worked for Rob. Do you know of a Mora Losley?"

He made the sound again. "Mora Losley? Bloody Rob! Bloody Rob! He took everything! Took you! He's up *here* now!" Alf was suddenly gleeful, swinging back and forth, though the effort made his voice crack up. "In his own Hell!"

"Dad, how can we . . . get her?" She'd nearly said "nick," but that would have sounded wrong.

He seemed to gaze up into something that Ross couldn't see. As if he was looking over things, and into things, reading distant signs. "What haven't you seen? What haven't you seen? Oh, you've done stuff. You've done such a lot." She tried not to feel pride at hearing that. "But . . . Oh, there. The empty boxes."

"What, from his office?"

"Yeah. I was shown him from up here, when he was alive and I wasn't. They showed me what he was up to, as he took over my old life. I don't know how much it'll help, but it's something. Sometimes he *drove* out to his lock-up—"

"His lock-up?! We haven't found that. Where—?"

"And sometimes, when he could get away with it, he . . ." He looked quickly around, as if something was approaching. "Can't stay," he said. And he turned, looking scared like a child, and twisted out of the way before something could see him. And the ceiling vomited shut, and he was gone.

Ross's legs collapsed under her. She fell to the floor and stayed where she lay, looking up. She could see his face still against the white. She felt the horror of it washing over her. She started to sob. She felt she should remain here, that she should always be here to talk to him, to offer him some tiny comfort.

Her Tarot card reading had turned out to be true. She had found an ongoing hope through someone who had been a sacrifice. She had found something that could help. And she had found something for all seasons that she could return to. That she *would* return to. She could tell him about her revenge and that would make it better for him. And his being here was horrifying, but it would also make her life better. They still had each other. Slightly. Horrifyingly.

She stood up, and she left the room, and she walked faster and faster down the stairs of her childhood, with her phone already in her hand, making the call to Quill, and she got all the way to her car and drove off without once looking back.

TWENTY-SIX

It was early morning when Kevin Sefton parked in a space which only someone with a permit was entitled to occupy, put his job logbook in the car window, to keep the traffic wardens at bay, and stepped out into the tidy streets where he had grown up. An old lady walking her dog looked him up and down, noting the way he was dressed, then his face. She'd soon be on the phone to the Neighborhood Watch, he thought.

He walked along the wide pavements, down the tree-lined avenues leading to the main road. He saw school kids walking past, and he stopped himself thinking about his own childhood. He was either about to escape who he was or about to fall victim to it. Dwelling on it wouldn't help either way.

He went to the deserted bus stop, and looked straight down the road. He tried to focus every aspect of the Sight into the distance, where the low sun glinted off pools of water in the potholes. He could hear it now: the distant sound of an engine that was different to those of the cars and lorries passing by. It slowly came into view, for just him. The number 7 to Russell Square, running on its Sunday timetable, with those silhouettes inside it, the darkness pulsing from within it.

He suddenly had doubts. Was he now committing suicide? He steeled himself, having never deliberately walked into anything worse than this. But he knew he could do it. The kids who'd spat at him, at a place just like this, would never have imagined that. They didn't understand what they were creating when they made him.

This was his sacrifice.

He stuck out his hand. The bus slowed and came to a stop right in front of him. It waited, its engine idling. It was full of darkness. He knew, absolutely, in that instant, what waited inside for him. But, in a moment it would move off again if he didn't act now.

He made himself put one foot in front of the other. He stepped onto the platform at the rear. He couldn't see inside, and it was cold in there. Of course it was. He was about to enter a ghost. He took a deep breath and stepped forward into the darkness.

It was like being squeezed into something awful inside his own head. It reminded him, for a moment, of the horror they'd all been suspended over in the attic. And then he was through that, and into—

It rushed at him. Oh God, oh God, he'd stepped straight into Hell! He'd deliberately stepped into Hell! Because he hadn't believed in it! Every inch of the bus was full of them, and it was more of a bus than any real bus could be; it was his school bus and every other sort of bus that had ever transported things that fought. They were on him, a mass of children, bigger than him, and yet he was still an adult. They put their fingers into his eyes and mouth, and down his trousers and up his arse, and they told him all that was wrong with him, pushed it into him like shoving wads of wet paper into his ears and brain until he knew it. They made him eat the whole bus, pushing it down into his throat until his body bulged and his muscles locked and cramped around it, until he curled himself up round it. And all the while the laughter directed at him was like white noise, them above him and pissing down on him like continual British rain.

This was going to go on, he realized, forever. And he'd deliberately sought it out! He put his hands up to shield his head, and then they started on his hands instead. Tiny nails scrabbling into every pore. Was he only trying to punish himself?

No, absolutely not. I'm not doing this to myself. You're doing this to me.

He felt a slight give in the pressure around him. He conjured up another thought of what he could compare this to: the act of being born. The ultimate violence. The ultimate passage from comfort to horror. It hadn't been the pain that he'd needed to go through; he had to face the fear. Understanding that now made him realize he could hear a real engine noise under the horror that was controlling his body. If he fought his way backward, and he could, then he could reach the rear platform, and let go of the rail and just escape. The choice was clear.

But no. *No.* He'd come here for a reason. He'd come here because this bus went somewhere beyond anything he knew, and because getting on it would be a sacrifice that was just a tiny way toward what Losley had suffered. He pushed forward instead of back. He'd made use of this knowledge before, hadn't he? He remembered the bookshop. This wasn't just his school bus, this was an old London bus too. What did London buses have that his school bus hadn't?

He kept his eyes open even as things spiked into the corners of them . . . made himself see past the pain that left pools of blood in them . . . made out a figure amid the purple blotches. There, among the hazy shapes of seats ahead, was the shape of a ticket inspector. Sefton brought him closer, closer again, trying to ignore all the pain. And closer still, until the figure turned and saw him, and paid attention.

A cold shadow fell across the bundle of struggling flesh that was now more clearly defined, but yet somehow all himself. Sefton was a shape made up of fighting children that were pricking and consuming him. Sefton realized that he couldn't look up at that figure. He could just see what might be a hand thrust demandingly close to his face. He'd been caught out. He was on this bus under an arrogant assumption. Even if he could make it the right sort of bus, he still didn't have a ticket. He didn't deserve to be here. He had to be his UC self now, quickly and, bluff his way through—

No, here he had to be honest.

What would his mother have said? What did all the stories say?

He knew. He put a hand into his pocket that he made exist, and took out a pound coin that he made the bodies struggling among him not steal from him.

One coin, not two, not small change. You have to pay the ferryman. He still couldn't make himself look at what this force amounted to, standing before him. And this was just something arising on the way to wherever he was going to end up. That was what this manifestation was saying to him: *This is only the beginning.* He reached out and put the coin into something cold and deep.

And then the "ticket collector" was gone. And he was sitting on a frozen seat in something which felt and smelt like a frozen London bus, and it was only him sitting here, and all his tormentors fled in a flapping of flesh into the surrounding structure, and there was just him in here, kept safe from pure hot darkness outside.

Sefton lowered his hands slowly to the seat and felt its protective cold. Again he breathed. Again he was free to do that. The colors outside the window suddenly changed. A real light streamed in over him. The tone of the engine changed, too. The sense of motion slowed. The bus was coming to a stop.

Sefton got unsteadily to his feet. Everything now seemed to be waiting for him. He could simply stay onboard, he realized, rather than go into the frightening unknown yet again. He could return home the same way. Again the choice, but what would be the point of that now, after he had done so much to get this far? He made his way along to the back of the bus. He could see light beyond the step. But nothing more.

He moved quickly and stepped off into nothing.

Sefton landed on his feet on a paved road with a sufficiently high camber to make him stumble toward the mud to one side of it. He turned to look around: with a roar of its engine that too quickly became inaudible, the bus had gone. He glanced at his surroundings. It was the same sort of day he'd come from, morning becoming afternoon. On his left stood the pillared front of a building whose top was obviously open to the sky, because clouds of vapor were rising from it. The pillars looked old, brown, weathered. A row of low wooden buildings, houses and shops, ran down both sides of the street. There was obviously a large town made up of such buildings all around him. The street went off into the distance in both directions until it reached a higher-level city wall. Signs in . . . that was Latin? Gaudy daubs of paint brightened everything up: traders' lures and graffiti. Had he . . . gone back in time? It didn't feel as if he had, somehow. But how could he know that? This didn't feel like anywhere real. It was like a computer game, only the world around him appeared perfect, every bit as detailed as the world he'd come from. He bent down and felt the soil. It felt like soil. So why that sense of unreality?

He took a few steps in the direction of where he'd got off the bus. Right, there was nobody about. Not a single person. No smells of cooking or fire, just mud and brick and distant agriculture, and clean air above it. *Utter* silence. Not even the sound of birds or animals. No, wait a sec—from ahead of him there sounded a gentle trickling. A river was running along a cut between the buildings, fording the road, which had a few larger stones placed in it to allow passage. He stepped over. The water looked murky. He walked ahead for a while, looking carefully around him, waiting for the trap but not sensing it. There was a turning into an open square on his left now, and across the square stood a long, low building, again with that weathered stone and the columns. He could hear a noise coming from it, the sound of someone . . . singing. That was where he was meant to go, then. He walked up the building's muddy steps, noticing no other footprints, and pushed open the enormous doors.

It was like being inside a church. The dim interior was lit by candles and torches to enhance the low light filtering through the high, narrow windows. Two rows of pillars defined a central aisle, while the stone floor was covered with dried plants, rushes or grasses that crunched under his feet. At the other end of the hall was a raised area, and there sat a man, and it was he who'd been singing, something sad and passionate in Latin. And now he'd suddenly stopped, and was looking at Sefton with keen interest. He was dressed in a toga, and had his hair brushed down over his forehead, in that Roman way. He slowly smiled.

Sefton felt he should say something, but didn't know what. The man stepped down from his raised chair, and walked toward him, studying his face intently. Sefton then realized that he recognized the man but, like in a dream, still didn't know who he was.

"Are you an actor?" he said.

The man reached out a hand and laid it on the side of Sefton's face. Then he leaned forward and kissed him on the mouth . . .

Until Sefton took a step back. He wasn't comfortable with that. He wanted to know what that gesture meant here.

The man chuckled. "Yes," he said, "I suppose I am." And his voice was English and upper class. Of course. "I'm Brutus."

"Brutus?" Sefton was thinking how this was absolutely the last person he'd expected to encounter on this journey. "As in . . . ?"

"Marcus Junius Brutus. Or Brutus of Troy. Or Brutus Greenshield."

Sefton tried to remember what he'd seen on telly about Roman history. "What, you're the bloke who killed Julius Caesar? Was he—?"

"From Troy? No. Those three names I gave you are those of three different people."

"Do you mean that you aren't . . . real?"

Brutus sighed. "You've probably realized there's an element, to all this, of you finding what you set out to find—"

"I've never even *heard* of Brutus Greenshield!"

"—and there's also an element that was chosen by me. I need you to realize that this isn't entirely an expedition into your own mind. The Romans never had any difficulty in seeing omens. In fact the call from outside themselves was something they welcomed. But people from your time do have this tendency to regard everything as internalized. You think you're making the world yourselves, at every moment. Sorry, but no."

"I didn't think that at all," Sefton said carefully. "In fact I came here to find out things I don't know."

"Excellent. So where do you think you are?"

"London. Roman London?"

"Correct. Well, to the extent that it's what this place is pretending to be at the moment: the city I founded in the country I founded. Britain, the country of Brutus! Did you know that was what people once thought? I thought it would be enjoyable to make the place look like that for you. But really, this is one of many . . . yes, places—let's call them that, since there's some truth to that—places that *orbit* London. They *affect* London, they make it the way it is because of their proximity." He looked playful all of a sudden. "Did you notice that while you're here you've lost the Sight?"

With a jolt, Sefton realized that it was true. It was why he'd felt no threat from this place. To be told he'd lost one of his senses made him feel—instead of the relief he'd been anticipating—suddenly vulnerable.

"The definition of the Sight is being able to sense something that has a connection to, that takes power from, one of these other worlds I spoke of—like this one—while you're in your own world.

That's meaningless here because we're actually in one of those other worlds."

"So this is, like, another dimension?"

Brutus put a finger to Sefton's lips. "You only get one question, so don't waste it on physics."

Sefton closed his mouth.

"You were very brave to come here without understanding where you were going. You've obviously realized that the quest isn't a matter of tramping over hill and dale, but that it's within you. Your world—I mean the planet—is getting smaller and smaller with so many people living on it, slower and slower as everything runs out, also hotter and hotter, and that's your own fault. You may have to start to find new adventures to aspire to, to find new shapes for stories. To overcome the inertia of history will be tremendously difficult for you. And there are those who are meanwhile taking advantage of this time of transformation and opportunity and horror—who are trying to turn the wheel in their own direction." He put a hand to Sefton's face again, turning his head left and right, as if examining a horse. Sefton let him do so. "You know what Hell is?"

"I don't believe in it."

"Good. It is *time* that defines whether something is real or not. Time is what makes what people experience a tragedy or a love story or a triumph. Hell is where time has stopped, where there's no more innovation. No horizon. No change. I sometimes think Hell would suit the British down to the ground, and that, given the chance, they'd vote for it. You'd better make sure they never get the chance, eh?"

Sefton took the hand from his face. It felt cool to the touch. He took care not to frame what he wanted to say now as a question. "I wish you'd just tell me who you are. So far, you keep contradicting yourself. You're pleased I don't believe in Hell, but then you tell me all about it. You're playing with words . . ."

"I *am* a word." Brutus leaned forward and kissed him full on

327

the lips again. This time Sefton let him. The kiss continued, long and hard, and Sefton started to wonder if this was going to be a significant part of whatever this out-of-body experience was. But, as he started to connect emotionally with the man he was kissing, to think about what Joe might have to say about this, to let his guard down, he thought he glimpsed something in his mind's eye: the answer to who this was!

He stepped back, staring and panting. But he couldn't afford to ask the question.

The man's voice turned gentle, supremely careful. "As the song goes, I am what I am. At the moment, just for where we are now, I'm that Roman chap who killed his friend for the sake of the law, to save the people and to let their will prevail. I have all those memories, of a complete life spent in Rome, including its end. But, clearly, that particular Brutus didn't talk as I do, and he had all sorts of dimensions to him that I don't represent. Because I'm also something else that has continued further, and that goes back further. I also remember being that other Brutus, the Trojan, making that first footprint on that muddy British shore, with my expedition of Romans behind me, all following me, their noble foreign captain, as we arrived in a new land for the first time. And, in yet another direction, I also remember my father, King Efrawg of the Britons, who raised me in Britain, in the British tradition, to carry a green shield. Do you see what I'm being here, what I've decided to be, in order to meet you safely? I'm the son of the British, and the father of them, and also someone entirely separate from them."

"Are you saying that you're . . . ?" Sefton stopped himself. That had nearly been a question, and he didn't want that to be his permitted question, because he didn't want to hear the answer. This was crashing against things he knew to be good. "I won't . . . I won't believe in some sort of higher power, you know . . . ever."

Brutus drew closer again. He smelt clean. Sefton could see the smallest pores in his face, the hard line of his jaw, the depths in his eyes. He so wanted to feel that connection again, to feel that love. But he was angry at it, too. He didn't know how you could avoid being angry with something so much bigger than you were. Not a lot of difference between this thing and Losley, not at his present size.

"Kevin," said Brutus, "I wouldn't expect anything more or less of you. This information you're taking in while you're here, it's rough stuff. It's being pulled screaming out of nature only because of what you've undergone to get here. I'm just something that intervenes sometimes to make it all a bit easier. For you, I'm a slippery stepping stone in a very choppy river, not a bridge you have to cross." He gestured around him. "Things are complicated. Not everything is known . . . and not everything will pass through this conduit. Although I've tried to make this communication as easy as I can, by giving you a place in which to have it, a person to have it with, some of it was always going to be garbled, incoherent, contradictory. Now, come on, you're ready. So ask your question."

Sefton wondered if he should ask something about the nature of the smiling man or, more practically, about Losley's location. But, no, he hadn't come here with any grand desire for illumination, and finding her was the only objective on the Ops Board they might be able to accomplish on their own. He'd come here with a specific purpose. He'd come here to save Quill's child. "How," he asked, "do we defeat Mora Losley?"

Brutus inclined his head in approval. "You remember the bookshop? What you felt there?"

"What about it?"

"That's another question."

"Tell me! Just bloody *tell* me!"

Brutus wandered away, shaking his head and laughing. But it was good laughter. He was laughing at Sefton's courage, the policeman realized. "If you want to find me again, you'll have to find another way. It must get harder every time, because otherwise, what would be the point of wisdom? You're now an initiate. You have an instinctive understanding of these things. Now you must work."

"But I don't know if I've understood . . . almost anything here."

"You were brave," said Brutus. "That's always a good beginning."

Sefton woke up with a start. He jumped to his feet and looked around. He was at the bus stop, he'd never left the bus stop, he'd leaned back against the wall of the shelter and fallen asleep!

No, he was actually somewhere different. He was leaning against the metal edge of a bus stop, but . . . it was a completely different one. The sounds and smells of London flooded back. People were walking past, all around him, glancing at him, wondering what was up with him. He took a few faltering steps and saw that he was just along from Cannon Street tube station, near a mobile phone shop and a business that called itself "London Stone."

Well, maybe that was someone's way of saying that what he'd just experienced had been real. But he felt disappointed, unfulfilled. He didn't know if he'd discovered anything that could help Quill. He felt the Sight back inside his head, but there was a difference now. Just a slight one. He felt more confident about it, as if he'd calibrated something inside his head by . . . switching it off and turning it back on again.

He'd gone down into the hole and he'd faced his fear and he'd come out changed. He'd taken a first step. Already a lot of what he'd experienced felt like a story, something that had happened to someone else. He took his special notebook from his pocket, and started to write down all he could remember. But he didn't know if he'd ever be able to show it to anybody.

TWENTY-SEVEN

With the cage holding the cat, Costain stood at the empty Boleyn Ground, in the gap where Losley's and Toshack's season-ticket seats had once been. Match day was tomorrow, and there were already preparations being made. He unbolted the cage. "All right," he said, "out you get."

The cat looked at him in surprise for a moment, then did so, dropping lightly on to the concrete. "Are you releasing me?"

"Yeah."

"Why?"

"You've got nothing further to contribute to the inquiry. And maybe I'm looking for some good karma. You'll know from your radio plays that Brits always treat animals decently, even when they're being shits to each other."

"Oh, thank you. Another unexpected kindness."

"Will you go back to her?"

"I'd like to, because I agree with her that she should have me around. But that all depends on whether or not she spots me here. It was a reasonable choice of site on your part. As any true Irons fan would, she does look in on the ground from time to time, remotely as it were. I shall remain here and see what transpires."

Costain squatted to smooth the creature's head. "Good luck, Tiger Feet."

"Thank you. You have been very kind. You are not as bad as you have been painted."

Costain smiled and headed out of the ground. When he'd driven a significant distance away—further, he hoped, than Losley would ever notice if looking in on her beloved turf—he stopped the car, and took the receiving station for the locator bug from out of the glove compartment. The GPS showed the tiny flash of light at the Boleyn Ground repeating. He didn't know how long it took for food to make its way through a cat's digestive system, but he hoped Losley would take the bait before then. She would surely want to retrieve something that she'd invested so much in creating. And there the cat would be highly visible, in a place she paid great attention to, and seemingly free to take back. She might even think she could learn a few things about the coppers from it, but Costain hoped that the friendship he'd so carefully developed with it would protect them from any devastating revelations. And, to be honest, they were utterly vulnerable where she was concerned, anyway. Losley would take the cat back to wherever she was hiding, and the locator bug would then tell them where that was, so they could all swoop in and save Jessica. That was his plan. But, standing here now, it seemed a pretty distant hope.

His phone rang. "If you've finished your own secret project," said Quill, "then get your arse back here. Ross has called in, and she's got us a solid lead."

"Me, too," he said, and managed to describe what he'd just done without committing the sin of pride. Not much. As he drove off, though, he wondered about sins committed against cats, and whether or not whatever went around really did come around. He hoped he'd get a chance to prove otherwise.

Ross marched into the evidence room to find Quill, Costain and Sefton standing surrounded by all eighty-three stationery boxes. "Still can't find anything," said Quill, looking at her almost angrily. "Who's this source of yours?"

For a moment, she wanted to lie or say nothing at all. But then she realized that it was just a ridiculous reflex, that she had no reason to. So she told them everything. She saw that Sefton was looking as if he understood, as if he'd been through something enormous himself. Costain looked somber as she described her dad's circumstances. When she got to the bit about the boxes, she went and picked one up, and turned it over in her hands. She put her hand inside it, feeling all the way around. Frustrated, she put it aside and picked up another.

"So what are we looking for?" asked Costain.

"It must be something . . . *normal*. Last time we looked, we were so into having the Sight, but Toshack didn't possess that . . ." She stopped and realized that, as she'd been talking, she was actually looking straight at what she'd been talking about. "Look."

In biro, on one side of the box, there was a tiny X.

"X marks the spot," said Costain, uncertainly.

"See if you can find any more," said Quill.

They found twenty-nine boxes with Xs marked on them. They made a pile of them. They worked fast, aware of the ticking clock, the football match approaching, and what any single goal would mean. Ross discovered that most of them had two Xs, on opposite sides. Four of them, like the one Ross had picked up first, had only one X. The Xs came in two colors, blue and red. Always the same color on both sides, except—

Ross held up the special box and spun it to show them all four sides: two blue Xs opposite two red ones. "Do you see?" she said. The others watched as she put it all together. The special box, with four Xs, went in the middle of the space they'd cleared on the evidence room floor. She placed a row of boxes, red X adjacent to red X, running right through it, so the special box remained in the middle. Then she did the same with the blue-X boxes.

They now formed a single large X.

As soon as she shoved the last box into place, something happened. There was a little noise . . . as the boxes all shunted closer together. She gently tried to move one of them. But it was stuck against the box beside it, and also to the floor. She stood up and looked at the others.

"Kick arse," said Costain.

Sefton sniffed. "What's that smell?"

"Fresh air," said Quill. "Didn't recognize it for a second."

It was coming from the boxes, Ross realized. She leaned over to sniff . . . and leaped back as the construction . . . started to *move*. It was spinning on the floor, like something badly animated in a children's show. The lines of boxes were sweeping around, faster and faster, without making any sound to suggest their bases scraping against the concrete. She blinked . . . Okay, so the concrete underneath the boxes seemed to be moving too. The X spun faster and faster until it was a silent blur, just a circle of movement on the floor. At the same time a pleasant wet winter breeze was wafting into the stuffiness of the nick.

They kept watching it. They waited. It kept going. Nothing else happened.

"What's this for, then?" said Costain.

"I think it's some sort of . . . travel thing," said Ross. "Dad tried to say it was Toshack's way of getting himself to a lock-up that we haven't yet found."

Costain picked up one of the other boxes. "I think I heard him working this," he said, "through the door to his den. This must be why he spent so much time up there." He took an awkward run-up at the spinning shape, and threw the box into the air above it.

The box vanished.

They walked around the spinning boxes for a while.

"We've got to see if it sort of . . . does it all in one go . . ." said Quill ". . . or if someone's going to get their arm chopped off if they make an extravagant gesture." He got a mop and, holding it gently, moved it toward the air above the spinning boxes. The end of the mop vanished into thin air. He pulled it back, and there was the end of the mop again. Ross felt relieved. There was a line around the circumference of the boxes: outside it, things were visible; inside, they weren't—and those things could be safely retracted again.

"So that leads to—?"

"Still somewhere in Greater London, judging by his travel time when he used the car instead," said Costain.

"Wait a sec," said Sefton. He ran out, and returned a few minutes later with his holdall, from which he produced the vanes that Quill had taken off the bloke who'd attacked him in Westminster Hall. "I've been wondering if these were meant to be a weapon, or if . . ." He held them toward the spinning boxes as if they were dowsing rods, and took a step forward. The vanes turned in his hands, crossing each other. "X marks the spot again," he said.

"And does that mean this is safe?" asked Costain.

"How should I know?"

"Could you find Losley with those?"

"I think it's kind of short range. So . . . only if she's right in front of me. And then I think I'd know."

"All right," said Quill, chucking away the mop, "who's up for doing this? Oh, right, no time to draw lots, so that'd be me." And, before anyone could say anything, he'd taken a few steps back and then run at it.

Quill had jumped while hoping that, if they were wrong about this, then at least it'd be quick. He was thinking of Jessica. Of how little he knew of Jessica. Of wanting to get to know her.

And then suddenly he was somewhere else.

He hit a wall. He swore . . . fell . . . landed. And looked around him, scrambled to his feet, exulting.

*

They came through one by one: Ross then Costain then Sefton. They took standing leaps.

"Don't take a run up at it!" Quill had shouted back to them.

They all landed against the wall and steadied themselves with their outstretched palms.

Quill stood there watching them, holding his bruised nose. They found themselves in a lock-up, what looked like the inside of a unit in a storage compound somewhere. The only light was from under the door. He found a switch and suddenly he could see properly. They'd come out of a vortex that looked just like the one they'd jumped in to, except that it seemed to revolve just the concrete floor here, rather than any boxes. It kept going, now they'd exited. It operated in a space that looked specifically cleared for it, because every inch of the rest of the unit was full of other cardboard boxes, metal chests and shelves packed with books.

"Aladdin's cave," said Quill. "There you go, Harry." He saw Ross looking around with that expression on her face which said she was inside yet another part of what she'd grown up among, and yet of which she'd been unaware.

"This is where Toshack vanished to all those times, when he wanted to consult his 'advisers,'" said Costain.

"Meaning," said Sefton, "he had a way of finding Losley from here."

Quill looked to Costain, who checked the locator bug monitor, and shook his head. "Let's get to it," he said.

As they began to search at high speed, with Ross taking the lead, Quill found himself working beside Sefton. "What about your expedition?" he asked. "Did you find anything?" The young DC had come in earlier, gone up to the Ops Board, stared at it for a while, and then just ended up doodling surreal swirls around the outside of it. Quill was still wondering if he'd gone a bit mental.

Sefton turned to him, still with that bloody Obi-Wan Kenobi expression of his. "I don't know," he said. "I'm still working it out."

*

The GPS on Costain's phone indicated they were in a trading estate near Heathrow. The contents of the lock-up turned out to be frustratingly mundane, which wasn't how Costain would have seen it just a few weeks ago. Back then they'd have thought of this place as the mother lode of all evidence. There were records of bank accounts that they'd never dreamed of, a full set of accounts books, too. There were bundles of cash, in Euros and Canadian dollars. It was the most thoroughly equipped bolt-hole, containing what a boss put aside for his last rainy day.

"Look at this," said Quill, having heaved open a metal chest with a crowbar. He lifted out boxes of ammunition, an entire stack of them.

"All different calibers," said Costain, taking one from him, "for all sorts of different types of guns. Not like him to bother, since the soldiers tended to keep their weapons at home."

Sefton pointed to a note on the boxes—the manufacturer's address. "Made in London," he observed. "Like at the New Age market. It's the London stuff that works."

"Bloody hell, Rob had obviously worked out enough about Losley to get himself a bit of an insurance policy, ammo for what-ever he was packing at the time that might actually give him the drop on her. Only we nicked him and he couldn't use it."

"Objective seven on the board," said Ross, stepping over. "Maybe we *could* have her with those."

"If," said Quill, "we could ever persuade an Armed Response Unit to shoot an unarmed granny. And maybe shoot her many times." He looked between them. "What . . . any of you lot got guns at home? Thought not."

They went back to their work. Costain found himself feeling desperately conflicted. There was currently something he had to do urgently, as a way out of everything that loomed above him, but what they were in the middle of was just as urgent. As he searched along the shelves of one of the metal units, suddenly Sefton was beside him, working the other way.

"Listen," he said, "I'm sorry."

"What?" said Costain.

"I kept trying to . . . write off what you experienced. And I've just discovered that . . . some of this stuff presents itself in different ways to different people, yeah? I still think there's only science. I still don't think there's a God—at least not like people think there is. I'm going to keep on being proud to say that. I have to. I think I've started to . . . know something about that now: what Rabbi Shulman called a 'deep understanding of the natural world.' Only I'm just starting, at that. I've got a lot to sort out and that might take me forever. But . . . when you saw Hell . . . I think it might be one of many things that aren't hanging over just you, but over all of us. I know what'd be in my own version. I'm saying . . . I think you saw something real."

Costain stopped, not wanting to reveal how he was feeling. "Mate," he said, raising a hand.

"Skip." Sefton clasped it.

They looked round at the sound of Quill's sudden exclamation. They went over to see, along with Ross. He'd just found a cluster of five much smaller cardboard boxes, the kind you'd keep business cards in. He'd put them together in an X, as with the larger boxes, and, as they watched, this also began rotating. And from the air above it fell a steady stream of white powder.

Costain took a pinch of it between his fingers. "Heroin," he said. "Rob's supply."

"And I don't think it's being made out of thin air," said Ross. "Losley must have set that up for him—and the one that got us here too. On the other end of that'll be somewhere in Burma or Thailand—"

There was a sudden noise from the smaller boxes. It was an outburst of foreign voices. "Bloody hell," said Quill, "they heard us!" He reached out suddenly, as if to grab whoever was on the other side—

Costain pulled him aside at the last moment, as the boxes flew apart and the heroin puffed up into the air with a sudden release of pressure.

Quill looked furiously at where the boxes had been, rubbing his hand as if his fingers had been nipped. "Ta," he said, "could have been nasty."

They tried to put the same boxes back together, but they wouldn't shunt into place. Presumably, whatever was on the other end had been pulled apart. This sudden resumption of interest after such a big gap in communication, Ross thought, would have made the suppliers immediately suspicious. Bloody shame, though. If they'd known that was going to happen, at the very least they could have thrown a locator bug through.

Aware of the clock ticking down toward the start of the match, they got back to work.

Ross was making her way along a row of books, mostly ledgers, when she felt it. It was a feeling born of the Sight. It involved a gravity about this one particular nondescript volume resting beside her hand. But it was more than the familiar feeling that there was something unusual about this book. She called the others over. "Do you feel it too?"

They all took turns to touch the book. Right up close to it, and only then, there was a kind of . . . nausea. Not sickness, but—

"It scares me," said Sefton, "just on its own. It feels like . . . the edge of a rooftop. My eyes keep trying to work out where the threat is."

"Booby-trapped," said Costain. "Like that tile."

"There's something . . . familiar about it," persisted Ross.

"You mean you saw it when you were a kid?" asked Quill.

"Not saw it, but I think it must just have been around sometimes . . . in his pocket."

"My day for doing this," said Quill. He grabbed the book by its spine and threw it off the shelf and onto a nearby desk, as if it was hot. They all leaped back, but nothing happened. Then he took a step toward it, and nodded when Ross asked if he was okay. They all leaned over the desk. The book was *The West Ham United Football Book, No. 2*, by Dennis Irving, with a foreword by Geoff Hurst.

"Why is that evil?" asked Costain.

Ross pointed at the top edge of the book. There were some pages of a different color sticking up at the back of the text. "There's something else in there."

"We need protection," said Sefton. "What is there we could use for protection?" He fumbled for his special notebook, and started leafing through the pages. Ross noticed that they were covered with notes added later, so that it looked as if it was starting to become a bit of a grimoire itself.

"Salt," he said finally. "That's the best I can do. The Met chaplain said that was always regarded as a protection against evil. 'Always' is good for me. And my mum always threw some over her shoulder, to get in the eye of the devil." The twist in the floor was still revolving, making a breeze that, when combined with the cold air coming in under the lock-up door, fluttered everything that wasn't boxed up. Sefton gingerly jumped back into the middle of it, and returned a few minutes later with some salt from the Gipsy Hill canteen. "We're going to be looking at manufacturers' addresses a lot, yeah?" he said, pointing at the container.

"*Packaged* in London?" said Costain. "Is that going to be enough?"

"That means it's got a *bit* of London-ness about it," said Sefton. "And what else have we got?" He poured some of the salt in a circle around the book, to no effect that Ross could sense. Then he poured some over it. Ross then felt maybe a slight diminution of the power of the thing. Sefton put on his evidence gloves, and gently opened the book, sprinkling salt over every page. "It is exactly what it says it is: no marks made on the pages. I'm going to turn to the back." He threw a larger amount of salt onto the last page as soon as he got there, and stepped back. When nothing happened, he opened the book again. Inside it were two flattened-out pages of very old paper, brown, cracked at the edges, brittle like leaves. "Don't even breathe on them," he said.

Ross could feel the threat crackling from the first page, which looked to be handwritten in some form of old English. She could still make out a few words underneath the salt, but it was the diagram that made her stop and stifle her reaction. It was a drawing of some oddly calm-looking medieval peasant hanging by a noose from the ceiling. There was a wound on his head, and a wound in his side, which was oozing huge drops of blood. A similarly calm man in a robe stood back, a sword in his hand, the other hand in the air, fingers splayed in an unusual gesture. To the left of the hanged man there stood a horned, dog-legged devil with a forked tail, his tongue curled ornamentally. He was spilling coins from a sack, obviously intended as a reward to the man in the robe. Sefton pointed to the page of text facing the loose sheets, where the picture of some long-haired footballer holding a cup had been stained brown.

"This has been concealed in here for a very long time," Ross declared.

She closed her eyes. So this was it, the idea that had killed her father. She could imagine Toshack finding this book in some antique shop. Had it been left there specially for him to find? Maybe. Or maybe this temptation was waiting around to snare just anyone, but Toshack had been ready to receive what was hidden in its pages: a guide on how to sacrifice a man and gain power in return. She could imagine him glancing, curious, at these strange ancient sheets, then starting to read them in detail. The ancient words they contained would have spoken to him, got into his head, whispered to him—as she felt them whispering now. *Here's how you reverse the fortunes of the firm, my son. All it'll take is the sacrifice of your own brother.* That sacrifice of her father had got Toshack his meeting with the smiling man. And the smiling man had then given him Mora Losley. And all Toshack's riches had flowed from that.

Someone put a hand on her shoulder. She opened her eyes and saw that it was Costain. "The fucker," he said, and she knew that he'd understood what she must be feeling, having finally seen the cause of her misery all this time.

Sefton turned over the page and scattered the salt again. Something golden and fearful bloomed out of the book. It was a name, scribbled in a hand that looked much more modern than anything else here, written right across the diagrams and words of the second page, as if none of that remained important now. It said "Mora Losley."

"That's Toshack's handwriting," said Ross, for she could see it now. Him taking this book along to the match that the smiling man had told him to attend; Losley sitting in the seat beside him; the conversation they would have held in whispers, her telling him to take out his pen and write down her name.

"There's some power to the paper itself," observed Sefton. "She must have got him to write it there in order to use that. And now it's like . . ." He dared to move his finger closer to it, then pulled it away, suddenly more careful now. "I can feel it tugging at me. It feels like . . . being on the perimeter of those rotating boxes we used to get ourselves here. I think this is . . . sort of like a hyperlink on a Web site. You touch it and go somewhere else."

"Losley wouldn't be up for him summoning her," said Costain. "He'd have to go to her."

Before any of them could stop him, Quill slammed his finger down on the golden words. Then, with a yell that shocked Ross, he withdrew it. He made as if to stick the finger in his mouth, but Sefton grabbed his hand to prevent him. "Stop doing things like that!" The finger was badly burned. Ross looked back at the sheet of paper. The name on it was swiftly fading, as the power dissipated. Then it was just ink.

Quill was shaking his hand in the air, furious with himself. "Of course that didn't bloody work. He came back here before we nicked him, so he would have tried that if it would! And I didn't see a burn on his fingers, because he knew better than to . . . knock on a locked door, or something! Fuck!"

Costain was again checking the monitor. When he looked up from it, it was obvious that nothing had changed. Except that his own expression had hardened, and he looked to have made a decision. "Listen," he said, "we're going to have to move as soon as this bug shows the cat's been picked up. *If* it is. So"—he handed the monitor to Ross—"there's something I can't put off doing any longer."

And, before anyone could stop him, he stepped over to the spinning boxes and vanished.

TWENTY-EIGHT

At 6 p.m., with twenty-six hours to go until the start of the match, Costain marched toward the office unit of a plastic-sheeting company on an industrial estate in High Barnet. He'd kept his phone switched off. He didn't want the others to know where he was or what he was doing. Not yet. The manager of the company was trying to keep up with him. "It's now been a few weeks, and nobody's been in touch. But you needn't worry. We didn't disturb anything. We don't even know what you left in there. Please could you . . . could you pass that information on, higher up the . . . organization?"

Costain turned to look at this nervous little man, lost in his baggy suit, unexpectedly having to deal this evening with someone to whom his usual signifiers of power didn't apply. He'd called earlier to summon the man over here from his home. And he tried not to enjoy the experience of dominating him, while looking him up and down. Perhaps he should say something reassuring? That would be the good thing to do. But, no, that would be breaking character, and also working against a greater good. This man still thought of him as an enforcer called Blake.

"Leave it with me," he said instead, and reached out a gloved hand. The man put a bunch of keys in it, then quickly retreated to his car.

Costain unlocked the door of the unit, and locked it again behind him. The interior smelt of newness. Certainly it didn't feel as if anyone had been in here lately. So that meant he was still safe. *Hmm*. The thought made him smile grimly for a moment. He ignored the office and found a back room with an aged carpet, a sprinkle of loose plaster, a stack of three chairs with a corporate desk calendar on top, and a kettle. He pulled aside a thick-piled rug that smelt of dog, uncovering a stack of metal chests of the sort photographers used. He opened the first with one of the annoyingly many keys, and inside saw . . .

They were still there. He let out a sigh of relief. He'd picked this place because the manager had been on Rob Toshack's protection list, after a few of his illegal Chinese employees had suffered nasty accidents, but had only had contact with himself and a couple of the other soldiers. At this stage, the man didn't know who he was paying off, and that's how it would have stayed until Rob had got confidently used to his reliability. Then this site might have indeed become a drop box for Rob, for certain items that needed to be kept far away from Bermondsey. "Anthony Blake," on the other hand, had *immediately* decided that it would do for his own purposes.

He pulled the two Heckler & Koch MP7 personal defense weapons from the case, possessing the firepower of an assault rifle, but easily concealable. And now, having just seen boxes of ammunition in the lock-up they'd accessed by the spinning boxes, Costain had a supply of it for these babies. Rob must have commissioned that London ammo manufacturer to make suitable rounds, ones that could potentially take down Losley.

Costain put the guns on the table, then found the second box. He couldn't resist a smile at what he'd left hidden inside it: six kilo bags of cocaine hydrochloride. Not cut with *anything*. It would have been assumed, by whatever remained of the Toshack set, to have been stashed in a particular satellite house when the final raid against the firm went down, and thus now seized in evidence. But actually it had been here, as a result of a little juggling act that could only have been performed by someone with his facility of access. He'd set this up as his last payday and, if required, his emergency exit. Two hundred and forty grand of coke, and who knew how much value for the guns? It had been a game he'd been looking forward to playing, taking them to a port somewhere up north and spending a weekend operating as an arms dealer. Yeah, his comrades had been, to some extent, right about him all along. But now he had to do the right thing—with a gun to his head, as Sefton had said.

He stopped suddenly, stock still. He could sense that there was someone else in the room with him. There had been just that little change in the air pressure, a little moment of cold. It was something derived from the world of the Sight, but it was very subtle. Was it that smiling bastard come for him, now he could be found red-handed? No. He'd always appear red-handed to that one. And, anyway, he knew who this was going to be, didn't he? He'd known it when Ross had told them about seeing her dad. He knew who, in his own life, filled that special place of pain.

He stood up slowly and turned to look. "Look at you," he said, "my very own ghost."

The deceased informer Sammy Cliff stood there, the original Tiger Feet, his arms wrapped round himself, shivering. Not so triumphant as when Costain had seen him waiting for him on the edge of Hell. But a good deal more whole than when he'd last seen the same man in the flesh: a corpse hanging from the ceiling with his feet burned off. Actually, though, Costain realized that now he could see straight through the man. The figure was wavering like a mirage, but the expression on his face said there was still something of the real Sammy in there. Costain watched calmly while that pathetic fear turned to fury, as Sammy realized he hadn't got the rise out of him that he'd wanted.

With a shaking hand, the ghost pointed at him. "You'll be joining me soon," he said. It sounded like a user playing at amateur dramatics. Doing his best and failing. Like they always did.

Costain supposed that he should feel either fear or pity, those being the options that would keep him out of Hell. But now that he saw what he'd expected to see, he didn't feel either. "You reckon?"

"'Reckon?' Of course I do! Look at you, you're a fucking liar. You just set people up and let them take the fall for you. And now you're doing it to your friends, too!" He was getting more and more solid as he yelled at Costain in that screeching, lost voice that demanded some sort of justice that just wasn't present in the world. He was a lot like Harry's dad, and Costain wondered distantly what the difference was between a ghost that was made by being "remembered" and some genuinely dead individual. Because, right now, Sammy seemed bloody artificial, as if he was a story rather than a person. All the time Costain had known him, Sammy had spoken and acted for something else, either for Costain or for the smack. He was continuing in that pattern now, doing this because that smiling bastard wanted him to.

Costain knew now that he could never be someone like that, someone who just played a role, said the expected lines, felt the expected emotions, in response to someone or something that was itself acting. Costain knew himself to be a shit, but inside that— *because* of that—he was honest.

"Sammy," he said, "Tiger Feet, old mate, let me explain something to you. No, tell you what, let me show you." He grabbed the box containing the bags of coke, and hauled it through the door to the toilet cubicle in the little hallway. He could feel Sammy watching him as he ripped open each bag and dropped it into the toilet bowl, flushing between every one, until he was down to the last bag. Then he looked up, into those eyes that always sought to appear so demanding and always failed so completely. "You're only a ghost for me, you sad fuck, if I *let* you be." He flushed away the contents of the last bag, too, leaving just a pinch in the bag's bottom corner. Then he marched back into the room he'd come from. He dropped the remnant of the splendidly fine product onto the table, extracted the blade from his multi-knife, and started to line it up and chop it. "It all depends on what I think of myself, on what I can live with—that's *my* standard. I'm not going to let you or anyone fucking else judge me when I came out here to help save the life of a child."

He took a drinking straw from the storage cupboard, looked the astonished ghost in the eye, and snorted up the last of his emergency exit. He felt it surge into his head, then he straightened up and laughed. "You know who I am, Sammy. You remember me. I'm not someone who lets himself get fucking *haunted*." He marched forward until he was looking right into the ghost's empty eyes. "And I'm not someone who plays at being a nice young man just to get a free pass out of Hell. If I'm doing the right thing, I'm doing it for real. And if I go to Hell, I'll end up fucking *ruling* it." And he stared at Sammy as the ghost faded further, and further, simultaneous with the rush of exultation in Costain's veins.

"Just remember," Costain said finally, when the ghost was nowhere in his consciousness, "who's the star of this picture."

He gathered up the guns, turned on his heel, and headed back to Gipsy Hill.

Sefton watched as the Goodfellow coppers entered Toshack's lock-up through the conventional doors and started yelling to each other about what they saw there. He felt distantly glad for them. He looked over to where Ross kept checking the monitor to see if the cat had yet moved. Quill was pacing about, shaking hands without joy. Twenty-five hours to go, and he had to find a way to turn his experience into something that could help.

After the three of them got back to the Portakabin, while Quill and Ross started to add the details from the manuscript pages to the Ops Board, Sefton got out his special notebooks and checked through everything he'd written down about his encounter with . . . whatever Brutus had been. "I was proceeding in a mystical direction

348

when I encountered a six-foot-two Roman male, with whom I shared a certain sexual tension." That's what it should have read. His actual account still squared with Sefton's memory, but it felt like a dream now. Brutus had said that he had to remember the bookshop. What he'd *felt* there. Again that word, a weird one to see in any copper's record of events. He found the page that covered the night referred to. He read the notes in every way he could: poetically, as if they were metaphors rather than description; like a word puzzle that hid a code. He read every third word; he even ran the pronunciations over backward. They merely became nonsense. Brutus had been very clear that he had to work for this, that he had . . . *continually* to offer a sacrifice of work, of himself, and of the sort of work he did. That was going to mean a sort of continual background pain, the inability ever to relax. *Pain is what this is about,* said a small voice in the back of his mind. What was the most painful aspect of the bookshop? That one was straightforward: being in the dark, having to save the others, when he'd had to make such an effort to make the darkness itself forget the horrors and be something else. It had taken great effort to make it forget.

And there suddenly was the thought, now so perfectly framed in his head. As it always was in a cop show, the phrase that completed the resolution of the mystery. Except this had taken work. This had taken him on another step toward . . . whatever he was trying to be. Brutus had called him an initiate, and he supposed that now he was. Because he now had something to contribute.

"Jimmy," he said, "could you give Lofthouse a call? I think there's something she could do that might help."

It was properly night when Costain returned. Ross saw Quill's eyes widen as the DC put the guns on the table in front of him. He considered them for a moment, then just nodded. "I'll get the ammo sent over from the lock-up," he said.

*

They took shifts in watching to see if the cat's locator bug had moved. Quill got some sleeping bags brought over. The person checking the monitor sat by its light while the others lay in the darkness, getting what little sleep they could. Ross wasn't sure if she got any proper sleep at all. Every now and then she heard a small noise or movement nearby, and realized that a nightmare had woken one of her comrades.

But then she must have found some way of drifting into sleep, because it was suddenly bright and cold and she ached all over, and Quill, his head in his hands, was looking up from the monitor. He'd just put his phone down. She'd heard him, she realized, at the edge of sleep, talking quietly to his wife.

"Match day," he said. "Shall we forgo the bloody tea and get straight to the coffee?"

They took showers in Gipsy Hill, finding whatever change of clothes they could. Ross actually got to the end of the bills list, using it to eat up the hours, saw the last page of it depart her screen, like the last train. Nothing found. If Losley didn't take her cat home, then, when that football match started, when bloody Manchester City, with all their firepower, with the bloody smiling bastard on their side, couldn't resist a goal . . . then Quill's child would be put in a pot by those unyielding, ancient hands and slowly boiled to death. And, beyond that, into the Hell she gave these infants to. As something cold seized her stomach, Ross realized how debilitating it would be if she kept thinking about that, and made herself get up and start to walk around. Exactly as Quill did.

"You realize she might not even look at the ground, so might not see the cat," said Costain, standing beside her, "until the match starts?"

Ross bit her lip, and drew blood.

It got to an hour before the game. Leaving the Portakabin, they went and sat ready in a car. Everything they needed, from Sefton's holdall to Costain's guns, was already in the back. They had the radio on, listening to the match. Otherwise they were silent. Quill had been on the phone to his wife many times that morning. He kept saying that he wished somehow she could be here, that she ought to be part of the effort to save her daughter. From what Ross overheard, she kept saying "Then, let me." It was the strangeness of there just being the four of them who knew about this stuff that meant Sarah Quill was suddenly closer to this operation than any of the rest of the Met were. But Sarah still couldn't see what they could see.

Ross felt the tension building in her neck. They weren't at all well-armed enough. Yes, they had a few new ideas, but no secret weapon. They were going to have to go after Losley anyway. If they got the chance. She kept her eyes fixed on the monitor on her lap. The locator bug was still resolutely fixed at the Boleyn Ground.

"The opposition today . . ." Alan Green was saying on the radio, *"well, they've just about said that they're not going to try to score. Which is against the rules of the league, and could get them fined, points deducted, or kicked out even. But would anyone here disagree with them? There was talk of fans staying away, too, but every seat is filled. Who knows what they've come here to see? Certainly not a proper football match. I hope it might be more of a demonstration of the common sense that the authorities seem to be lacking. The mere fact that this match is being played at all is insanity. No matter that meaningful images—reminders of the victims of Mora Losley—will be shown on the big screens around the ground at half time."* Ross looked over to Sefton, who exhibited slight relief on his face. *"No matter that a memorial service to the victims will be said in the middle. It's not an act of defying terrorism on the part of the football authorities, as they're making out, but participation in it. And, saying that, well, maybe I won't be around for the next match myself, either. Those empty spaces around where Mora Losley's season-ticket seat used to be, they represent a blot on this ground now, like a wound. Everyone*

can see them, everyone keeps staring at them, even now as the players are coming out . . ."

Quill's mobile rang. He answered it and then listened for a moment. "The uniform we told to watch the cat, he says he's lost it." Quill sounded as if he didn't dare hope. "He says he was looking right at it."

Ross stiffened in her seat. She looked down at the monitor screen, and suddenly, as she watched, it started scrolling wildly, trying to find the signal, previously at the ground but now . . . coming from somewhere else in London? Sefton must have seen her expression. He bent over to look.

"Losley's taken the cat away," he said. "She bloody took it."

"Waiting," said Ross, and the screen was still scrolling. "Waiting for signal acquisition . . ."

On the radio, the match had started. The roar of the crowd sounded strange, fearful, as tense as they were. Ross imagined a ball being gently passed, defended, while the West Ham players either genuinely attacked, or showed the same courtesy in return. Various interviews had hinted they'd either play a real game or that they wouldn't, sometimes both versions from the same player at different times. Ross was keeping her mind busy as she watched the map on the screen scroll uselessly, helplessly, around London. Surely that now meant the signal had been lost completely? Surely, after so long . . .

The map suddenly changed to show a particular borough of London and the signal tag appeared above a building. "Peckham!" she shouted. "She's in Peckham!"

"Go!" shouted Quill. Costain put his foot down, and the car accelerated off into the darkness.

They sped north, the lights on the roof and behind the radiator grill flashing. Costain took them over red traffic lights, cars pulling onto the pavements to get out of their way. She wished she could feel that the people they were passing were all on their side, cheering the good guys who were out to slay the wicked witch. But it felt as if those people would never sufficiently understand the world in which the team had now found themselves. She pulled up Peckham on Google Earth but, even looking straight down at the roof of the building where the GPS signal was located, the Sight said nothing to her. "She's gone stealthy," she said. Which was why none of their random sweeps through London aerial maps had yielded anything. "Remembered or not, she's afraid of us."

"She fucking should be," said Sefton.

Quill was on his phone. "Ma'am, we are on our way to Losley's location. We have precise whereabouts, and we're passing that to you now. No, no back-up. No armed response. Yes, thank you, ma'am." He clicked off the connection.

"What did she say?" asked Ross.

"Just yes, yes to everything, like always." Quill was looking out into the night, as if he could make the car go even faster. "I don't know how, or why, but thank Christ."

The building on the corner of what was otherwise a civic shopping street looked dull, formerly something official, but with one of those hardcore sheet-metal doors that Quill associated with crack houses. There were rugs hanging up to curtain the windows on an upper floor, and an attempt at artistic graffiti on the lower wall. The street lights made everything shine. "She's moved herself into a frigging squat!" It had taken them less than ten minutes to get here. The pedestrian streets all around were almost deserted. The sound of the match came out of every pub, out of every window boasting a satellite dish. The spectacle, the unknown, all of London was centered on them. "She in there?" he asked Ross.

Ross looked up from the monitor. "Yes."

Sefton unzipped his holdall. Costain and Quill reached into the pockets of their coats. Quill had offered Sefton the gun he was carrying, but he'd turned it down in favor of his normal bag of tricks. The man had a weird certainty about him now. He saw

Ross also check something in her pocket. After all they'd been through, he'd still balked at giving someone who wasn't a police officer a gun, but if she'd brought some sort of weapon along, good luck to her. "You all open up when you feel like it," Quill decreed. "Who knows if I'll be in a position to give the order."

"Guv," said Costain.

"You know who she . . . well, you know everything, don't you?" He found he couldn't look them in the eye. "I don't have any speeches, but I'm glad you lot have . . ." He looked around at them, and found their expressions satisfied him. And there was no further need for words. "All right, then."

Costain led them over to the door and knocked on it demandingly, but quickly, civilian-like. "Steve, mate!" he called. "Fuck's sake, you're missing the match!"

A hard-looking man opened the door, after a minute or so of pounding. He looked blearily at them. "There's nobody called—"

Costain grabbed hold of him and threw him out into the street and they were in through that door and locking it behind them, before he had a chance to leap back up and slam his fist against it and yell. And now they were in. There was a stairwell that had also been painted with graffiti, a kitchen full of hippies who were staring at them in shock. Costain pointed at them, then upward, to indicate where they were going, and that it was nobody else's business. They happily stayed put. Quill led his team slowly up onto the first landing. A distant radio commentary wafted through an open window. Still revealed the same level of tension. Still no goal. But, coming from above, there was an echo of the same sound.

Quill put his hand on the banister. "Here, you see what these stairs have?"

"Newel posts," said Sefton, indicating the flat surface of the upright at the turn of the landing. "That's what they're called." He produced a piece of blue fabric from his holdall and, poised to act, started slowly upward on his own, trying to look up ahead around the corner. Quill waited.

There came a sudden sound, a cut-off shout, and then a muffled yelling. Quill made a gesture, and the others followed him softly upward. On the next floor, Sefton was standing beside a newel post, on top of which sat a head, presumably, but it was now covered entirely by what had been an anorak hood, pulled tight and secured by wrist ties at the bottom. Granules of salt were spilling out of it.

Quill nodded in approval, and stepped forward toward what had obviously once been an office. The remains of an old sofa, burned in some accident, took up most of the corridor outside. The graffiti were everywhere. But, over it all, Quill could see the shades of Losley's typical house, applied here and there. That effect grew more pronounced, until the doorway itself looked exactly like the door they'd been through twice before, like a front door bizarrely located in an office corridor. The head had found its new position, presumably, because this was where the surrogate house's stairs were meant to be. The sound of the radio commentary came loudly through the door, and Quill guessed that someone had been turfed out of their home to make way for Losley. Which probably meant another skeleton somewhere, and that bunch of people downstairs never being quite certain who was in occupation here now. And this was also a way in which she could be sure that there were no edits to show up in the tax records. Either for this "house," or for who-knew-how-many she had left, all empty and waiting to be filled by the sudden arrival of her rooms?

They formed up in front of the door, in the way they'd rehearsed. No battering ram this time. Costain aimed the gun at the lock. Quill looked to the others, saw they were ready. His own anger radiated back from them, looking more certain than he was, even. Seriously strung out. At the end of everything now. Ross looked determined, as if she was ready to die. He turned back to Costain and nodded.

*

The noise was loud in the corridor. The lock flew off and the door was smashed open under Quill's kick. They dived inside.

Quill felt as if he was moving in slow motion, in a nightmare. He heaved the gun up to firing level, remembering the words of his instructor on the range: not opening fire from the hip, but stock against shoulder, ready to fire one shot then assess again; not waiting for a sight picture to fire the gun, but going by sense of direction . . .

But then he saw the cage, and the child inside it. She sat curled up and terrified. She'd been left on her own here, Losley needing only one now she was remembered, one who was so important to Quill, because—although he still didn't know her, still didn't feel their connection—he saw her face and knew she was meant to be his.

"Daddy!" she yelled.

Losley herself was standing over the cauldron. It was bubbling, boiling. She was already turning. The cauldron was sparking, had started suddenly blazing with noise, he realized. He heard the thunder distantly from beside him. And then the same roar was exploding off Losley herself, Costain letting off a full burst at her, sending her staggering back, pieces flying from her body, making her scream. Quill tried to join in, tried to fire, but all he could think of was the ricochets, and where all those rounds were going. Costain was yelling something as he fired. Sefton was now ahead of him, Ross beside him, both rushing at the tub of soil. They had in their hands condoms full of London holy water. If the spray hadn't worked, then maybe this holy hand grenade would. Quill saw them fly aside, bouncing off of whatever was protecting the tub, as the bullets had bounced off of the cauldron. He skidded to a halt and made sure he could aim properly, and Losley was swimming back through the air toward him, flesh hanging off her, her face and body unprotected, but somehow still invulnerable. He fired. He kept it aimed straight at her as she rushed forward, the missiles ripping apart her clothes and her body. He fired it into her face.

With a great scream, she spread her hands wide.

Quill flew backward. He hit the wall, and the gun was wrenched from his hands. He tried to heave himself up, but he was pinned there. *Thump-thump-thump* from around the room, and there they were, all four of them stuck up against the walls. Sefton threw something from one hand, but it fell back over him.

Then there was only the noise of the radio. The bubbling of the cauldron. The screaming of the child. The terror of *Jessica*. She was standing at the door of her cage, saying "Daddy" over and over, in between howls that he'd never heard from a child before. Quill deliberately looked away from her, and finally spotted the cat. It was at the window, covered by fine drapery in here, by rough rugs from outside. It was staring in horror at Costain, looking as if it was wondering if this could somehow be its fault.

"You keep trying." Losley stepped toward them. Her flesh was hanging from her in folds, great sidelong scars of it, ripped from her by the bullets, as if she'd been savagely scourged. Her face was a skull with one eye, the other eye a mass of blood. Her thin muscles held together visible bones. She was like something from a museum, or animated out of a plague pit. "I can repair damage. This doesn't hurt. This is good. Now you can watch with me. Let us wait for a goal."

"There won't be a goal," said Quill.

"I know men. There will be a goal."

And, at that point, the whistle blew for the end of the first half.

Sefton knew this was the moment. His holdall lay across his feet. He couldn't reach it, but that didn't matter. All that was in there, anyway, was a bunch of London stuff, more bloody marker pens. Those were just things. He had to go beyond. "That must take some doing," he said, looking Losley up and down. "Holding yourself together like that. And you haven't had a sacrifice lately."

"But I am remembered now." She sounded tremendously proud

of it. "They all know who I am. I can feel the tide of London supporting me. I knew it would, one day. I knew, if I waited long enough, it would come to me."

"The Witch of West Ham."

"Yes!" She laughed and moved her hands in a gesture which made them all flinch, but turned out to be the first move of some ancient court dance, which spun her about the floor, making bloody spirals from the severed gristle trailing at her ankles. The dance took her to the cage, where she stopped, a smile on her face.

"Don't you touch her!" screamed Quill.

"Tell me again not to." She reached down and unbolted the cage, picked up the child and held her, as she squirmed and squealed. "Look at this new thing. What everybody thinks is so wonderful. But it's got no history. People fool themselves into thinking it does, that it'll be more of them, a new branch on a tree. But it could be anything. You don't decide. It's just chaos. A football team or a city, *that's* growth, *that's* a proper use of time. Never all of it replaced at once, always a tradition, always memory. I could dash this thing against the floor and you could just make another one." She raised the child, as if to do it. Quill yelled something again, thrashing against the wall. But she shook her head. "But that's the last thing I'm going to do. I need her for the sacrifice. The pot is ready. Your feelings on hearing her screams, on understanding how long I can continue them with proper care and use of the ladle . . . that will be a magnificent sacrifice to my lord."

Sefton waited to hear what he needed to hear.

Ross was trying to contain her fury. She was only pleased that it wasn't fear. "We know who you are," she said. It was nearly a playground thing, a pathetic attempt to demonstrate some childish power. "We know who your mistress was, where you lived, so don't you tell us this is just business."

Losley cocked her head on one side. "What?"

"You were a victim, someone who had all their power taken away from them in a terrible way. Like every serial killer. Now you want to hurt someone else who's powerless, just to get even with the world. Like every serial killer. What goes around comes around, that's you. The witch bit, that's just a bonus. You know how many movies and TV shows about your mistress there are? They remember her. Sometimes they say *she* was a witch."

Losley screamed at her. "She was *not!*"

"—and sometimes she's a victim. And, I tell you what, Henry VIII? Jolly fat bloke. Threw meat over his shoulder. And you're not in it. Where are you in it? I read that Anne Boleyn was never at that house of yours at all. How are you in it, again? You're not a witch, you're just a serial killer. You're a scared little girl who started off by hurting animals. Not done *for* anything. Not for a mistress who left you—" Ross's head was slammed against the wall with such force that it left blackness rolling around the edge of her vision. But she bellowed against the pain and heaved herself forward again, and found that in the pain there was certainty to her words now. "You're not doing it to me *again*, you bitch! Don't you *dare* think everyone in that phone book's on your side! You're not even fooling yourself, so how can you fool us?!"

"These are just words." Sefton watched as Losley, carrying the child, turned to look between them all. "You cannot *wish* me away! I am . . ." And she actually paused, as if needing to take a breath.

Sefton realized what had started up on the radio: "Chasing Cars," by Snow Patrol. The commentator said it was being played at the ground as images redolent of missing children, Losley's unknown victims down the years, abandoned toys and empty nurseries, appeared onscreen. That was what he'd got Quill to ask Lofthouse to arrange. Now—he had to do this *now*! "What's the matter, Mora?" he called out. "Is it taking more of an effort to make them all forget? Now that they're all trying so hard to remember? 'Cos you've got to work at it, haven't you? All those victims, over all those years, anyone who's still alive, you've got to keep on spending your energy to do it." He saw her expression falter, the realization starting to creep over her face. "Yeah, I've got it right, haven't I? That's how it bloody works! And it's not just the ones at the ground now. It's the ones watching on telly, maybe a lot of them who're only just realizing that they're missing someone. Maybe a lot of them, all over London, starting to pull more and more energy from you. You can't help it, you set it in place, so you can't just let them remember!"

Mora was actually starting to stagger now. Sefton understood it in that moment: he'd found his voice. He was changing the world with every word. And they were words about London, words often said in the accent of his school tormentors. London was giving *him* power now. The very ones who'd tried to hurt him had given him this weapon. They'd made his tongue into a sword.

He heaved himself away from the wall. He saw the others trying and managing to do the same. Losley didn't know which way to turn. Clutching the child, she looked as if she couldn't believe it. "How's it feel now, then?" he asked. "Still feel that all London's on your side? They're not all remembering you now—they're trying to remember something else!"

Suddenly she looked right at him. "You understand," she said. And it was with a look of such amazement, as if she was seeing him for the first time as a person.

He stopped himself from goading at her further. In the same way Muhammad Ali had stopped himself landing another punch once he saw, in his most famous fight, that George Foreman was already falling to the ground. He had been made this way by his tormentors. But he was not like them. Or like her.

"No," he said.

All Quill could see was Jessica trapped in Losley's hands. He had just one moment. One moment now that Losley's power was being undermined by what was going on at the stadium, and while she didn't seem to know what to do next. He dragged a breath into his lungs. "You, Mora Losley," he bellowed, giving in to everything he was and wanted to be, "are nicked!" And he threw himself forward at her, intending to rip the child from her hands.

But in that second just before he reached her—

Her hand slashed across. The room was suddenly falling sideways. Quill tried to throw himself across the gap, but now he didn't know which way he was falling. "She's trying to leg it again!" he shouted. "Stop her!"

But the room was folding up again, angling toward that red door, which had again become the plughole at the bottom of the world.

"Stand like coppers!" yelled Sefton. "Compose yourselves!"

The room folded around them, missed them, became an arrow darting for the door, with the streak of what had been the mounted head outside bursting in at the last moment, and then—

They were standing there in the tattered shell of a squat. Losley had gone. And she'd taken Jessica with her.

"No!" bellowed Quill. "No, no, no!"

TWENTY-NINE

Costain heard the noise, under whatever Quill was shouting. He looked over to the inner door, and then he ran toward it.

The cat was lodged in the gap. The force of the inner door had bent it almost in two. Blood was pouring from its mouth. Costain grabbed the door and pulled. The cat fell, breathing heavily. "I . . . tried to follow her. I was too slow. And then something went from its eyes, and it lay there empty. Costain found the blood pounding in his head. He squatted down and put his hand on the cat's body. It was utterly cold, immediately. He couldn't feel for it. He couldn't find anything in himself to do that. After all, it was just a cat.

He made himself stand up. He grabbed the door again and swung it wide open. The force that had tried to close it had cut off once the cat got in the way. Some sort of inbuilt safety mechanism. He made himself step through first . . . into complete darkness beyond.

The others followed, Sefton using a wooden stake as a wedge to hold the door open. Quill got his torch out of his pocket and switched it on. They were at a T-junction in a corridor made of . . . Costain couldn't work out what it was made of. It was like rock, but utterly smooth, as if it had been made of something artificial.

The surface showed no natural blemish or roughness. The corridor smelt of old houses.

"Which way did she go?"

They tried left, then right, and found themselves with further options branching off from both directions. If they were now in a tunnel between Losley's houses, it was between many of them, presumably all of them. Of Losley herself there was no sign. They made themselves be silent, and listened. There was no sound in the distance.

Sefton looked down. "Soil," he said, squatting to touch a thread of it that ran down the center of the corridor, looking strange on the material. "Which, of course, means West Ham soil. Which means she needs to take power from it for some reason. So this line would form a sort of . . . power cable. Connecting all her houses. What goes between those houses? Her home, the furniture, all that stuff. So these lines must provide energy for . . . for moving all that."

"Didn't help her much in Brockley," said Quill, "when she could only appear down in the street."

"Because you put that rubber wedge in the door then," said Sefton. "She must have sort of shorted out this system, by pushing against it. She had got all her stuff away, but not herself."

Quill looked at his watch. "The match restarts in five minutes."

Sefton reached into his holdall and produced the vanes. "These work with stuff that's right in front of you," he said. "Like this soil is right now. If there's power flowing through it . . ." He held the vanes as he had before. Everyone fell silent. The rods moved, just a touch, toward the left.

Sefton set off in that direction at a jog, and they all followed.

It was, thought Ross, as if they were running inside London itself. Not like in the underground, but inside something fundamental. She could imagine these routes connecting houses like spokes of a wheel, an alternative tube map where the distances were even less related to real geography. She wished her dad had got to see some of this, had got to try the amazing things Toshack had discovered, instead of being used as . . . fuel for them. If that had happened, would she herself have become part of the crime family? Had her desire for revenge just made her choose another gang? She pushed that fragile thinking down inside her. She would do this anyway. *This* would complete her life. Fuck everything else. Fuck everything afterward.

Quill ran, following Sefton, aware of time running out, aware of that possibility that he could one day love his child or, being more honest with himself, of that other possibility of terrible emotional harm being done to his wife.

He had still said it, though: "You're nicked," had still been that bloke, and maybe he'd never change.

He heard a sound from ahead. The radio! They all broke into a sprint together. Quill followed Sefton, his heart pounding, left–right–left down choices of corridor. And there was a closed door ahead. And the sound was coming from behind that door.

Quill suppressed a great yell and rushed at it.

He smashed down the door and raised the gun to aim . . .

. . . at his own child.

Losley, or the tattered bloody mess that remained of her, was standing over the cauldron, still bubbling, now in a different shape of room. She'd spun with Jessica in her arms, astonished upon astonished. Jessica hung over the water.

"And it's still nil–nil," the voice from the radio was saying, *"and let's hope it stays that way."*

Quill and the others moved steadily forward, Quill and Costain both keeping their weapons trained on Losley.

"Put the kid on the floor," said Costain.

"Of course not," said Losley. "The ceremony is complete. I am ready to make the sacrifice that will give me the power to once again avenge my football club." But she made no move to attack them. Her face had a terrible stillness to it. Maybe she had nothing left.

"Zoretska's retrieved the ball, he's going to knock it to the young defender, Faranchi. It's like a training exercise out here, West Ham hanging back as much as the opposing team. There were a few early forays at goal, but there seems to have been a dressing-room talk at half time, and nobody's had a go in the second half."

"Human nature seems to be doing all right," said Ross. "They're not going to score for you. Are you sure you know men?"

"We can make a deal," said Quill. "Make everything right again. You remove the Sight from us, serve your time for the murders, and we'll—"

Losley's laughter drowned him out.

"Yeah, you fucker," he said, nodding along with her, "but I felt I had to make the offer."

"West Ham developing this strong left side of the field, which can— oh no!"

Quill froze at the sound in the announcer's voice. A huge roar was coming from the stadium.

Losley tensed in anticipation.

"It bounced off Faranchi's boot! And the goalkeeper's taken by surprise! He's running after it. It's rolling into . . . ! It's gone in! West Ham have scored an own goal!"

Losley whirled round and stared at the radio. She looked as if she'd been physically struck by something that had impaled her at an angle to all her world's rules.

Quill leaped at her. She threw a gesture at him that was little more than a slap, but it still sent him sprawling. But the others had rushed in, were between her and the cauldron. Costain had his gun up, ready to try for a shot, but Jessica was in the way.

Suddenly, Losley ran for the outside door, taking Jessica with her. "Hold your fire!" yelled Quill. He rushed after her, and the others ran too.

*

Ross was just behind Quill as they burst out onto a balcony, the sudden chill of night air providing a shock to her senses. Losley was standing on the parapet along the far edge, a three-story drop below her, open land stretching behind her, leading across to another long low apartment building. The sound of match commentaries echoed from a thousand satellite dishes all along the balconies, a sea of lights glowing behind curtains. And already people were stepping out of their doorways, yelling and pointing, turbans and burqas, football shirts and chav caps. Losley grasped Jessica, with a small gleaming knife set against her ribs. She had a coil of twine already wrapped around the child's neck, the noose held firmly in her other hand.

"Daddy!" screamed Jessica.

"Wait," said Losley, as Quill took a step forward. "This is to keep you there." She let go of the noose, but kept the knife where it was. She made a gesture with her free hand as if she was pulling the world into her, the remains of the flesh of her fist sucking on the air.

Ross felt the result as much as she saw it. Something was rushing into Losley from all directions. She could see the images now: all the different versions of Losley, the visions from the front of the newspapers, the haunting photographs, they were smashing into her, plastering themselves over her, putting flesh back onto her bones new, skin forming out of newsprint, muscle from the three colors of television.

"Is that her getting her power back?" whispered Costain.

"I think it's her cashing her last check," said Sefton. "She's leaning on being remembered, taking it all at once."

Losley's newly healed eye looked balefully at them. Unreal because it looked black and white. She put her free hand into a bag at her hip, and threw a handful of soil over her left shoulder. Ross, impossibly, heard it land on mid-air. She wondered how much of this those people leaning out from their flats were seeing. Losley stepped back off the wall.

"No!" shouted Quill.

But she was still standing there. In mid-air. On a trail of soil that stretched out into the gap between the buildings. She took another step backward. "I must continue to do as I have always done," she said. "I will have to kill Milo Faranchi, even though he is on my team, even though he is beloved by me. You see, I said I would now kill every scorer. Such are rules. We all have to make sacrifices." She continued to move backward, higher into the air, her hand tightening again on the noose around the child's neck. "A blow to her head, a wound to her side, one quick swing of the rope. The threefold death. An even better sacrifice. Especially with her father here to watch."

Quill bellowed something incoherent at her. Costain had taken up a firing position on the wall. But Ross couldn't see how he was going to get a chance at a clear shot.

"I've made sure I have enough left," she said. "I have my soil on me. I have these people remembering me . . . oh, look at them, how they're remembering me now! I have enough to do this!" And she spat out a sudden noise that could easily do the work of a gesture. A very London noise.

Ross pulled the knife from her pocket as the noise burst past her. Her knife split the noise. The noise hit the others. It hit Quill and Costain, and even Sefton, who was starting to turn it away as it hit, and it broke them from their bodies. She saw their personalities fall, screaming, endlessly through the infinite depth of the housing block, pulled by the gravity of something beyond London. She saw their bodies collapse where they stood, their souls blasted out of them. But she could still see a connection, still see that they would return if she did something quickly. She saw how this happened between time, as all the watching public just started to react, but would never understand every moment of it.

Her knife had split the noise.

Losley stared at the knife. Losley stared past it, toward her.

367

Ross became very sad and very sure. It was just her now. She had only moments left to save the others. She could feel the heat starting to blaze from their bodies behind her. She could hear the sound of their falling. In moments their bodies would explode into blood.

She jumped up onto the wall. She stepped out onto the soil bridge.

She didn't look down. She knew there was a long fall beneath her, but that didn't matter. Losley held the child before her as a shield as Ross got close to her. "Come on, then," she said. She jerked suddenly as if about to drop the child or to stab it or hit it.

Ross slashed out.

Jessica yelled in terror.

The rope around the child's neck parted and fell into the dark below. Ross looked Losley in the eye, wrong eye to wrong eye. "This," she said, "is my knife for freeing fathers."

Losley lashed back with her own knife. Ross caught it with her blade, sending the blow swinging aside. Losley screamed in defiance, and turned that swing into a long, downward, sacrificial stab—

Ross cut Losley in her side. She cut her on her brow. That blow set the witch swaying on the spot, with blood flying from her, spattering all down the child held in one arm. Losley was still trying to deliver her own killing blow. "If I die or I flee," she yelled, "this bridge will collapse and you will fall, and the child too!"

"I know," said Ross. And slashed her across her neck.

Losley tried to keep the blood in. She tried and nearly succeeded.

Ross's sudden punch caved in her nose.

The witch vanished. The soil dropped away from under her feet. And from under Ross's feet. And the child screamed in mid-air.

Ross grabbed the child. They fell.

Quill slammed back into his body and hit the wall of the balcony—

Just as Ross fell, with Jessica in her arms.

Costain and Sefton were there a moment later. The small clinging mass of two bodies plummeted to the ground far below. Quill rushed for the stairs. Costain and Sefton ran immediately after him.

Quill shoved his way through the crowd that was gathering around a bundle lying in the dark, torches casting light over the wet grass. There she was, there was Ross, lying flat on her back with a bush crushed underneath her. Her eyes were closed, one leg projected at the wrong angle. It took a moment for Quill to find what else he was looking for. Something was screaming. It wasn't Ross screaming. It was what she still held tight in her arms. What had landed on top of her.

Quill pulled Jessica from hands that would loose her only to him. She was screaming for her daddy. Quill felt horribly, distantly, that that wasn't him. He looked back toward Ross.

Fumbling, Costain had found her pulse. "She's alive!"

"We called an ambulance," said a woman. "She just . . . threw herself off."

"No she didn't," said Quill, frustrated to the point of anger at what these bloody people hadn't seen. Suddenly, from all the flats around them, the crowd noise on radios and televisions became very loud indeed.

"Something's happening at the Boleyn Ground," said Sefton.

Mora Losley had run to where she felt most safe. She was dying. And soon. But she still knew how to save herself.

She threw herself off the wave as it entered the West Ham stadium. She found herself stumbling forward onto the blessed pitch, the floodlights washing over her. Blood was pouring from her wounds, and she couldn't stop it now. Meanwhile the match was continuing. But now she was on the sacred turf! Her blood was mingling with it. In a moment, power would surely come to her. She started heading into the midst of the West Ham team, and there he was, Milo Faranchi, stopping now, slowly turning to stare in horror at her approach. She waved the dagger at him, so sadly. But it had to be. She had to do what she had always done. The dagger would have to make do until the power came.

She was suddenly aware of the crowd all staring at her, of shouts and screams going up, in a roar louder than she had ever heard, even here, and on the screens there still were images that spoke of the children she had boiled, of her glorious sacrifices. It was as if this moment was made only of her. She thought absently of the coincidence in where that girl's blows had fallen, without apparent intent on her part. Or had it merely been coincidence? That thought was worrying. Mora increased her speed, marching determinedly toward Faranchi. His team mates parted like sheep before her—

She was attacked from behind.

Her face hit the turf, she sprawled on the ground, the knife bounced away from her. She lay there, shocked, her face and fingers pressed in that beloved soil. She tried to take power from it. But she found there was . . . nothing!

She had been severed from it. She had been betrayed.

Or . . . *sacrificed*?

She looked up as what turned out to be the steward who'd tackled her grabbed her once more, manhandling her, started hauling her up. She raked his face with her fingernails. He cried out and fell back, but then another two were on her, trying to restrain her. Both were wearing the club badge, and she hesitated at the sight of it.

She looked past them, saw the entire stadium. And she stopped her struggling in astonishment. From every direction, spectators were fighting their way onto the pitch, a great concert of them bursting over the barricades. The stewards couldn't stop them, and then they came at her, too. They were roaring now, enough to drown out the tannoy. They were fast converging on her, hundreds of them, converging on the center spot where she stood. She spun slowly in the circle, feeling the mob all looking at her and, for the first time, taking nothing from it. "Don't you understand?!" she screamed. "I did it all for you! I'm on your side!"

Being *remembered* had turned out to be a two-edged sword.

The mob rushed in. She threw the stewards down. She picked a direction. She started to hopelessly hobble away.

The fittest men reached her first. One struck her round the shoulders, and while she was scratching at him, another grappled her around the waist. She could hear screaming now, the screaming of women, coming in on the next wave, women howling for her blood. Something heavy struck her round the head. She spun away, toward the beloved floodlights and the blank dark sky—

She encountered a second attack, from the other way. Hands grabbed at her, from every direction. What hair she had left was wrenched out. They yelled in triumph that they'd got some of her hair. Feet lunged into the backs of her knees. Childish blows rained on her back, delivered by those who ran forward and then fearfully back again, just to say they'd got her. Long nails raked her face, and tried to get into her eyes and tug her ears.

She hadn't expected the knife. She felt a final weakness flood into her, in a terrible instant, as its blade entered the existing wound in her side. A large hard man and his mates pierced the wound again, and then again, their blades through her ribs, catching on the organs inside her. They were shouting obscenities, rage on their faces, calling out things about kids—when their words were recognizable at all. For every one of them she wounded and flung away, the rest of them grew more shrill, more ecstatic. Their blood on her hands was everything they had seen in their dreams for weeks, and now, she realized, they had found a release for all that fear, all that hatred. She had made herself the thing they hated. And now they had her. And, just for once, just for once, she heard the actual words, hissed through clenched teeth: they were going to give it back, give someone what they deserved.

A large hand got the back of her head and twisted it and forced it down into the mud. She writhed, she spluttered, sucking mud down into her lungs. She felt something tighten around her throat. A belt. Thin leather. Too tight.

She saw now why this had to be like this. But she was not willing. But that didn't matter. What a terrible thought. Three blows to the head, three wounds to the side, three suffocating attacks on her throat. The threefold death three times. She was to be a great sacrifice.

Still a victim! Still!

She wrenched herself up, and felt all her limbs held, and her body being hacked at. If there was rescue, it was far beyond this crowd that spun around her, around and around, and every one of them reaching in to add to her punishment. Fists punched at her face. Blood covered her vision. An eye exploded. Her ribcage burst open. She tried to twist away. Just an animal now. But every part of her was being pulled. Her intestines, she was dimly aware still, were being hauled out, beautiful silver-peppery in the gold and green light.

Hands plunged in. Hands got hold of her heart. And she had one last thought, which was that she knew where she was going. And who would be waiting for her there. And she thought she saw him—in the last moment she could still see—standing there apart from the crowd and smiling.

And then the mob ripped her fucking heart out.

The wave burst from the stadium. Ripples raced out from it in concentric circles. The ripples hit other waves and rebounded, set up interference patterns that bounced off the nearby buildings. They rushed invisibly, instantly, to the very boundaries of the crooked circle of the conjoined cities of Greater London. And then it reflected back to the center again. And burst out again fivefold, in five directions, forming the great knot of something being pulled suddenly tight.

The smiling man exulted in it. He stood at all the places in London where he could stand, and watched as the wheel of his ambition turned a full circle on this dark winter day, toward what he had in store for London. And he found it good, my son.

He held the pieces of Mora Losley in his hands. Because in the moment of her death he had arranged for her good work to continue. For the image and the fear of her to imprint themselves on everyone.

He scattered the notions of what she was into the hidden rivers under London. She was swept underground, through the caves where the remains of older civilizations were built upon, each city standing on the shoulders of some older giant. She passed along the back of St. Thomas's hospital, and under Elephant and Castle, alongside New Kent Road, and then she was lost amid that plummet into the modernity of all the new sewers, and he felt the roar of despair in her—

—and then the sense of accomplishment as she emerged again, part of the pattern, to splash upon the mud of the old rookery of Jacob's Island, where they used to hang the pirates, and there she became the last victim lost in that murk.

And so she was watermarked into the hearts of men.

Ghosts of her would appear this very night, and often, as the stories would spread, and people would look out for her and believe. At her houses, and at the West Ham ground, she had done great service in life, also in the moment of her death, and now she would continue to turn the wheel for him afterward, in his own borough. "No rest for the wicked," he declared.

And then he washed his hands of her.

Quill was feeling totally useless as the paramedics got Ross into the back of the ambulance, gazing into her unconscious face as they got the collar on—the three of them looking down at her, helpless but horribly caring. He felt sick at what he was hearing from the radio, and from the police reports coming out of Upton Park. He kept holding the child who was a stranger to him, as the ambulance drove away, feeling that he was frightening her with how blank his face must be compared to whatever she was so desperately needing.

He wanted to hand her on to someone else, but he couldn't, and he felt guilty even at the thought. He saw how Sefton and Costain were standing about uselessly too. A copper thought saved him: they had done what they set out to do. Well, they had achieved Objectives one to three and seven, anyway. He felt ridiculously proud of his team, of what each of the other three had done to get them here. And proud of Ross, at the end: her sacrifice. For a moment, he thought that this must be what it was like to be a father.

And then, suddenly, he knew what it was like to be a father. That thought came crashing down on him, as if it was released out of the sky. Because there was no longer a will in this reality to block it.

And he fell to his knees under the weight of it. And he stared into Jessica's face. And he knew exactly who she was.

Terry and Julie Franks, at home in Brockley, suddenly looked over to where Charlie, aged five, Hayley, six, and Joel, seven, sat watching television, because Terry and Julie had kind of felt the children would take themselves off to bed when they were ready. The kids had adapted a little already to how their parents were now. They were starting to deal with the shock, starting to accept the awkward, desperate trying-to-care they'd been offered as simply how things were now, part of the hugeness that had happened to them. Terry and Julie had been doing their best, buying them loads of stuff, because they felt they had to do the right thing. They had neighbors to fend off, too, people who they'd never realized were their neighbors until the TV crews started showing up.

It had been like one of those dreams where you're called on to be an expert, only you're really not.

But now there was suddenly this great lump of pain and history within their bodies.

They now knocked over furniture to get to those three children, because suddenly they needed to hold them so much.

*

When she was born, James Quill had put his enormous rough fingertips on the side of his little daughter Jessica's red face, and felt how incredibly soft she was. She'd smelt like a butcher's shop. A good butcher's shop. He had put his nose in her hair so many times in the last year and a bit. She would hand him things when he was sitting beside her, as if he was just a convenient keeping-things-handy thing. Or she would just leave things falling in the air, expecting him to catch them.

She could drive him to fury because she was stubborn, exactly as her mother was, and would raise her voice higher and higher until she was screaming at him. And he could never be fully angry back, because he was her world, and that world should never be completely angry at the little one inside it. And that wasn't something he had to try to be or not to be; it was just what he was.

And Jessica and Sarah . . . that smaller, shaking her head violently, putting her hands over her eyes, putting her arms over her head, impossible to get into her pajamas, louder, small-explosion version of the woman he loved. A little clone of her. Them looking at each other, the little one not knowing a thing about love, as if Mummy and Daddy were her friends, and everyone in the world was like this, not understanding the way Sarah looked at her.

Quill grabbed for his phone just as it rang. "I want to talk to her!" Sarah sounded as if she was crying, and he thought he was probably crying, too, but whatever *he* was doing had now suddenly rushed into the background and become so hugely *unimportant*—

"Daddy," said Jessica, looking up at him as she said it to both of them.

"Hello, girl," he said.

He was sure that, at this age, the witch would eventually be forgotten.

THIRTY

That night in the hospital, with two broken legs, three broken ribs and numerous vertebrae waiting for a specialist verdict, Lisa Ross had a dream.

She, Quill, Costain and Sefton were standing together in the tunnel that led from the home dressing room to the pitch at Upton Park. They'd been there for real, of course, so there was loads of authentic detail. Ross looked around, amazed at the clarity of it. There was a framed picture on the wall of the tunnel. She went to it, and smiled when she saw that it was a picture of the four of them, with their names neatly inscribed, standing like four proud hunters, their feet on top of . . . the corpse of . . .

No, she *was* proud. She expected to meet her dad somewhere in this dream. She really was proud. Under the picture were written two words in longhand:

The Present.

She didn't know what that meant, as she couldn't find any information to analyze there. She looked to the others, and then walked up the tunnel.

Kev Sefton had a dream that night too, while he was lying in bed with Joe. He was standing, with Ross, Costain and Quill, in the tunnel that led from the home dressing room to the pitch at Upton

Park. There were pictures of famous players on the wall. Up ahead there were full-length ones, shining. He started forward . . . No, not pictures. Mirrors. They were going to walk through a tunnel of mirrors. He went ahead. He did it first. He carefully didn't look to his left or right. He was being offered the opportunity to see himself as others saw him. To be judged. Did he think he was up to that? Those mirrors would reflect each other. Those visions of himself would go on forever. Wouldn't that be grand? To see himself so thoroughly, so brilliantly—to shine gloriously like that?

Sefton was tempted. And then he realized he was being tempted. And, in stories, being tempted was never good, was it?

He shifted his feet a little. He kept his gaze straight ahead. *Don't know what you're talking about, mate. Got the wrong bloke. I'm here by accident. I'm not in charge of anything. I don't even know what I'm about.*

Not yet.

He got to the other side, then he looked back to his friends, and he instructed them how to proceed.

Tony Costain, asleep in an uncomfortable chair a few feet away from Ross, also had a dream that night. He was standing with Ross, Sefton and Quill at the end of the tunnel that led from the home dressing room to the pitch at Upton Park. They didn't want to take the last few steps out onto the pitch, because of a figure that stood in the shadows of the floodlights. It was breathing heavily, as if it couldn't do it any other way. It was shaped roughly like a man. It felt like the smiling man. Because this was a dream, he knew that was who it was. But it was bigger than him now. And for Costain to see any more than he was seeing would be bad. He understood he was being deliberately spared that. *More fool you, then, son.* He led the others of his team to the door and then, as they went carefully past, he turned to look straight at the thing. It was hanging on here, he realized, to watch something, to check on the show it was staging. He made himself keep looking at it as the others headed past him. He was on guard. He was offering the big boss a challenge. The fear was still huge, but it stayed steady. He couldn't discern any more detail, no matter how hard he looked. Sure, it was keeping itself concealed from him . . . but maybe that wasn't entirely for his benefit. He nodded to it. Respect. *We'll see.* Then he followed his mates onto the pitch.

At home, in bed with Sarah and Jessica, James Quill was having a dream. He was on the pitch at Upton Park, with Ross, Sefton and Costain. A handful of uniforms were hanging around. From the streets outside, there was the distant sound of continuing violence, shouting and sirens. Multiple arrests, he knew, because of a riot that had spread out from here. At the center of the pitch stood a cluster of police spotlights. He led his team over.

A plastic sheet lay across the center circle. This was a dream, so he wouldn't be disturbing evidence, therefore he lifted up the corner of it. Underneath were the splintered remains of Losley. The clothing had been ripped up, and much of the body had been too. The intestines were spread out and had burst under people's boots. There was shit, blood and offal fanning out. There was nothing left of the eyes. The skin was burst open all over, where every blow had fallen. The heart lay as an explosion of meat across her broken chest. It looked as if they had even taken some of her bones. There was still something of the Sight about her, only slightly. But, as Quill watched, the sparks of information that had been written into her and into London, all those centuries ago, slowly became as mundane as the frosty grass on which she lay.

"It wasn't a suicide," said Ross.

Sefton looked startled, as if he hadn't expected anyone to speak in his dream. "What?"

"She came here with one last, desperate wish, thinking she'd find at least *some* love. But by then that had all gone. When she went for one of their own players she became 'the other.' That's how they're always going to see the people who deal with this stuff. If we keep seeing it, if we keep having to deal with it, we'll never be cheered on as witch hunters. Even if we wanted to be. *Because we're* the other *now*."

"So no change there," said Costain.

"You know," said Sefton, "that this is *my* dream?"

Ross blinked. "No, it's mine."

"Mine," said Quill and Costain together, and looked at each other.

"Oh," said Sefton, looking around fearfully, "this isn't a dream at all, is it? Not really. I mean, it's in our heads, but—" They instinctively drew closer, forming a copper's square, back to backs, Ross doing it as second nature now.

"Hullo, Tone, Kev," said a voice from right beside them.

He stepped out of nothing. He was wearing a shabby suit, and had small burns on his hands and face.

"Well, well," said Quill, "Rob Toshack. Fancy seeing you here."

Ross took her time in looking Toshack up and down. It occurred to her that maybe there was something to be said for this world in which they found themselves, if there was the possibility of some justice in it. Or after it. But, then, if it was justice at the hands of the smiling man, then it was no justice at all—not with this man and her dad lumped in together. She was sad to find she still hated him, even with him now looking so pathetic. She still didn't feel let off the hook, she'd wanted him in *their* hands. Under *her* judgment. She kept her face an impassive mask.

"Yeah," said Toshack, noting their expressions, "I suppose what goes around *does* come around."

"You're in Hell, then," said Ross.

"Yeah, and I must say, it's . . ." he had to think for a moment ". . . way beyond anything you might assume it is. It's like . . . the first time you come, pardon my French, the first time you fuck, the first time you break a bone. A whole different thing."

"So this visit is a bit of a holiday for you? Let's not stretch it out too long."

"I'll be seeing you soon, girl—after the betrayal and all." He glanced at Sefton and Costain. "You two and all."

"Yeah, but you would say that, wouldn't you?"

Quill stepped between them. "Why are you here?"

"My boss sent me, to offer you your reward."

"We know who he is," said Sefton. "We know how that story goes. We don't take gifts from him."

"He said that's what you'd say. Sends his regards to you, especially. And, may I say, I never had you for a poofter, Kevin. Came as quite a surprise, that one."

Sefton kept his silence.

"No, you see, it wouldn't really be a gift. You did him a favor by getting rid of Losley. You've actually helped him in this whole process he's putting together. And, like any good head of the firm, he don't see why people who've got nothing to do with it . . .'cos you haven't, have you, not really, and you're just a bunch of coppers . . . he don't see why you should have to worry yourself about it. Anyhow, the way he sees it, he owes you. All you have to do is ask, and he'll take the Sight away from you. Now, wait a sec." He held up his hand, as if requiring silence. "It has to be from all of you, or none at all."

There was silence.

"We could take a vote on it—" began Costain.

"This isn't a democracy," said Quill, "but all right."

"—and I vote," Costain finished, "we keep it."

Toshack looked surprised. "If you keep the Sight," he said, "something *will* get you."

Costain strode forward and glared at him. "Not if *we* get *it* first. I'm not going to end up in Hell, whatever that takes. I'm going to need to *see* what's coming after me."

Toshack, a mocking smile on his lips, glanced to the others. "Boys and girls, trust me, I've seen it all now. So far, you've only run into a fraction of what's out there. You're joining the game long after my boss has moved the goalposts. It's all going his way."

"This is something I can do," said Sefton. "Something I'm well into now. It's given me a voice. I'm not losing that. So I vote keep it."

And then Quill looked to Ross. "What about you?"

She'd worked out her own answer, way back. Looking at Toshack now just made her more certain. "There's something I have to do, and I'm going to need the Sight to do it."

"What would that be, then, girl?" asked Toshack. Was it her imagination or did he actually look worried?

"That, you fucker," she said, "is an operational matter."

Quill had felt relieved that the others had said it first. But now Rob Toshack had turned to him, and he considered his words for a second. "The attestation we read out when we become coppers," he said, "it says we'll do our duty to 'the best of our skill and knowledge.' You see what that means for us lot? Even if we can't see it, this stuff would still be going on. We'd *know* it was going on. We'd hear about something mad and think 'Oh, is it that?' We'd know there were leads we couldn't follow, evidence we couldn't see. Someday we might find a body, or lose a mate, and know that whoever did that was *definitively* out of our reach. Already, we've acted on intel concerning major crimes, found a way to approach an operation, sourced information, planted an informer and, whether or not we caught our suspect, closed the case and achieved four of our operational objectives. We nearly had her." He walked up to Toshack and put his finger under his nose. "And, however much front your boss is putting up now, about this all being his game, about how he owes us a favor . . . well, we know how reliable a source he is, don't we? If this *is* the Old Bill versus Old Nick, we'll have him too, sunshine. You tell him *that*, eh?"

*

Toshack looked back at them almost sadly, as if they'd chosen the most awful path. Ross saw an echo of her dad's pain in his face. But she held herself steady. "All right, then," Toshack said finally. "All right. You'll still find you've got an appointment with him." He turned, took a last look at them, and walked off into the darkness. A second later, his guised dignity vanished into a scuffle and a scream.

Ross felt pleasure at the closeness of the other three, as if they were standing around the kettle in the Portakabin, instead of inside who-knew-what in some cosmic who-knew-where.

"What's this plan of yours," asked Quill, "that you need the Sight for?"

"Hostage situation," said Lisa Ross. "In the fullness of time, I'm going to propose an operation to get my dad out of Hell."

And then she woke up.

It was daylight. A nurse came over to check her vital signs on the monitor. "We didn't expect you to be awake yet."

Ross could just about get her parched lips to form words. "Stuff to do." She looked over to the other side of the room. There sat Costain, looking startled. Then he managed a smile. He'd just woken up too.

Quill woke up to see Sarah glancing down at him. He looked quickly to his side, and saw Jessica curled up, snoring.

"I'm going to need to know everything now," said Sarah.

"Yeah."

"Terrifying as that's going to be."

"Absolutely."

"You're just agreeing with everything right now, aren't you? You've got your happy copper face on."

He put a hand to her face. "I realized what I was missing."

*

"It was giving them the memories back," said Sefton, lying against Joe's chest. "That was the win Brutus was talking about. That was the moment when I felt I'd won."

" 'Cos you're a good bloke."

"Yeah," said Sefton. "I think my mum would approve." And he kissed him.

And then they started to argue about who was going to get up and make the coffee.

While Ross was in the hospital, Costain found himself faced with the strange prospect of being on leave. He didn't know what to do with it. He went to a couple of movies, and found he really didn't like 3D now. And when a movie did take him out of himself, let part of his brain relax, he found other parts kept taking him back to thoughts about an informer and a cat.

One day he went up to Kilburn and, using the carte blanche that Lofthouse seemed to have established for the four of them, visited the local nick. He walked around, nodding wisely at things, perplexing his uniform escort. He took a piece of paper out of his wallet and asked her about a specific shoulder number. He found the officer in question standing by his marked car, parked in a bus stop outside a kebab shop. He was finishing up talking to the owner about a missing pane of his window, now replaced by wood.

Costain watched him for a while. Still a constable. Bit paunchy. Going by the book, bit of a smile as encouragement for the owner. Costain then went over, walking in such a way as to be looked at. He hadn't visited this nick in his business suit, but wore his hoodie, and now he put the hood up. He did a slow cruise past the uniform, looking him up and down. The copper clocked him, suddenly turned his attention toward him. "All right, sir?" Blandly said, with no spin on the "sir." Nothing about him that connected to what Costain had remembered for so long: that stop-and-search, that racial slur. There was nothing for Costain to build on here. No rage he could make a new version of himself out of. He was going to have to find something. But maybe his way forward had to be based in the future, not in the past.

Costain shook his head and moved on. Reaching the corner, he took the piece of paper with the man's shoulder number on it from his wallet, and chucked it in the bin.

Ross stayed in the hospital for a week, until the doctors were certain there were no spinal injuries, and that she could start walking on crutches. She got on to them like she'd wanted a pair all her life, and was soon doing laps round the hospital, pushing her muscles until they begged her to ease up.

The other three, having visited in shifts, were all there on the designated day to take her home. Quill stepped forward, took her head in his hands and planted a kiss on her forehead. "The life of my child," he said. "I'll never forget that."

They drove back across London, taking the Rotherhithe tunnel under the Thames. Sefton signed one of her bandage strips. She'd been trying so hard not to start laughing or crying or something. She felt chemically all over the place, and she was finding it hard to deal with all this concern. "So now Toto will be wrapping up?"

"Lofthouse wants us to stay together," said Quill. "That last house of Losley's stayed put, so there's enough evidence to try and put some sort of reasonable narrative together. The media have almost made it all sound possible. We 'flushed her out,' they say. And, thank God, we were nowhere near the riots, so we're the flavor of the month. I should think Lofthouse may well have turned down medals on our behalf. It's causing havoc in the Met, but it looks as if you lot are on permanent attachment to a squad they're still finding a name for, headed by yours truly."

They passed, on one of the narrow thin pavements that ran down the side of the illuminated concrete tunnel, a bag lady pushing a supermarket trolley loaded with her possessions. Behind her, Ross noticed, skipped a row of small creatures wearing hooded brown robes.

"What's going on there, then?" asked Quill, having noted it the same moment she did.

Sefton stopped the car. He put the flashing light on the roof, and set the warning lights to ward off passing vehicles.

The four of them walked back to where the woman was already panicking, looking as if she was about to run. "I'm not supposed to be down here—!"

Costain smiled at her. "Relax, ma'am, it's not you we're after." He reached down and grabbed one of the little creatures, which reacted with a squeal of shock to be torn from what it had obviously thought was its invisible cavorting. Costain slammed the entity against the wall of the tunnel. The bag lady just stared. To her, it must be like they were harassing her darkest imaginings.

Quill stepped up to the thing in Costain's grasp and addressed it. "Are you bothering this lady?" It hissed at him. "Well, you can stop it now, shortarse," Quill continued "Put this out on your grapevine. No, tell you what, I'll do it myself." He got his mobile out, and found a particular number. Ross, looking over her shoulder, saw it was the same one that had been displayed on the Ops Board. The same one from which the darkness had texted them at the bookshop. Unfamiliar dialing code, but she was sure it was a London number. From the most distant borough of all. "The number of the beast," said Quill, and hit it.

They all waited through the ringing tone. Then it was picked up. From the other end of the line there came silence.

"Yeah," said Quill, "enough of the heavy breathing. We've got a few of your lads down here, causing trouble and, before we give them a good kicking, I thought I'd have a word. Two points here. One: fuck. And two: you. It may not have occurred to you, but us policing the London of the Sight, it's sort of liberating. We won't need to be doing so much paperwork. We won't have to worry too much about the rights and needs of little sods like this lot. We won't have to watch our Ps and Qs with the cautions. We're going to be a bit more like policing was when my dad did it. We're going to be able to kick in a few doors and say, 'You with the tentacles, you're nicked.' There's *law* now, for you and yours. The same law as for everyone else. Have a nice day, sir." And he clicked off the phone.

Ross found herself grinning, and saw the others were too. Costain threw the thing back among its fellows.

Quill turned to the old lady. "So, love, where to?"

They got her stuff into the boot, with a struggle. They drove her to a night shelter. They were so forcefully jolly at her that it worried her. They tried to answer her vague questions with the best reassurance they could: that they were on the job now. They left the creatures, whatever they were, running about in the tunnel behind the car, bellowing ancient and unintelligible threats as other cars flew through them, unaware. They'd probably catch up with the old lady. But meanwhile they'd given them something to think about.

EPILOGUE

THREE WEEKS LATER

Quill finally dismantled the Ops Board. He left the photofit that they'd renamed "the smiling man" on it, and the Concepts list that could be applied more generally, but got rid of just about everything else. He ticked the operational objectives they'd achieved before filing that section of the chart. Last but not least, he stuck an X of black tape over Losley's face, and, with great ceremony, transferred her photo into a file box.

"In order to justify our existence and minuscule budget," he announced, "we'll need to become, in effect, a targeted crime squad. So, that means we need to find some other nasty buggers." He pinned a new blank card at the top of the board, with a question mark on it where the name of their next operation would be indicated.

Sefton had come in that morning with the idea of further experimenting with the vanes as dowsing rods. Quill assimilated that suggestion in tandem with Ross's desire to take a closer look at the Thames, since it had seemed such a source of strange activity during her drive across London. "I've started a dirty great database," she said. "We don't know what half of what we've been seeing *means.* Think of all those . . . stories we glimpsed across London on that first night. The coffins, the bridge gatehouse, those ghost ships. That's our patch now. And then we have to find out what that bastard's done to it. What Toshack meant by moving the goalposts. Why he wanted rid of Losley, and why he was glad we did it."

"And," said Sefton, "we never found out why it was us who acquired the Sight." He put his finger on the word "protocol" on the board. "Losley didn't use that word very much, and when we heard it from her, it sounded awkward. I reckon that's someone else's word, an expression she heard once."

They went down to Wapping nick, and Sergeant Mehta of the Marine Policing Unit took them out on the fast-response boat *Gabriel Franks.* Now they'd got used to having the Sight, there wasn't so much to shock them during the daytime, though those heads sticking out of the mud under certain docks were a bit unnerving. They all took their own special notes, but there was just a bit too much of the pleasure cruise about this jaunt for Quill to feel comfortable.

"This is just a pause," said Costain, looking up at the sky, where the sun was struggling to make London anything other than cold and blustery. "The world's still fucked up. They're still taking the piss. This city's still going to Hell."

Quill could only nod. "It's hard for it to escape the past," he said. "That's why they call it 'being haunted.'"

"How are you feeling now?"

"Much like you lot, I suppose. But I've had a lot more sleep. I'm enjoying Jessica so much, as if she was just born, that she's wondering why all the sudden attention. That is positively a good thing. And as for all this . . ." he gestured around him. "If I was previously missing having a meaning to life—which feels bloody weird and selfish now, considering I had her—well, here it is. There *is* a meaning to the world—or at least to London. Granted, it's a *bad* meaning, but you can't have everything, can you?"

Costain got the binoculars out, and every now and then he'd call one of the others over. Sefton noted the way the vanes turned when encountering every new oddity. Seeing that going on, Quill felt content to just observe with a sense of purpose.

Maybe that was why he was the first to see it. It was because he'd got used to his "new eyes," he assumed later; because he'd started to integrate them with his copper's instinct of when something was wrong. He still didn't have too much of an imagination to get in the way. But, seconds later, Sefton was at his side, indicating there was something important over there, and then the others joined in too, the Sight pulling on them all, in its different ways.

It stood on the left bank, the Rotherhithe side of the river, and it looked completely out of place. "Weird that they've left that in such a mess," he said, pointing it out to the others. "Prime real estate—or is it a historical thing?"

Sefton looked with surprise at the vanes in his hands. Quill could see they were almost jumping toward what he was pointing at.

"What?" said Mehta, looking straight past whatever Quill was talking about.

He then looked puzzled at them when they all turned and smiled at him at once.

Quill left the sergeant with the boat, docked beside a floating restaurant, and led his team off to have a look. They walked at a pace Ross could manage on her crutches. The anomaly stood on the edge of a great commercial plaza, where new skyscrapers rose, all tall Byzantine curls and gestures toward the nautical. There was a giant anchor here, a flock of seabird silhouettes on the paving.

Among it all, beside a well-tended little garden, were the remains of a square of walls punctuated with gaps, the hint of a roof surviving at one corner. All of them were bleached white, and it was impossible to tell how old the ruin was. Inside it, now they were up close, Quill could see, to his surprise, a stone table, split in two, and beside it the remains of some chairs.

"Are we sure it's not some kind of art?" said Sefton.

As Quill watched, a young man in a suit, hurrying on his way somewhere, swerved right around the outside wall, without breaking step, contorting his body as if he was water flowing around an island, but with a lack of expression that suggested nothing unusual.

He hadn't even noticed there was anything in his way.

They checked over the ruins.

Quill was all the time aware that, to any passers-by, they must look like some demented group of mime artistes pretending to look into nooks and crannies in mid-air. By the way the others were looking but not touching, and occasionally straightening up when someone laughed, they felt much the same.

"If we're going to carry on in this job," he said to them, "embarrassment is going to have to be the least of our worries." To underline that, he called over some distant private-security personnel who'd started to take an interest, and showed them his warrant card. A quick chat with them revealed no local problems except some disturbances involving youths, in the evenings.

The adjacent garden annex apparently belonged to the nearby firm of De Souza and Raymonde.

Quill swept his hand over the surface of the table. It seemed to be made of granite. There were traces of a floor underneath it, on which could be glimpsed signs of . . .

"The same pattern that's on the table," confirmed Sefton. "That's a pentagram, such as is used as a protective symbol."

"Obviously a not *very* protective symbol," said Costain, gesturing at the ruin around them. "Have you been taking occult evening classes?"

"I've been reading up on this stuff," Sefton admitted, "wanting to, you know, survive."

"Come on, then," said Quill. "Give me the who, what, when, why."

"Relatively recent," said Ross, studying the table. "There's bird shit on this thing—"

"Do you reckon the birds can see it?"

"—and, comparing it to this car that's been sitting outside my flat for the last few months—"

"That's really the limit of our useful forensics now?" remarked Costain. "That's going to be an issue."

"—this has been open to the sky for quite a lot longer than that." She put her palm on the surface. "But it's hardly weathered, so we're talking only a few years that it's been exposed, not centuries."

"If I was asked to guess what we're looking at," said Sefton. "I'd say it's some sort of meeting room, with a stone table out of *The Lion, the Witch and the Wardrobe*, out here all on its own—"

"Not on its own," said Costain, standing at the far corner and looking toward the long shadow of the De Souza and Raymonde skyscraper. "Look at where that path leads. This little room belongs to that enormous building."

"Right, so we'll be having a word," said Quill. "That could be the *who* of who owns this—scary architects."

"Masons," suggested Sefton. "And now we're in the *Da Vinci Code*."

"And as for the why," said Quill, "this place doesn't look like a bomb's hit it. No scarring anywhere, not even on this lovely table; no sign of concussive debris; no fire damage . . ."

"Even if it was attacked with hammers," said Ross, "where's the rubble? That's what makes it look like a historical ruin—"

"Because someone's tidied up," said Costain. "Which kind of implies this place was subject to some sort of . . . special attack."

"But if they could do this," said Quill, "they could have just left it flattened, couldn't they? Or left it as a mountain of candyfloss or something."

"Which then implies," said Sefton, "that it was left here like this deliberately as—"

"A sign," said Ross, "a warning."

They walked the entire floor, each taking a quarter of the small area, treading with care, staring down at it as they went. Costain brushed some leaf mulch aside with his shoe, and then called out to the others.

It was a small loop of rope, connected to a metal ring set into one of the larger floor tiles. Costain bent down to pull it—

Sefton called for him to stop, and went over.

"Okay," said Costain, "what sort of extra protection have you got for me?"

Sefton thought about it for a moment. "Nothing," he said. "Sorry."

Costain let out a long breath and put his fingers into the loop again. "I wasn't feeling as scared, before you did that." He heaved on the loop. He grabbed his straining wrist with his other hand and put his full weight into it—

A row of several tiles flew up, leaf mulch falling from them, and slammed onto the ground like the lid of a chest. The team looked down into what was below. A dark space, that smell of a library—

"There are books down there," said Quill, aware of the copper's relish in his voice. "Documents."

Ross clomped over to a chair standing in her quarter of the area and moved it aside. It had been in front of a small post with a metal rotary lever on it. "I was waiting to mention it until after I'd finished examining my section," she said. "Could someone please—?"

Sefton turned the handle. It, too, took a little effort. He leaned on it with all his weight. "Rusty," he said. There was a sudden noise from under them, and then something rushed up out of the gap in the tiles and into the ruins—

And came clanking to a halt with a solid click of machinery. Wooden racks that looked to form part of some Victorian library.

Containing row after row of cards and documents. Quill let out a long, exultant breath.

They found spindles full of information, too, that had to be hauled out of the ground, and then spun so fast that, when they slammed to a stop, they swayed as if they were going to collapse. Sefton found himself excitedly moving back and forth between all this information, exchanging glances with Ross, both of them interested by virtue of their own speciality.

This was what he was now: a police specialist in . . . well, call it the London underworld. "There are gaps," he announced. "Look at it, someone's been through this." He opened up a polished wooden case with brass handles, and found a velvet interior with . . . he put the vanes he'd used to find this place into the gaps, and they fitted perfectly. "There's been a bit of looting but, of course, it's only been by those who've got the Sight. We might get a lot of evidence here, but the site'll have been filleted for anything that's powerful in itself."

They were going to need at least a large van to take away this haul. The light was failing them, the big shadows of the skyscrapers obscuring the ruin, more and more people passing through the square as they headed home from work. They all looked at them curiously.

Quill and Costain went to commandeer bags and boxes from anywhere they could, and Ross called Mehta to tell him to take his boat back to his nick. There was no authority onto which they could pass this crime scene, if it was one; no experts to examine all this in situ. Forensics just would not *see* anything out here, so this had to be their business now, thought Sefton, and theirs alone.

They started to put everything into the bags and boxes systematically. Until suddenly Sefton realized that, in his hand, he was holding something like a personnel file. He called everyone over. Inside the file were just photographs of five people. The looks on their faces were proud, almost smug. "The 'Continuing Projects Team,'" he said, reading aloud. He had a quick look through the job descriptions on each photo and raised an eyebrow. "A brief, an architect, a priest, a senior civil servant, even someone from the BBC."

Ross looked up from her phone. "None of whom are recorded anywhere."

"All of whom," said Quill, "have been forgotten."

"Think of the energy," said Sefton, "that someone is putting into keeping that going." He gestured around him. "Into *this*."

They ended up reading by torchlight amid the ruins. They were all too interested to wait until they got it back to the Portakabin. "It's all about . . . buildings," said Sefton, "shapes. Nothing much here about people."

"And this lot," observed Quill, "go on about 'protocols' all the bloody time."

"I think they," Ross flapped the folder, "must be the 'old law' that Losley talked about."

"And maybe this," Costain gestured at the ruins around them, "was when those goalposts got moved."

They thought about that in silence for a while. Sefton was about to suggest that it was time to pack up and summon that van over, when Ross made a sudden noise. She held up a personnel file with nothing inside it, which she had just found between the remains of two filing boxes.

On the front of it was written: *Detective Superintendent Rebecca Lofthouse*.

"Oh, bloody hell," said Quill.

There was a noise from nearby, and they all looked up. Standing there was Lofthouse herself. She looked very uncertain, and was holding what looked like an ancient key. It had a gravity about it. It was a thing of the Sight.

"Oh," said Quill, "and I'd seen that on her charm bracelet so many times." He stood up, and they all did.

Sefton suddenly remembered his sensation, inside the circle in the bookshop, that there should be five of them, rather than four. He looked back to the pentagram on the broken table: there had been five members of this team, too. And there had been that weird moment when Lofthouse had got them to sit at very particular places around that meeting table. "Five," he said to Ross, under his breath.

"Five is better than four," she replied. "Like the fortune-teller said."

Lofthouse stepped forward, looking between them and the key in her hand.

"There's something here I can't see, isn't there, Jimmy?" she said.

Quill could only nod.

"Well," she said, "now I know why I've been supporting you all this time. *This* explains *a lot.*"

GLOSSARY

the Admiral Duncan—gay pub in Soho

Airwave—a type of police radio

baggy—a plastic bag containing cocaine

batty boy—West Indian derogatory term for a gay man

'blige!—North London expression of laughing astonishment, perhaps short for "obliged"

the Boleyn Ground—alternative name for Upton Park, home of West Ham Football Club

brass—slang term for a prostitute

butcher's, have a—slang for "take a look"

CAD number—Computer Aided Dispatch reference number, which allows police on the move to keep those that need to know informed of their whereabouts

Chelsea tractor—sports utility vehicles that the upper classes use incongruously to get around London

chisel—slang term for cocaine

chop shop—a garage where stolen cars are illegally serviced and altered

CID—Criminal Investigation Department, the branch of a police force consisting of plain-clothes detectives

CRIMINT—a national crime database

DC—detective constable

DCI—detective chief inspector, senior to a DI

detective superintendent—or "super," senior to a DCI

DI—detective inspector, senior to a DS

DPS—Department of Professional Standards—see below

DS—detective sergeant, senior to a DC

estuary English—the sounds of modern working-class speech in South-East London, and areas bordering the River Thames

five by fives—a grading system with which analysts assess the importance and reliability of intelligence

Flying Squad—mobile detective unit within the Met

FME—Force Medical Examiner, the on-call doctor covering several police stations

Grindr—gay dating Web site

Hendon—location of the police college

39 Hilldrop Crescent—home of infamous murderer Dr. Crippen

I2 link chart—analysis tool to show links within criminal organizations

IBO—Integrated Borough Operations, a police department within a borough, which handles communications and gives out pocket books

"I'm Forever Blowing Bubbles"—a song associated with West Ham Football Club

Intelligence Cycle—a standard model of how intelligence is processed in professional organizations

the Irons—nickname for West Ham Football Club

kettling—police crowd-control tactic of isolating groups of protest marchers and containing them

Kojack—police slang term for an electrical socket only found on the dashboards of police vehicles

marked car—a police car with police insignia on it. An unmarked car is a car without insignia.

Metvest—body armor that also identifies the wearer as an officer in the London Metropolitan Police

Nagra—an outdated form of undercover recording device

National Intelligence Model—a formal declaration of how intelligence should be applied to policing

NDNAD—the United Kingdom National DNA Database

OCN—an organized criminal network, a gang

OCU—Operational Command Unit, a division of police forces not on a geographical basis

Professional Standards—the department of the London Metropolitan Police that deals with police wrongdoing and corruption

PRO-FIT—software that lets a witness build up an image of a suspect's face

punt—slang term for a bet or a liaison with a prostitute

10 Rillington Place—home of infamous murderer John Christie

RV point—rendezvous point

SCD 4—the police department that examines the scene of the crime

SCD 7(2)—the police department that deals with special projects within Serious and Organized Crime

SCD 10—the police department that runs undercover operations

shebeen—an illegal and unlicensed bar, usually in a private house

shout—paramedic and fire service slang for a call out

SOCO—a Scene of Crime Officer

spod—slang term for an intellectual

the thirty-three boroughs—all the boroughs that together make up Greater London

tom—slang term for a prostitute

Tyburn Tree—the gibbet where criminals were hanged, in what is now central London

UC—undercover police detective

Acknowledgments

I've been helped by a great many people in writing this book, a number of whom chose not to be named, being serving undercover police officers and intelligence analysts. Where I've got it wrong, or used artistic license (for instance in keeping Gipsy Hill police station open and hugely increasing its size) the fault is mine, not theirs. Decades ago, these characters were first created for a television series pitch overseen by the tremendous talents of Steven Moffat and Beryl and Sue Vertue. The story has changed out of all recognition since those days, but their support and encouragement remain, and I owe them many thanks.

I'd particularly like to thank my editors Julie Crisp, for a life-changing set of notes, and Bella Pagan, for her continual good stewardship, as well as Chloe Healy, the publicity genius. I couldn't be happier to be part of Team Tor. And this book wouldn't have happened at all without the support and friendship of my agent, Simon Kavanagh.

I'd also like to thank:

Rob Appleby; Ali Blackburn; "DC B" of the Specialist Crime Directorate; Liam Brison; Tracy and Darren at the Faringdon Coffee House; Cerys Clarke; Rev. Sheena Cleaton; Hywel Clifford; Simon Colenutt; Jessica Cuthbert-Smith; Robert Dick; Jac Farrow; "SJG"; David Gifford; Toby Hadoke; Joanne Hall; Jennifer Heddle; Lyn

Holmes; Simon Holmes; Tom Hunter; "JPL"; Matthew Kilburn; Paul Kirkley; Rabbi Markus A. Lange; Peter Lavery; Tony and Tracy Lee; Patricia MacEwen; Seanan McGuire; Mike Maddox; Inspector Dick Malcolm; Laurie Mann; Harry Markos; David Matthams; Ian Mond; Mike Perkins; Rabbi Danny Rich; Claire Ridgway of www.theanneboleynfiles.com; Al Robertson; Guy Robinson; Fazana Saleem-Ismail; Graham Sleight; Chief Inspector Andrew Smith and "T."

About the Author

Paul Cornell has written some of *Doctor Who*'s best-loved episodes for the BBC. He has also written on a number of comic book series for Marvel and DC, including X-Men and Batman and Robin. He has been Hugo Award–nominated for his work in TV, comics and prose, and won the BSFA Award for his short fiction. *London Falling* is his first urban fantasy novel.